KILLER WAVES

KILLER WAVES

BRENDAN DuBOIS

THOMAS DUNNE BOOKS
ST. MARTIN'S MINOTAUR ≈ NEW YORK

After many years, this book is for
Jed Mattes,
for so many reasons.

THOMAS DUNNE BOOKS.
An imprint of St. Martin's Press.

KILLER WAVES. Copyright © 2002 by Brendan DuBois.
All rights reserved. Printed in the United States of America. No part of
this book may be used or reproduced in any manner whatsoever
without written permission except in the case of brief quotations embodied in
critical articles or reviews. For information, address St. Martin's Press,
175 Fifth Avenue, New York, N.Y. 10010.

www.minotaurbooks.com

Library of Congress Cataloging-in-Publication Data

DuBois, Brendan.
    Killer waves : a Lewis Cole mystery / Brendan DuBois.—1st ed.
       p. cm.
    ISBN 0-312-28487-X
    1. Cole, Lewis (Fictitious character)—Fiction. 2. New Hampshire—Fiction.
3. Journalists—Fiction. I. Title.

PS3554.U2564 K46 2002
813'.54—dc21

                                                          2001058550

First Edition: June 2002

10   9   8   7   6   5   4   3   2   1

CHAPTER ONE

The night I saw the dead man began loudly enough, with my clock alarm at my bedside chiming at one in the morning. I slapped it shut and stared up at the dark ceiling, listening to the waves of the Atlantic Ocean crash in on this portion of Tyler Beach, New Hampshire, that belongs to me. Remembering why I had set the alarm at this ungodly hour, I swung out of bed, put on a thick terry-cloth robe, and padded downstairs in my bare feet. The living room was barely lit up by a quarter moon and I found my way to the couch and flicked on the television. The channel had been preset to CNN and I waited in the near darkness, huddled in my robe. Embers glowed from the nearby fireplace. The sound on the television was muted, so as I watched grainy television footage of refugees in some far-off place fleeing their bombed homes, I had no way of knowing if it was in Russia or Kosovo or Colombia or about a half dozen other places. It had been that kind of year. Then the footage broke away to a CNN "Breaking News" logo, and there it was, more than a thousand miles to the south of me, the space shuttle *Endeavour*, about two minutes away from being launched into space. I switched the mute off and watched the countdown flick its way down to zero, feeling my chest tighten as each second flashed by. Seven astronauts were aboard the *Endeavour,* and some months ago I had met the mission commander, a New Hampshire native, at a Tyler Rotary Club function. We had talked for a while and he seemed like a nice enough guy, until Paula Quinn, a reporter for the Tyler *Chronicle,* asked him why he had entered the astronaut corps. His answer—which I'm sure he was glad didn't appear in the next day's paper—was bitter: "I joined up to go to the moon or Mars, and instead I'm a truck driver, going to the same place a couple of hundred other men and women have gone to, low-earth orbit. A hell of a deal, don't you think?" Then he smiled at the two of us and that had been that.

I looked over at the coffee table. Two empty wineglasses were in the center, where Paula had been not more than six hours ago, sharing a dinner and good conversation with me. Not a bad night, and I was hoping this shuttle launch was going to put a nice cap to the April evening.

"T minus thirty seconds," came the voice from shuttle launch control, and I found myself leaning in toward the television, clenching my fists, my chest quite tight, knowing that sitting on top of those millions of gallons of explosive fuel was a slim man with a mustache with whom I had shared breakfast and quiet conversation last fall. Then it began, with the three main engines starting up with a roar, and then the camera showed the twin solid-rocket boosters lighting off, and up she went in the Florida night sky, rocketing up and then slowly rolling over as the shuttle began its long and quick climb into orbit. I watched for about another minute or so, and then I got up and headed toward the sliding glass doors that led outside. From the kitchen counter I retrieved a pair of binoculars, and after sliding open the glass doors, I stepped out to the rear deck.

My feet were quickly chilled on the cold wood of the deck, and I thought about going back in to put on some footwear, but it was too late, too damn late. I shivered and looked out on the ocean, where I saw the running lights of some freighter, probably heading up north to Porter, the state's only port, but my focus was on the south. The night was clear, with the moonlight washing out some of the stars, but it was still fairly dark. Toward the south I made out the muted glow from the lights of Tyler Beach, and the only sound came from the waves and the wind. I picked up the binoculars, scanned toward the south. Nothing. I shivered and stamped my feet. Maybe something was wrong. Maybe it had already gone by.

I brought up the binoculars again. Nothing. Just the stars.

I put the binoculars down and was going to rub my hands together, and there it was.

A small, fast moving dot of light just above the horizon, heading to the north.

"I'll be damned," I whispered.

In the binoculars the light was a large dot. I could make out a small, fuzzy triangle of red and orange at the dot's rear, and I tracked the space shuttle overhead as it raced into orbit. Usually the shuttles don't come up the Atlantic Coast, but a certain orbit had to be achieved for this mission, and I had lucked out. By now the twin solid-rocket boosters had dropped off and all that was left were the main fuel tank and the shuttle itself. I kept them in view, willing my hands not to shake, and then the little triangle of flame disappeared. Then there was a small flash, and then another, and I kept on watching the little dot until it disappeared. My throat felt heavy, knowing what I had just witnessed: when the flame went out, it had meant the shuttle engines had shut down. The first flash was when the fuel tank had broken away, and the second flash had been a quick burn of the shuttle's maneuvering engines, pushing it away from the now empty tank.

And I had seen it all.

With the binoculars now resting around my neck, I wiped at my eyes. Some years ago, what I had just witnessed would have been news enough to be the lead story on all the networks and on the front pages of the newspapers. And now? I glanced through the sliding glass doors at the television set. The five minutes or so of coverage had ended. A taped interview with some movie star had taken its place. No doubt a more important thing in some people's minds, but not in this one's. I looked up at the stars and then noted an orange one, high up in the sky. How appropriate, and how ironic. Mars, waiting up there patiently, waiting for

3

whenever we decided it was time to stop sending truck drivers into space.

I rubbed my hands again and thought about how warm my bed would be, and I turned and headed into my house, and then I spotted the lights. I stopped, looked to the north, past the low rise of hills and trees that marked the boundary of the Samson Point State Wildlife Preserve. In the years I have lived here in Tyler Beach, not once have I ever seen lights up there in the preserve at night. But now there were flashes of blue and red, rising and falling, and being reflected on a low band of haze. Up again went the binoculars and I tried to focus in on what was going on, but I couldn't make sense of it. Blue and red, rising and falling. I rubbed one cold foot against the other. What did make sense was to crawl back into bed. That would have been the smart thing. But having just seen a spaceship go overhead and now faced with the little mystery of these colored lights just up the coast, I knew it would be a long time before I got sleepy again.

I went back inside, got warmed up for just a minute, and then got dressed.

When I stepped outside and started walking up to Samson's Point, I felt the odd and nervous energy of being wide awake when most of the surrounding world is fast asleep. I had a small flashlight and picked my way through the rocks and boulders that marked this part of the shore, and then I scrambled up to solid land that formed the outer boundary of the nature preserve. Years before, Samson Point had been the site of a coastal artillery station, ready to defend Porter and its harbor from a long series of enemies—Spaniards, Germans, Germans again, and then Soviets—and after it had been deactivated and its big guns hauled away, it now belonged to the state. Besides giving New Hampshire all of the buildings, bunkers and underground tunnels, the federal government also thoughtfully left behind a couple of toxic-waste sites, which meant not many tourists got to this part of the park, which suited me fine.

In the woods I made my way along a dirt path, using the

flashlight beam to guide me. The branches on the hardwoods were still bare, though buds were beginning to form, and I could hardly wait for the annual explosion of green and life this spring. It had been a long winter, filled with a lot of dark and long nights, and I was beginning to feel bored and disconnected. I had a reasonable job as a columnist for *Shoreline* magazine, but writing and researching those columns took about five or six days a month. That meant a lot of hours left over, with the snow piled up high to the windows and the wind racing down from Canada to batter at the house, hours where you began to think too much.

The faint light from my flashlight caught an overgrown bunker, off to the right. There were two huge concrete gun emplacements farther up into the park, but scattered throughout the land were other bunkers as well, marking either storage areas or spotting stations or installations for smaller artillery pieces. At the top of a rise of land I stopped and looked back. The ocean's waves looked almost metallic in the light from the stars and the moon, and I could also make out the lights of my home, standing there alone on the shore, almost like a sentry, before the faint glow in the sky that marked the town of Tyler Beach. An apt thought, for throughout the Atlantic coastline and especially these New England miles, the shores had always been places for forts, naval bases, and other icons of war.

I resumed walking, and disturbed something in the underbrush that skittered away in the old leaves. It startled but didn't scare me; the only animals one had to worry about out in these woods had two legs, not four.

Within a few minutes the woods thinned out and I was in an area of grassland, and that's when I noted the sounds of engines running. The lights were now brighter, flickering at an even faster rate, and by now I was pretty sure of what was going on. I yawned. All this walking, and for what? Probably to see the local cops roust some high schoolers, out drinking and smoking where they shouldn't be. I went up a small hill and looked down at the parking lot for the nature preserve, to the west of the point itself, and shut off my flashlight. Not a high schooler in sight, but what was there did look like trouble.

There were two police cruisers and an ambulance, their lights still flashing. I could see two cops and two ambulance attendants, all clustered around a parked car, their flashlights examining the interior. There was a shape in the car, a shape I couldn't make out, but the fact that the ambulance attendants were talking to each other, hands in pockets, seemed to indicate that their services as EMTs were not required. I shivered. I write for a monthly magazine, not a daily newspaper. The type of articles I write for *Shoreline* don't usually involve dead people in cars. Whatever was down there was not really my business. But still . . . I was wide awake and maybe I could find something out for Paula Quinn. By the time she got to work tomorrow, the cops would have a sanitized press release about what had happened here. I could get her some on-scene notes, and then . . . well, she would beat the competition and be grateful to me, and that wasn't a bad result.

I switched on the flashlight again and made a production of going down the hill toward the parking lot, whistling and making a lot of noise. The nature preserve was in North Tyler, the next town up from Tyler and its beaches, and while I knew all the cops in Tyler and was best friends with the town's sole detective, I didn't know the North Tyler force all that well. Plus, I'm sure both cops were pretty wired at the moment, and I didn't want them to overreact by having a stranger pop up in their midst.

Sure enough, by the time I got to the parking lot, both cops were on me, the one on the left yelling out, "Hold it right there! Hands up! Right now!"

I did exactly as I was told, flashlight still in my hand, and the cop on the right circled around to come at me. Not a bad job. He did that so his partner had a clear shot in case I did something stupid, but I wasn't feeling stupid at this hour, so I just stood there. The cop came up to me, shining the light in my face.

"Who the hell are you? And what are you doing here?"

I guess I could have asked the cop to get the light out of my face, but I didn't want to push the matter. "The name is Lewis Cole. I'm a writer for *Shoreline* magazine. I live over on the beach, just south of the park. I saw all the lights and thought something was going on."

"Uh-huh," he said. "Outside at one in the morning. You do that all the time?"

Only when spaceships fly overhead, I thought, and I struggled to come up with an explanation that wouldn't make them even more suspicious, when the other cop said, "Cole? Lewis Cole?"

"That's right," I said.

He lowered his flashlight and came over to us, and said, "Yeah, Tom, I know this guy. He spoke to my son's class last fall, about writing for magazines. Tyler cops know him well. He's okay."

I could sense the tension ease away with those last two magic words. When one cop says to another that somebody's "okay," you've made it. The first cop just nodded and lowered his light, and then I looked at the guy who had pronounced me okay, and after reading his name tag I said, "North Tyler Elementary, right?

"That's right. The kids said you did a good job."

Hurray for kids, I thought. My rescuer's nametag said REMICK and his partner's said CALHOUN. Both had on leather jackets and looked to be regular patrol officers, and knowing how small North Tyler is, I was probably looking at the entire on-duty police force. I couldn't make out their features well in the poor light, but it looked like Remick was younger than Calhoun. I motioned with my flashlight and said, "What do you have over there?"

They started walking back and I joined them, and Officer Remick said, "What we got is a dead guy in a rental car, that's what. Tom here was on patrol and stopped by, saw the gate was open. We've had complaints of kids using the lot to drink and raise hell, and he spotted—"

"Greg," came the other cop's voice, "you talk too much."

"Ah, hell, that'll be in all the papers tomorrow. What's the difference?"

We came up to the cruisers and the ambulance, and the two EMTs looked my way and then continued talking to each other. I wasn't in handcuffs and I wasn't bleeding, so I didn't count. The car was a white GMC, one of those clones that look like a half dozen other models. There was a slumped shape in the front seat, barely illuminated from the sole streetlight for this part of the parking lot. Off to the east, where the waves rolled in, were a couple of park administration and visitors' buildings, and beyond the buildings a hill rose up, and nearly hidden in the trees at the top of the hill was another concrete bunker.

I said, "Mind if I take a peek through the windshield?"

"Knock yourself out," Officer Remick said. "But stay a couple of feet away and don't touch anything."

"Greg . . ." came the other cop's voice, and his partner said, "So what? Besides, we can't do anything until the State Police get here, and you know it."

I left them there talking and went over to the car holding my flashlight. From my dealings with my best friend, the Tyler police detective, I knew Officer Remick was right. In cases of suspicious death, the State Police always responded with their Major Crime Unit and essentially took control of the investigation. So I probably had a couple of minutes to look things over before the very large and very polite and very insistent State Police detectives arrived and told me to get the hell out.

I switched on the flashlight, and felt myself take a quick breath. There was a man in the driver's seat, dead. His head lolled to the left, up against the closed driver's-side window. The right side of his head was smeared with blood. His skin was dark brown and he had a mustache, and he wore a black suit and a white shirt and no necktie. Blood had also stained the right side of his coat, smearing over a small lapel pin that he was wearing. I tried to step closer, but the first officer called out: "Hey! Remember what we said!"

I nodded and kept on looking from a bit of a distance. The pin appeared to be yellow and what I could see past the blood-stain looked like a thick black exclamation point standing on its head. I moved the light around, saw nothing in the rear seat, and nothing in the front seat as well, nor on the floorboards. Just a dead man. An apparently murdered man, right in my neighborhood. I switched off the light and looked around. Save for this car and the vehicles from the town of North Tyler, the large parking lot was empty. Lots of acreage out there to lose yourself in, and I felt a shiver, thinking that maybe when I was on my back deck, watching the shuttle go overhead, someone put a bullet in this man's head. Just a number of yards from my home someone had been murdered.

I didn't like the feeling.

The two cops were talking and I made a production of walking around in a big arc, and when I could make out the rear license plate I took my reporter's notebook out and quickly scribbled down the number. Putting the notebook away, I walked over to Officers Remick and Calhoun.

"Any ID yet? You said it's a rental car; they must know who it was rented to."

The older cop just grunted and Officer Remick said, "Yeah, rented out today at the Manchester Airport. By a guy named Smith. Doesn't sound too promising, does it?"

"No, it doesn't," I said. "Guess you poor guys will have to start doing a canvass of the motels and hotels once the State Police get here."

Officer Calhoun said sourly, "Yeah, if they don't make us go on coffee or doughnut runs in the meantime, that's what they— hold on, looks like they're arriving."

I turned and looked over at the park entrance, which was a simple wooden gate and guard shack, and which opened out onto Route 1-A, also known as Atlantic Avenue. Route 1-A runs the entire eighteen-mile length of the New Hampshire coastline, and on this particular few yards, three cars came barreling into the parking lot at high speed. They braked to a halt and doors flew open, and they were all dark blue Ford LTDs with New Hampshire license plates. Officer Calhoun said, "You know what, those guys sure don't look like the State Police."

His partner agreed, saying, "Tom, I don't particularly like the look of this."

Neither did I, but I kept my mouth shut.

I counted six individuals getting out of the LTDs, five men

and one woman. She talked to the crowd for a moment, and then three of the guys switched on their own flashlights and began fanning out across the open fields of the park. Two of the guys and the woman came over. All of them had on business suits and dark blue or black raincoats, and they surely did not look as if they received their paychecks from the state of New Hampshire. The woman had on dark slacks, flat shoes and a white turtleneck, and her fine black hair was cut shoulder-length. As she came over, she got right to the point.

"Who's the officer in charge here?" she asked, looking at the three of us. The EMTs had slunk against their ambulance, as if trying to gain some shelter there, and then Officer Calhoun spoke up and said, "I'm the senior officer, until the State Police show up. Name's Calhoun."

"Goody for you," she said, "and just so you know, the State Police aren't showing up for a long while. Officer Calhoun, a moment, if you will."

She took him by the arm and walked him away from us, leaving behind two of her male companions. The one on the left had a crew cut of red hair and a merry little smile, as if he couldn't think of anything else he'd rather be doing than being in a nearly deserted parking lot at two in the morning. His companion was about a foot shorter and a foot wider, and he wasn't smiling, not at all. His eyes bounced between me and the other North Tyler officer, as if he were hoping one of us would reach for a gun or knife so he could snap a few finger bones.

Officer Remick cleared his throat. "You thinking what I'm thinking?"

"I'm no cop, but I'm guessing these gentlemen and that lady belong to the federal government."

"My thoughts exactly," he said, and then he spoke up. "Hey, can anyone of you tell us what the hell's going on?"

The squat man said nothing, but the taller guy with red hair said, "Your partner's getting the whole deal. Just relax, all right?"

I looked over at Officer Calhoun and the woman, who were standing near a wooden guardrail that bounded the parking lot.

Officer Calhoun was saying something with dramatic effect, hands waving, jaw moving, and all the while the woman was standing there with arms crossed, not moving at all. It looked as if she had done this a number of times, coming into a crime scene and taking control from the locals, and she looked bored. She said something and walked back to us, Officer Calhoun following, not looking happy at all.

She stood and looked us over. "Officer Remick, is it?"

He stepped forward. "Yep."

She smiled, a tired-looking expression. "Would you please accompany Mr. Turner here and give him your statement of what's transpired? It shouldn't take too long, should it?"

The crew-cut guy came over, still grinning. "Nope, not at all."

Officer Remick then walked away, and I was there by myself. Officer Calhoun was standing behind the woman, hands in pockets, face now quite red, looking seriously pissed off. I looked at the woman and she managed a tired smile again. "And you're Mr. Cole, correct?"

"You have me at a disadvantage," I said. "I don't know your name."

"So you don't," she said. "I understand that you're a magazine writer, live down the road a bit. Officer Calhoun said you came upon this scene just a while ago. That you didn't notice anything else. Is that correct?"

"That's true."

She nodded. "Good. As of now, we've taken control of this area, Mr. Cole, and I'd appreciate it if you'd leave."

"And who might 'we' be, if I can ask?"

Even though she looked tired, there seemed to be a bit of a sparkle about her eyes. "You may ask. And I'll say again, would you please leave?"

I looked around. Officer Remick was talking to the guy identified as Mr. Turner. Officer Calhoun just stood there, his angry expression having not changed one bit. I saw that one of the three guys who had gone out across the fields had come back and was talking to the two EMTs from the North Tyler Fire Department. And the wide and burly man with the woman was still staring at me with distaste.

"Well, there's a problem with that," I said.

"And what's that?"

"This happens to be a state park. Public property. Perhaps I like it here."

"Perhaps you do. And perhaps if you don't leave, I'll ask my associate here to escort you off."

Now the burly man had a little smile on his face, as if he had finally been told he could do something he liked. I looked at him and then at the woman. I said, "Your associate may find it might be harder to escort me than he thinks."

She said, "Oh, I doubt that. Tell you what. Would you please leave then as a personal favor to me? Please?"

I looked over the scene again and then felt tired. There are times to fight and times to call it quits and go home. By now a stiff breeze had come up and my face and hands were getting cold. Maybe I was wrong, but I could tell by their attitude and self-confidence that these people were in fact the feds, maybe the FBI or something. A long time ago I had been in the middle of their little world, and I didn't want to go back. The woman wanted to play games. Good for her. I had seen all that I was going to see this early morning, and now I wanted to go to bed.

I shifted, managed a smile. "Oh, all right then. As a personal favor to you, and your smile. How's that?"

I think I embarrassed her, if only for a moment. "That would be fine. Thank you, Mr. Cole. I trust we won't see you again, will we?"

"Not tonight, that's for sure."

Then she nodded crisply and said something to the bulky man, and I turned and started walking away from the parking lot. I went back onto the field and up the slight hill, and then I looked back. It was a busy scene, with the dead man's rental and the three Ford LTDs and the ambulance and two cruisers. I walked up the hill, and when I noted a large boulder I squatted down so that I couldn't be seen by the sharp people back down at the parking lot.

With the small flashlight held in my mouth, I opened up my reporter's notebook and quickly wrote down three license plate numbers I had memorized when the LTDs had come barreling into the parking lot.

She had said something about not seeing me again. Maybe she was right. But maybe I had other ideas.

I shut off the flashlight and put the reporter's notebook back in my coat, and when I emerged from my little hiding place I looked down to the lot.

One by one, the blue and red lights that had brought me to this place were being switched off.

I shivered again and headed home.

CHAPTER TWO

The offices of the Tyler *Chronicle* are set on one floor of a two-story white clapboard building near the center of town, right by the town common. The newspaper office shares space with a dentist, a legal firm and a realtor, and on this late morning I parked out back, near a set of old B & M Railroad tracks. I noted Paula Quinn's Ford Escort was there, and I ducked in through the rear entrance, the door usually reserved for staff. I didn't want to go through the front door and the hassle of dealing with whatever receptionist happened to be working this month.

Once inside, I went past the subscription area and piles of bundled newspapers and found Paula at her desk. There were no cubicles or private office areas, just a wide area of industrial-strength green carpet and metal and wooden desks that didn't have a chance of being matched. A couple of other female reporters—freelancers whose names I forgot about thirty seconds after meeting them—worked at their desks, typing hesitantly on the Digital computer terminals. Paula was on the phone as I came up to her, and I sat down at a spare chair and looked around.

Up toward the other end of the large area, near a closed door for the conference room, something new was hanging from the tile ceiling. I folded my arms and looked it over. It was the front pages of the two local daily newspapers that the *Chronicle* was competing against, the Porter *Herald* and Foster's *Daily Democrat,* and each front page had been mounted on cardboard. Stuck through the center of each front page was a plastic dagger, and some red fluid had been smeared across the newspaper, suggesting blood. Considering what I had seen not more than eight hours earlier in a certain rental car, the color wasn't even close. Suspended below the front pages was a small plastic banner stating: IT'S WAR!

Below this delightful little display was the unoccupied cluttered desk of the paper's editor, Rollie Grandmaison, and I also noted a new desk had been butted up against Rollie's. While Rollie's desk was messy and piled high with newspapers, press releases, envelopes and other editorial debris, the companion desk was a shiny black behemoth that was empty except for a telephone, a computer terminal, two pens, a pencil and a legal pad.

By now Paula was saying, "Uh-huh, uh-huh," in the kind of tone that meant she was desperately trying to get away from whomever she was talking to but at the same time didn't want to tick off by being too dismissive. She caught my gaze and rolled her eyes upward, and I gave her a smile. She had on tight dungarees and a simple black sweater with a faux pearl necklace, and her blond hair this spring had been trimmed back somewhat. Still, her ears stuck through the side of her hair in a manner I found charming and that she found distressing. There was a smudge of newsprint ink on her slightly pug nose and I had a quick urge to wipe it clean with a soft touch of my thumb.

Instead, I leaned over and said in a loud voice, "Paula, editorial meeting in thirty seconds. Don't be late!"

She grinned at me and then said, "Well, Chick, you heard the word. Gotta go. Bye."

Paula dropped the phone down and said, "Jesus, thanks a lot, Lewis. That woman can talk a hole through a tin pot."

"Somebody important?"

"Oh, she thinks she's important, which is all that counts.

She's the new day dispatcher from Wentworth County. Thing is, if I can keep her happy and glad to talk to me, then I can get better news about what's going on in the other towns, like Bretton and Eaton. Otherwise I'd have to spend half the day trekking back and forth to county dispatch, seeing what happened the previous night."

I remembered our long conversation from the previous night at my house about her and her job and the changes contained within, before the space-shuttle launch and before my long trek out to the state wildlife preserve. I motioned to the two newspaper front pages hanging from the ceiling.

"More motivational signs from the new regime?"

Paula leaned back in her chair, her own computer terminal at her elbow. Her desk was as cluttered as Rollie's. "New regime. Yeah, I like that word. Regime. Makes me think about the guillotine coming out, the nobility and merchant class being obliterated."

"How's Rollie doing?"

"Rollie? A company man through and through. He's a few years away from retirement, and if the new powers-that-be told him to start putting alien babies and Elvis sightings on the front page, he'd snap to it and make me paranormal editor."

Somewhere a phone started ringing and then was picked up. "Okay, more important. How are you doing?"

She started playing with a pen on her desk. "Like I said last night. I'm doing okay. It's just that—"

I didn't have a chance to hear what was next on Paula's mind, for then the door to the conference room slammed out and Rollie Grandmaison came out, his face red, what few black hairs on top of his almost-bald head in disarray. His dark gray slacks seemed bunched around his waist, and the sleeves of his off-white shirt were frayed. Whereas Rollie looked as if he had gotten dressed in the dark, the man coming out of the conference room behind him looked as if he had spent the previous day with a tailor. Black slacks and black loafers with tassels, blue-striped shirt with suspenders and a red bow tie that was definitely not a clip-on. His black hair was thick and slicked back, and his nose prominent. He noticed Paula and me and strolled right over, just as I heard Paula mutter, "Christ, here we go" under her breath.

"Paula?" he asked, looking down at her, the same kind of look a hungry hawk would give a plump little hare.

"Yes, Rupert?"

He stood as if he were at attention, with hands clasped behind his back. "You'll note that it's one hour and ten minutes to deadline. Will you get the stories listed in this morning's budget submitted by then?"

"I will," she said, putting about a ton of disdain into each word.

"Grand," he said. "Is this gentleman here assisting you with a story on that budget list?"

"No, he's not," she said. "Rupert Holman, this is Lewis Cole. He writes for *Shoreline* magazine."

Now his look was aimed in my direction, and I aimed right back with a look of my own. He gave a quick nod. "I see. Mr. Cole, do you have any desire to write for the *Chronicle?*"

"Not today," I said. "My schedule is pretty full-up."

"I see," Rupert said, and then he turned his head back to Paula. "Then it would appear to me, Paula, that this is a social visit, and a social visit so close to deadline—"

I was opening my mouth to tell him what he could do with his upcoming deadline, when Paula beat me to the punch. She reached behind herself and pulled her black leather purse free from the rear of her chair. "Actually, Rupert, Lewis is here to visit during my morning break. I haven't taken it yet."

"Mmm," he said, nodding his head again, and I imagined little gears and cams behind that impassive face. "All right, then. Ten minutes. Don't be late."

"Don't you worry," she shot back, but by then he was halfway back to his desk. Rollie looked up and gave Rupert the look of a scared steer, seeing a butcher in a bloody white apron heading his way.

Outside, she slipped her arm inside mine and said something in a low voice that would probably shock about half the elected officials in Tyler. We headed across the small common to a tiny brick building that once held Tyler's first post office and was now the Common Grill & Grill. She pushed her way in and we sat at a booth in the back. The place was nearly empty, save for the owner, John Thiakapolous, a large bulk of a man who was sweating behind the grill, and a waitress and a couple of retirees, who were making their late-morning breakfast stretch out. It's one of the smallest restaurants on Route 1, and its name comes from the fact that the previous owner lost his bar license. When John bought the place some years ago, he had a spare neon "Grill" sign, which he used to replace the hole left when the "Bar" sign had been taken down.

Remembering what Paula had said last night, I said, "So that's the famous Rupert the Ruthless, the hired gun sent in to set the *Chronicle* in the black, and to drive out the heathen competing newspapers from your territory."

She gingerly blew across the top of her coffee cup. "Yep, and to drag this little daily newspaper kicking and screaming into the new, bold newspaper age. When I started here, the paper was part of a chain of one daily and two weeklies. Now, three owners later, we're owned by a conglomerate based in London. Can you believe that? London! And to make sure they squeeze every potential penny out of each newspaper, we get an efficiency expert like that clown to make our lives miserable for the next six months."

I took a sip from my own cup of tea. "Tell me again about the circulation wars, and what he's got planned."

"Huh," she said. "Pretty basic stuff. We've got to increase circulation and drive back the Porter and Dover papers who want to home in on our territory. To do that, we need stories, lots of stories. So we're getting pushed to do things we've never done before. Like community reporting. You know what that is? It means if there's no hard news to report, you get to make news. Stories about how to be a better parent. How to be a better student. Spring decorating tips. Mush like that. Plus, Rupert here has hitched his star to the New Puritans to stir up things in town."

"The new what?"

Paula made a show of rolling her eyes. "Didn't you listen to anything I said last night, or were you too busy ogling my new leather skirt?"

"I wouldn't exactly call it ogling," I replied, trying to make my voice sound hurt.

"Whatever," she said. "Look, town meeting last month, we got a couple of new selectmen. Both of them are so conservative they think Ronald Reagan and Barry Goldwater were charter founders of the ACLU. And they want to stir things up, and Rupert's glad to help them out. They've already had one victory, if you can call it that. The assistant school district superintendent. You do remember that, don't you?"

I surely did. "Yeah, he was fired after using the school computer to look at certain Web pages."

"On his lunch break," Paula pointed out. "And the pages he was looking at . . . okay, they were odd, but if a guy wants to spend thirty minutes of his free time looking at pictures of women's legs in stockings and high heels, why should I care?"

"There was a deal in the works, wasn't there, to save his job?"

She nodded, took another swallow of her coffee. Back at the counter, John started muttering to himself in Greek as he flipped over a couple of eggs. Paula said, "The school board was going to give him a couple of weeks suspension without pay, but one of the school board members is married to one of our New Puritans. One meeting with Rupert and a couple of front-page stories and editorials later, the poor bastard's lost his job and has moved back in with his parents in Oregon. Let me tell you, this is turning into a hell of a business."

Then she looked at me, her eyes now bleak. "And I'm afraid it's going to get worse. Unless you can help me."

I looked back at her. "Go on."

She sighed, looked at her watch. "Jesus, only five minutes left, and you wouldn't believe how tight this guy watches our time. Look, Rupert's told me that he wants me to do an in-depth profile of our own Diane Woods. She's one of the few woman detectives in the state. Okay, a standard profile, I could practically do in my sleep. But Rupert wants more."

Oh my, I thought, and my hand trembled as I put my teacup down on the table. "I see."

"Do you?" She looked around and leaned forward, lowering her voice. "Look, I've known for a couple of years that Diane has a certain sexual preference. Big deal. Except for the usual runarounds you get from cops, she's treated me okay. But now Rupert's heard something about Diane, and his blood's up. He told me he wants something juicy, something sexy, something that will put the *Chronicle* on the map. You know what he's talking about?"

"Sure," I said, thinking back to just a few minutes ago, when I was in the newspaper's office. Instead of thinking of something sharp to say to the man, I should have just stood up and slugged him in the face. Get rid of the unnecessary steps. I went on. "Typical tabloid story. Police official with secret life. How can you trust her to prosecute certain sex offenders? How can you trust her, period? What kind of role model for the children? A few quotes from the new selectmen, maybe a minister who believes the Earth is still flat. And all wrapped up with a couple of grainy long-distance photos of Diane with her lover."

Paula now looked miserable. "Exactly. And Rupert's told me I've got just over a week to wrap it up."

"And I suppose he didn't listen to reason, did he?"

She shook her head. "Nope. I tried a couple of times, and then it just came down to recommendations. He told me that when he left in a few months, it would be his task to recommend who would stay and who would leave from the *Chronicle*'s staff. And it would be my decisions that would put me on either one of those lists."

"A charming guy. All right, you said something about me helping you out. What do you have in mind?"

Another glance at the watch. "Not much time . . . Lewis, I know you're good friends with Diane, and you know what will happen if I do a story like that. Her career would be ruined, and

every cop and firefighter in town and probably every other surrounding town would stop talking to me. Forever. I told Rupert
that and he just shrugged, saying it was one of the challenges of
journalism. Afflicting the comforted and comforting the afflicted,
or some crap like that."

"And I can do . . . ?"

"Talk to her. Warn her about what's up. Maybe we could
work something out. Maybe she's got some ongoing investigation
that she can give me an exclusive on. Or maybe she can promise
me a front-row seat the next time there's a major drug bust. Or
something. Anything. I don't want to do this story."

I finished my now cold cup of tea and said, "But you will if
you have to, won't you?"

Now she glared at me. "Time's up. I've got to get back to
the office. Walk me there, will you?"

Outside I gently rubbed the back of her neck as we made
the short walk back to her office. "All right, here's a story I might
help you with. You heard about the dead guy found at Samson
Point?"

"Yep," she said. "Even had a faxed press release from the
North Tyler Police Department waiting for us when we got into
the office this morning. A male subject found dead in a rental car.
Self-inflicted gunshot wound. Identity not made public until next
of kin notified. End of story."

"Self-inflicted? You sure?"

"That's what the press release and the follow-up phone call
I made to the North Tyler chief all pointed to. Hey, how did you
hear about it?"

"I was there, about a half hour or so after the first cops
showed up."

She stopped by the white wooden door into the Tyler
Building, looking at me with a slight smile. "And what you were
doing out there so early in the morning?"

I didn't want to get into a lengthy explanation so instead I
said, "I had my reasons. And I got a look inside the car. I didn't
see a weapon."

She shrugged. "The cops said there was one there, which was good enough for me. One of the few policies I like here at the paper is that we don't do suicide stories."

"So no follow-up?" I asked, thinking about the three Ford LTDs and their mysterious passengers.

"Nope, no follow-up. Hey, I've got to run. Thanks for the coffee and conversation."

I reached up and squeezed her hand. "My pleasure. Tell me, is the paper doing anything about the mission?"

"What mission?"

"The space-shuttle mission. The one that was launched this morning."

Paula shook her head. "Unless there's a cabal of gay or Communist astronauts aboard, this newspaper now doesn't care. Look, call me?"

"I promise," I said, staying there until I saw her go through the door and pass by the main windows, heading back to the newsroom. It looked as if she waved at me, and so I waved back at her fleeting image.

A few minutes later I was on Route 51, heading toward the main beach and the police station, and for the first time in months I got stuck in traffic. A line of about fifteen to twenty cars were in front of me, at the sole traffic light on this road between Manchester, about 35 miles away to the west, and Tyler Beach. I rolled down the window, enjoying the scents of the warm day. Another sign of spring: the leaves come out, the grass turns green, and tourists start coming into Tyler and its beach, clogging the roads and taking the best parking spaces. Toward the south and the east were the wide flat marshes, still tan and brown after a long winter and spring. Seagulls spun and swirled up in the light blue sky, and when the traffic eased up, I continued heading to the beach.

I rubbed the steering wheel a bit self-consciously as I drove. This month I was driving a new Ford Explorer, replacing a Range Rover of mine that a couple of months ago got in the way of a few dozen rounds from a couple of semiautomatic weapons, and I was still getting used to the new vehicle's feel. While I probably could have had the Range Rover replaced, insurance companies do tend to report to the local police how one's vehicle got full of bullet holes, and I didn't want the attention.

At the intersection of Ashburn Avenue and Route 51, I turned right and in less than a minute was pulling into the rear parking lot of the Tyler police station. Despite years of plans and budget proposals and votes, the station looks pretty much as it did thirty years ago: a squat, single-story white cinder-block structure that could have been a command bunker in some obscure war. As I walked across the bumpy ill-paved parking lot, I noticed how the adjacent town parking lot was only about a third full, and smiled, thinking that in less than two months drivers would sometimes engage in fistfights over the last few available spaces.

The on-duty dispatcher at the glassed-in booth recognized me, and after she had buzzed open a metal door I went down a narrow corridor to an office marked "BCI," for Bureau of Criminal Investigations. When I went inside, I found the entire criminal bureau of the Tyler Police Department on her hands and knees, looking for something under a metal desk.

I leaned against the doorjamb. "On the trail of a major crime?"

Detective Diane Woods slowly backed out. She was wearing sneakers, faded jeans and a brightly colored rugby shirt. Looking up, she gave me a slight smile, a pen in her hand.

"Sure I am," she said. "The problem is, the crime is the same one, committed year after year: not enough bodies, not enough budget to do the right kind of job. Gets to the point where even pens are valuable, so much so that you can spend fifteen minutes looking for one after you've dropped it."

Diane got up and sat down at her desk, which was pushed against one of the cinder-block walls painted a light, sickly green. The desk was covered with file folders and photos and notebooks. A plaster skull cast served as a paperweight. This spring she was letting her thick brown hair grow out, and her face was still lightly tanned from a trip some weeks ago to Key West. At the base of her chin was a short white scar, earned one night when she was on patrol and a drunk banged her head in the booking room. One of the few times I had ever heard of when someone took advantage of her while on duty, and I still think it made her more cautious in doing her job, in not leaving her back exposed.

She played with the pen in her hand and said, "What brings you here this lovely spring day?"

"Wondering if you're interested in lunch."

"I'm always interested in lunch, especially if you're buying, but I've got a previous commitment. It's career day at the Main Street School and I'm gonna tell the little darlings about the glamour of small-town police work. About going to car accidents at two in the morning and diagramming the place where their drunk older brother or sister was ejected through the windshield. Or going into a small cottage to look in after their grandma or grandpa after they've passed on a couple of weeks earlier. Or about trying to do your job when elected officials who would've fit right in at Salem three centuries ago start sniffing around your personal life."

"Gee," I said seriously. "You'll be a hit, I'm sure."

She stuck out her tongue and threw the pen at me, and I'm grateful she's better with a gun than a pen, for it ended up in the hallway somewhere behind me. "Why don't you take Paula out to lunch? Word is, maybe you two are finally on track after all these months."

"I just had tea with her a while ago. Didn't want to overstay my welcome."

Diane reached up to scratch her side, raising the rugby shirt and showing a tanned, flat belly, and a holstered Ruger .357 and detective's shield pinned to her waistband. "Well, ain't that nice. How is the young Miss Quinn?"

"The young Miss Quinn is fine," I said. "But her new boss isn't. Look, I don't know how to say this, but—"

She held up her hand. "Forget it. I already know. Their hired gun is here to stir things up to increase circulation, and it looks like I'm next on his hit parade. I already know the drill. Slobbering dyke detective on the public payroll, put in a place to corrupt the youth of our fair town. Blah, blah, blah. It was bound to happen one of these days. I guess now's the time."

I felt a flash of anger toward that well-dressed and well-oiled man back at the newspaper office, sitting there comfortable and well-fed, waiting to toss my best friend's life into a threshing machine of publicity.

"Any idea what you're going to do?" I asked.

"Do? Me? Well, I had thoughts of firebombing the place, or maybe tailing that Rupert guy and arresting him on suspicions of being a professional jerk. But since firebombing is against the law and being a professional jerk isn't, it looks like my options are limited."

"Paula wants you to know that if you can help, there might be a way to avoid her doing the story."

Diane's eyes narrowed and her little white scar seemed to whiten, both dangerous signals indeed. "Like how?"

"I'm not sure. But she said if there's some investigation that you're doing that she can report on, some big story that will focus attention away from this profile piece, then she'll be glad to do it."

"I see. Give her one exclusive in exchange for not doing a tabloid story about my love life. Your girlfriend definitely has a reporter's sense of ethics."

"She's not my girlfriend," I said, the words sounding ridiculous right after I said them. "A dear friend, but nothing romantic."

"Yet," she observed.

"Yet," I agreed. "But she's willing to help you, if it's possible."

Diane shook her head and got up and went out to the hallway, retrieved her pen and then sat heavily down. "You tell Paula . . . okay, I won't go there. Look, I appreciate where she's coming from. Honest, I do. But I'm not in the business of trading that kind of favor. In anything else, yes, I'll do that. Exchange an exclusive story on a drug bust for some good publicity for the department. That I'll do. But not when it comes to what kind of woman I am and who I love. That's not up for trade. All right?"

It wasn't time to press the matter. "All right, it is," I said. "And speaking of who you love, how's Kara doing?"

Her face widened in a smile. "Better, much better. She still gets the occasional bad dream about the assault and all, but she's got a new job at Digital. Involves some travel, which I hate, but she seems to thrive on it. I think because it gets her away from the memories here. She promises that the travel won't last long, but she's doing better. Honest, she is."

"Good."

"And you?"

Diane looked at me with the face of a friend, but the face was also backed up by the look of a professional interrogator. I struggled for a moment about what to say, about the strange sense I had this spring of being disconnected, of feeling that nothing I was doing was making any kind of impact, was making a difference in anything at all.

I said, "Okay."

"Okay? Just okay?"

"Well, there's something going on that I'm curious about, if you don't mind me asking."

"Go on."

"You hear about the dead guy the North Tyler police found up on Samson Point?"

"Yeah, heard a brief news report. Something about a self-inflicted gunshot wound. What about it?"

"Well, I was there—"

She sat up. "You were there when the guy killed himself?"

"No, no," I said. "I was out on my deck and saw the lights of the cruisers and the ambulance. I walked over and checked it out. And it just looks strange, that's all."

"Why strange?"

I told her about the three Ford LTDs and the crew of five men, headed by a woman, who quickly secured the scene, and she nodded a couple of times. "Yep, that sure sounds strange."

"What does it sound like to you? The feds?"

From nearby the door to the booking room clanked open, and I listened to a couple of Tyler cops drag in somebody who

26

was yelling about calling his lawyer and congressman. Diane turned to the noise for a moment and said, "Sounds like a good guess. The feds. But what kind, I couldn't tell you. Maybe it was the Marshal's Office. Those guys are pretty closed-mouth. Maybe that was a witness they were suppose to be escorting, or some guy in the witness protection program that decided to end it all. That kind of stuff can be very embarrassing. Not the kind of story you'd spill out to a local magazine writer who happens to stumble by on the crime scene."

I reached into my coat pocket, took out a piece of notebook paper. "Well, could you help me satisfy my curiosity? These are the license plate numbers off those three Ford LTDs. If you could do a trace . . ."

Diane laughed and pulled the paper from my hand. "If I charged you for each plate I ran, I could afford to take you out to lunch. Hold on, I'll walk it out to dispatch."

She went out and headed to the dispatcher, and I stayed there and looked around the office. Another sign of how much she trusted me. Any other detective wouldn't have allowed a writer to stay unescorted in a detective's office. All those files, stuffed full of confidential information about ongoing cases. Little fruits of stories, just waiting to be picked. If I had been a true professional magazine writer, I would have stood up and started looking down at what was on Diane's desk.

Instead, I sat in my chair and thought of other things. About the times I had spent here with Diane in this little office. A snowy night in December, going out to a Christmas party somewhere in town, agreeing to be her date and watching her as she came out wearing a black evening dress that looked spectacular. The times I had been in here, either seeking or giving information, both of us in the pursuit of what passed as justice these days. Sometimes sharing a take-out lunch on her desk, laughing about local politics or the misadventures of tourists. And that horrible time a couple of months ago, after her lover Kara had been assaulted—the furies and the angers that had been coming from her, sometimes directed at me, sometimes ending with the demand that I never see her again.

Yet I had come back. I always came back.

Diane entered the room sipping a Coke, saying, "I could have saved time by calling the dispatcher, but I needed a drink. Sorry, Lewis."

"Sorry? Don't worry, I'm not thirsty."

She shook her head, sipped gingerly at her straw. "Nope. Sorry about the license plate numbers. Fred ran them and they all came back negative."

"Negative? In what way?"

A noisy slurp of soda. "Negative in that the plates don't exist, that's why. The State Police and a few federal agencies have an arrangement with the Division of Motor Vehicles in Concord. They can get plates that don't show up on the DMV records, so that nosy police detectives or magazine writers can't trace who they've been assigned to. And to answer your next question—no, I'm not going to pursue it, unless you can show me that they committed a crime in Tyler. Okay?"

"Sounds fair. What's your guess?"

She smiled at me. "Best guess is that I have to leave in two minutes, and that you're going to have to satisfy your curiosity somewhere else."

I nodded. "I guess I will."

Diane turned and put her Coke down on her desk, shoving aside a few envelopes to make room. "Then be careful, my friend. These people seem to be working in some deep and dark places. I'd hate for them to start paying attention to you."

I stood up, suddenly feeling antsy, as if I had to be on the move. "Thanks. And I'll be careful."

"I have no doubt you will. I just worry about the other guys."

I said, "I always worry about the other guys."

"Good," Diane said.

CHAPTER THREE

I drove north on Atlantic Avenue, passing the section of Tyler Beach that's known as the Strip. The shops and restaurants and motels were crowded in together, and while the developers years ago didn't quite build on every open bit of space, they sure did give it a try. The traffic was moderate and a lot of the shops and arcades were open, nervous business owners trying to get a jump on the official start of the summer season.

Near my home I passed the Lafayette House on the left, a large white Victorian-style hotel, and in a matter of minutes I had crossed over into North Tyler and turned right at the entrance to the Samson Point State Wildlife Preserve. From here, the ocean was some distance away, past the open lawns and park buildings. The ticket kiosk was still closed—the state of New Hampshire not having officially opened the place—and I found a parking spot easily enough.

I got out and walked around the pavement. A couple of dozen cars were scattered across the lot, and people were walking and flying kites or playing with dogs, and a couple of hardy souls were actually sunbathing. I wandered over to where I thought everything had happened the previous night and sat down on a wooden guardrail, looking out across the parking lot. Several hours earlier, a man in a rental car had come right here and had been murdered. Not more than a ten-minute walk from my house.

I folded my arms, let the sun warm my back. I am not a vigilante nor a guy who goes seeking trouble. Many years ago, trouble had found me and had injured me and had killed a number of friends, and this trouble had eventually sent me here, to my new home on Tyler Beach. For the most part, my new life had been a good one. I should just let this whole thing drop and get on with things, whatever things were out there.

Still . . . I had the image of that dead man, in a car, so close to my home. Almost insulting, really. And then there was the matter of the intense men and the very intense woman who had come upon the crime scene and had taken control of everything. I didn't like the way they had acted, and I especially didn't like the way that woman had ordered me out of there. Even if she did have a pretty smile.

A young girl raced by on pudgy legs, a balloon trailing from a string wrapped around her wrist. Her parents chased after her, laughing, not trying too hard to catch up to her, and they ran right across the empty space where the dead man had been, and I shivered. Something bad had happened here, and for whatever reason, from the murder so close to my home to those officious people, things were out of balance. And I felt an urge to set them straight.

So I got up and got back into my Ford, and drove out.

The North Tyler police station is in a small wooden building near the town hall. While smaller than the Tyler police station, it was more charming, with lots of wood clapboards and black shutters. By producing my official state of New Hampshire press identification card—complete with a photo almost as unflattering as my driver's license picture—I wangled a few minutes with the chief, an amiable man named Roy Tallinn.

Roy had on a white uniform dress shirt and black trousers

and black shiny shoes, and the collars on his shirt had four little gold stars on each of them. His office was smaller than Diane's, but considerably neater, and he had a beefy look about him, from his thick wrists to the flesh that spilled out over his shirt collar and red face. His gray hair was buzz-cut short, and he offered me coffee, which I declined.

"*Shoreline* magazine," he mused, rubbing his thick hands together. "Sorry, I can't say that I've ever read an issue. Does it make it up to newsstands up here?"

"Apparently not," I said. "But I could send you over a few sample issues if you'd like."

He ignored my gracious offer. "And you're interested in doing a story about the suicide victim found last night at the state park."

"I'm considering it," I said. "And are you certain it was a suicide?"

He smiled. "Very certain. There was a revolver found on the floor of the car, and a suicide note in the glove box. Fingerprints found on the revolver, and gunpowder residue found on the man's hand. About as straightforward as it gets."

"And you're not releasing the man's name?"

"Standard procedure. It's a suicide. Not a murder, or even an apparent murder."

"And the revolver. On the floorboards, right?"

A slow nod, but the smile was still there. "Right."

"But Chief," I said, trying to keep my voice friendly, "I was there right after your two officers got there. I got a good look in the car. I didn't see a revolver."

His smile seemed to match mine. "Oh, right . . . You're the magazine writer that walked in on my guys. Yeah, Lewis Cole. Should have noted that before. Then you must have missed seeing the weapon."

"Yeah, maybe I did," I said, replaying in my mind's eye what I had seen that night, doubting very much that I could have missed seeing a weapon. "By the way, who were the other responding units there this morning?"

"You mean the State Police Major Crimes Unit?"

31

"No," I said, beginning to feel a bit chilled in this sunny office. "Three other Ford LTDs came in, with six people, a woman and five men. Well-dressed, arrogant, seemed to enjoy shoving their weight around. Looked like feds."

"Hmmm," Tallinn said, slowly going through papers on his desk, looking like a bear who had just woken up from hibernation and was looking for his first meal. "Here we go. Incident report. Hmmm."

As he started reading, I noted that the palms of my hands were getting moist. I wiped them down on my pant leg, just as the chief finished reading. "Sorry, Lewis. No mention of anybody else in my guys' report. The first officer saw the vehicle on routine patrol, and then my second officer responded. A brief mention of you, and then I show up, and then the State Police. There you go. Like I said, pretty straightforward."

"Officer Calhoun and Officer Remick," I said quietly, "are they on duty today?"

The chief's expression hadn't changed for a moment since I arrived. "No, they're not."

"Will they be in later tonight? Or tomorrow?"

"I'm afraid not," the chief said. "They're both taking some vacation time."

Now I looked back to the office's doorway, gauging if I could make it out to the parking lot in time if the good chief did something silly, like pull his weapon. I kept my voice even. "Gee. What a coincidence."

A slow nod. "Yes, a coincidence. A nice word."

I tried to see what was going on behind that chief's merry expression, and I failed. He was good. I said, "What did they offer you?"

He blinked. Maybe that was as good a response as I could expect. "Excuse me, I don't understand what you mean."

"What did they offer you?" I said again. "New cruisers? New weapons? A hefty contribution to the Police Relief Association? Some other goodie to keep it all a secret? Come on, Chief, I was there. I saw the other people. Saw the three LTDs. I saw it, your cops saw it, and so did the EMTs."

The chief's gaze at me didn't waver for a moment. "I'm not sure what you saw, but my cops and the EMTs didn't see anything unusual last night. And if you try to talk to the fire chief next door, you'll get as much satisfaction as you did here. Which is zero. Now, is there anything else I can do for you?"

Leave, a voice inside of me said. Leave now and be thankful you can get out. I stood up, shook his hand. "Chief, one of these days, it'll come out. I don't know when or where, but it will come out. It might prove pretty embarrassing to you and the department. You can see this as an opportunity to let a member of the press in on what was going on."

A sad shake of his head. "Sorry. There's nothing I can do for you."

I turned and headed out to the office, feeling better with each step taken, and then the chief called out to me. "Lewis?"

"Yes?" I said, turning by the door.

He was still behind his desk. "Want to hear a secret?"

"Sure," I said, wondering what was coming next.

His smile widened. "Four years ago, I cheated on my wife. At a police convention in Atlanta. With a woman SWAT team leader from Oregon. There. Satisfied?"

"Not really," I said, and then I left.

In my Ford I locked the doors and started the engine, and then I started shivering. It wasn't cold, damn it, it wasn't cold at all, but still, the shakes wouldn't stop. I turned on the radio and started listening to the news at the top of the hour from WBZ-AM in Boston, and that calmed me down some. The fifth story in was a ten-second report about last night's successful space shuttle launch, and I wiped my face and hands with my handkerchief, and felt a little better.

This part of North Tyler had the police and fire stations and a little town hall, and a store in a converted train station that was next to the old B & M Railroad tracks. About as peaceful as a place as one could expect, almost as peaceful as the parking lot of the state park, just a few miles away.

But something had come traipsing into these peaceful areas, something that didn't belong, something that scared me to death, and something that, for a while, several years ago, I had been a part of.

When my shivering stopped, I drove out of the parking lot and headed home.

My home is across the street from the Lafayette House, near the border between Tyler and North Tyler, and I pulled into the tiny parking lot across from the hotel. A large sign at the entrance said PRIVATE PARKING FOR LAFAYETTE HOUSE ONLY and I went to the north end, passing a few parked cars, BMWs and Volvos and Lexuses. At the end of the lot was a low stone wall with an opening where some of the rocks had fallen free. There was a narrow dirt-covered path there, just wide enough for my Ford. The path went to the right, past two homemade NO TRESPASSING signs, and my home came into view. It's a two-story house that's one step above a cottage and has never been painted and which has a dirt crawl space for a cellar. The scraggly lawn rises up to a steep rocky ledge that hides my home from Atlantic Avenue, and I parked in the sagging shed that serves as my garage.

Inside I had a quick lunch of tomato soup and bread and cheese, and as I ate I watched CNN, hoping against hope that they would have a lengthy update about the shuttle mission and its crew. Instead, they had some sort of legal affairs program, where they dissected yet another court case where an overpaid and undereducated football player got away with murder. As I washed the dishes, looking out to the ocean, I had an odd feeling that I was glad I was near a window that overlooked the empty water. There would be no way that quiet men with long-range binoculars could keep watch on me from that vantage point.

I then retreated upstairs to a nice hot shower, and when I was done I mechanically went through my daily routine of checking my skin for bumps, for swellings, for things that did not belong. As I did this, I also noted the two scars on my left side, one on my left knee and one on my back, near the coccyx. Daily reminders of how I had come to be here.

I got tired all of a sudden and sat down on the toilet, towel wrapped around my waist. Then the shakes came back and I felt nauseous, and it all came back to me, like a movie in the VCR set on fast forward: my previous career as a research analyst with the Department of Defense, the friends I had made. Carl Socha. Trent Baker. And my darling Cissy Manning. Then a weekend in Nevada. A training mission, trooping around in the desert. We got lost and ended up in the middle of a test range. A test range that didn't officially exist. And out of that group, only one person came out alive.

Alive, with memories and scars and the threat of an odd disease coming back at any time to strike me down. Which explains my daily skin searches.

The shakes continued, and I knew why. Once I had been in the middle of a dark and deep world, with missions and projects and tasks that were classified ABOVE TOP SECRET and which were never made public. A world of intelligence briefings and missions and black budgets. A world that didn't exist in any newspaper or magazine or TV or Internet report.

I thought I had safely left this world behind me, and for the most part, I had been right.

Until last night. With those LTDs and that crew of people, and that smug woman who looked as if she knew all the answers.

I bent my head down, rubbed at my face with a towel. Two options, then. To forget everything that had happened, or to stay awake nights with questions and concerns, waiting for that phone call or knock at the door, to see if the almighty Them had finally decided to do something about a witness who had been on the scene of something highly classified.

Or to do something else.

I cursed and got up and got dressed. I wasn't about to forget a damn thing.

The only person I know well in North Tyler is Felix Tinios, a native of the North End in Boston. I'm not sure if he chose the town because it had the word "North" in its name, but it's as good a reason as any. Felix lives a couple of miles north of the Samson

State Wildlife Preserve, on Rosemount Lane, a road that extends off to the east and which contains six houses. As I made the short drive north, I kept on glancing up at my rearview mirror, as if I was expecting to be tailed by one of the cars I had seen the night before. But the only traffic behind me was a bright red pickup truck, and I made the turn onto Felix's road with no problems and no mysterious cars behind me. Five of the homes are clustered together, but Felix's house sits by itself, on a bluff overlooking the Atlantic. It's a low-slung ranch and parked in the driveway was his blue Mercedes convertible.

I got out and felt again that twinge of anticipation that comes from the scents of spring, and then I felt another twinge of guilt as I walked up to the house. I suppose I should have called first, but I didn't want to talk to Felix over the phone. I wanted to see him face-to-face before I unburdened what was troubling me.

I rang the doorbell twice, and as I waited I looked out across his lawn. While my own lawn is the size of a couple of postage stamps and is a collection of weeds and whatever, Felix does take no small pride in his own turf. Even this early in the year the lawn looked good, and Felix had told me once proudly that since growing up in a crowded brick apartment building, he had always dreamed of a wide green lawn to call his own. Of course, his lawn also contains no shrubs, trees or brush that could obscure a gunman crawling up to visit Felix. He once told me that a door-to-door census taker had asked him his occupation, and when Felix had replied, "Security consultant," the teenage girl asking the questions just shook her head quickly in terror and walked away. Felix sometimes has that effect on people.

I was about to ring the doorbell for a third time when the door flew open and there he was, dressed in gray sweatpants and a white tank-top T-shirt, nearly soaked through with sweat. "Jesus, Lewis, haven't you ever heard of the phone?"

"Sorry," I said. "I was driving by, thought I'd stop by for a quick visit. Did I catch you working out?"

He ran a hand across his thick black hair and grinned. "Yeah, you could say that. Jesus. All right, for a few minutes, but only if it's important."

I followed him in through the foyer and then stopped. Piled up by the doorway were a horse saddle, knee-high leather boots and a riding crop. I gave him a look and asked innocently, "Taking up a new hobby, Felix?"

He laughed. "No, not really. It's, uh, well . . ."

Then I made out the sound of a shower at the other end of the house, just barely drowning out a woman's voice, singing. "I see," I said, now feeling embarrassed, like a small child breaking into his parents' bedroom at an inopportune time. "Look, I won't keep you—"

He waved a hand and led me into the living room. "No matter. Her name is Michelle, but she likes to be called Mickey. Met her a few days ago up at Sandtree Stables. She's a horse trainer and her boss hired me for a situation."

"What kind of situation? Somebody skimming the oat bags?"

Felix turned, still smiling. Fine black hair ran up both muscled arms, the skin a light brown, and his feet were bare. "No, not really. A stablehand was threatening to torch a barn or two unless he got some back pay he thought was owed to him. I convinced him otherwise and now he has a new and satisfying career as a fry cook, over in Keene." Felix sat down on a couch, motioned me to an easy chair across the way. "Of course, his career will be more satisfying once the cast comes off his arm. What's going on?"

While my house is old antiques and creaking wood flooring, Felix's is relatively modern and up-to-date, with Scandinavian-type furniture and polished hardwood floors. Even sitting still, Felix seems to dominate a room, which was certainly the case now. I looked at him and wondered where he kept his weapons hidden.

"What's going on is a murder that took place in North Tyler last night," I said. "Hear anything about it?"

With the showering and the singing continuing, I now had Felix's full attention. "No. Tell me more."

"I was out on my deck about one A.M. this morning—"

"Doing some stargazing?" he interrupted, and I nodded. No use in trying to explain it any more than that.

"That's right. Then I saw some lights, over at the state park. Police and ambulance lights. I took a hike over and saw what was going on. A rental car was parked in the lot, and there was a guy in the front seat, with what looked to be a gunshot wound to the head."

His eyes narrowed some and he rubbed at the blue-black stubble on his chin. "Don't like the sound of that."

"Why?"

"Don't be coy," he said. "You know where I've been, what I've done. Most murders in this lovely state of yours occur between friends or lovers. It's domestic-related, usually fueled by coke or booze, and it takes place in the home or at a bar. A knife, a baseball bat, and sure, maybe gunfire. But not like this. Not a guy alone in a rental car with a tap to the hat. That shows a level of professionalism you usually don't see in the Granite State. Go on. What next?"

I would have thought that the singing and the water running would have distracted me, but it almost made me feel calm, at peace. "What's next is that I talked to the cops at the scene and they had squat. The guy rented the car from the Manchester Airport, under the name Smith. I went over and took a look. Guy was in a suit, no necktie. Dark-skinned, mustache, blood down one side. No weapon in sight. And then, while I was waiting there, it got weird."

Felix now seemed tense, like a hunting dog, detecting a foreign scent. "I can hardly wait to see what your definition of weird is."

"These three Ford LTDs came racing into the lot, like they belonged there. Five muscled guys and a sharp-looking woman came out, took control of the scene. The cops and the EMTs have been shut up, and when I had the license plates of those LTDs traced, they've been faked up. The official story today from the North Tyler cops is that this guy killed himself. The police chief said a revolver was found on the floor of the car, even though I didn't see anything. There was also a suicide note in the glove box, he said, and because it's a suicide, no more information's coming out."

"This crew that came in, did they ID themselves?"

"Nope. And the chief said I was imagining the whole thing,

that there wasn't a crew there in three cars with fake license plates. So there you have it. Dead guy in a rental car and all's quiet."

"Yeah, I guess that's weird all right," Felix said, shifting some on the couch. The sounds of showering and singing were continuing. "It seems like Uncle Sam has an interest in this guy. That make sense to you?"

"Right from the start," I said.

"Then that's probably why you didn't call me, right? Wanted to keep things confidential, in case there are electronic ears out there."

About then I felt about as thick as a plank. "You know, you're absolutely right. I just had this odd feeling that seeing you face-to-face made more sense than calling you up."

"Fair enough. So what's your interest?"

Good question, and about the only answer I had was a weak one. "I don't like having guys murdered next door to my house, and I like it even less when I'm told to pipe down and pretend it didn't happen."

"Might make the most sense—pretend it didn't happen."

"Sometimes what I do doesn't make sense."

"True," Felix said, smiling. "And what would you like me to do?"

"Damned if I know," I said. "I thought maybe these feds are with the FBI or Department of Justice, something like that. If that's the case, then maybe you can find out if anybody down south in Boston has a dad or brother missing, somebody that fits the description."

He nodded confidently, as if a challenge had been issued and he was glad to pick it up. "Sure. Easy enough. You know, I don't like guys getting whacked in my adopted hometown either. Okay, let's say I do find out it's mob-related. Maybe a meet gone bad, maybe somebody's been removed for gross stupidity or having sticky fingers. What then?"

"Then I do nothing," I said. "That kind of rough justice . . . well, not much point to me finding out any more."

"And if it's something else, something that's not related to friends or family of mine?"

"Then we'll go from there, won't we."

"Hah," Felix said. "Not sure why you're mentioning 'we,' I don't recall agreeing to—"

Then the shower stopped, as did the singing. Then a pleasant, clear woman's voice came calling out, each syllable stretched for effect: "Felix . . . will you come wash my back?"

I looked over at him and he was trying hard not to laugh. "Sure, Mickey, in a minute!"

"Hurry up," the unseen woman said. "I'm getting cold . . ."

I got up from the easy chair. "You go ahead, Felix. Looks like you've got some washroom duties to attend to."

He stood up and slapped me gently on the shoulder. "Well, we've all got our burdens to bear. Tell you what, I'll give you a ring tomorrow, let you know what I found out. And I'll keep it low-key. If nothing's there, I'll just say I went out last night and had a bad dinner. If there's anything else, I'll just make a lunch date with you. Sound okay?"

I headed for the door, not wanting to keep Felix from his appointed rounds any longer. "Sure, sounds great."

"Good," he said. "Now get the hell out of here so I can get scrubbing."

Outside, the sharp smell of the ocean seemed to settle around me like an old and comfortable blanket. Walking back to my Ford, I felt good. Felix was on the case, and Felix was quite smart, and quite deadly when he wanted to be. I'm sure he'd get the answer I was looking for soon enough. I had full confidence in his abilities.

It was a good feeling, one that was due to expire in less than twelve hours.

CHAPTER FOUR

The next morning the weather gods decided that winter would come back for a day or two along the New Hampshire seacoast, for the clouds were thick and dark and a stiff wind whipped up the ocean, causing whitecaps and little sprays of foam. A short walk up and back from the Lafayette House, bundled in a heavy coat that I had to retrieve from a storage closet, secured my morning newspapers, and I had a breakfast of tea and toast as I scanned the front pages and the editorial sections.

The New York Times and the *Boston Globe* had the usual customary stories about world atrocities, and little flashpoints that seemed to pop up every now and then, mostly concerning rogue nations and weapons of mass destruction. Refugees were also on the move this spring, being bombed either by rebel movements or governments, the bombs and bullets and shrapnel still doing their bloody work, no matter whose slogans or dollars paid for them.

Closer to home, the Tyler *Chronicle* was taking a decidedly local approach, by the second in a four-part series on what was called "The Hidden Danger: Porn In New Hampshire's Playground." The stories in the series were prominently played on the front page and focused on the few adult bookstores and video stores doing business in the small towns around Tyler. The meat of the stories was that none of the stores did a very good job in checking IDs of young males who were skulking in, and that the stores were mostly owned by a guy who lived in Massachusetts, and who had a dreary criminal record consisting of drug offenses and a couple of burglaries.

The stories, not written by Paula Quinn, had a nice moralistic tone—I imagined the Rupert character heavily editing them for the right flavor—but the tone was offset by the photo illustrations on page one that went with the stories: color reproductions of adult magazine and videocassette covers with black bars covering what British television delicately calls "naughty bits." Not a bad job, if you were trying both to raise circulation and run a moral crusade at the same time.

After breakfast—the rain hadn't started yet—I retreated upstairs to my office. It's the smallest of the two upstairs rooms, and it was full of bookshelves on every wall, save the one with the window overlooking my sparse lawn. I settled down at my desk and got to work setting up my new Apple computer. My previous computer had been more than four years old, and in computer years, that's equal to a century. So it had been time to upgrade, and the old computer with its files dumped sat forlornly in a corner. I had tried to donate it to a couple of the local schools, but something so ancient was no longer of any value. Just as I got one cardboard box opened, the phone rang.

"Lewis?" came the voice.

"Yeah, Felix," I said, feeling the need to sit down. "How's it going?"

"Oh, not too bad," he said, his voice cheerful. "Hey, I had dinner last night with Mickey, the place you recommended up in Porter."

"How was it?" I asked, staring at the nearest bookcase, not trying to think of anything much.

"How was it?" Felix repeated. "How it was, it sucked. Sorry to tell you that, but man, it's been a long time since I've eaten in a place so bad. Lobster and soup were both cold, the salad had brown leaves . . ." Then he laughed. "About the only thing good about the night was the dessert, and I got that at home."

"I'm sure you did."

"Well, I'll talk to you later this week. If I have another bad meal, that is."

"Understood."

We talked a couple of more minutes about the Red Sox actually securing a good pitcher for this season, and then, after hanging up, I went back to work.

A couple of hours later I was still looking at the brightness of my new machine, trying to get used to the neon-like blueberry color. In a room with wood flooring and books and bookshelves, the plastic and bright colors seemed as out of place as a circus clown at an Amish social. I sat in my chair with manual in hand, and started putting the new machine through its paces. As I worked, I was also trying to figure out what to do next about the man who had been murdered some yards away from this comfortable place.

So far, all I knew was that the death—murder or suicide, of course, depending on your point of view—had attracted the attention of some very interesting people. I had no idea who these people were, but the guesses of Diane Woods and Felix Tinios dovetailed into my own: people in the payment of Uncle Sam. But with Diane unable to trace those license plates and with Felix striking out on my organized-crime theory, I wasn't sure what I could do next.

Oh, in the long term, I knew what I could do. After a couple of weeks or so, I could start putting a little pressure on the North Tyler cops and EMTs who had been at the scene. Knowing cops and firefighters and how they are the very best of storytellers, I knew it wouldn't take long for some information to dribble out about what had been said to them by that nighttime crew in their Ford vehicles.

In the meantime, well, in the meantime I had a new computer to try out, and after an hour of that, testing some of its abilities, from sound to video recording to Internet surfing and word processing, I sat up and looked out the window. It was almost time to have lunch, but with a start, I knew lunch would have to wait.

I had visitors.

I leaned over in the chair, continued looking out the window. My lawn rises up to dirt and a rocky ledge that hides my house from Route 1-A, and a man in a suit was there, looking down at me, talking into a handheld radio. I looked up my dirt driveway and saw other men running down, followed by a certain woman, a woman I had only met two days ago.

I sat back in my chair, crossed my arms, played some more with the computer. It looked as if some of my questions were about to be answered.

Pounding sounds came up to me, from someone at the door with a heavy fist. I sat there, waited. I looked out the window, and the guy on the ledge was still there. I waved at him. The guy scowled and he went back to his radio.

I worked some more on the keyboard, and then there was a loud noise that made me wince. Splintering wood and protesting metal, and that quick sound was drowned out by stampeding feet coming up the stairway. I put the computer in a screensaver mode and then rolled the chair around, so that I was facing the open door. Two men sprinted into view, pistols held up in the air, and I tried to sit there calmly, my hands in my lap. I recognized the two men as part of the crew the other night from the parking lot of the wildlife preserve.

"Clear!" the guy on the left called out, and then he moved back and the woman came in, nodding to both of them, as if she was congratulating them for a job well done.

"Mr. Cole," she said, sitting down in my spare chair, which I usually use to hold printouts of my column before mailing them off to *Shoreline*. She was dressed the same as the last time I saw her, but it didn't look like the same clothes. I imagined she had an identical wardrobe of black slacks and white sweaters, kept somewhere in a large suitcase. In the light of my office I could tell that her skin was tanned. She placed a soft black leather shoulder bag on her lap.

"The same," I said. "Let me guess. Itinerant home repair-men. Am I right?"

For the first time since I had met her, the look on her face faltered. "I'm sorry, I don't understand."

"Well, why else would you break down my front door? Unless you want to repair it now and charge me about twice as much as I should pay."

She crossed her legs. "Sorry, but we broke your door down because we needed to talk to you, and you wouldn't answer."

"Isn't that my right, to be left alone?"

"Not today."

"I suppose it would be too much to ask for a warrant, or anything else similar," I said.

I could make out the sounds of the other men walking around my house, and I tried to keep a calm expression on my face. There were debts being incurred at this very moment, and I knew that one of these days, these debts would be paid. Then one of the men came to the door.

"Interim weapons inventory completed," he said, looking at a piece of paper in his palm. "One FN eight-millimeter assault rifle, one nine-millimeter Beretta pistol, one twelve-gauge Rem-ington shotgun, and one Smith and Wesson three-fifty-seven revolver. Ammo for all, as well."

"Thanks, Clem," she said, turning slightly to talk to him. She turned back to me and said, "You've got a lot of weapons."

"I have a lot of needs," I said. "Which brings me back to my point about the warrant."

"If you would prefer a warrant, Mr. Cole, I'm sure I could secure one within a few hours," she said. "But time is of the essence, and we were hoping for your assistance."

"Some hope," I said. "The other night you couldn't wait to get me out of your hair. What's changed since then?"

She smiled at that. "Well, that was before we found out a bit about you, Mr. Cole. Like your inquisitive nature, asking about our activities with the Tyler and the North Tyler police. That made us curious, and we soon found out that you had quite the interesting life before becoming a writer for *Shoreline*."

"I don't know if I would call it interesting."

"Oh, I would," she said, pulling out a sheaf of papers from the leather shoulder bag on her lap. "Like your service in the Department of Defense. The comments in your personnel file, showing a high intelligence quotient but poor team skills. Your posting to the Room Three-twelve Subgroup, also known as the Marginal Issues Section. And the dreadful event that resulted in the deaths of your colleagues, and your eventual retirement to this beach resort. Have I covered enough, or should I go on?"

The words came out of my mouth almost mechanically. "I'm afraid I can't comment on what you've just mentioned. Whatever service I performed for the Department of Defense, I signed a non-disclosure form when I left prohibiting me from discussing it."

She nodded, still smiling. "Like this one?"

I was almost afraid to touch the paper, remembering where I was when I signed it. At a government hospital facility in the middle of the Nevada desert, following my first surgery and recovery, desperately ill and desperately frightened that I would not leave the hospital alive. I quickly gave the paper a glance, almost imagining that the sense of horror and despair that I had felt back then was still clinging to the paper, like some old odor.

And there it was. My scribbled signature, from all those years ago. I could barely recognize it. I passed the paper back. My mouth had had been quickly getting dry with each syllable that she had pronounced about my past service. It had been a very long time since anyone had mentioned those phrases in my presence. I tried to clear my throat. "Like I said the other night, you have me at a disadvantage. I don't know who you are, even though I have a pretty good idea who you work for."

She laughed. "Sorry to be so cloak-and-daggerish. The name is Laura Reeves." From her bag she pulled out a slim leather wallet, which she passed over. "I work for the Drug Enforcement Agency, as do the other members of my little task force here." I glanced at the identification and then passed it back to her.

"Your picture looks good," I said. "Better than your average license photo. And what brings the field agents of the DEA trooping into my house on this fine April day?"

Reeves put her identification away. "Simply put, we need your help, Mr. Cole."

"Really? Well, parking isn't much of a problem this time of year, though you have to be careful around The Strip down at Tyler Beach. A lot of the restaurants are overpriced and overreviewed, but I could—"

"Not that kind of help. Something else."

I tried to smile back at her. Damn it, why was she looking so cheerful? "I'm sorry, Miss Reeves. That's the only kind of help I'm prepared to offer."

"But that's not the help we need. Mr. Cole, the man who was found in the parking lot of the state park was there for a meeting with someone we believe is responsible for a major heroin shipment coming into the New Hampshire seacoast over the next several days. The gentleman's name was Romero. He was from Mexico. Without getting into too much detail, obviously the meet didn't occur as planned."

"So if the man was murdered instead of committing suicide, why the cover story?" I already knew what the answer was going to be, but I wanted to hear what kind of spin she was going to put on it.

"You can imagine, I'm sure," Reeves said. "A suicide means lack of news media attention. Without the news media attention, we can work better in the background, without being forced to answer a number of questions. Something as delicate as this, we don't need the attention."

I folded my arms. "Then here's a question for you. Why me?"

Her hands were gently playing with the flap to the carrying case. "Like I said, we prefer to work in the shadows. We can do a lot dealing with the local law enforcement agencies, but sometimes that's more work than it's worth, handling their egos and problems. We're looking for your help because you're familiar with the area, you have a great cover as a magazine columnist—which allows you to ask a lot of questions—and because of your past experience."

"All I did in my past experience was read and write government reports."

She shook her head. "You're too modest. You performed some admirable intelligence work, coming up with conclusions that others had missed. If it hadn't been for that unfortunate accident in Nevada, I'm sure you could have gone far."

"No," I said.

"Oh, I disagree," she said. "I think that—"

"I wasn't responding to your statement about my abilities," I said. "I'm just cutting off this lovely discussion so that we're not wasting each other's time. No, I'm not interested in working with you, for you, or even in the same room as you. All right?"

It was as if she hadn't heard me. She went on. "All we know about the contact in this state is that he's associated with the Porter Naval Shipyard, up the coast, and that the man's nickname is Whizzer. We're sure you can do well with that information, give us some leads—"

"No," I said.

"We'll pay you an attractive day rate. One thousand dollars a day. When can you start?"

The noise of the other men in the house was still going on, as they searched for God knows what. "Never," I said. "I worked once for this government. At the time, it seemed to be the patriotic thing to do. I was younger and full of vim and vigor. Now, all I have is a few scars and a lot of nightmares, plus a little vigor and no more vim."

She made a point of looking around my office. "Plus this house and an attractive monthly pension."

"Which doesn't even begin to compensate me for what happened in Nevada," I said.

"That was a different time, a different administration. Because of those past mistakes, do we have to—"

"The space shuttle," I said, interrupting her.

"Excuse me?"

48

"The space shuttle mission going on right now," I said. "Do you and your folks have any connection with it at all?"

"Of course we don't. What's the point?"

I leaned forward in my chair. "The point is, Miss Reeves, that the shuttle mission going on right now is one of the few areas in the federal government where I would gladly volunteer to assist. If you had come to me from NASA, we could have worked something out. Since you're from the Department of Justice, no deal."

"Is that your final word?"

"My solitary, last and only word. No."

A quick, chilly nod. The smile had gone. Oh well. She reached once again into her leather bag and passed over a business card. "Here. My card. If and when you change your mind, you can contact me at any hour of the day."

I put the card on my crowded desk. "As the saying goes, if the phone don't ring, you'll know it's me."

She got up and I followed her out of my office and down the stairs. Three of her men were waiting outside my shattered door. One of the men was the redheaded fellow with the merry smile from the other night, the one she had called Mr. Turner. He looked over to Reeves and said, "Well, is he on board?"

Reeves said, "Nope," as she went outside.

Turner shook his head. "Man, you don't know what you just did. Nobody says no to Laura."

"I feel honored to start a new tradition."

He shook his head again and went outside. The cold wind was still blowing and the sky was overcast. Frozen rain pellets started spitting down at us. I looked at the broken door and the splintered doorjamb. I said, "Can I expect you strong fellows to come back later to fix this?"

He laughed. "Get the door fixed and submit a claim. You should be paid by the end of April. Of next year, if you're lucky. After all these years, have you forgotten how the federal government works, Cole?"

He joined the procession of DEA folks, trooping back up to the parking lot. I saw Reeves had a cell phone out, was talking urgently to someone by the way her free hand was waving about. I looked back to my ruined door.

"No," I said. "I haven't forgotten how the government works."

Later that night I was sitting alone in my living room, listening to the wind whistle through the broken door, feeling a cold draft upon my feet. The rains had begun in earnest and I had started a fire in the fireplace. My back and hands hurt, for in addition to working on the door I had also spent the past couple of hours cleaning house. The DEA crew had trooped in a lot of mud and dirt, and I didn't want anything left in the house to remind me that they had come in here, violating my peace and my privacy.

I looked over at the door, where I had stuffed old blankets in and about the doorjamb, trying to keep the wind out, though my feet told me I had done a lousy job. Tomorrow I would pay a visit to Tyler Village Hardware to see what else I could do, but right now I was too tired to do anything but brood.

Besides disturbing the nature of the day and my home, this little squad from the Department of Justice had also stirred up old thoughts and memories. It had been like taking a stick and moving it around rapidly in a shallow lake bed: scum and dust and bits of debris were now floating about, obscuring what had once been clear. Old memories and thoughts and fears and passions were rumbling through my mind, and I didn't like it, not one damn bit.

Some years ago I had come to this place, tired and thin and achy from surgeries and too many bad dreams. This little home on the side of the Atlantic Coast had begun as a haven for me. When I first moved in here, I had eaten a lot of take-out food and read and gone for walks along the pounding surf line. But though I had recovered physically after some months, my mind was still there, wounded, dissolving my better nature with the acidy feeling of guilt. Guilt that of all the people I had worked with in that little intelligence group, only I had survived the accidental exposure to an experimental biowarfare agent.

Eventually I was fortunate enough to find a way of tamping

down the guilt, before I got the urge one day to start swimming out to Great Britain from the front of my house. I began to do research for columns that would never appear in print, about matters in and around Tyler that were on the fringes of law enforcement. I was also quite fortunate to find a friend in the sole detective for this town, who partially understood my need to get involved, to set things straight. A few days ago, I could have rightfully said that the day in Nevada, gasping for breath on the sands of a test range, seeing my friends and co-workers vomit blood as they died about me, was far in the distance, like my memories of grammar school and high school and college.

But now that damn woman had to show up and shove that piece of paper under my nose, showing me that shaky signature, reminding me with brutal quickness of how weak and scared I had once been, and now it was all coming back. The smell of the desert air. The smile from Cissy Manning, my dear love. And the sounds of those damn helicopters, swooping down upon us, spraying out a fine mist . . .

I shivered, got up and switched on the television. After about a half hour of channel surfing, from one end of the cable spectrum to another, I caught what I was looking for: a quick update on the *Endeavour* mission, including an interview with the shuttle commander. He was grinning as he spoke into a hand-held microphone, saying everything was just fine, the mission was going great.

But remembering what he had once said to me, I knew better.

"Not all of us get to do what we want," I murmured to the television screen. "Not all of us get to go to Mars. Or even the moon."

I watched for a little while as the cold wind from my poorly repaired door whipped around my feet.

CHAPTER FIVE

Two days after my door had been broken down, it was now again secure and firm in its new form. Earlier I had gone to Tyler Village Hardware and had talked to a couple of the workers there. After a bit of discussion and some folded green had been passed around—my hardware skills typically begin and end with fixing a leaky faucet—they had come down to my house during their lunch break and had made everything right.

Now I was back in the center of Tyler, looking to have lunch with Paula Quinn, but when I pulled into the parking lot I saw that her Ford Escort was missing. I stayed there for a couple of minutes to see if she would show up, but the only thing that did appear was a slow-moving train on the nearby tracks, rumbling its way north. I got out and went through the rear entrance of the *Chronicle*, thinking that maybe her car was in the shop or was parked in the municipal lot across the street, but the newsroom was empty save for the hired gun, Rupert Holman. He looked up at me as I went up to his polished desk and said, "Paula Quinn about?"

Today he still had on those red suspenders, but his shirt was different, one of those blue-striped ones with white collars, popular among bond traders who are about five minutes away from being indicted by the SEC. He shook his head no. "She's down at Falconer, near the harbor. There's just been a fire at an apartment building, so I imagine she'll be there for a while."

"Oh," I said, and I was about to turn around and head out when Rupert spoke up again.

"Tell me, Cole . . . It *is* Cole, isn't it? Tell me, if you don't mind, why you just went through the 'Employees' Only' entrance just now."

That's when I decided to sit down in front of his desk, which I did. "Because it was there, that's why."

Another shake of the head. "Unless I'm mistaken, you're not an employee of this company. You should go through the front entrance, just like everyone else."

"Well, I'm not just like everyone else," I said. "I've been coming through that door long before you got here, and I'll be coming through it long after you're gone. And I don't like having to announce myself to whomever you've hired this month as a receptionist. Maybe I'm just being cranky, but that's the way it is."

He managed a slight smile as he rubbed his fingertips across the smooth wood of his table. "The way it is, Cole, is that the owners of this newspaper have given me full and total authority here. I like that, very much. What I don't like is you undermining my authority among the members of the staff, including Miss Quinn. And speaking of Miss Quinn, I have her last month's expense report right here. I could sign it and send it along to accounting, or I could misplace it. And knowing what I know on how much she's paid, a few bills that she owes probably won't be paid on time this month if that expense report gets lost."

I tried to imagine what he would look like if he were on the floor and I was busy twisting an arm out of its socket. "Just so that I'm clear—unless I start being a good boy around the newspaper office, you're going to make life miserable for Paula."

He just smiled, said nothing. I went on. "Man, you sure are a peach. What rock did you crawl out from under of to get here?"

"Just here to do a job, that's all," he said.

"Some job," I said. "I mean, what's the point of all this hoo-ha this past month—the special reports, the big headlines and photos?"

"My job is to raise circulation. Since I've been here, it's gone up one point five percent. I intend for it to go up another two full points before I'm finished."

"Must be lots of laughs, to go after people's private lives, to print stories about porn and sex rings and all that," I said. "Here's a thought for you. Why not do some real stories for a change? Like how many senior citizens have to sell their homes each year in this county because of our property-tax system. Or how a handful of business people actually own the best property on Tyler Beach, and how their great-grandparents basically stole that land from the town last century. Or a story about a couple of the corporations in and around Tyler, and how much they donate to local charities, all while they're busily storing toxic waste in barrels out in the open. There's enough real stories out there to report on instead of all this tabloid nonsense."

He picked up a paper clip on his desk, examined it as if he were trying to be sure that it really was a paper clip, and then placed it in the top drawer of his desk. "We do the stories I want to do, the ones that will fulfill the requirements of the newspaper's owners. In my professional opinion, we're doing the right type of stories here in Tyler. This paper goes where I send it."

"And who elected you?"

A sharp smile. "Nobody. Ain't that a kick?"

"People in Tyler might not like where you're taking their local paper."

"Remember what I said, Cole. Circulation is already up one point five percent. The fine boobs around here are telling us what they want with their money, and so far, it's what I'm offering. Now, if you'll excuse me." He bent down and scrawled his signature across a sheet of paper, a rather simple scrawl for such a piece of work.

"I'd like to think of an excuse myself," I said, standing up, "but I can't come up with one."

About twenty minutes later I was in Falconer, the next town south of Tyler and the last town on the New Hampshire seacoast before crossing into Massachusetts. I took Route 286 down to the small beach area that Falconer had, and along the way I stopped at a sandwich shop near the wide expanse of marshes that fill the area between the beach and the mainland. The smell of hot meat and grease filled my Ford by the time I found Paula, at an apartment building on Atlantic Avenue. About fifty yards up the road was the drawbridge that spanned Tyler Harbor, and entered the southern end of Tyler Beach. Two fire engines and a ladder truck were parked out on the road, causing traffic to back up. I parked in a fireworks store—Falconer is one of the few places in the state where you can buy porn, gold jewelry and fireworks in one quick walk—and I found Paula talking to an older man and woman. She was writing on the hood of her Escort, and just as I went over she nodded and said something to the couple, who then walked over to a cheerful-looking heavyset man wearing a white Red Cross coat.

"Feel like lunch?" I said, passing over a paper-wrapped package.

Her smile touched me. "Lewis, that would be so wonderful . . . thanks."

We unwrapped our lunches on the hood of her car as we watched the firefighters continue their cleanup. The apartment building was three-story, and a couple of windows on the second floor had been broken. Some light gray smoke still seeped out of the broken windows, and firefighters trooped in and out of the entrance, stepping over hoselines that had been stretched into the building. The rumbling noise of the fire trucks was still loud, as was the chattering noise of the radios. A Falconer cop was directing the thin stream of traffic, no doubt thankful that this was April and not August, when the line of backed-up cars would have stretched deep into Massachusetts.

I took a healthy bite of my sandwich—steak-and-cheese sub, plain—and managed to ask, "What happened?"

Paula chewed a bit from her own meal—steak-and-cheese sub with every vegetable known to man included—and said, "Simple thing, really. Elderly guy living alone up on the second floor decides to reheat a meal for an early lunch. Falls asleep watching TV, fire breaks out on stove. Elderly guy okay but now en route to Exonia Hospital with smoke inhalation. His dozen or so neighbors evacuated for the morning, should be back in this afternoon after the smoke and water damage is cleaned up some."

"So, a simple thing. A simple story?"

She took a swig from a Diet Pepsi and gave a quiet, very unladylike belch before proceeding. "No, not hardly. Last month, this would be a nice little straightforward story, with a photo. On page one if it's a slow news day, otherwise on page three. 'Stovetop fire forces evacuation of a dozen Falconer residents. One injury. Everybody back in by end of day.' But not now. I've been informed that my writing isn't sexy enough. So I've spent the past hour or so talking to the residents, trying to get juicy quotes about how they narrowly escaped death this morning. How this brought them into a new realization of how precious life is and all that crap. So instead of a simple stovetop fire, by this time tomorrow the readers of the *Chronicle* will be reading about a blazing holocaust that almost claimed the lives of dozens of people."

Another chew of the sandwich and a swallow, and Paula pressed on. "The thing is . . . if I had the time and the backing, I could do a really good story about this fire, one that involves the owners. You see, some of these apartment buildings are owned by some shadow corporations, making lots of money for investors in Boston and New York City. And the on-site management is pressured to keep improvement and maintenance costs down, so you've got a lot of code violations. With those kind of violations, these places should be shut down. Problem is, they generate a good chunk of tax revenue for the town, and if they were forced to close, bang, the town budget gets faced with a shortfall. Oh, it's not a blatant corruption, but if I had time, I could make this into one hell of a story."

"But your new editor is more interested in other kinds of stories."

She wiped her chin with a paper napkin. "Yeah, he is. Spice and sex and blood. His mandate is to get circulation up, no matter what. Hell, I'm no newspaper absolutist. Without a healthy circulation, there's no newspaper, so what's the point of bitching about plans to raise it? Which reminds me . . . have you talked to Diane yet about the story Rupert wants to do on her?"

"That I have," I said. "Simply put, Detective Woods appreciates the heads-up but she's not in a mood to do any kind of favors regarding her personal life. Including passing on a juicy story to you that will offset any planned story about her and what kind of woman she is."

"Lewis, that's not good enough."

"I know."

"Damn it, the things this holier-than-thou guy wants us to do . . . He sees himself and the rest of us as moral beacons of the community, all working toward one big-ass goal: more papers sold. And you know what's funny? Last year we got stock options as part of our compensation. An increased circulation means more money in my pocket, but that increased circulation is going to depend on ruining some people's lives. You think there could be a healthier way of doing it."

I finished my lunch, watched as the Falconer firefighters drained their hoselines and then began the tedious job of rolling them up. "If there is a healthier way, I don't think Rupert is interested in hearing about it. I had a little visit with him about an hour ago. He surely does take his job seriously, especially the part of being in control."

Paula frowned, began stuffing soiled napkins into a paper bag. "Yeah, he does. Each week we have staff meetings, on Wednesday, at lunchtime. Casual little things, not too serious. But when he came aboard, he put a memo out—and I think it's the first time we've actually seen a memo in over a year—that said the meeting starts promptly at noon. Well, I got there on time, but a couple of our freelancers didn't, and when it came to the noon hour, he locked the conference room door. He practically made these two women—about my mom's age—beg forgiveness before letting them into the conference room, and he said that was his first and last lesson in promptness. Tell me, did you have a run-in with him?"

I thought for a moment about Rupert's threat to hold up

expense reports, and decided it wasn't worth getting her upset over it. "No, not really. Except he's a bear about non-employees using the rear entrance of the newspaper. Hell, if that's so important to him, I won't tick him off."

Paula smiled at me. "Tick him off as much as you want. That's about one of the few fun things I get to see in that newspaper office."

"And how long does he get to stay there?"

"Until the circulation reaches a certain level, or we murder him in the conference room. Whichever happens first." She glanced at her watch on her tanned slim wrist. "Speaking of murder, someone's gonna kill me if I don't get back to the office and start working on this story. Thanks again for lunch, Lewis. You're a dear."

I picked up her trash and said, "Next meal will be more proper. In a restaurant, with real tables and chairs and everything."

Another smile. "Such a deal."

Then I leaned over and kissed her, and she sighed and kissed me back. The sound of the fire trucks and radios all seemed to fade away as I tasted her lips and her mouth, tasted the sharp tang of onions, and not caring one bit. When I finally stepped back she reached over and stroked my face. "My, that was nice. Do call me, will you?"

"Without a doubt," I said. "Without a doubt."

With the traffic still being slowed from the fire apparatus blocking the road, I reversed course and headed back up Route 286, taking the long route back to Tyler. The two-lane road traverses through the marshlands and has a great view of Tyler Harbor and the squat and bulky concrete buildings of Falconer Station, the nuclear power plant in this part of the state that attracted thousands of protesters when it was being built three decades ago, and hasn't attracted a single one in the past couple of years as it quietly produced its power without killing or injuring anybody.

Along the way north were a number of bait-and-tackle shops, seafood places, and one store that had a number of people

58

parading in front of it, carrying signs. I slowed some as I went by. The building was one-story, wooden, with its windows blocked out by large sheets of brown paper. The place was called ROUTE 286 VIDEO and there were four people there, three men and a woman, slowly walking in a circle. Each of them carried a handmade sign on the end of a wooden stick:

FREE US FROM THIS FILTH
NO PORN IN OUR PLAYGROUND
GOD PUNISHES PORN SINNERS
PORN OUT NOW

I kept on driving for just a few seconds more, thinking not of those signs but of a certain newspaper man a few miles away, sitting confident and smugly, knowing in his heart of hearts that he knew what was best for this area.

I muttered something and then made a U-turn and drove back to the video store. I pulled over to the side and got out and deftly walked through the protesters as I entered the store. The woman among them called out, "Don't support these sinners; please, don't support these sinners!"

Inside the store there were racks of videotapes on the walls, categorized into comedy, science fiction, adventure, horror and family. Toward the rear was a counter where an older woman sat, reading a book and smoking a cigarette. She looked up at me and then went back to her book. By the counter was another doorway, with a sign on the closed door: ADULTS ONLY BEYOND THIS POINT. I went up to the counter and said, "People out there bothering you?"

She eyed me over the pages of her book. "Are you carrying a hidden camera for one of those TV blooper shows, or are you just asking stupid questions for no reason?"

Her voice had an accent, Eastern European, it sounded like. I glanced at the spine of her book. *Cancer Ward*, by Solzhenitsyn. "Not a bad book," I said. "I liked *Full Circle* better."

"Yeah," she said, taking another puff from her cigarette.

She had on a shapeless flowered dress and one earpiece of her eyeglasses had been repaired by a bit of tape. "I've been out of the old country for almost twenty years now, and I'm still trying to catch up on the banned books. Trying to figure out what really went on. And I don't know sometimes why I do that, you know. What difference does it make? But still . . . I read. I want to know. That's all."

"Not a bad reason."

She motioned with her cigarette out the door. "Those people . . . they think they know it all. They think they know black and white. They see a place that is a source of all evil. They don't see a store that just serves a need. They don't see an old Russian woman trying to make some extra money. They don't see all that. They are righteous and full of conviction, and I wish I could take them to my old home, where many people filled with righteousness and conviction slaughtered millions." She shrugged. "Enough of my talk. You're here to rent videos, are you not?"

"Yes, I am," I said.

"Then get to it, please." And she went back to her book.

I looked around the small room with the standard videos, and feeling a bit unsure of myself, I opened the door marked ADULTS ONLY and walked in. If you're going to make a stand, sometimes you have to do it in the mud, I thought. I stood for a moment, surprised at what I saw, and then I closed the door behind me. Luckily I was alone, for I thought that if I were with anybody else in here I would probably ignite from embarrassment at being in public with somebody else with so many video box covers showing naked people in various activities, some of which looked as if they were still illegal in some states.

The room was easily three times as large as the one I came from, and like in the first room, the videos were placed on walls and racks in different categories. But while the categories earlier had been horror or science fiction, the groupings here were quite different: straight, gay, bi, European . . . I went around the room, not looking at anything in particular, but just amazed at the quantity and the variations. Who were these people? How did this all get produced and duplicated and shipped? Oh, I'm no prude and

I've always been aware that one of the largest industries in the country—especially in a couple of California counties—is the sex industry, but the sheer magnitude of what was available out there stunned me.

After a few minutes the naked bodies and forced smiles and silicon-enhanced breasts all began to blur together, and I picked five videos at random and then went back out to the counter. I felt another hot flush of embarrassment, but the old Russian woman just went through the motions, as she no doubt did dozens of times a day. Since I was a new renter, she asked for a name, address and phone number, which I provided, and then I scribbled a signature on the receipt and went out the door. Thankfully by then the videos were in black plastic cases, so I didn't have to go through the picket line openly displaying my rented wares. Even then, they booed at me as I went back to my car, put the videos down on the seat and drove away.

I shivered, from the embarrassment of having been there in the store, and the feeling that whatever I was doing made absolutely no difference at all. The twenty dollars I had spent on renting these videos wouldn't make up for whatever lost business was there, and besides, defending the First Amendment was fine in the abstract. It got a little more gray and grittier when you looked at the wares the Route 286 Video shop was peddling.

Twenty dollars. I thought back to what I had also spent on the lunch for Paula and an earlier gas-up of my Ford, and when I got back into the center of Tyler, about fifteen minutes away from home, I turned right onto High Street and drove up into the branch of the First National Bank of Porter. I pulled up to the drive-up ATM, right behind a red Toyota. A man with a baseball cap on backward was looking at the machine for a long bit, as if the instructions had been printed in Sanskrit. Then he pulled out an envelope and began writing on something in his lap. I waited. A Chrysler minivan pulled up behind me. I was trapped. The man in front kept on writing and scribbling. He shook his head, tore the envelope in half, and went up for another one. From behind me a horn blew, and the man in front ignored us all. He returned to his life's work. I had thoughts of men out there in suits keeping an eye on me, weapons in hand. In this location I was out in the open; I couldn't move.

Finally, the man in front of me triumphantly made his deposit and drove out, and I pulled up to the machine, braking a bit too hard. I slid in my ATM card and punched in a withdrawal for sixty dollars, and I looked about the parking lot as I waited. The lot was empty. The machine bleeped at me and I looked over. The card was hanging out of its slot, as well as a white receipt, but there were no twenty-dollar bills. Not a single one. I looked at the slip, where it showed my request and below, in a fancy blue script, INSUFFICIENT FUNDS.

A tickle began at the back of my throat. Back the card went into the machine, back again went the entry of my access code and the request for sixty dollars. Sixty bucks! I knew that my checking account easily had a hundred times that amount available, and I thought that perhaps something had gone silly in the ATM's innards, but the second round was the same as the first round.

INSUFFICIENT FUNDS.

Now it was my turn yet again, and another horn started blowing from the line of cars behind me. I pulled out and stopped in the parking lot, looking dumbly at both receipts. Then I went through my wallet, pulled out an ATM receipt from the previous week, from this very same branch. The account numbers matched. Last week my balance had been $6,032.41.

Today it was zero.

I got out of my Ford and walked straight into the bank branch.

The branch manager was a woman in her mid-thirties with short, dark hair, named Gloria Harrison. She wore a dark blue skirt and a white shirt with ruffled collar and a Victorian-style brooch at her throat. On her desk were pictures of her husband and two young sons, a stack of free calendars, and a little glass jar that offered lollipops in a variety of colors. She wore half-rim glasses and was warm and pleasant and helpful and not able to get one dime of my money back.

"I'm so sorry, Mr. Cole, but this is what our main office

received yesterday afternoon," she said, passing over a fax that had bleeped through her machine a few minutes earlier. "It's an order from the Treasury Department. They're fairly cryptic in what they say, but it does look fairly clear. There's an audit being performed of a certain activity within the Department of Defense, and because something . . . untoward has been found, they've seized your accounts as a precaution. Do you receive a monthly pension from the government?"

"I do," I said, trying to keep my hand steady as I read the cool legal words on the sheet of paper.

"Were you in the service, then?"

"No," I replied automatically. "Just in the DoD, working out of the Pentagon."

Yeah, just like that, I thought. A monthly pension, to keep my mouth shut about what I saw happen to me and my friends in the Nevada desert, and the columnist job through *Shoreline* magazine basically to launder the funds. Mighty Uncle Sam had turned on this particular spigot some years ago, and now he and his minions had just shown me how easily they could turn it off.

Off. Not only off, but drained.

I looked up at her. "My savings accounts as well?"

A slight nod in reply. "Everything in this bank. I'm sorry, Mr. Cole, but we had no choice. We had to follow the directives of the Treasury Department. We've sent you a registered letter, explaining what has happened . . ."

Living the way I did, my mail ended up in a post office box in Tyler, and usually a twice-a-week visit was good enough. But not today, apparently.

"What's next?" I asked.

"I imagine they will be in contact with you, Mr. Cole. But I can't tell you when. In the meantime, I suggest you get a lawyer. A very good one. And prepare, well, prepare for a long haul." She lowered her voice some, as if afraid the banking gods would hear her. "When you get caught up in the gears of something as large as the Treasury Department, it can be a very long time before something is resolved. A very long time, even if eventually it is resolved in your favor."

She paused. "A very long time," she repeated.

I paid very little attention to what was on the road ahead of me as I headed east, back to Tyler Beach and my home, the day now overcast again. The little gang of DEA agents and their head, Laura Reeves, had just shown me what they were capable of. In spite of my now-serious financial condition and my anger, I was impressed. Just a couple of days. That's all it took to seize my funds and stop my monthly stipend. Fine, I thought, making a left hand turn onto Atlantic Avenue, heading up to the Lafayette House. On my property was a hidden safe, and contained therein was about fifteen thousand dollars. I also had a couple of credit cards with zero balances that allowed cash advances. If need be, I could live off those resources for a year or two, until Reeves and her friends got tired of waiting and went on to something else.

I made a right into the Lafayette House parking lot, now almost feeling a hell of a lot better than I did back at the bank branch. I had taken a hit, but it was survivable. And if Reeves wanted to play hardball, well, I could take up the challenge. I could get one of the lawyers in town that I was acquainted with to take up my case, to start raising a fuss. Publicity? Reeves had said she was doing everything to avoid publicity, and I could show her in a day or two of my own what I could do in return. Hell, I could even come clean with Paula Quinn, and that would be a story I'm sure even her new boss could be interested in.

Down I went, over the bumpy dirt path to my house, and I thought I saw something on the front door as I parked my Ford in the garage. I got out and made my way across the thin lawn. The wind had picked up some, and the booming sound of the waves was comforting as I saw my brand-new front door and three white business-sized envelopes flapping in the breeze. All three had been stapled on the door, and I reached up and tore them free.

I looked at them in the late-afternoon light, the wind still making them move in my hands. The first envelope was from the Internal Revenue Service. Inside was a receipt for cash funds seized at my residence in the amount of $15,113.12. These funds were going to be held in escrow until the completion of an investigation into a matter involving disbursements from the Department of Defense. So much for my well-hidden safe. I closed my eyes for just a second, and then went to envelope number two. It was from the Department of the Interior. This one was a bit longer and more in-depth than the IRS note, but boiled down, the message was pretty simple. When I had come out here years ago, the title to the house and property—which had once belonged to the Department of the Interior—had been been transferred to my name. Now, the Department was politely telling me that they were taking the house back, and I had seven days to move my belongings out. Have a nice day.

I sat down on the stone steps, looking at both messages. The wind was making me cold, quite cold, and I shook myself free and got up, let myself into my house—my house, damn it!—and flipped on the entranceway light. Nothing happened. I flipped the switch up and down again, and then looked at envelope number three. It was from the Exonia & Tyler Electric Company. I made a mess of the envelope tearing it open. Inside, the letter said at the request of this particular home's owner—the Boston office of the Department of Interior—all power had been switched off.

Back into the house I went, and in a matter of minutes I had lit a couple of candles. I sat down on my couch, feeling the coolness about me. With no electricity, there was no oil furnace, and no heat. The three envelopes were in my lap. I thought back to what the bank manager had said. I had just got caught up in the gears of something large and black and nasty indeed. Reeves and her crew wanted my cooperation, and they had just demonstrated what they were going to do to ensure it. A more noble and stronger man than I would fight them, would fight them on the beaches and landing fields and cities. He would move into a tiny apartment on the beach and put his belongings in storage, and get a job as a dishwasher or something, and eat lots of rice and beans and fight, fight, fight the good fight.

I sighed, looked about my house. My one sanctuary, the one

place that had really belonged to me after a lifetime of renting apartments and condos. The memories and good times and quiet peace that had been offered to me here . . .

Noble. Strong. Not two adjectives that applied to me at this particular moment. I got up from the couch and picked up a candle, and guided by its flickering light, I went up to my office. I looked around my messy desk for a moment before finding the business card that had been left here, and I picked up the phone. I got the reassuring sound of the dial tone. At least she had left that, but knowing what she had just done, I'm sure that this was part of the plan.

I dialed the number on the card, and the phone was picked up on the second ring. "Four-seven-four-six," came the man's voice, merely identifying himself by the last four digits of the number I had dialed.

"Laura Reeves, please."

"May ask who's calling?" the man said.

"Lewis Cole," I said.

"Hold one."

There came the sounds of clicks and buzzes, and I stood there, the candle in one hand and the phone in the other. Blue wax began to drip down the candle and onto my fingers, but I didn't move.

The phone seemed to ring again. "Hello?" came a different male voice.

"Laura Reeves, please," I said, and wanting to move things along, I added, "This is Lewis Cole calling."

"Just a moment."

There was a cluttering sound as the phone was put down, and then it was picked up. I took a deep breath. For a moment I was going to hang up the phone, but then I pressed on.

"Hello?"

"Laura?" I asked.

"Yes. Is this you, Mr. Cole?"

"It is," I said.

"What can I do for you?" she asked, in an innocent-sounding voice that was quite good. She had been trained well.

"I think you know already," I said.

"Maybe I do," she said. "Go on."

I looked around my dark office. "You got me," I said. "You've won."

CHAPTER SIX

For the next few minutes, Laura Reeves of the Drug Enforcement Agency tried to be gracious about the whole damn thing. I guess she had read Lincoln's Second Inaugural Address, for she certainly was being magnanimous in victory. The first thing she said right off the bat was, "No, no, we haven't won anything," her voice sounding almost shy. "This isn't about winners or losers. This is about working cooperatively together for the good of your state, and for the nation."

I guess I should have hung up the phone on that twisted statement, but I said, "You want my cooperation, you have it. But I want everything else taken care of. The Treasury Department, the Interior Department, my bank and the power company. Understood?"

"Fine," she said. "Let's get together now and talk, and when we're done, it'll all be settled."

"I'd rather have it taken care of before I troop out somewhere and meet up with you."

She laughed. "It wouldn't be a long troop. We're right across the street."

"Excuse me?"

"The Lafayette House," she said. "We've rented some rooms. I'm in five-twelve. We'll be expecting you."

And she hung up. I stood there in my dark office, the candle flame flickering bravely, the hot wax trickling down my fingers. I blew the candle out and in the darkness made my way downstairs and outside of my home.

The Lafayette House began its life as a tavern in the early eighteen hundreds, and is named because the Marquis de Lafayette, during his famed tour of the young United States in 1824–25, had supposedly stopped there for a drink on his way to Boston. Of course, if Lafayette had stopped at every public house and tavern that claimed his presence back then, his liver would have had the consistency of leather by the time he got back to France. I huddled in my winter coat as I trudged up my dirt driveway, and then walked across Atlantic Avenue. Since then, the place has been expanded, built upon, almost completely destroyed by fire a couple of times, before it reached its level of Victorian splendor back in the late nineteenth century.

Now, though it had suffered some during the 1970s and early 1980s, it's a touch of old money and class that exists for those people who still think there's something grand and glorious about spending an average year's wages to summer at the shore.

I went into the glass-and-marble-decorated lobby and took an elevator up to the fifth floor. I was by myself, which suited me fine. The corridor was wide and there were small mahogany tables along the way, each one bearing a vase with fresh flowers. At room 512 I rapped on the door and one of the larger men in the DEA group opened it up. He gave me a quick once-over—no doubt evaluating my physical condition, weapon-carrying status and current voter registration—and stepped back. I walked in and Laura Reeves came up from a couch, sipping a Diet Coke. She had on gray sweatpants and an MIT sweatshirt. Her feet was bare and her toenails had been painted red.

"Thanks, Doug," she said, walking over to me. "I can take it from here. Come on in, Mr. Cole. We've got things to discuss."

"You should stop speaking in understatements," I said, "or people will stop taking you seriously."

"Not being taken seriously is something I haven't had to worry about since I gave up cheerleading after high school," she said, without a trace of humor in her voice.

Doug went to one of the easy chairs and picked up a *Wall Street Journal* and started reading. The room was huge, with a conference table in the center, two couches, a handful of easy chairs and a couple of coffee tables scattered around. There was also a large-screen television and a kitchen setup off to the left. On the conference table was a mess of notepads, envelopes, papers and photographs. Another table set up against the windows had two computers and some communications gear. One closed door to the right, I imagined, led to sleeping quarters for Reeves. The other probably led into another room.

I sat with her at the conference table. "Nice to see what my taxes are being used for."

She put the Diet Coke can down on the table, picked up a thick file folder. "I've not been home for two months. Most of my crew can say the same thing. We're on the road constantly, eating bad food, sleeping in hotel rooms or motel rooms. Sometimes we're in places where cops don't like to travel except in pairs. So when I have a chance to make things a bit better for me and for them, I take it, with no apologies."

"All right, no apologies accepted."

As she went through the file folder, I looked at her sweatshirt and said, "Your school?"

"Nope, my boyfriend's. I went to Cal Tech."

"Is he in the DEA as well?"

"Nope," she said, removing a few papers and a thin stack of black-and-white photographs from the folder. "He's dead."

"Oh. I'm sorry, I should have kept quiet."

"No matter," she said, rubbing at the side of her face for a moment. "Sam's been gone for six months now. He was a pilot in the Air Force. He was flying a drug surveillance aircraft in

Colombia when it was shot down by narco guerrillas. Did you see it in the news?"

"I remember seeing something about that," I said. "But I thought the aircraft crashed in the mountains."

Her lips just managed a thin smile. "That usually happens when a Soviet-built Grail 7 SAM takes out one of your engines. We're in an undeclared war down there, Mr. Cole, one that the current administration is trying desperately to keep out of the news. Let's begin, shall we?"

I shifted in my seat, saw Doug was still staring intently at his newspaper. Surprisingly, his lips didn't move as he read. "Let's begin with a few other things first, all right? First, by the time I leave this room, everything will be set back—my power, my finances, my home title—correct?"

A nod.

"Good," I said. "My cooperation means just that. Cooperation. No miracles. And one more thing. For God's sake, please stop calling me Mr. Cole. It makes me feel like I'm ready to start wearing an adult diaper. Lewis will work just fine."

Another nod. "All right, Lewis. That's all acceptable. And we're not looking for miracles, not at all. We're just trying to button up this little battle of ours in the drug war on your home turf. The narco guerrillas move on a lot of different fronts, from most of Colombia to states in Mexico to islands in the Caribbean. What they're looking for are safe and secure routes to bring their product into the States, their most profitable market. What we do is to make it more expensive for them. That's all. We're never going to stop it, not ever, but we can harass them, make their lives difficult, force them to be on the defensive, all the time. Which is why we're here. For a while New York City was their favorite destination, but we've had too many successes there for them. Boston would be a logical choice, but from what we've learned, they've decided to go one step farther up the coast. Here."

"I find that hard to believe. Why not up in Maine? Portland would seem to be a logical choice."

"True, but they've chosen this little stretch of seacoast to set up shop. Probably because you're just a few minutes away from I-

95. From here, you can be in Portland or Boston in an hour, in Hartford and New York City in a few hours more."

Looking down at the conference table, I could see what was depicted in the black-and-white photographs. "And this dead man, up at Samson Point, who was he working for?"

"A cartel out of Medellín, Colombia, where else. He was from Mexico City, was due to meet up with his local contact at the wildlife preserve. We were late in catching up, we thought they were meeting somewhere else. And damn it, we weren't even going to make an arrest. We were just going to observe their first meet."

"The first meet obviously didn't go too well, did it?"

She said, "And you accuse me of overusing understatements. Yeah, that was one royal screwup, and we're not sure why. Best guess is that another cartel decided to move in on this little turf, and decided to eliminate a rival, before going up to the local people and offering a better deal."

"And who's the local people?" I asked.

"Ah, that's where it gets tricky. From intelligence intercepts, all we know is that the local contact is someone associated with the Porter Naval Shipyard, someone nicknamed Whizzer."

"What do the shipyard folks tell you?"

"Not a thing," she said. "They have more than a thousand people working at the yard. What work we've been able to do there has been quite preliminary, by contacting some of the management at the yard. We've been hobbled by two things: First, if the word spreads throughout the shipyard that someone named Whizzer is being looked for, then that person will no doubt go to ground, never to be seen again. The second thing is that if word gets out that the DEA is looking into a drug ring involving workers who do maintenance work on nuclear-powered attack submarines, well, I'm sure your local papers would have a lot of fun with that kind of story."

"Without a doubt," I said. "And that's why you folks had the bright idea of bringing me aboard, right?"

"Maybe not a very bright idea, but the best we could do,"

she said. "Like I said the other day, back at your house. You know the area. You can ask questions without people thinking you're part of law enforcement. You can go places we can't, because of your magazine job."

I looked at the table and the pile of materials, and I looked over at Doug, still leafing through his newspaper. Reeves leaned over. "What are you thinking?"

I sighed. "I'm thinking that when I first came here, I was offered several positions as employment, besides the magazine job. One was running a grocery store. Day like today, I wished I had taken it."

Reeves said, "Lots of days like today, I wished I had never heard of the federal government. Here, a reminder of what we're up against."

She fanned across the black-and-white photographs of the dead man, and I looked at the photos, each freezing a point in time where the body of a dead man slowly cooled in his rented car in a state parking lot. Somehow, in the photographs he looked more real, as if the man I had seen the other night had been a fake. I went through each of them, looking at the closed eyes, the finely trimmed mustache, the bloodstream going down the front of his suit, the white shirt stained as well, no necktie. Each photograph was part of a series, and soon I got sick at looking at a dead man from a variety of angles.

"Name's Romero, correct?" I asked, putting the photos back down on the table.

"Yes."

"When did he get to New Hampshire?"

She went to a legal pad, took another sip from her Diet Coke. "Got into Manchester the same day he got killed. Arrived at three P.M. on a commuter flight from Boston. From Boston, we've traced him back to JFK in New York, and from there, back to Mexico City. Apparently traveled by himself, no checked luggage."

I pushed the photographs back to her. "When was the time of death?"

"Maybe an hour or so before he was discovered. No matter

what the novels or TV shows say, it can be a hellish thing to set the time of death."

"All right," I said. "It takes about an hour, at the most, to get from Manchester to the seacoast. Any idea what he did or where he went during those extra hours?"

There was a soft rustle of the newspaper from Doug, and Reeves said, "No, though we've been quietly canvassing all of the bed-and-breakfasts, motels, and hotels in the area. You have any idea how many lodging establishments are in this part of the state?"

"Not a clue."

"Lots, believe me," she said. "So far, we've turned up nothing. Hell, for all we know, Romero might not have bothered with setting up a room reservation."

"And the rental car?"

"Under the assumed name of Smith, with a credit card issued by a Mexico City bank that's practically owned and operated by the narcos. We're also trying to backtrack his movements, to see if he communicated with anyone along the way. Still nothing."

One of the two side doors opened and Turner came in, his face looking excited. "Laura, we've got our hands on the Fehler debrief and—"

Reeves turned and said, "Button it, Gus."

Gus stood still, now looking slightly humiliated. "You told me to come get you the minute it came in."

"Right," she said, "and I'm telling you I'm busy here. Look, I'll be there in a sec. Okay?"

He said nothing, his face red, almost matching the color of his hair, and he went back through the door. I caught a glimpse of another room, almost as large as this one, and also stuffed with tables, computer gear, and, in this case, two unmade beds. The door slammed shut—a touch too hard, I thought—and I looked back at Reeves. She said, "Gus is a bit eager, but then again, once we all were. Is there anything else?"

"Yeah," I said. "This Whizzer character and whoever he represents. Are they local, or are they recent moves to the area?"

"Why do you ask?"

I thought about Felix and said, "I might have an ability to track him down if he's originally from Massachusetts, that's all."

She shook her head. "All we know is the name and the shipyard. I'd focus your attention on that, Lewis."

"Well, I'll also focus your attention on the fact this Romero character came to my home state and got killed for his troubles. That's the kind of thing that makes me sit up and take notice."

She played with the top of her Diet Coke can. "In our recent visit to your home, I was impressed with the number of firearms you possess."

"I'm an avid supporter of the Second Amendment."

"So it would seem. So I would think you'd have no problem defending yourself, if the need arose."

"Thanks for your confidence," I said. "I'd much rather have better intelligence on what I might be facing out there."

"Whatever we find out, we'll pass along to you. You can reach me right through the hotel's switchboard, or through the number on my business card. Either way, I'm eager to find out what you've learned."

I sensed I was being dismissed, so I got up. "Oh," she said. "Three more things." She slid across a sheet of paper and tossed a pen after it. "Another non-disclosure form. I'm sure you'll understand."

"Oh, more than you'll know," I said, not even bothering to read the damn thing, just scrawling my signature on the bottom.

She reached over into her shoulder bag, pulled out something small and black and tossed it to me. I caught it with one hand. A pager.

"Just so that we can contact you when we need you."

I nodded, putted the pager in my coat pocket. Then an envelope came sliding over, bumping into the form I had just signed. I picked it up, peeked inside. Reeves said, "Like I promised. A thousand dollars a day. There's your first check."

"Thanks," I said.

Making sure she was looking at me, I held the envelope in both hands and tore it in half, and then quarters. I would have gone further except the scraps of paper were too thick. I let it all fall to the table, but a couple of torn pieces fluttered to the carpeted floor.

"Fair or foul," I said, "you've got me. Don't insult me by trying to make it better with something like this."

And when I walked out toward the door, I was sure that Doug, the burly man reading the *Wall Street Journal,* gave me a quick smile.

On the short walk back home, I stopped at the slight rise that marked the beginning of my driveway, and looked around. Behind me was the well-lit splendor of the Lafayette House, and I played a game for a few moments, trying to determine which lit window marked the suite of Laura Reeves and her merry band of pirates. I was pretty sure I had the right window fixed in my mind, and I spent another few moments thinking fun thoughts of what those burly young men back there would think if I came back to this place with my FN 8-mm rifle and started pumping rounds into those chosen windows.

A pleasant thought, though not very productive. I turned again and looked out to the dusk of the ocean swells. As the light faded, the ocean's color seemed to broaden and deepen. I shivered for a moment, then looked down to my house. There were lights on there as well. Reeves's word was at least good in this little respect.

I put my hands in my coat pocket, felt the foreign presence of the pager, and started trudging down the dirt driveway to the faint light from my home. On any other night, this picture would cheer me up and lighten my step, but not tonight. Not after I had been brutally shown how simple it would be to take everything away from me. I headed home, head down, just putting one step in front of another.

A couple of hours later I was sitting on my couch sipping a glass of red wine, looking into the dancing flames within my fireplace. Earlier I had eaten—a ham-and-Comté-cheese omelette, nothing too fancy—and for dessert I had cleaned and loaded my 9-mm Beretta. I thought about the dead man in the parking lot and Whizzer and Reeves and her crew, back there in the

Lafayette House. Eating and cleaning up and working on my weapon had made my sour mood subside a bit, and the fact the power was on and there was a pile of cash in an envelope on my kitchen table—exactly in the amount of $15,113.12—had helped as well. Plus, though I wouldn't admit it to Reeves or anyone else, a part of me that had enjoyed working in the shadows liked the sensation of being back on the job.

I took another sip of wine, leaned forward and tossed a dry piece of split maple onto the flames. The fire faded out for just a moment and then the flames roared up, fed by the new fuel. Still, something was bothering me. Something about the whole setup. Everything she had said and shown me had made sense, about who they were and what they were doing. Everything.

But what did she show you? a voice asked me. Any documents? Any supporting papers?

Nope. Just the photographs of the slain cartel rep, Romero. Photographs.

I put the wineglass down on at side table and padded upstairs to my office in stocking-covered feet. In my office I switched on the overhead lights and tried not to blink at the neon-type glare coming from my new Apple computer. I rummaged around on my desk for a moment, until I located a certain notebook. I flipped back and reread the cryptic handwriting from a few days earlier, when I had left a crime scene.

There. I had described the driver (dark-skinned, middle thirties) and the wound (apparent entrance wound to the right temple) and what he was wearing (black suit coat, dress pants, white shirt, no tie and lapel button).

"Bingo," I whispered. I put the notebook down and slowly went down to the first floor of my house. I remembered the lapel button, a yellow circle with a thick line down the middle. Partially obscured by a streak of blood, I had noted it right away.

But it hadn't been in the photographs. Not at all.

So what happened to it? Fallen or moved? And if moved, was it moved because it was evidence, or because of something else?

Back to the couch I went, thankful for the warm fire and the taste and texture of the wine, for they would all help me sleep tonight, help me sleep when so many unanswered questions out there would try to keep me awake staring at the ceiling, listening to the steady boom of the waves coming in, one after another.

CHAPTER SEVEN

When spring had officially arrived to the New Hampshire sea-coast a couple of weeks earlier, I had splurged and purchased a new gas grill for my outside deck. Now it was burning merrily along and I stood out in the cool early afternoon flipping two thick hamburgers, and then checked my watch. This grill was expensive but it was constant in the heat it produced, which meant making a perfect cheeseburger every time. I put a slice of cheddar cheese on each burger, and then closed the lid. There. In four minutes, lunch would be ready.

The door to the inside slid open, and Diane Woods poked her head out. "When are we eating?"

I looked at my watch. "In exactly three minutes and thirty seconds."

"How do you know?" she asked, smiling.

"Because this is a no-fail grill that produces perfect cheese-burgers, that's why."

She shook her head. "Where's the adventure in that? No-fail grills are fascist."

I politely pushed my way past her into the kitchen to get a plate. "When it's making the trains run on time or making a perfect cheeseburger, cooked medium rare, then fascism does have its attractive points."

As promised, lunch was completed in the allotted time, and we ate at the kitchen counter, eating small carrot sticks and a fistful of potato chips with our burgers. About halfway through Diane made contented noises and said, "You're right, these are perfect. I take back everything bad I said."

"The day's improving already," I said, and we finished up a few minutes later. As she helped me clean up and wash dishes in the sink, she said, "While the food is as good as any restaurant at the beach, I sure as hell don't have to wash up afterward."

"Think of it as the price you pay for my charming company."

She bumped her hip into mine and was going to say something when we both heard a high-pitched beeping noise. Diane glanced at her side and said, "That's a pager going off, but it sure isn't mine."

"Uh-huh," I said, wiping down a plate.

"No, I'm serious. There's a pager going off in here. Lewis, why in the world would you have a pager?"

I put down the plate and washcloth. "That's an excellent question. Excuse me for a sec, will you?"

I left the kitchen and went upstairs, taking two steps at a time. In my bedroom the little black pager was chiming at me from the top of an oak dresser. I looked at the display and recognized the number as belonging to the Lafayette House. I juggled the pager in my hand a few times and then went over to the small second-floor deck that juts out from my bedroom to the south. I slid open the glass door and stood on the tiny deck, and then let the pager drop from my hand.

I leaned over the deck railing and watched its progress. It fell straight down onto a collection of rocks ranging in size from an egg to a bowling ball. From this height, the pager seemed to explode in tiny black pieces of plastic. I took a deep breath of the ocean air and went back downstairs.

We had small dishes of chocolate ice cream for dessert and I said, "How goes the battle between you and Paula Quinn over the newspaper interview?"

She licked the spoon clean before going in for another bite. "Oh, right now I'm being a caustic little bitch, not returning her phone calls, not bothering to help her set up an interview."

"You figure you can keep doing that for a while?"

"Why not? About the only time it'll change is when that new editor over there gets on the horn with the chief, and he orders me to cooperate. Until then, I'm like the morning fog. You can see me but you can't hold me."

I rattled my own spoon on the edge of my ice cream dish. "And what will you do once the interview begins?"

The phone began to ring, and Diane looked at me quizzically. "Don't worry," I said. "I'll let the machine pick it up."

"Aren't you being mysterious today," she said.

"And I intend to be a bit more mysterious before the day is over. So, back to my original question. Once the interview gets underway, what will you do then?"

She seemed to think about that for a moment, and then she idly licked her spoon. "Oh, hell, I suppose I could seduce her and see what happens . . ." Then Diane laughed, and I smiled with her. "No, really, I know Paula. Nice young lady, enjoys playing with nice young boys like you. Besides, I'm not one to cheat. No, you know what I'll do, Lewis? I'll do the interview, discuss my background as a cop, how I grew up in Porter, so forth and so on. I'll be extremely polite and cooperative. And when the time comes that she feels compelled to ask me who and how I love, I'll politely say it's none of her business."

I finished off my own dessert. "Unfortunately, her boss believes it's his newspaper's business to know."

"Then they can publish and be damned," she said.

"I'm pretty sure Paula's previous offer is still open," I said. "Hot story in exchange for dumping this profile story."

"And I'm positive that my previous position hasn't changed as well," she said. "I'm not going to trade professional favors as part of my personal life. Won't happen. Now, if you'll permit me, I'd like to change the subject for a moment."

"Go ahead."

"Earlier, you said something about being mysterious today. What do you mean by that?"

Almost as if on cue, my phone started to ring. She looked over to the phone and at me, and said, "What's going on?"

"I'm working on a new story," I said, as the phone stopped ringing and the answering machine did its thing.

She eyed me skeptically. "A real story, or one of those stories that will never appear in print?"

"One that will never see the light of day, which makes it mysterious. Look, what can you tell me about the drug activity around here?"

"Around here meaning Tyler Beach, or around here meaning the seacoast?"

"The seacoast."

"Well." She stretched out her denim-clad legs and plunked her feet down on my coffee table. "Tyler being Tyler, you can use that as an example for the rest of the area. Most of the stuff is low-key, marijuana or party drugs like Ecstasy. We do what we can—and please note, I'm speaking in the royal 'we'—to keep a lid on it. That's all we can do. There's harder stuff like coke or heroin, but so far, not that serious a problem."

"How about dealers?"

She looked over at me, eyes a bit merry. "What are you doing, looking for the proverbial Mr. Big, sitting in a luxurious mansion with a fistful of gold chains around his hairy neck and an AK-47 across his lap?"

"The thought's occurred to me."

She gently slapped me on the leg. "Then forget it, friend. Most of what occurs here is done on the sideline. Some loser will have a hobby of breaking into cars or houses, and will deal a little on the side. Probably drives over to Manchester or down to Lowell or Lawrence to pick up his supply, which he immediately cuts with oregano if it's marijuana and baby powder it it's cocaine. In the off-season, it's mostly locals, and when the tourists invade, it's still the locals, plus a few out-of-staters looking to make a few extra bucks on their summer vacation."

"Nothing coming through the harbors?"

"You mean Tyler and Wallis? Lewis, please, you're making me laugh! This isn't south Florida. What goes through those harbors are tour boats, whale watchers and fishermen. Both harbors are so small that if somebody is bringing in something that isn't a tourist or a dead fish, people will know. It's a clannish group, those fishermen, and if someone is doing something like smuggling to make an extra buck or two, then by the next day our phone tip-off line would be filled with anonymous tips, telling us who's smuggling what."

"How about Porter, then? It's a big-enough city."

Diane put her empty dish on the coffee table. "Porter's just a grown-up version of Tyler. You can take everything I mentioned about Tyler and just multiply it. Just a bunch of losers and young kids who don't know any better. No Mr. Big, no grand schemes of smuggling in stuff from boats."

"Even with a harbor as big as Porter?"

"The harbor doesn't matter," she said, as the phone began ringing again for the third time since she had come by, and this time she ignored it. "What matters is the shipping that brings your stuff up from the Caribbean. If you're going through the islands down there and heading to the States, you're taking a trip of a day or two. Easy to slip in and out. Going up the Atlantic coast is another thing entirely. More time on the open seas means more time to be followed, to be spotted. Plus, down there, you've got lots of small craft and charter boats. Delivery is laughably easy. But not up here. No, you need a ship that can make the haul from the Caribbean up to the North Atlantic. And then what? Courier watercraft to bring stuff in from the supply ship? No, not hardly. Too difficult. The ports up here are working ports. Drug smuggling is too much of a losing proposition."

"Even if there's pressure on the other ports down south?"

She glanced at her watch. "Jeez, look at the time. Hey, walk me up to my car, will you?"

"Sure," I said, and I grabbed a light green L.L. Bean jacket and we went outside. She slipped her arm inside mine and said, "This supposed story you're working on. I'm going to use my keen detective skills and say that it has something to do with that guy who ended up dead in his car a while ago, and those fed types who came in with their license plate numbers that don't exist."

"You deserve a raise," I said.

"Then please write a letter to the town manager, will you? And what's so important about this dead guy anyway?"

Lots of possible answers to that one, so I gave her the first one that came to me: "He practically died on my doorstep, and I don't like that."

As we walked up the bumpy dirt driveway, the Lafayette House gradually came into view to the right. I imagined that whoever was calling and paging me this day was having a lousy time, and that thought made me smile.

"Pressure," she said. "You said something about pressure, on the other ports down south. Care to explain?"

We had reached the edge of the parking lot, where Diane's dark green Volkswagen Jetta was parked. It still had the thirty-day temporary paper plate attached to its rear.

I said, "If the cartels and smugglers were getting pressure from the other ports down south, wouldn't they think of expanding to ports up here? Like Porter or Portland?"

She shook her head sharply. "Those guys do what they like, and what they like is down south. If the pressure on the ports increases, they go to bringing it in on airliners. If pressure builds on the airlines, then they try driving it up I-95. Look, pressure and getting intercepted is part of their business. It's like a supermarket assuming that a certain percentage of their goods is going to be shoplifted. It's nothing surprising, nothing out of the ordinary. It's what they plan for. All right?"

"Sure," I said. "You're making a lot of sense. But tell me, is there somebody I can talk to at the shipyard?"

"Nope, sorry," she said. "I can't help you there."

"How about the Porter police, then? A fellow detective?"

"What, so he can tell you what I just said? Man, you are being mysterious today."

"Part of my alluring nature, which so far hasn't worked on you."

She laughed and patted my cheek. "It's going to take more on your part to make yourself alluring, no offense intended. Some surgery and hormone therapy, to start. Look. Joe Stevens. A detective in Porter. I've had some dealings with him. He's young but good. I'll make a call."

"Thanks."

As she headed toward her car, I thought of something else. "Hey, Diane?"

"Yeah?" she said, turning and zipping up her coat.

"The Porter Naval Shipyard. I thought you had a fair number of relatives who worked there."

Now she seemed cold and tiny in her coat. "I do. But you said you wanted to talk to someone who could help you. Lewis, those relatives of mine who work at the shipyard, I haven't talked to in years. Let's just say that they could become bosom buddies with the new boss at the *Chronicle*, if they knew what he was up to. Clear enough?"

I nodded. "Clear enough. Thanks."

But she didn't say anything else as she went to her car.

Back home there was a little red numeral 4 on my answering machine, which meant that I must have missed another call while walking out with Diane. Gee. I erased them all and went over to the television set and the cabinet that supported it, and opened the bottom door. Past my collection of videotapes from such subjects as the Apollo moon landings to D-Day were the five tapes I had rented the other day from the Falconer video store. I took out the unviewed tapes, removed the receipt, and then put the tapes on the counter.

The phone started ringing again. Time to get moving, before Reeves and her boys came bursting through the door.

A half hour later, I was at another store in Falconer, this one on Route 1, just south of the main gate for the Falconer nuclear power plant. This store was in a small plaza that had a jewelry store, a pet store, and a place where one could drop off packages to be delivered. The clerk was a sullen-looking youth who was smoking what smelled like clove cigarettes. The adult section this time was past a doorway blocked by long streams of beads, and I pulled another five tapes to be rented.

Once again, since I was a new renter, the clerk asked me to fill out a form, which I did, and within a couple of minutes I was out the door. Shivering slightly in the cool April afternoon was a heavyset man holding a cardboard sign crayoned with the words FORNICATORS WILL PAY THE PRICE. He looked at me and called out, "God bless!"

"If you say so," I said, and left Falconer, a lonely soldier in the battle for something or another.

I was lucky this afternoon, for Felix was home and willing to chat. We took up residence in his kitchen, and he offered me a bottle of Molson Golden Ale and poured himself a glass of wine. He had on jeans and a long-sleeved black turtleneck shirt, and I made a show of cocking my head, as if listening to something.

He sat down in a captain's chair across from me by the kitchen counter, noting my look. "Something wrong?"

"Nope," I said. "Just listening to see if anybody's taking a shower and needs to be rubbed down or something."

Felix laughed. "Oh, Mickey. She's working at the stables this afternoon, and I'm going up to see her in a few minutes. She's trying to teach me to ride a horse."

"And how's she doing?"

"She's doing well, but unfortunately I don't get much time in the saddle, so to speak. Something always manages to come up to interrupt the lesson."

I tried to act innocent. "Does that mean you get your lesson fee back?"

Another laugh. "Hardly. What's up with you?"

"Trying to get a handle on something," I said.

"Something to do with the dead guy in the parking lot?"

"The same," I said, taking a satisfying swig from my Molson.

"Well, I did some work on that, like you know. Whoever he is, he wasn't connected to anything that I'm familiar with, or with friends of mine. An out-of-towner in every aspect. What else do you need to know?"

I looked around the clean kitchen, where cooking pots and pans and culinary instruments of all types hung in plain view. I've always said Felix should do a shooting-and-cooking show—a unique concept, one I was sure would be a surefire success—but he always demurs, saying he doesn't need the publicity.

"Drugs, as clichéd as it may sound," I said. "I think the guy was connected somehow to the unofficial pharmaceutical business, and I want to know more."

Felix rubbed a thick finger around the rim of his glass. "What makes you think I know anything at all? You know what I've always said and done: Nothing to do with drugs, at all. Too many crazies."

"True, but I'm just looking for some information. Is the trade around here so attractive that someone would be killed for it?"

A shrug. "People get killed all the time, sometimes for pocket change or because somebody stepped on somebody else's sneakers. But a death over the local drug market . . . Lewis, it doesn't sound right."

"How's that?"

He rubbed the finger again across the glass edge. "Too diffuse, too penny-ante, too low-level. Even in Boston and New York and Hartford, there's hardly any gang-banging activity at all. Those cocaine and crack wars, they're mostly over, and that's in the big cities. Up here? Never even came close to that level of violence, either then or now. Which makes me suspicious if somebody told you that guy was whacked over the local drug trade."

I took a cold swallow of the Molson. "Suppose the guy was connected to a cartel, looking to come up here and expand their business?"

"In what way?" he asked, suspicious.

"Start importing their materials around here. Like Porter Harbor."

Felix said, "Excuse me for being blunt, but are you losing

your mind? Forgot where your sock drawer was this morning? Putting orange juice in your breakfast cereal?"

"No, no, no, and thanks for the concern."

"Well," he said, hunching himself over so his elbows rested on the polished kitchen counter. "I don't doubt that some stuff moves in and out of Porter, but it's a commercial port, and a small one, at that. The guys from the cartels, they like to work in familiar turf, familiar ports. This far north and something this small doesn't make any sense whatsoever."

He looked up over the kitchen sink, where a small clock rested on a shelf, next to a row of spices. "Running out of time, my friend. Anything else?"

"Yeah, if you don't mind."

He smiled widely. "Knowing where I'm going and what I'll be doing with the dear Mickey this afternoon, I'm feeling particularly generous. Go ahead."

"I'm trying to find someone in the local area, somebody associated with the Porter Naval Shipyard."

"You got a name?"

"I've got a nickname," I said. "A guy called Whizzer."

"Whizzer?" he asked.

"Whizzer," I confirmed.

He finished his glass of wine, slapped his hands against his flat belly. The sound almost echoed in the house. "I'll give it a go, Lewis, but it sounds like a guy who has a bladder problem. Not somebody hooked up with the drug business."

"Maybe so, but if you could find him, I'd appreciate it. Even tell a few lies about you to Mickey the next time I see her."

"Sure, I'll see what I can do. In the meantime, hurry up and finish your beer, so I won't be late."

A couple of minutes later we were outside, and he started walking to his blue Mercedes convertible. "By the way, you okay on this?" he asked.

"Okay on what?" I asked.

"Whatever it is you're looking for. I know you like to poke and pry at things mysterious, usually when it interests you or involves a friend. Whatever for, I've never been quite sure why. Must be your law-abiding nature."

"Must be," I said.

"But this thing sounds too nutty, even for you. Dead guy in a car, fed types crawling around, looking for a guy named Whizzer. You working for the feds on this, Lewis, or is this freelance?"

I said, "Let's just say I'm working."

He gave me a straight look. "Okay. I understand. But understand this. Be careful. Feds always have their own agenda. Always. And most times, they don't share their agenda with us little people. So watch your step."

"I intend to."

"Good," he said, slapping me gently on the shoulder, which is about as expressive as Felix gets. "I'd hate to think of the conscience of Tyler Beach getting into trouble."

"Too late for that," I said, and went back to my own vehicle, thinking of him and Diane giving me direction, giving me clues. I sat in my Ford for a moment, watching Felix drive away, confident and sure in his skills and his future. He had been shot at, knifed and beaten up on several occasions, and no doubt his name existed in several law enforcement agency files, but right now I envied him.

For he wasn't afraid.

I started up the Explorer and went home.

CHAPTER EIGHT

When I got home the lights were on downstairs, and somebody was waiting for me as I walked through my new door, still smelling fresh and alive from its recent arrival from the hardware store. Laura Reeves was on my couch, wearing a white turtleneck and a short black skirt this time, her black stocking-enclosed legs tucked underneath her. She had a Sunday *New York Times Magazine* in her hands and she nodded at me as I took off my coat.

"Thought you'd be home eventually," she said. "How was your day?"

"Gee, dear, it was swell," I said, walking into the living room. A fire was burning its way in the fireplace, and I looked around. "All by your lonesome tonight?"

"Rest of the crew's working," she said. "Out there doing the nation's business, which is why I'm here. To see what kind of business you've been up to. For example, how's that pager working that I gave you?"

"It's not."

She nodded, as if she had already figured it out. "I see. And how's your phone working?"

"Phone's working fine. I guess my phone answering skills ain't what they used to be."

Another crisp nod, and she unfolded her long legs and sat up. "I see. Tell me, do you think this whole thing is a joke, something put together for your amusement?"

I went over to the fireplace, tossed in a chunk of wood. "Oh yeah, it's been a barrel of laughs."

"Well, think about this before you start laughing," she said, standing up. "We took several things away from you—from your house to your funds—to get you on board. Now that you're on board, we're expecting results. And results don't mean goofing around, hoping we'll lose attention or move on to something else. And if I think you're not serious about providing results, we can be right back where we started from. Understood?"

I looked at the sharp look on her face, her self-assurance, the way she held herself. I stood up and held my hands behind me.

"Understood," I said. "Care to stay for dinner?"

There. I think I disturbed her, just for a moment, for her eyes moved away from mine. "No, I would not." A slight smile. "Thanks for asking, but I must be going."

Reeves went past me to the door, and as she stood on the stone steps she said, "Whenever you next leave your house, please advise me. And one more thing, Lewis. Please answer your phone, all right? We're not the enemy."

"Sure," I said. "I understand."

And I waited until she was a distance away before I said, "You may not be the enemy, but I'll be damned if I know what you are."

Then I closed the door.

It was 2 A.M. I was wide awake, staring up at the ceiling. Sometime earlier I had spent a couple of hours on my new computer, surfing the Net, enjoying the fast modem I had with my new machine. I had gone to a lot of different places on the Web, one of which was responsible for my getting up at this hour.

Still, I had thirty minutes. I rested, listening to the ever-present sound of the ocean. During the day and when I'm out and about in the daylight, the noise of the waves rolling in is like a low humming, a soft background noise that I can hardly make out. But at night, with the lights out, with nothing else demanding my attention, the waves always take center, always demand attention.

Just like this little adventure I had signed up for. From the way Reeves and her boys had roared in, to the reaction of the North Tyler chief to the way they had shanghaied me to play in their little world, not a lick of it had made sense. And Felix and Diane had also told me as much. I continued staring up at the ceiling. Be careful, Felix had said, be careful.

I checked the clock. Time to get up. I yawned and got dressed in the dark and then went downstairs, where I put on a heavy coat and stepped outside. It was a clear and moonless night, and even being in one of the most heavily populated parts of New England, I could make out the faint veil of the Milky Way spanning overhead. In the dim light I went up my driveway, stopping only when I reached the parking area of the Lafayette House. I then walked across the silent parking lot, sitting on one of the boulders that marked the eastern boundary of the lot. I sat and let my legs dangle, the waves of the Atlantic just yards away. I had seen winter storms where waves would reach the rocks I was sitting on, but not tonight. It was too calm for such anger.

I looked at my watch and then looked over to the southeast. Right on time. A bright dot of light that appeared to be moving slowly, and then gaining speed the longer I looked at it. The space shuttle *Endeavour*, once again circling the globe from more than 160 miles up. I crossed my arms and just stared at that little dot, signifying more than a spaceship, signifying a little bubble of air and pressure and light where seven people were living up there for a week. Impressive, but yet, when I was a child, we had the energy and will to send similar little bubbles of humanity more than a quarter million miles to another world.

A similar trip wasn't on the agenda tonight. Tonight we were just busy orbiting the blue planet, and I kept on watching, paying tribute in my own little way, as the bright dot descended to the northwest and then faded from view. I sighed and got up and rubbed my face, and then started walking.

But not home. I walked across the street, to the bright lights of the Lafayette House.

I was lucky, for the main lobby doors to the Lafayette House were open, and there was no security on duty this early in the morning. Maybe in a couple of months, when the thousands of tourists and the assorted hangers-on showed up, those few who try to take advantage of the tourists and their money, then would security be an issue. But at this early hour on this April morning, I took the elevator to the fifth floor without any problem, any challenge.

At room 512 I started pounding on the door, and when no one came to answer in a minute or so, I resorted to using my feet.

Then the door popped open and one of the musclemen—Clem, I think his name was—stood there, barefoot, wearing a white terry-cloth robe with the Lafayette House crest over the breast. Quite a cheerful sight, if you overlooked the black automatic pistol clutched in his large right fist.

"You . . . Jesus, what the fuck are you doing here?" he asked.

I stepped in, trying to act confident, trying to look like I belonged. "I need to see Laura Reeves. Right now."

He rubbed at his eyes, stepped back. "Christ, do you know what time it is?"

"The time doesn't matter," I said. "The fact that I need to see Reeves does. Take care of it, will you?"

"She's next door, you jerk," he said. "Why did you come here?"

"Made a mistake, I guess," I said, as I stood by one of the tables set up in the room. I looked about. A bedroom door was open, which probably belonged to Clem, who was now on the phone, a grumpy look on his unshaven face. I looked down at the table. Writing pads, more photos of Romero, and a pile of badly photocopied documents. They were upside down but still, looking at them, I could see that they weren't in English.

But they weren't in Spanish, either. Clem hung up the phone, yawned. "She'll be right here, you moron, and it better be good."

"It'll be better than you expect," I said, and then the adjoining door to the other room opened up, and Reeves was there. She also had on a white terry-cloth robe but she looked awake and alert, as if she didn't need sleep at all, just a dusting and an oil change every ten thousand miles.

"Yes?" she asked, her arms folded.

I smiled. "When last we spoke, you told me to inform you whenever I left my house."

"And?"

"I wanted to let you know that I left my house about fifteen minutes ago."

She slowly nodded. "I see. And where did you go?"

"In the parking lot across the street. To see the space shuttle go overhead."

Clem started muttering some curses involving me and my intelligence, ancestry and sexual habits, but Reeves just nodded again. "Very good. Is that all?"

"For now," I said.

"Then I'm going back to bed. Clem, be so kind as to show Mr. Cole the door."

So now I was back to being Mr. Cole. Oh well. "Don't bother," I said. "I know the way. Talk to you soon."

But I was talking to a closed door. Clem was also getting up, and I managed to sneak one more look at the documents on the table as I left the room. I whistled softly as I went back down on the elevator and out into the cool April night, thinking about what I had seen in the room. Besides seeing two grumpy and sleepy federal agents, I had also figured out the language on those documents.

German. Not really the language of choice for drug cartels from Colombia.

I was still whistling when I got home, and before I went to bed I disconnected my telephone, just in case Reeves or her boys had an idea of getting me up with the sun.

Maybe I wasn't playing fair, but who were they to complain?

Some hours after my nocturnal visit to Reeves and her crew I was at the police department in Porter, New Hampshire, one of the few cities in our state and also the state's only major port to the Atlantic. The police station is on a hill near the center of town, in a former hospital that had been closed some years earlier. The city hall and the police department and a few other city agencies shared the large quarters, and I knew that Diane and other police officers up and down the seacoast could barely hide their envy at the relatively luxurious quarters the Porter police enjoyed.

While Diane and other local departments had to make do with concrete buildings that flooded out in the spring, or the basement of the town hall where the ceilings leaked, the Porter police had a building large enough to contain an exercise room, a shooting range in the basement, and private offices for their detectives.

The detective I was meeting today was Joe Stevens, who looked to be in his late twenties. He was a bit shorter than I but his dress shirt and pants barely concealed a well-muscled young man who seemed confident in being a detective in what passed for a big city in the region. His black hair already sprinkled with gray was cut short, about a quarter inch away from being a crew cut, and his nose was a slight pug, as if it had been broken at an early age.

Unlike Diane's office, with its files stored in cardboard boxes and the concrete walls painted a sickly green, this one had neat file cabinets and wide windows that overlooked the old brick buildings of Porter. I took a seat next to his desk as he sat back, a coffee cup in his hand. On the wall behind him was a monthly calendar from Smith & Wesson, a few photos of him in SWAT gear, and one of him with an attractive brown-haired woman who looked to be his wife.

"So," Joe said. "Diane Woods gave me a ring yesterday, asking me to give you some time, Mr. Cole. Since I owe her a couple of favors, ask away. What can I do for you?"

"I'm a writer for *Shoreline* magazine, out of Boston," I said. "I'm considering doing a story about the local drug activity on the seacoast."

"*Shoreline,* eh? Not a bad magazine. I gave a subscription last year to my mom. What kind of articles do you write?"

"I do a monthly column about New Hampshire, called 'Granite Shores.'"

He shrugged. "Sorry. Can't say that I've ever seen it. Mom likes the magazine, but I don't have time to read it."

"I hear that a lot," I said, my reporter's notebook unopened in my hands.

"So, a column about drug activity. Anything in particular?"

"I was thinking of starting my way north here in Porter and working my way south, comparing and contrasting what's going on in the different communities."

"And you want to start in Porter, is that it?"

"Actually," I said, "I wanted to start a bit farther north, but Diane wasn't able to set something up for me. At the shipyard."

The Porter detective looked incredulous. "Our shipyard? The Porter Naval Shipyard?"

"That's right."

He laughed, took a sip from his coffee, put the cup down. It was black with red lettering, the red letters spelling out D.A.R.E. "No offense, Mr. Cole, but in the day-to-day business, that shipyard is in its own little universe. We have no jurisdiction over there, the good people in Kittery, Maine, think it belongs to them anyway, and I think I've been to the shipyard maybe twice in my career. And both times it was because the shipyard had some surplus blankets and office equipment to donate to us, and both times I met a shipyard official in a parking lot to transfer the gear. The shipyard's not a place we deal with that much."

"Why's that?"

"Because it belongs to the Department of Defense and the Navy, that's why, and they like running things their own way. Look, for a time that place built a hell of a lot of submarines, subs that sank a lot of Jap freight back during World War Two. But you know what they do now?"

"Overhaul and refits," I said. "Mostly of Los Angeles–class attack submarines."

"Right you are," he said, smiling. "Most people have their

heads up their butts when it comes to the shipyard. Okay. That's their job, overhauling and refitting attack submarines. You seem to be an intelligent guy for a reporter, and you come recommended from Diane. Anything special about those subs?"

"Besides the fact they're powered by nuclear reactors, and no doubt most of them carry nuclear warheads of one kind or another?"

Stevens smiled. "This is the most fun I've ever had on an interview. Most reporters I know couldn't find their ass with both hands and a road map. Yep, nuclear materials, all around. So you're the Department of the Defense and you're the Navy. Care to think how much tolerance you'd have for drug dealing and drug use around nuclear reactors and nuclear weapons?"

"None," I said.

A quick nod. "A number of companies around here now have programs to counteract drug abuse. Random searches of offices, urine-sample analyses, that sort of thing. Well, that's kindergarten compared to what I hear they do over at the shipyard. Not to piss all over your story idea, Mr. Cole, but if you're planning to do an article on drug use in the seacoast and you're going to start with the shipyard, it'll be a mighty small part of the story."

I turned the notebook over in my hands a couple of times. About what I had expected, but still, I had to go to the best source I could and find that out firsthand. "One more thing, and then I'll be out of your hair," I said.

"Go ahead."

"This might be a bit delicate, but in the course of my research, a name came up of someone that might be playing a key part in the drug trade around here. Somebody who's connected with the shipyard."

His voice seemed a bit flat. "And you'd like me to check out this name?"

"Purely on background," I said. "Not for attribution or for use. Just to help me in my research. And I'm sorry to say, it's not a full name. Just a nickname. Whizzer."

"Whizzer?" he asked.

"Whizzer," I said.

He smiled and wrote something down on a scrap of paper. "Okay, I'll give it a shot, but don't hold your breath."

"I don't intend to hold anything right now," I said, standing up. I held out my hand and he shook it, and I said, "This favor that Diane Woods did for you, it must have been a good one."

"That it was," he said, his voice now quiet. "Last year one of our senior patrolmen found out he had cancer. Incurable and inoperable. He decided to end it all, and did it in a motel room at Tyler Beach. Diane helped us a lot, helped us keep it out of the papers. We still owe her big."

"So do I," I said. "So do I."

When I saw her later that day, Paula Quinn was not having a good time of it. I had parked my Ford in the rear lot of the newspaper as always, and as I started heading toward the rear entrance of the newspaper, I stopped, looking at the closed door that led into the circulation department and from there into the newsroom. Some battles are worth fighting for, every minute of the day, and others deserved to wait. I decided to wait, and swung around and went to the front of the paper.

The receptionist was a young woman with dyed-blond hair and an earring through her left eyebrow—I was wondering if they were now called brow rings, if that's where they were placed—and she was studiously working on a crossword-puzzle book. It took her two tries with the phone system before she contacted Paula, and then she smiled up at me and said, "You can go right in. Do you need to know where her desk is?"

"I'll make a wild guess and stop at the one where she's sitting at," I said, giving her my best *Chronicle* customer smile and walking into the newsroom. The place was empty save for Paula, who was at her desk, which looked as if it had been attacked by a roving gang of junk dealers. She had on a light gray UNH sweatshirt and blue jeans, and her hair had been pulled back from around her face by a thin black bandanna. The two chairs near her desk were piled high with folders and newspaper clippings, but I found a spare chair and dragged it over. The desk of her editor, Rollie Grandmaison, was empty, as was the desk of the new guy, Rupert Holman. The front pages from the *Chronicle*'s competition still hung from the ceiling, complete with fake blood and plastic dagger.

"It looks like you're the one who got left behind at the junior prom," I said, and she looked up at me, her eyes sharp like crystal, and said, "It's been a sucky day, so please don't start."

"All right, apologies," I said, looking around the place. "Where the hell is everybody?"

"Out having a lengthy victory lunch, that's where," she said. "Latest circulation report came in and we exceeded our new weekly goal by three. Can you believe that? Three newspapers purchased at a newsstand, and we beat quota. Rupert was so thrilled that he took the whole cast and crew of this little adventure out to a nice long lunch to celebrate. Three strangers within five miles of this newspaper office, they decide to buy a Tyler *Chronicle* because of a story or a photo on the front page, or because they need something to wrap their dead fish in, and because of those three strangers, here I am, alone in the newsroom."

I looked at her and her desk, at the mess of papers, files and other debris that accompanies being a daily newspaper reporter. "Okay, so you won't ask the question; I'll still answer it," she said. "The reason I'm not at the lunch is because I've been remiss in meeting one of our newsroom goals. Goal number four, if I recall, to have an orderly and clean working space. According to Rupert's anal compulsive mind, I had not even begun to meet the goal, let alone achieve it. So here I sit, while my fellow workers go out and enjoy a free meal."

"Must be heartwarming, to see how many of your coworkers stood up for you."

She wiped a strand of hair from her eyes. "Around here, Lewis, standing up just makes you a bigger target. This place is usually either somebody's first job or last job. In any event, it's a job they don't want to jeopardize. And I hate to admit, that means me right about this point. Which is why I'm here, hungry and angry, cleaning out my desk and file drawers." She reached over to a filing cabinet, pulled out a cardboard box filled with pencils, pens, buttons and bumper stickers, which she threw down on the desktop.

She continued. "You know, you'd think he'd appreciate the fact that I'm his best reporter, that I always meet deadlines, and that I haven't made that much of a fuss in doing those kinds of stories he's been asking for. Speaking of making a fuss, friend, why in hell aren't you returning my phone calls?"

"Excuse me?"

Out at the receptionist area, the phone started ringing. It rang six times before it was picked up. Paula looked at me, another strand of hair across her face, but this time she didn't bother to move it. "You heard me. I called you yesterday and left a message. No reply. I called you this morning, same thing. Something going on?"

I thought of the four messages I had erased yesterday without listening to them, and how I had gone out of the house this morning without checking messages after my morning shower. Damn. I tried to make light of it. "Sometimes I just forget, that's all. I'm sorry, I haven't checked messages in a while."

Paula didn't seem to be in the mood for light. "Well, sometimes . . . sometimes I need to talk to you, especially when the day's not going well and I'm beginning to doubt my own journalistic skills. And I'm not being whiny or needy or greedy or any damn thing, but I sure could have used a talk last night."

I slowly nodded, looked over at her. "Apologies again. Look, can I help you sort through this mess? Clean some of this stuff out to the rear dumpster?"

She managed a smile. "No, that's okay. For one thing, this is my mess and I only trust my own eyes for deciding what stays and what goes. Plus, I'm enjoying sitting here, stewing and plotting revenge on Rupert when his time comes up. Tell you what—you can buy me a drink later, if you'd like, 'cause I'm sure I'll be in the mood for one."

"Deal," I said, and Paula picked up the small cardboard box and looked in and rattled it around. "My word," she said, "sometimes I can be such a pack rat. Time to dump this stuff and go on to the next pile."

In front of me was a half-full wastebasket, and Paula turned the cardboard box over to empty it. Paper clips, pens and other debris tumbled out and I was going to ask her where she would like her drink when something yellow and black flashed by me. I felt my breath catch and waited until she had turned and gone to another filing cabinet drawer before I leaned over and looked down in the now full wastebasket, saw the little color of yellow. I gingerly reached down and picked up the yellow button with the black insignia that looked like a fat exclamation point. I was surprised my hands didn't tremble at holding the little bugger.

Paula noted me and smiled. "Things so tough back at the ranch that you've got to go through my garbage for spare paper clips?"

"This button," I said, holding it gingerly, as if I was afraid it was going to fly out of my hand and disappear, "do you remember where you got it from?"

"Sure," she said. "But you're holding it wrong. Turn it about halfway . . . there. That's the way it should look. Yep, got that up in Porter, a couple of months ago."

I now looked at the button, saw the way it was suppose to be displayed. The black mark no longer looked like a fat exclamation point. It was now the silhouette of a submarine. "At the shipyard? Did you get this button at the shipyard?"

"No, I didn't," she said. "I got it at the Porter Submarine Museum, which is on the waterfront. By the USS *Albacore.* Their grand opening was back in late February and I was part of the press contingent when they had their ribbon-cutting ceremonies. That button is what you wear after you pay your admission. I'm surprised you haven't been up there yet, knowing your interest in things historical."

"Me, too," I said. I rolled the metal object between my fingers. The Porter Submarine Museum. Maybe Reeves and her intel was wrong. Maybe nothing to do with the shipyard, but something to do with the submarine museum. Wrong intelligence from a federal agency? Made one feel like writing a stiff letter to *The New York Times.*

I said, "Is it a big place? Do you know who the director is?"

"Director? Lewis, the place is in a little converted brick storage building. Has two floors and you can get through the whole museum in under fifteen minutes. There's an old guy who runs the place, looks about ninety years old, and from what I gathered, he runs it by himself."

"Can I get a copy of the story you did?"

Her face flushed for a moment. "Oops, another secret revealed from the secret archives of being a newspaper reporter. Don't be shocked, but I was up in Porter that day for a dentist's appointment. It was late in the afternoon and I decided to go over to the museum, see if I could get something to eat from the reception before heading home. I did a little news brief, if that. Not much of a story. You know we really don't cover Porter that much, especially if it's something like the museum."

I held the button in my hand for just another moment, and then let it fall into the wastebasket. I looked at the newsroom clock. It was four o'clock in the afternoon, and I was about thirty minutes away from Porter, if I pushed it.

"Sure I can't help you in cleaning up?" I asked, hoping she would turn me down again, which she did.

"Sure I'm sure," she said. "Unless you want to stay here and keep me company until my fellow members of the working class stumble back in from their free meal."

I made a show of looking at my watch. "Well, I was thinking about running a couple of errands. How about I do that and then come back for that drink and conversation?"

If she was disappointed, she managed to hide it quite well. "A drink and a conversation would be wonderful. Especially after today."

I got up and said, "This Rupert guy. In addition to keeping tabs on what you do and how clean your office is, do you think he does video surveillance?"

"Here? In the newsroom?"

"Yeah, here in the newsroom. Any chance of video cameras in here?"

She laughed, started flipping through a number of newspaper clippings. "He's hard to work for in a number of ways, but I don't think we can accuse him of spying on is. Not yet, anyway."

"Good," I said, and leaned over to give her a kiss. She was surprised but then she laughed against my lips and kissed me back, quite well and diligently, thank you, and her hand gently tugged at the back of my neck.

"Hmmm," she said. "Any reason for this little PDA?"

I pulled back, glad to see the smile on her face. "Is it really a public display of affection if we're not in public?"

"Shoo," she said, waving a handful of clippings at me. "Before I fall behind even more and Rupert sees what a bigger mess I've made."

I touched her lips quickly with my fingers. "Drinks and conversation, very shortly."

"Good. Now, go."

I got.

CHAPTER NINE

The quickest way to get to Porter from Tyler is to get on Interstate 95, which I did after leaving the *Chronicle*'s offices, moving quickly only when I was out of view of Paula and the newsroom. Heading north on the interstate, I joined the other streaming crowds of cars, trucks and minivans heading home on their daily commute after another day of doing whatever it is that normal people do.

Normal people, I thought, looking ahead, trying to remember which exit was the closest in Porter to get to the USS *Albacore*. Normal people don't end up getting dragooned to working for the Drug Enforcement Agency, and normal people don't try to chase a spirit called Whizzer, and normal people don't go to Porter twice in one day, asking questions and prying and ignoring the attentions of a lovely young newspaper reporter who just recently tasted of cinnamon.

But I've never claimed to be normal. Near Porter the interstate splits in two, one way heading to a traffic circle—a free one-ring circus that can provide long minutes of terrifying amusement as four lanes of traffic merge into one place—and the other way heading up and over the Piscataqua River, heading into Maine. I took the last possible exit before I ended up in the Pine Tree

State, helped by the exit sign that said PORTER WATERFRONT. The exit is elevated and I got a good view of the harbor—the salt and scrap piles, the small tankers heading up to the oil and gas terminals in Lewington. Many places in New Hampshire have been gentrified and yuppified and turned into theme parks that would make Walt Disney proud, but this port was still a working port, and I felt an irrational sense of pride at that.

At the end of the exit I turned right onto Harborview Road, and then I turned right again after fifty yards or so, at the submarine, the USS *Albacore,* now landlocked and a tourist attraction. Before I came back to New Hampshire years ago, the locals in Porter had asked the Navy if the city could have the decommissioned *Albacore* to use as a tourist attraction. The experimental submarine had been built at the Porter Naval Shipyard in the 1950s and was destined to be scrapped. The Navy agreed to donate the submarine, and through lots of planning, criticism and scrambling, the city had pulled together to bring the sub in. One creative bit of planning included digging a ditch across four lanes of highway and building a temporary canal, so that the submarine could be placed inland.

At the entrance to the submarine and the museum, a small blue-and-white OPEN flag was flying, so I knew I had some time. The parking lot only had a few vehicles parked there and to the right was the submarine, with a ramp leading into the side of its hull, where a door had been cut away. The white numerals "596" were quite bright. I parked and sat there for a moment, thinking about the man called Romero, who had died so near my home. He had been here, without a doubt. To do what? Meet up with his contact? And why continue wearing the little button as he sat in the parking lot of the state park? Being forgetful? Or was it used as an identification of some sort? And why was the button missing from the crime scene photos that Reeves had shown me?

Lots of questions, and I got out of my Ford and walked over to the museum building. But no easy answers, none yet.

The museum building looked like a small two-story brick schoolhouse, and many of these buildings still exist in some of the smaller towns in this county. Inside, a tall older man was talking loudly into the phone. A couple of tourists were examining brochures at the other wall. I looked over at the info sign, saw that the place closed in less than an hour, and that an admission to the museum and the submarine cost five dollars. The man with the phone was behind a counter fronted by a glass display case and I walked over to him. At his elbow was a cash register and he looked at me and gave me an exasperated look, as if he would rather be anyplace than here. He looked to be in his mid-seventies, and wore black slacks, a dungaree shirt and red suspenders. A name tag on his chest said JACK EMERSON. Behind him was an open doorway into an office area packed with a small desk, chair, filing cabinets and some framed photos and certificates.

"And I'm telling you," he said, "I do have spaces for two tour buses. But I don't have a place to feed your people. You'll have to make arrangements in town."

To the right of the display case was a short archway made of brick, and a sign overhead said EXHIBITS. Glass windows overlooked the parking lot, the harbor and the silent black shape of the *Albacore*. I slid a five-dollar bill across the glass counter.

Without missing a beat, Jack picked up the five-dollar bill and rang up the cash register. "Well, there are plenty of restaurants in Porter; I can't go ahead and book you in one. Best I can do is fax you a list of restaurants in walking distance."

He reached underneath the counter and I heard a clicking sound, like poker chips being rubbed together, and then he brought up a yellow button, just like the one Paula had had in her office, just like the one Romero had on his lapel when someone shot him in the head. It was almost as if I were picking up some kind of cursed voodoo fetish as I took the button and pinned it on my shirt.

"Well, we do a lot of things here at the submarine museum, but we're not a catering outfit," Jack said. "That's the best I can offer you. I know you're bringing in seventy-five people and I appreciate that, but right now, you're being more of a pain than I need."

Hoping I would have better luck with this button than the

man called Romero, I went through the archway into the museum.

Right away, I was transported back in time, back to 1800, when the first ships were constructed in the harbor for the U.S. Navy and the shipyard had been officially opened, though shipbuilding of all sorts had taken place in Porter since the place was first settled in 1623. The first part of the museum showed various displays and exhibits on the shipyard's early years, when it built all types of vessels for the Navy. And then, in 1914, the submarine work began for Porter and its navy yard.

I went upstairs into the main exhibit, highlighting the submarine work that the yard had been so famous for during World War II. I walked quietly and respectfully through the exhibits, which showed the different types of submarines that were built here in the 1930s and 1940s, as Porter supplied seventy-nine fleet-class submarines for the Atlantic and Pacific naval battles of World War II. All of the photos were black and white, some were large and mounted on the walls. A lot showed submarines, draped in bunting, going down the slideways as they were launched, and others showed men at work, pipefitters and welders and steamfitters; and for a time, during the height of the war, the men were joined by women, standing there proudly in their boots and overalls.

Another wall contained small ribbons commemorating all the submarines that had been built and launched here, name after name: *Aspro, Ronquil, Requin, Odax, Diablo, Piper, Pomfret, Sea Owl, Piranha.* I smiled as I remembered a book I had read about when the new nuclear subs were being built, and Admiral Hyman Rickover began naming submarines after states and cities. The old salts in the Navy had sniffed about tradition, about how the tradition was to name the underwater craft after marine creatures. And in a snappy response, Rickover noted that fish didn't vote; residents of cities and states who had submarines named after their hometowns, did.

Thus endeth the argument.

There was a smaller display, titled TRANSITIONS, which covered the time during the 1960s and 1970s, when layoffs struck the shipyard, and when it became a yearly battle for the New Hampshire Congressional Delegation to keep the yard open and its thousands of jobs safe. But before I entered the TRANSITIONS gallery, I came to a full stop before a small display that showed a different type of submarine, with a "U" designation on the side.

German subs, docked at the Porter Naval Shipyard.

I stopped for a long while at the exhibit, and learned a lot in just a few minutes, long minutes where I read and reread the exhibits and wondered what in hell I had gotten myself involved with.

When I got back down to the main entrance, the old man called Jack was locking up the cash register. What little hair he had was white and cut short in a crew cut, and he had on black-rimmed reading glasses. He looked over at me. "Sorry you didn't get to walk through the *Albacore,* but we're closing up. Tell you what. If you want, you can come back tomorrow and I'll let you sneak on in."

"Thanks," I said. "I might just do that." I reached into my wallet, pulled out a business card that identified me as a columnist for *Shoreline* magazine. Jack looked it over and I said, "Do you have time for a few questions, Mr. Emerson?"

"Jack, please," he said, pocketing my business card and extending a hand, which I quickly shook. His hand was dry and wrinkled, and it felt like old paper.

"Lewis Cole," I said.

"Are you planning on doing a story on our little museum?" There was a familiar eagerness to his question.

Here it comes, I thought. Another in a series of the Great Lie, where I get perfect strangers to open to me, to trust me, to answer my questions. The Great Lie I had done on numerous occasions, and it still made me feel like I should wash my hands when I was done. I took a breath.

"To tell you the truth, Jack, I'm just doing some research, some poking around," I said. "Sometimes it results in a story, sometimes it doesn't. If you really don't have the time, I understand."

He laughed, took out a glass-cleaner sprayer and a roll of paper towels, and started wiping down the countertop. "At this stage in my life, time is the only thing that I have plenty of. Go ahead and ask away."

"Well, are you the director here?"

Another laugh. "Director, exhibit manager, scheduler, tour guide and janitor. All in one. This is pretty much a one-man show, and while being a a one-man show means not much in the way of staff discord, it can wear on you after a while."

I looked around the lobby, at the entrance to the displays, and the enormous landlocked submarine out there beyond the parking lot. "Really? I mean, well . . ."

"I know what you're thinking," he said, wiping carefully from one end of the countertop to the other. "You're thinking that this museum is important, that it highlights the vital military contribution this port has made to the nation and the world, and that a place like this, that honors the men and women who built submarines to defend this land, should be well-funded and well-staffed."

I caught the sharpness in his tone. "One would think."

He put his cleaning supplies back under the counter. "Well, once upon a time, that was the case. When this place opened up, years after the submarine got here, I was on the committee that raised the money and did the organizing. We had a number of volunteers who came in here and helped me out. The fund-raising went well for a year or two. And then things changed. Some of the volunteers moved away, others passed on, and still others got involved in other things. And most of these volunteers were my age or older. The younger generation . . . well, don't get me started. So we make do with the admission and a few donations here and there. Just enough to keep the place open and pay my magnificent salary."

"It may be small, but there's a lot of good information in those exhibits," I said.

"Ah, so there is, but we have lots more items that I'd love to display, but we don't have the space for it. Old uniforms, blueprints, submarine models. We could triple the size of this place and still not have enough room."

He reached over to a wall behind him and started flipping off light switches, and the *click-click-click* sound was loud in the lobby. "And what brought you here today, Lewis of *Shoreline* magazine? Got a hankering to learn more about Porter and her submarines?"

"A bit," I said, "but I'm also looking to see if you remember a visitor you might have had here a couple of days ago. A dark-skinned man, wearing a two-piece black suit, white shirt. He had a mustache. Might have spoken with an accent."

He rubbed at his chin, and I could hear a faint scratching sound as his skin went across his chin whiskers. "No . . . I'm afraid I can't, but that doesn't surprise me. Most of these days I've been on the phone from the moment I come in to the moment I leave. Tour groups, God help us all, getting ready for their summer season. They call up and say they're going to come, and then they start dickering around. Looking for a group dis-count. Looking to combine a tour here with a tour at another museum, and couldn't I get a discount for them at that museum as well. Looking for a cheap meal right next door. When it gets that busy on the phone, I hardly even look up. Just take the money and pass over the lapel pin. This guy with a mustache a friend of yours?"

"No, not really."

"Then why the questions?"

"Something I'm working on, something just a bit confiden-tial. Sorry."

He waved a hand. "Ah, don't worry about it. I knew a lot of confidential things when I worked at the yard. Got so that my late wife learned to stop asking so many questions when I got home from work. What else do you want to know?"

"Ever hear of a guy at a shipyard or volunteering here at the museum with a nickname called Whizzer?"

He grinned. "Sounds like a lot of guys my age with prostate problems. We're whizzers all right, day and night, especially when we've settled down in bed or on the couch. Nope, can't say that I do. I'm afraid this isn't being a very productive trip for you."

Jack ducked into the small office at the rear and came out, struggling to put on a tan jacket while grasping a metal cane in his hand. "How long were you at the shipyard?" I asked.

"Spent ten years in this man's navy, working on the old diesel pig boats. When I got out, spent another twenty years at the yard, following what my dad and my uncles had done, until I dinged up my leg. Got out on disability and puttered around until I joined up here."

He went around the counter, leaning heavily on the cane. "I've really got to get moving along, if you don't mind. You can walk me out to the parking lot, if you'd like."

"That would be fine," I said.

Outside in the parking lot were my own Ford Explorer and his Dodge pickup truck. With the light growing dim, somehow the *Albacore* looked even bigger. Jack noticed that I was looking at it and said, "One of the first subs I helped build, back in the mid-fifties. You want to hear about secrets. We were all sworn to secrecy when we built that baby, because of the hull design and other new features."

He walked a bit over to the *Albacore,* raised his cane and started using it as a pointer. "All the subs we built during World War Two followed the same design, but this one was radical. It served as a prototype for every type of sub that followed, from the Polaris to the Trident missile boats and the Los Angeles and Sea-wolf classes. More of a teardrop shape, enables the boat to move faster and quieter through the water. Boy, did she ever. You know, even now, almost a half century later, the speed and the depths this boat reached are still classified information? Unreal, isn't it."

I joined him, looking at the boat, thinking over what I had seen in the museum that had caught my attention. "Something that strikes me as unreal is that little display I saw, right before the Transitions gallery. About the German U-boats that came here in 1945."

"Ha, yeah, that's a heck of a story, one that still isn't widely known." Jack started walking slowly back to his truck. "You see, back in May '45, when the war in Germany was over, the U-boats were ordered to surrender. Most did, except for one that went all the way to Argentina. Supposedly there were rumors that that boat carried Hitler or some other Nazi mucky-mucks out, but that story was a load of crap."

"Why's that?"

"For the most part, the Nazi leadership didn't like or even understand their navy. For them to spend months in a U-boat, eating canned food and smelling each other's farts and sweat, no, there's no way they would have put up with that."

We reached his pickup truck, which was rusting and whose tires looked as if they were about a month away from being officially classified as bald. There were two faded bumper stickers on the rear. One simply said, SUPPORT THE PORTER SUBMARINE MUSEUM and the other, THERE ARE TWO KINDS OF BOATS: SUBS AND TARGETS. He unlocked the door and climbed in, and I helped him with his cane.

"The four subs that came here after the war, where did they surrender?"

"On the high seas in the North Atlantic," he recalled. "The U-boats were to surface and announce their location in the clear over the radio, and fly a large black flag, if I recall. Destroyers from the British and the U.S. Navy came by and escorted them here. It was the nearest military port and a good secure place to look things over."

He turned the key in the ignition, and the engine didn't do a thing. There was no clicking sound, no grinding of the engine, not a thing. He looked at me and he was embarrassed. "Damn thing's been giving me fits all month. My idiot son Keith, he promised me he would take care of it, but . . . damn."

Jack turned the key again and again, and nothing happened. By now I had found that I liked the old man and his stories, and I quickly said, "Look, if you need a ride, I'll be glad to give you one."

"No, that'll be a bother. I'll give Keith a call and have 'im come up—"

"I insist, really," I said, thinking of what it must have been like to be young and strong and in the Navy, defending your country, not knowing what your future would be like, probably not wanting to know that you would end up in Porter, disabled and alone, depending on the kindness of tourists to support you.

He nodded, smiled. "I would greatly appreciate that, honestly I would." As Jack got out of his truck, I checked the time, and a relatively fresh promise came to mind, about a drink and conversation.

"By the way, is there a phone around here I can use? I need to call up a friend."

"Over there," he said, motioning with his cane. "There's a pay phone by the doorway."

I left him by my Ford, and at the pay phone I called the offices of the Tyler *Chronicle*, and on the fourth ring I slipped into voice-mail hell, where I had to press numbers and stars and pound keys. It was one minute past five o'clock, and I'm sure the receptionist at the paper I had earlier met had gone out the door about fifty-nine seconds earlier. The fourth time I called the paper I surrendered and got Paula's voice mail, and left a message. "Paula, it's Lewis. I'm stuck up here in Porter for a little while. I'll try you at your apartment. The drink-and-conversation offer is still open, and I should be back in Tyler in a half hour."

I called her apartment, got her answering machine. I left a similar message there, and then hurried back to my Ford.

As we drove through the one-way and somewhat twisting streets of Porter, I said, "The German subs that came to Porter. Any Nazi officials and bigwigs on those boats?"

"Nope, not at all," Jack said, holding his cane upright between his legs, like an old king holding on to his staff. "Three of the boats were regular attack subs, staffed by kids. I mean, average age of a U-boat captain back then was twenty-one or twenty-two. Can you believe how young all of us were back then? Teenagers, fighting and dying for our country. Now, I can't even trust my boy Keith, who's almost forty, to remember to fix my truck. Here, take a right at this street."

We were in a part of Porter that looked as if it didn't get too many tourists. The street was narrow and the homes were old and jammed together in tiny fenced-in lots. This time of the year what lawns existed were still brown and dry. "Okay, that house up there. The small white one."

I pulled into the narrow driveway. The house was two-story but about half the size of my own home. The porch had a sagging couch and a rusting refrigerator flanking the door.

"The fourth boat," I asked. "Did that one have anything special about it?"

"Ah, it certainly did," he said. "That U-boat was one of their big supply boats, and it was headed for Japan. The U-234, I think it was called. On board it had lots of strategic supplies, from electronics to optics to medicine."

Thinking of Reeves and her agency, I said, "Drugs? Like opium, morphine?"

His thin shoulders shrugged. "Who knows. But it was other things on board that got the military here all spun up. A jet aircraft, disassembled and in crates. Plans for the V-One and V-Two rockets. Some mercury. And there were even a couple of Japs who were going along for the ride, who committed hara-kiri out in the Atlantic instead of surrendering. A hell of a story."

Jack reached over and shook my hand. "Appreciate the ride home, Lewis. And if you ever decide to do a story on the museum, or you decide you've got more questions about subs and such, give me a ring."

"That I will, Jack, that I will," I said.

He stepped out onto the driveway and then stopped, stuck his head back in my Ford. "Oh, yeah, one more thing about that last U-boat. The one with all the supplies."

"What's that?" I asked.

"Uranium, that's what," he said. "The boat had several hundred pounds of uranium that the Germans had processed, for their own atomic bomb. With the Allies closing in, they decided to give it to their Axis comrades in Tokyo. Pretty important stuff."

Uranium. Atomic bomb. "I'd say."

He laughed. "And another thing. That uranium went missing, right after the U-boat was interned at Porter."

My hands were on the steering wheel and the skin on the back of them started tingling. "Missing? How?"

"No one knows publicly, and whoever knows privately ain't talking. There was a story in the *Boston Globe* a few years back, about some nuclear-weapons specialist doing a book on World War Two. She was trying to trace all the uranium that we and the Germans and the Japs had, and this shipment from Porter . . . just went missing. No records of it being disposed, no records of it even existing, except when it was logged in when it came to Porter. Poof! All gone. Just like that."

"Just like that," I repeated.

"Yeah, well, the end of the war, a lot of funny things like that were going on. Hey, thanks again for the ride, Lewis."

"Jack, you are very welcome."

And as I watched him walk slowly up to the porch, relying steadily on his cane with every step, I recalled my last visit to the rooms that Reeves and her crew had rented back at the Lafayette House, and the documents I had seen, the documents in German.

Then I backed up my Ford and went south, to Tyler.

CHAPTER TEN

The offices of the Tyler *Chronicle* were dark and closed up tight. I drove slowly through the parking lot and then continued out and made my way to High Street in Tyler. Paula lived in an apartment building about five minutes away from the center of town, and her car was in the building's tiny lot when I got there. Abutting the parking lot was a two-story motel, its windows and doors boarded up. A couple of months ago the place had been hit by an arsonist, and Paula told me that the owners were taking the chance to turn the place into condos instead of taking their insurance money and rebuilding the motel.

As I got out of my Ford, Paula was coming out the main door of her building, black leather purse over her shoulder, wearing a short white jacket.

"Hey," I called out. "Sorry I'm late. Did you get any of my messages?"

"Sure, Lewis," she said, striding over to her car, "I got all three of them."

I followed her over to the car. "Sorry, but I only remember leaving you two messages."

She turned to me at the car, a tired look on her face. "Sure,

I got the message on my office voice mail and the message on the answering machine at home. And there was a third message there, too, my friend. You see, earlier I wanted something simple. Conversation and a drink. That's all. Something friends and companions and occasional lovers—whatever the hell that means nowadays—can do without thinking, without even planning it. But those two little things didn't seem important to you tonight. That's the third message I got tonight. That what I needed wasn't important."

I held my hands behind my back and clasped them tightly. "It surely was important," I said, speaking low and even. "Which is why I called you when I knew I was going to be late. If I didn't care or if I didn't think it was important, I wouldn't have made the effort."

"And why were you late?" she asked, in the same tones she used when interrogating the town manager over discrepancies in the town's budget.

"I was involved with somebody at the Porter Submarine Museum, for a story I might be working on."

"Ah yes," she said, opening the door to her car. "Another story for *Shoreline* magazine that never appears. It must be tough, trying to keep track of your mysterious life."

"I manage," I said. "Look, I'll make it up to you. Dinner instead of a drink. Right here and now."

"You know what night it is, right? Tuesday night. Guess where I'm off to in an hour."

Houston, we have a problem, I thought. "The weekly Tyler selectmen's meeting. I should have known, you're right. Look, I'll come along, sit next to you. We can write catty notes to each other about the town fathers as they drone on."

There, a small victory, as a smile flickered across her face. "Nice offer. But not tonight. You go do your things mysterious. I'm off to have dinner with the new town counsel and then to work. Take care, Lewis."

And then she got in her car, started it up, and was gone.

An incurable romantic would have followed her, I suppose,

and continued the debate, continued the argument, continued whatever it was that had been going on. But I had other commitments, other things to do.

At the Lafayette House I could detect the odor of dinner being prepared in the fine kitchen of its restaurant, and my stomach started grumbling as I took the elevator up to the fifth floor. I went to Room 512 and knocked, and then knocked again. No answer. The door to Room 510 opened up and the redheaded member of the team, Gus Turner, poked his head out.

"Oh, it's you," he said. "Looking for Laura?"

"That I am," I said, walking over to him. "Is she about?"

"She's . . . she's on the phone right now," he said. "What do you need?"

"I just want to give her an update."

"Oh. Give it to me, then. I'll pass it on."

"No offense, Gus," I said. "But I'm working for her. I'm not working for you. If I'm giving anybody an update, it'll be her. When she gets off the phone or whatever, she can give me a ring at home. That's where I'll be."

He grinned as he closed the door. "No offense taken, Lewis. And you want to know why?"

"I'm sure you'll let me know."

"Because I predicted this, the first time we came to your house. Nobody says no to Laura. Nobody. It was just a matter of time before you came aboard."

"Aboard what? The *Titanic?*"

He smiled again, started closing the door. "I'll let her know. Have a great night."

"You, too."

I took the elevator back down to the lobby, and then made a detour to the dining room.

A half hour later I was back home, sitting at the kitchen counter eating a Lafayette House lobster pie, which was the meat of two lobsters, sliced and soaked in melted butter, plopped right down in the middle of a seafood stuffing mix. The Lafayette House doesn't do take-out dinners, but I have an understanding with the evening chef, an understanding that involves some cash donations on my part.

The American Heart Association would probably collectively shudder in horror at what I was eating, and I was trying to balance the assault on my cholesterol level with a salad and a glass of red wine. It wasn't probably much of a balance, but we all have our fantasies.

Just as I was finishing up, the phone rang, and it was Laura Reeves. As she started talking, I knelt before my fireplace and got a small fire going.

"Lewis? Laura here. What do you have?"

I struck a match and started burning a rolled-up editorial page from the *Boston Globe*. Some days, being used as fuel was its best use. "Gee, it's nice to talk to you, too, Laura. How was your day?"

I could hear her sigh over the phone line. "My day was horrible, as was the day before and no doubt the day tomorrow. I'm sorry if I'm offending your delicate little sensibilities, so here I go again. Hello, Lewis. How nice to talk to you. I hope you're well. Did you do any fucking work today? Lewis?"

I smiled, watched the flames dance up from the dying *Globe* and into the small pile of kindling. "How nice of you to ask. Yes, I'm fine, and I did have a busy day. I've talked to a detective at the Porter Police Department, the curator of a submarine museum in Porter, and an acquaintance of mine who's been known to be involved in things criminal. I've also talked to a local newspaper reporter and another detective with the Tyler Police Department. No Whizzer, no lead on Whizzer, but many promises to see what they can find."

"All right," she said grudgingly. "A fair start. And what will you do tomorrow?"

I picked up a length of oak, put it in across the growing flames. "More of the same, I suppose. And I'll probably talk to the same people again at the end of the day, to see what's going on. And what about you?"

"Don't you mind what we're doing," she said. "You do your own little piece. We'll do our own."

"Thanks for the vote of confidence," I said.

"Confidence has nothing to do with it," Laura said. "I'll use a phrase I'm sure you'll remember from your days at the Pentagon. Need to know. Right?"

I sat down on the couch, extended my feet to the flames. "There are many things I've tried to forget about my years at the Pentagon, and you and your crew keep on bringing them back to me. Thanks a lot."

"You're welcome," she said. "And do talk to me tomorrow, will you?"

"You can count on it."

After she hung up, I sat there on the couch, phone in my lap, just watching the flames rise higher and higher, the fuel from the dried wood giving the fire life until they, too, gave up all they had, and the flames began to die.

Then I went upstairs.

In my office I went through my collection of books, until I found what I was looking for: a two-volume history of Hitler's U-boat war, expertly researched and written by Clay Blair. I also took down a couple of other books about the Battle of the Atlantic during World War II, and then started looking up information about what was going on in this nearby stretch of the ocean as the European theater of World War II ground to a halt. Armed with this basic information, I fired up my computer and started racing down the grand old information superhighway, to see what I could learn about U-234.

And it didn't take long.

The U-234 was more than three hundred feet long, and had been designed as a submarine that would lay mines. For its final trip, its mine-laying equipment was torn out by German engineers so that it could carry more cargo. Among the cargo it carried in its intercepted voyage were tons of strategic materials—from lead to steel to mercury—and as Jack had mentioned, a disassembled twin-engine ME-262 jet fighter aircraft. There were also optical glass, medical supplies, antiaircraft ammo and equipment. The submarine left the great German naval base at Kiel on March 25,

1945, for Norway, where it picked up an additional passenger, a Luftwaffe general.

And stored forward, in ten cube-shaped metal cases about nine inches on a side, were more than twelve hundred pounds of uranium-oxide ore. Produced for the German atomic bomb effort, it was being sent to their Axis allies in Japan for their own atomic bomb project.

The heavily laden submarine left Norway on April 15, 1945, and in the middle of the Atlantic, when word came that Germany had given up on May 7, the U-234 surfaced and the crew surrendered to an American destroyer, the USS *Sutton,* on May 14. And, as Jack had said, the two Japanese officers had committed suicide rather than allow themselves to be captured.

At the Porter Naval Shipyard on May 17, the uranium oxide—which could be processed for use in an atomic bomb—was removed from the submarine. And there, the paper trail ended. No official government records existed on what happened to the uranium.

Oh, there were theories, the most popular one being extraordinarily ironic, in that the uranium was processed in the American Manhattan Project and was used in the atomic bombs dropped on Nagasaki and Hiroshima. German uranium used in American atomic bombs to shatter Japan. But nothing definite.

In looking through the documents and my books, I saw a familiar name. Fehler. Johann Heinrich Fehler, a thirty-four-year-old German navy lieutenant who was commander of the U-234.

Fehler. Just the other day, when I was first with Laura Reeves in her room at the Lafayette House, Gus Turner had come in saying he had secured the Fehler debrief. Which meant an intelligence document of some sort, debriefing Fehler after his surrender.

I quietly logged off, stared at the blank screen. I tried to think of any type of circumstance where a German U-boat and a U-boat captain and its load of uranium and weapons interned near here more than a half century ago could have anything to do with Colombians, Mexicans, and a drug shipment, but I had no success. After a while my head hurt, and I turned off the computer and went to bed.

The phone rang about thirty minutes later, and putting on my robe, I went downstairs, rubbing at my face. My portable office phone had been left downstairs, and although there's a phone jack in my bedroom, there's never been a phone there. It would be easy enough to set up another phone, but I've always felt a room with a bed in it should have the basics: a bed, a light, and plenty of books. Besides, by the time I got downstairs to answer the phone, I was usually awake enough to make sense in talking on the damn thing.

"Hello," I said, bringing the phone over to the couch, barely beating the answering machine. The fireplace was now dark. Even the last of the embers had died away to black.

"Hey, Lewis, it's Paula."

"Hey yourself," I said, looking at the time. It was ten past eleven.

"Did I wake you?"

"Not hardly."

"But you must have been in bed, the phone rang so long."

I tried to lighten up my voice. "It makes me smile to think that you know how many steps it takes to go from my bedroom to my phone."

There. A laugh. She went on. "I just got out of the selectmen's meeting, and they were still going at it when I left. They had fifteen items on the agenda, and number twelve—which they spent more than thirty minutes yapping about—was whether or not the town should have a park designated for dogs only. That way, the dogs have a place where they can poop while their owners run them around, and we don't have to worry about kids playing in dog doo-doo and getting it in their mouths."

"Democracy in action," I pointed out.

"Yeah, ain't it wonderful," she said, sighing. "Then a couple of people spoke up, said that taxpayer's dollars paid for those parks, and that everyone in town should have the same right to visit them. That it wasn't right to exclude people from a town park. Then somebody said didn't dogs have rights too. After all, their owners have to pay money to license and register them in the town. About then I was expecting somebody to bring Fido up to testify, and I started getting the giggles, thinking how Rhonda, the recording secretary, would put that in the meeting minutes."

"Did anybody see you get the giggles?" I asked.

"God, I hope not. That'd be another thing for Rupert to get pissed at. Anyway, the meeting got even stranger when people started arguing on why dogs have to get licensed, and cats don't, and cat owners are freeloaders when compared to dog owners. That's when I gave it up and decided to leave."

"Good choice."

"Then I got home and I started thinking . . . well, I decided I didn't want to be mad at you anymore. I'm much happier thinking about you and thinking about good things. But it's just . . . I don't know, Lewis. I was thinking as I was waiting for your phone call earlier today that I didn't matter, that you enjoyed getting caught up in those strange things you do, and that I was taking a backseat. Plus the fact that I didn't have a particularly good day at the paper worked its way into the equation. So. There you go. Apologies and all that."

"Apologies and all that accepted. And you're not in the backseat, not at all."

"Thanks."

"And how was dinner with the new town counsel?" I asked.

"Oh, it was all right. The name's Mark Spencer. Young pup, maybe a few years out of law school. Full of vim and vigor on how he was going to work for the town, serve the people and do good things, all before lunch every day. Didn't feel like telling him he'd be spending most of his time arguing before the superior court about arcane zoning regulations and septic permits."

"That was nice of you."

She laughed again and said, "What about you? Got anything good going on tomorrow?"

"Tomorrow? I've got a little trip planned."

"Really? Where?"

"Boston," I said.

"But you hate driving to Boston."

"That I do."

"Then it must be kind of important, to head off to Boston like that."

"It is."

She yawned and said, "Oops, where did that come from? Tell you what, why don't you get on up to bed and get some sleep, rest up for your exhausting trip on the morrow."

"And you do the same, so you can get to your newspaper early and write a scintillating story about parks and dog feces and cats' rights."

Another yawn. "Right now I don't even know what scintillating means, never mind spelling it. Night, Lewis."

"Good night, Paula."

I was halfway back up the stairs to my bedroom when I was startled to hear the phone ring yet again. I doubted it was Paula who was calling me, but I instantly thought of Reeves, across the way. Perhaps lightning had struck. Perhaps the mysterious Whizzer had walked over to the hotel and surrendered. Perhaps I wouldn't have to go to Boston tomorrow. I walked back downstairs and retrieved the phone.

"Mr. Cole?" came the woman's voice, which I couldn't identify.

"The same," I said. "Who's this?"

A pause, and all I could hear was her breathing.

"Hello?" I called out again.

It was as if she weren't there, except for the regular sound of her breathing. Then she cleared her throat and said, "I do hope you have your affairs in order." Then she hung up. I stared at the phone, dialed an asterisk and then 6-9, which Bell Atlantic claims will instantly reconnect you with whoever had just dialed. But Bell Atlantic must have been having a bad night or something, for when I dialed the ring-back combination, I got a high-pitched whirring sound that told me a lot of nothing. I hung up the phone, tightened my robe about me some more, and slowly walked upstairs.

In my bedroom I went to the top drawer of my oak bureau and pulled out my holstered 9-mm Beretta. There were two spare clips in the bureau, which I left behind. If I couldn't handle whatever was out there with the sixteen rounds in the clip, then I doubted additional ammo would do me much good.

I sat on the edge of the bed, lifted up the mattress some and worked with the holster, which had a short leather strap attached to it. With the mattress pinching the strap between it and the box spring, the holster and the pistol now were at fingertip reach from my bed. I took off the robe and crawled in, and then practiced a few times, to make sure I could get at the pistol if necessary.

Logically, I knew the call was just designed to rattle me. Logically, I knew if somebody really wanted to do me harm, then they would have come and done it already, without the muttered threats and such. Logically, I knew I was well-armed and that all my doors and windows were locked.

But logic was on vacation this evening. I was ticking off somebody, somebody who was concerned enough to phone in a threat, and I wondered why.

I was still wondering long minutes later, when I fell into a fitful sleep.

The next morning I showered with my Beretta resting on the edge of the bathroom sink. I had a quick breakfast of tea only—both to make penance for the huge meal I had consumed the night before, and because of the nervousness I felt, still thinking about the previous night's phone call. After washing up in the kitchen I made a call across the way, and got ahold of Reeves right off the bat.

"I just wanted to let you know that I am now leaving the house," I said, still hating each word I was pronouncing, as if I were a schoolchild leaving the campus and telling his principal. "Anything interesting going on at your end?"

"Not a thing, except I'm getting mightily sick of room service food."

"Well, maybe some morning you'll luck out, and I'll make you a meal."

I thought I heard a giggle. "Now, that's an offer I'd like to pass on to my supervisors. Go on, Lewis, and do good."

"That's what I intend to do."

I hung up and then grabbed the Beretta—placing it in a shoulder holster—and my L.L. Bean jacket. Outside, the morning air was crisp and cool, and the ocean's swells were low and smooth. I wished my own mood matched the look of the ocean, and then I got into the garage and backed up my Ford Explorer.

At the top of the hill, in the parking lot of the Lafayette House, I drove out on Atlantic Avenue and headed south. From Atlantic Avenue I took Route 51 out to the interstate, but instead of heading north, as I would if I were going to Porter, I turned south, following the huge sign that said BOSTON.

Getting on the interstate cost me two quarters. I felt my legs tighten in distress as I drove. The highway was crowded with southbound commuters, mostly high-tech or professional types who enjoyed making the relatively high salaries in Massachusetts and living in relatively low-tax New Hampshire, but from the looks of the commuters who passed me, it didn't look as though much enjoyment was going on. I spent a fruitless few minutes looking for something intelligent to listen to on the car radio, and finally secured a classical music station out of Rockport. The names of the Massachusetts towns flew by me as the morning wore on—Newburyport, Newbury, Georgetown, Boxford, Topsfield—and for the most part, we were in farm or suburban country. As I drove, I practiced in my mind, over and over again, what I would do and what I would say, once I got into Boston.

At Danvers I-95 jogged to the left, and I went right, onto Route 1, and in the matter of minutes I was in commuter hell. The traffic slowed and about me the land had been built upon, paved and transformed into a cold-climate nightmare of what parts of Los Angeles must look like. There were gas stations, strip joints, restaurants, malls, miniature golf courses, discount stores, sporting-goods establishments, bars, more gas stations, and acres and acres of parking lots. Scattered among this concrete-and-asphalt mess were a few lonely houses, the last survivors of what must have been a relatively attractive community about a half century ago, before the Boston sprawl moved north and swallowed everything in its path.

Cars and trucks and buses flowed around me, cutting in front of my Ford without hesitation, without using a directional signal, and I found myself caught in a vicious rhythm of braking and accelerating as I tried to keep up. I had no doubt that if I were to brake suddenly, the onslaught of the commuters heading into Boston would tumble my Ford over and over, cascading the wreckage and me into one of the side drainage ditches.

Route 1 suddenly went up a hill and I saw signs for Revere and for Logan International Airport, and there, just a few miles away, were the tall buildings and spires that marked the Athens of America.

But I only spared it a glance. I had a lot of driving left to do.

About forty minutes later, I found a parking spot near the building I was looking for. I turned off the engine and just let my trembling fingers ease themselves against the steering wheel. It had been a number of years since I had been in this part of Boston, near the harbor, which was gradually being brought back to life. There was an enormous construction project going on in this part of the city—a plan to eliminate most of the driving congestion, once and for all, at least for a year or two—and roads I remembered had disappeared, others had sprouted up in their place, and there were detour signs and blockades sprinkled here and there to make things interesting.

The driving a while back on the commute I thought had been bad enough, but the last half hour or so had been a wide-awake nightmare story of snarled traffic, ineffective traffic cops who leaned against trucks drinking cups of coffee, and drivers who flew through stop signs and red lights as though they were artifacts from another planet. I rubbed at my face and got out, locking the doors behind me. My Beretta was snug in its holster, but only gave me a small bit of comfort. I didn't expect anything bad to happen to me as a result of my mystery phone call last night, but the pistol served as a talisman of sorts, at least letting me know that I had a means of defense. Through connections of Felix's, I had a permit to carry a concealed weapon in this state, and knowing how hard it is to get such a permit, I always wondered what strings he had pulled to make it happen. I had never asked point-blank, but I had always wondered.

The brick building had once been a warehouse but had been rebuilt a decade or so ago, as the waterfront district of Boston became attractive property. I joined a bunch of commuters—feeling smug knowing that I could go home anytime I wanted to—and got off at the third floor.

Impressive. The last time I was here, the lobby area had been dark and cramped. Now, windows had been blasted through the brickwork and gave a nice view of the financial district, lighting up the whole place. The receptionist was an intense-looking young man with round black-rimmed glasses and short brown hair, and his collarless white shirt was buttoned up to his neck. He had on one of those telephone headsets, which made him look like a flight controller for NASA.

I went up to him and said, "I'd like to see Admiral Holbrook, please."

He looked up at me. "The editor? Admiral Holbrook, the editor?"

"That's the one," I said.

"Do you have an appointment, Mr. . . . ."

"Cole," I said. "Lewis Cole. No, I don't, but I'm sure he'll want to see me."

His face looked a bit prim, as if he were the smartest student in class and was about to show off in front of everyone. "And why's that, Mr. Cole?"

On his desk was a magazine, which I opened up and went past the advertisements for museums, bed-and-breakfasts, and Chambers of Commerce throughout New England. I found the page I was looking for and passed it over to the receptionist.

"Because I work for him, that's why," I said. "I write this column for him every month, and I need a moment of his time. See any resemblance in the photo?"

It's an old photo and I don't like it that much, but it did its job this morning. The receptionist's face flushed into the color of the old brick behind him. "Of course, Mr. Cole, of course. Have a seat and I'll see if I can get ahold of him."

"Thanks," I said, and I went over to one of the chairs set against an ivory wall. Through the glass doors—all marked SHORELINE—I saw the bustle of people moving around, working on putting another magazine out. My coworkers, I thought. These people were all my coworkers, and except for the editor, I didn't know a single one of them.

Not a single one of them. I sat back and crossed my legs and waited.

CHAPTER ELEVEN

It had been a long time since I had last been out to this office, and I felt like someone who had gone back to a high school reunion and was the only member of his class to have shown up. When I first came here, after driving east all the way from Nevada, the place had a rawness to it, as if the staff examined each issue with a cautious and critical eye, concerned that it do better than the previous issue. Now the place had a different feel to it, of success and doing well with increased subscriptions year after year.

I myself felt different as well. When I first came here, I was thin and nervous and still recovering from something quite bad that had happened to me out there in the high desert. Getting this job with *Shoreline*—along with my house at Tyler Beach and my monthly stipend—was payback for keeping my mouth shut about what happened to me and my friends in Nevada. I had once promised never to return to this magazine's offices, but like a lot of recent promises, this one had been broken.

A woman came out into the reception area. She seemed to be about Paula's age, and had on tight black slacks, a pink top, and thick black shoes that looked as if they could be used to walk across plutonium. "Mr. Cole?" she said, striding over to me, hand held out. "Libby Graham. I'm the admiral's assistant. Won't you come with me?"

"Of course," I said, standing up and going with her into the bustling sights and sounds of the *Shoreline* offices. As we walked, the pleasant young woman chattered to me about how much she liked my columns, how she and her boyfriend enjoyed visiting Tyler Beach every year, and how, if she was lucky, the magazine would publish an article of hers in an upcoming winter issue. I grunted and nodded at all the appropriate places, until we came to an office set against a far wall.

"Here you go, Mr. Cole," she said, opening the wooden door.

Inside, I blinked. The office had changed hardly a damn bit in the years since I had last been here. There were tall windows that looked out over the harbor, and by one window was a brass telescope on a tripod. The brick walls had framed photographs of the ships on which the good admiral had served during his long career, and one glass-fronted box lined with velvet held his service ribbons and medals. From behind his wide wooden desk, Rear Admiral Seamus Anthony Holbrook, U.S. Navy (Ret.), stood up and his wrinkled leathery face afforded me a grin. He had on a white turtleneck shirt and khaki trousers, and although he had lost some hair since the last time I saw him, he looked hardly changed at all.

He came from around his desk and shook my hand. "Lewis Cole . . . You know, I've always wondered if we'd ever see you again."

I took a chair in front of his desk, remembered the last time I saw him. After moving into my new home at Tyler Beach years ago, I had been offered a job as a columnist for this magazine and he had set the terms of the arrangement quite clearly: I would supply a column each month on the New Hampshire seacoast. If I submitted crap or didn't submit anything at all, they would substitute another column. Over the years I had found that I actually enjoyed the job, which provided a reasonable cover for the hefty monthly stipend I received from the DoD.

"Well, wonder no more, Admiral," I said.

He sat down in his leather officer's chair. "We keep on sending you invitations to our Christmas Party, but you never respond. You've got something against Christmas?"

"No, I've got something against driving in Boston."

He laughed. "Don't we all. What can we do for you? Planning to take a long vacation? Looking for a raise? Want to start writing about Maine instead of New Hampshire?"

"Not really," I said. "I'm looking for your help."

The easygoing features on his face disappeared and were replaced with the hard-edged features of a Navy admiral, retired or not. "What kind of help?"

"I need some information confirmed. You're my only and best source in doing this."

"What kind of information?"

I took a deep breath, wished that I could spend a few minutes using his telescope gazing at the harbor traffic, instead of doing what I was doing. "Last week a man was murdered in a state park near my home. People identifying themselves as members of the Drug Enforcement Agency are investigating the crime. They have requested my assistance with this investigation."

One of his hands was on top of the desk, rubbing against a legal pad. "That sounds highly . . . highly irregular."

"It gets better. If I didn't cooperate and assist them with the investigation, they promised a few things. Like taking away my house, my savings, and my monthly stipend. And just to prove that they weren't joking, they did that for about a day or so. Which means I'm not really thrilled about writing a column for *Shoreline* if the agreement reached with the DoD so long ago can be so easily breached."

He spoke carefully. "Lewis, you knew that the job with *Shoreline* was something I administered. It wasn't something that I was responsible for. You understand that, don't you?"

"Fully," I said. "But I need information. I don't think these folks are working for the DEA. I want to know who they really are, and that's why I'm here."

"And what makes you think I can help?"

I gazed straight at him. "When I first came here, you told me that you were part of an unofficial network that assisted the Department of Defense and the intelligence community in performing certain tasks. That means you've been doing favors for a number of people. I would think that you could call in a few of these favors."

His fingers kept on toying with the edge of the paper pad. "Perhaps you're right. But why should I help you?"

"Why?" I asked. "Because you owe me, Admiral. Right from the start I could have sat back and let you worry about the monthly column for this magazine. Right from the start I could have not done a damn thing for you and this magazine. But I did. I wrote the columns and fulfilled my responsibility, and when somebody comes along and kicks me in the teeth, I would think that I deserve a little bit more from you than just a 'why.'"

The admiral stared at me and I stared right back, and then he moved about in his chair and picked up a pen. "Okay. What do you have?"

"There's a group of five men and one woman. The woman's in charge. Her name is Laura Reeves. She's assisted by a Gus Turner. Of the other men, I know the first names of just two. Clem and Stan. They responded to a murder at the Samson Point State Wildlife Preserve last Wednesday evening. That's in North Tyler, New Hampshire. Here's the registration numbers of the vehicles they were driving."

From my coat pocket I took out a piece of paper, which I passed over to him. "Those license plate numbers have been traced and don't officially exist."

That got his attention, as he slowly said, "Uh-huh."

"Currently, they are staying at the Lafayette House Hotel in Tyler Beach. Supposedly, the death of this man has been linked to their investigation into one of the Colombian drug cartels. But I don't believe that story anymore."

"You don't?" he asked.

"I don't. I do believe they are working for the federal government, but I'm almost positive it's not the Drug Enforcement Agency."

"And what agency do you think they belong with?"

Here we go, I thought. Out in spookland, one more time into the breach. "I think they're with the Department of Energy. I think they're NEST."

The admiral's face now matched the color of the papers on his desk. "What makes you think that?"

"What makes me think that is something I should keep to myself, in case this gets kicked around. You've done good by me, Admiral, and I appreciate it. If you can confirm that, I'll be in your debt."

He started doodling with his pen. "If you're so sure they're NEST, why do you need my confirmation?"

"Because then I'll know, I'll know for sure. Any other way Reeves and her group might claim that they're FBI, DIA, or any one of a half dozen agencies. I need something solid to stand on. Something that you can give me, if you can."

He looked down at his desk for a long moment and then he looked up. "All right. I'll do it. But don't ever come back here again. Unless it's for the annual Christmas Party, I don't want to see you darkening my doorway."

"It's a deal," I said.

"Good," he said, picking up the phone. "Go out into the reception area and I'll get to work."

I nodded and found my way back to the place where I had entered and sat down.

The morning dragged on. I got hungry, and then I got thirsty, but before then, I was bored and antsy, all at the same time. The coffee table in front of me had one *Time* magazine, one *Newsweek* magazine, and half a dozen or so copies of *Shoreline*. I wasn't so hard up that I would reread the familiar words of *Shoreline*, so I went through both *Time* and *Newsweek,* and wrapped that up fairly quickly. Not one of them had a story about the space shuttle mission. I looked through the magazines on the coffee table again. Nothing. Right then I would have gladly paid ten dollars for a copy of that day's *New York Times,* just to keep my mind off what was going on inside that office.

I had an old feeling, one that I'd had back when I worked in the Pentagon. When the information was sparse or contradictory and a deadline was approaching, sometimes you had to make a leap of faith. The Great Leap, we called it. You didn't like to depend on a Great Leap because usually it would morph into a suicide leap, killing your career in the process, and maybe even some of your countrymen as well. But in the few times I had made the Great Leap, I had that inner sense that I was right, that all I had to do was wait it out until the confirming information came in.

I had that same feeling now, sitting in the office, watching the receptionist work his phone, watching the people stroll in and out, just sitting there, my hands sometimes rubbing anxiously against the backs of my legs.

The door to the offices opened up. The admiral looked out at me. I stood up. He just nodded and walked back inside.

I let out a slow breath.

Time to go home.

About a half hour later, as I left the confusing streets, warrens and lanes of Boston behind me, I switched on the radio and let the soothing sounds of classical music fill the car. Once I was on the interstate, I sat back against the seat in relief and let the Ford find its way home automatically. My stomach grumbled, and before I got too far, I slipped into the parking lot of a Boston Market and ordered up a chicken-and-cheese sandwich, on which I munched as I went back onto the highway. It had been a busy morning and the rest of the day would no doubt prove to be just as busy.

Plus interesting. Oh yes, the rest of the day was going to be interesting indeed, and despite the uneasiness of what I was going into, I felt well-armed and ten feet tall. This time, at least, I had good, solid information, and that was a great feeling indeed.

I finished my on-the-road lunch and crumpled up the napkins and waste and carefully deposited it all on the passenger seat.

When I got home I called across the street and this time I got Clem. I think. The heavyset men who were providing security for Reeves and her activities were all beginning to sound and look the same to me. When I asked for Reeves, he said that she wouldn't be back in town for another hour or so.

"But I've got word," he said. "She said that if you had something important, to page her and let her know."

"No, that's fine," I said. "It's nothing too important, but I do need to talk to her. An hour, you said?"

"That's right, an hour."

"Then I'll call back in sixty minutes."

When I hung up the phone I paced around the house, again feeling that nervousness I had felt in the reception room of *Shoreline*. But this time, there was no confidence in making a Great Leap. I was about to do something great indeed, but that feeling of self-assuredness was gone. All I knew now was that I had to get out of the house and waste an hour.

I was making the third circuit of the living room when I noticed the pile of unviewed videotapes, and I knew where those sixty minutes would go.

After returning those adult tapes to the Route One store in Falconer, I drove into Tyler Falls—a town just south of Tyler—and found another store that was under assault by the pro-whatever forces stirred up by Rupert Holman and the editorial pages of the *Chronicle*. It was in another group of small shops and stores on Route 1, and besides the video store, there were a lighting store, a place that sold antiques and old magazines and a yarn shop. Two young women with baby strollers were parked on the sidewalk, talking earnestly to each other. Homemade white cardboard signs hung from the sides of the carriages. One said, I'M NOT GOING TO GROW UP TO BE A PORN STAR, and the other, I'M NOT GOING TO GROW UP TO RENT PORN TAPES. They looked at me as I went into the store and resumed their talking.

Inside the store, a distracted teenage girl with a ring through her nose was on the phone, saying "uh-huh" a lot. I went through the door marked ADULTS ONLY and spent another few minutes in there, among the random tapes displaying random couplings. Entering the store, I thought I would be embarrassed to rent something from a woman so young, but she just nodded as I filled out the standard paperwork. I was even ignored by the two young women outside, who were talking about day care and such, and I looked at my watch as I got to the Ford. More time to kill. I went inside the antiques store and spent a pleasant twenty minutes going through piles of *Saturday Evening Post* and *Collier* magazines from the 1950s, boldly predicting colonies on the moon and Mars by the end of the century, and I thought wistfully of the space shuttle pilot I knew, up there in earth orbit on this day, going around in endless circles.

I bought three *Collier* magazines from 1955 that featured interviews with Wernher von Braun and great cover paintings by Chesley Bonestell of winged spaceships with bulbous fuel tanks, heading to the Red Planet. Outside, I went back to my Ford, and I saw that the two protesting women had left.

I also saw that my Ford Explorer was now resting on four flat tires.

I got home about a half hour later than I had planned. In the end, it wasn't as bad as it looked. The air had been let out of the stems—the women had thoughtfully not used ice picks or knives to damage the tires—and I only had to walk a half mile to a hardware store down the road to pick up a couple of cans of aerosol flat-tire-repair kits. Using those, I got enough pressure to drive slowly to a service station, where I managed to inflate all four back up to regular pressure. As I got my vehicle underway, I thought about how nice it was that the local moms were getting involved in the political and cultural activities of their area, but now I wished it hadn't forced me to expend time and money as a result.

My answering machine was displaying a comfortable zero, so nobody was chasing me, threatening me, or trying to ask me questions. Not yet, at least. I went upstairs to my office and got my new computer up and running, and then went downstairs to use the phone. I called across the way, and this time Laura Reeves was there, answering almost too eagerly, as if she had been staring at the quiet phone for the past hour.

"Yes, Lewis, what is it?"

"Laura, I need to talk to you. Right now."

"Well, come on over then."

"No," I said. "I need to see you here, at my house. And by yourself."

"Come on, Lewis, I've been traveling all day, I really don't need to get my carcass up and going again and—"

I interrupted. "It's about Whizzer. I believe I know who he is."

A quick response. "I'll be right there."

"And I'll be waiting, upstairs in my office. The door will be open. See you soon."

After hanging up, I walked over to a window by the door, counted the seconds. In less than a minute I saw a shape up at the top of the hill near the hotel's parking lot, saw it descend down my driveway. I felt my knees quivering a bit, so I got a move on and went upstairs and sat down in my office, my computer humming contentedly by my elbow, the screen now in screensaver mode. I set the spare chair near the door, so she wouldn't have far to walk when she got here.

The door from downstairs opened up, and she said, "Lewis?"

"Up here, Laura. In my office. Come on up."

The sound of her steps came from the wooden stairs, and there she was, at the entrance to my office. Black sneakers, tight jeans, and the same MIT sweatshirt. Her shoulder bag was in her hands and I motioned to the chair, and she sat down, smiling, eyes glittering with eagerness.

"Lewis, this is great, this is really great news, I wish I could—"

"Just a sec," I said, interrupting her again. "Before I go on about Whizzer, there's a couple of things we need to clear up first, all right?"

She nodded. "Sure. Go ahead."

"Okay," I said. "I'm curious about something."

"Which is?"

"Does the Drug Enforcement Agency get angry at you folks borrowing their identity and their good name?"

The smile, the eagerness, the bright look in her expression

had disappeared from one blink of an eye to the next. "I don't know what you're talking about."

"Of course you do, but you're too well-trained to say anything. I, on the other hand, am still a civilian. So I'll let you in on a little secret. I know you and your boys don't work for the Drug Enforcement Agency, or the Justice Department, or anything like that. You folks work for the Department of Energy, don't you?"

Silence, but I could see the knuckles on her hands whiten as she tightened her grip on her bag. I went on. "Not just for the Department of Energy, however. Right? Though I'm sure you probably have back-up identification that says you work for the Fuel Efficiency Program or the Strategic Petroleum Reserve or something equally silly. Nope, you and those other five, Laura, you work for NEST, don't you? The Nuclear Emergency Search Team. The quite secret organization that's used to hunt out nuclear weapons in this country in case we're threatened by terrorists. You're not here because of drugs, are you? You're here because of the uranium brought here into the country back in 1945 on a U-boat. You're here because somebody else is after that uranium, somebody else who either wants to build a bomb here, or build it back in their homeland. That's what this all about. Uranium. Not cocaine or heroin."

"You have really gone off the reservation," she said, still not giving up. "I don't know what you're talking about."

"Then I'll try to speak more clearly," I said, now warming up to the task. "The whole story you gave me about the Colombian cartel coming up here for alternative delivery spots is so much smoke and mirrors. I know this area. You don't. And the law enforcement types and others I've talked to all said the same thing. All the local drug activity is small-scale. There's no point in having a cartel rep up here in the area. It'd be as stupid as sending General Eisenhower and his staff in on the first wave at Omaha Beach. No sense at all. But what does make sense is the shipyard connection. And thinking that you and your high-powered friends would come here because of drugs connected to the shipyard is slim indeed. But thinking that the folks down in D.C. would send you up here because someone's trying to sell several hundred pounds of uranium—now, that makes sense."

She spoke slowly. "If I had my service weapon here right now, Lewis Cole, I'd shoot you dead."

"True, and there would be an awful stain on this floor for the next tenant to worry about. So you work for the Department of Energy. Based in Nevada, right? That explains the healthy suntanned glow you all have."

"I don't have to tell you a damn thing," she snapped. "All you have to do is do your job, what we agreed. That you find Whizzer. Nothing else."

I folded my arms. "But it's not that simple anymore. I made that agreement to help out with Laura Reeves of the Drug Enforcement Agency. I didn't make it with Laura Reeves of the Department of Energy. Assuming, too, that Laura Reeves is your real name."

"That is my real name, you idiot, and I don't care what you think; you're working for me. Don't worry what the department is. Now, tell me, who the hell is Whizzer?"

I shook my head. "Sorry. I'm on strike."

Her face was now reddened. "Then get ready to lose this house, your bank account, and quite possibly your freedom, Mr. Cole."

I shrugged. "Then get ready to lose your privacy, your anonymity, and the cover story that you're working for the DEA. I've made arrangements with a couple of members of the local media. They have the whole story, written up and sealed in envelopes, about you and your folks. About NEST and the Porter Naval Shipyard and the uranium off the U-234. Oh, you probably have low opinions of our local reporters—just as you have low opinions about the rest of us—but they can be smart and they can be sly. And all it will take is a phone call from them to a Boston television station or the Concord bureau of the Associated Press, and by this time tomorrow there'll be camera crews staked out in front of the Lafayette House."

"You're bluffing," she said.

"Try me," I said.

While her voice was remaining calm, her face showed the struggle that was no doubt occurring inside of her. She said, "You have no idea what we're up against, what we're trying to do here. Please, trust me on this, will you? Can't I appeal to your better nature? Your patriotism?"

I unfolded my arms, leaned forward in the chair. "Once before, you might have. Before rolling in here like you owned this place and had no time to talk to the locals. Before you threatened me with bankruptcy and threatened to take away my house. So no, appeals won't work this time. The truth will. NEST. Confirm what I just said, and then we start anew. Don't think we're all stupid up here because our area code is six-oh-three, and not two-oh-two."

She seemed to mull that for a moment. "Then you'll tell me what you know about Whizzer?"

"Absolutely."

"The non-disclosure form you signed, it still holds, Lewis. You repeat anything from what I'm about to tell you, and you'll disappear into a federal penitentiary, and I don't care what rat-ass local newspapers do or say. Understood?"

"Clearly."

"Shit," she murmured. "All right then, here it is. You're right, you bastard, about the enriched uranium. One of the many little secrets from the end of the Old War and the start of the Cold War. You know how much weapons-grade uranium and plutonium and other fissionable material have disappeared over the years since we first split the atom? I'll give you a guess. It's not in the pounds, it's not in the tens of pounds . . . try hundreds of pounds. More than fifty years' worth. Some of the early record-keeping was so sloppy, it would make you cry. Missing plutonium or uranium would be put down to accounting problems. Dissipation. Adhering to draining equipment or testing equipment. Unbelievable. And our job is to clean up these little messes, to make sure they don't end up in the wrong hands."

"I thought NEST responded to more direct threats, like someone sending a note to the President, saying 'Come up with

141

ten million dollars in a week or we destroy some city's down-town.'"

A firm nod. "We do. It seems like every few months or so, some idiot sixteen-year-old decides to make a million dollars by making a threat about putting a nuclear device in Omaha or San Diego or Washington. Our job is to analyze the threat, respond to it, and make sure that little snot-nosed sixteen-year-old gets in a world of so much hurt that he'll never go near a computer again. Our job is also to respond to the threats that come from some adults—to go into cities with detecting devices and search out where a bomb may be hidden. Thank God that particular scenario hasn't come up recently. It's not often that we get to respond to a real deal."

"The guy in the parking lot, shot through the head," I said. "Are the Colombians looking to get the bomb? Is that the real deal you're working on?"

"No." She looked around my office. "I can't believe I'm telling you this. No, he wasn't from the cartel. He was from Tripoli. Care to guess what his area code is?"

It felt like a draft in the room, for there was a cold tingle at the back of my neck. "Libya."

"The same. It's like a cycle over there. Every couple of years or so, while he's in a tent out in a desert, their supreme leader gets a vision that it's time for North Africa to get their own bomb. Usually it's the CIA or somebody else who nips that little beauty in the bud. A nuclear physicist goes missing. A ship transporting uranium-enrichment equipment founders during a storm. A truck with centrifuges gets blown up. The usual stuff. But then our friends with the big ears at Fort Meade—"

"The National Security Agency," I said. "Look, once upon a time I had clearance for this stuff, so don't get all fretful. Go on."

"Okay. The NSA, our great information vacuum cleaner, listening in to everything from fax machines to cellphones, got the message about the U-234 uranium. You know how the NSA works, right?"

"Sure," I said. "When it comes to message intercepts, they don't have the manpower to listen or to read everything. What they do look for is key words or phrases. Like anthrax. Or Hezbollah. I guess that U-234 and uranium were a key phrase, right?"

"Correct," she said, and I got a sense that she was eager to talk. "We've known for decades that this particular shipment has been among the missing. But so far, the cover story has always held, that this stuff eventually got shipped to Los Alamos and was used in one of the early atomic weapons, if not one of the two we dropped on Japan."

"And what's the story behind the cover story?"

"It arrived in Porter aboard the U-boat, just like the newspaper accounts and books described," she said. "Then it was taken off in the yard. Next paper record shows everything else being examined at the Navy Yard in Norfolk, but no uranium. It either never left Porter, or disappeared on its way south to Virginia."

"The optics, the weapons, the German jet fighter, that all got to Norfolk in one piece?"

She shook her head. "Yeah, all that stuff. Man, you are up to speed."

"I try. Okay, so the NSA got the news about the missing uranium. What next?"

"What next is that they started doing real-time listening, trying to find out why this missing shipment was being discussed. That's when we found out about Libya, and their contact here in New Hampshire. All we knew about his contact was the name, Whizzer, and that he was associated with the shipyard. That's when the great fight started. Some of our other intelligence agency boys, they wanted to snap up this Libyan intelligence contact the minute he got into the States. But since it involved potential weapons-grade uranium on our soil, it became our responsibility. We didn't care so much about spooks and spies and their agenda. It's the uranium we wanted, and bad. So it became our job. To track the Libyan and keep him under surveillance, and intercept the handover when he tried to purchase the uranium."

"And what happened?"

"The meet was on for a certain time, but he left early," she said. "Plus, he had swept his car before arriving at the state park and found our tracking device. We didn't think he would be so suspicious, but there you go. All we knew is that he'd be meeting in a park somewhere on your seacoast. Do you know how many goddamn parks you have in this stretch of coastline?"

"Enough, I'm sure. Look, you folks have any idea why the meet went bad?"

She shook her head. "No. Maybe they had a fight over money. Maybe they had a fight over religion. Who knows? But all I know is that we're going to stay here until we find this Whizzer and get that uranium back. My gut tells me that this Whizzer character might be trying to contact somebody else as equally charming as Libya. I'm sure you can think of a few countries who'd like this uranium. We sure as hell don't want to open up a weapons bazaar here. We've got to wrap it up, and quick."

I leaned back in my chair, feeling something creak, either my back or the chair. "So why didn't you tell me all this at the beginning?"

"Need to know; sorry," she said.

I said, "It would have saved a lot of time and effort on my part."

She shrugged, smiled. "So we lied, sue us. Now. I've done all the talking. It's my turn. Who's Whizzer?"

I looked at her with a steady gaze. "I have no idea."

Her face whitened. "You told me earlier that you knew who he was."

I smiled, shrugged. "So I lied. Sue me."

CHAPTER TWELVE

I think she thought about leaping out of her chair and coming over to strangle me. Her face reddened and her bag dropped to the floor as she said, "You son of a bitch, what kind of fucking joke is this?"

"No joke, Laura," I said. "I wanted to talk to you, and I wanted you over here, alone. I didn't want to be on your turf anymore, with your muscle boys and all the trappings of your job. I needed to get your attention, and I used the best way I could."

"You lied!" she said, her voice rising. "You lied about—"

"Ever hear the word ironic?" I put a hand on my desk, picked up my well-worn Merriam-Webster's dictionary. "Here. You can look it up. One of the most popular definitions is that of a government official, who's been lying from the get-go, complaining that the person she's been lying to has just returned the favor. Care to look it up?"

"Right now I'd care to see you choke on it," she said.

"Probably won't fit, no matter how hard you try," I said. "Look. I've done some preliminary work on this Whizzer character already. That's a given. Now that I'm up to speed on what you clowns are doing, I'll be even more serious in my efforts."

"What the hell do you mean by that little remark?" she demanded.

"Look, having me snoop around for a druggie, well, how much effort above and beyond do you think I'd expend? Now that I'm looking for someone who claims to hold enriched uranium and is willing to sell it to the Libyans . . . well, you've got my attention. Earlier you appealed to my patriotism. That wasn't going to work, coming from you. But it will work, coming from me. I don't like the idea of uranium ending up where it doesn't belong."

"So you're saying that me telling you all is a good thing?"

I nodded. "Best damn thing that probably happened to you today."

I was surprised to see a smile appear. "You're probably right." She suddenly rubbed at her face with both hands, and when she took her hands away she looked ten years younger and about a half foot smaller. "People just don't know," she said, her voice just above a whisper. "They don't care anymore. We no longer have those idiots over in Red Square and those big May Day parades and submarines lurking off the East and West Coast to worry about, and people no longer care. Our fellow citizens think they can earn their money and fatten their portfolios, and that nobody hates us anymore. To most of them, foreigners are just people who care about getting better Internet access. There's no threat out there, no threat at all."

Another rub of her face. "Last year I saw some public-affairs show about the lack of interest people have in current events. They talked to some surfer guy out in California, with earrings through his eyebrows. He said all he cared about was getting a buzz on and worrying about a nice killer wave. That's it. That's the kind of people I'm defending, day in and day out. Killer waves. I'd like to educate him about killer waves, like gamma rays from a nuclear burst. Gamma rays that can punch through almost everything and give you a death sentence from miles away. I'll bet there's some people in Baghdad and Tripoli and Pyongyang who know all sorts of things about killer waves, and would like to show them to that surfer dude and his friends."

"I'm sure," I said.

She looked at me. "I'm venting, aren't I? One of my many

faults. Pops up every now and then on my performance appraisals. I get fired up about something and I start venting. Blathering on and on, especially when I'm tired. And especially when I'm hungry. Which reminds me, I'm starved."

"Really?" I asked.

"Really," she said. "I think now I'd like to take you up on your offer."

"And which offer is that?"

"To make me dinner," she said.

I looked over at her, different things conflicting in and out-inside of my mind. I felt like someone being urged to pet a grinning rattlesnake. Then I smiled and said, "All right."

Downstairs I opened a bottle of Merlot and got my outdoor grill going. Earlier in the week I had purchased a nice piece of tenderloin steak for tonight, but it was big enough so I was sure that it would feed us both. She sat at the kitchen counter and said, "Anything I can do to help?"

"No," I said. "It's my kitchen and while it may not be much, it does belong to me. Just chat with me to pass the time, why don't you?"

"About what?" she said. "More secret information?"

"No, not at all," I said, washing some lettuce in the kitchen sink and placing the leaves in a salad spinner. "Give me some basic stuff. Like what a nice girl like you is doing in the service of her country, hunting nukes and nuclear material."

She poured both of us a glass of wine. "Quick and dirty story, coming right up. Grew up in Wyoming—"

"The great outdoors out west?"

"You didn't let me finish," she said. "Wyoming, Delaware. Did well in high school, very well in math and physics. Ever hear about women having a fear of math? Well, not this woman. I did great in my SATs and applied to CalTech, and there I went. Majored in nuclear physics, and before I graduated decided that working for the civilian nuclear program was a dead end. No offense to that lovely power plant you have down the coast, but nobody's building any more nuclear power plants, and probably won't think of doing it again until both poles melt from global warming and we have to build dikes around Miami and Manhattan. That's not a particular attractive time frame to build one's career around."

I started washing two baking potatoes, and after poking dozens of little holes in them with a knife, popped them into the microwave. "So there you were, in school, big loans coming due, your career options limited. Then somebody showed up from the government and gave you the Great Lie Number One."

She sipped from her wineglass. "How true. 'We're here from the government and we're here to help.' Which actually wasn't too far from the truth. After graduation, went right into the Department of Energy. Paid my dues, did the usual things here and there, and then I applied to NEST. Not to brag, Lewis, but only the best get to apply to NEST, and only the very best get chosen."

I took some more dinner fixings out of the refrigerator. "What do you think your selection committee would do if they knew that you've just revealed all to a civilian while you were on a mission?"

A defiant shrug. "If I can get that uranium secured and in a safe place, they wouldn't give a shit. Success breeds success, Lewis, and I haven't screwed up on an assignment yet. And this won't be the first one that I screw up on. Not by a long shot."

I got the potatoes out of the microwave and put them in the oven, juggling the hot spuds in my hands. "Care to tell me what other missions you might be on?"

"Sure," she said. "I would care not to. Sorry, you know the ins and outs of this little baby. I'm not about to tell you any more."

"Fair enough," I said. "Excuse me for a second, will you?"

I went past her and opened the sliding doors to the rear deck and went to my new grill to check the temperature. Almost there. I leaned against the railing, looked at the darkening sky. This morning I had been in Boston trying to confirm something I had guessed about, and less than twelve hours later, all had been revealed. Surprise, surprise. I looked through the sliding glass, saw her on the phone. Probably telling her workmates that she won't be home for dinner. How sweet. As I looked at her on the phone, I thought again about who she was and what she did. When I had first met her, she had seemed the very model of a federal bureaucrat. Now, looking at her form and hair and eyes . . . she still looked like the very model of a federal bureaucrat. But definitely one who did more than the average employee of the IRS.

Temperature check on the grill. Perfect. I went back inside, and Laura was at the counter again, wineglass in her hand. "Oh, the phone rang while you were out there. Some woman named Paula. She didn't leave a message."

Uh-oh, I thought. "Why didn't you come get me?"

"She insisted that I not do that, so I didn't," she said, eyeing me curiously. "Who is she, your girlfriend?"

I went over to the phone. "She's a woman and she's a friend. Let's leave it at that, shall we?"

I dialed, got a busy signal. Damn. "Did she ask you who you were?"

"Nope, and I didn't offer. Hey, is this messing things up for you and this Paula?"

I tried again. Still busy. I put the receiver back down. "Let's just say that we're working through some things, and I wished I had answered the phone and not you, no offense. It's time to start grilling. You still starved?"

A smile. "Famished."

Three more tries on the telephone later, I managed to get past the busy signals. But either she wasn't home or wasn't answering, but I did manage to leave a message for Paula to call back. By then, dinner was ready. Laura had ignored my instructions to stay out of the kitchen and she had found a couple of plumber candles, which I keep around to use when the power goes dead during an ice storm or blizzard. The meal of steak, baked potatoes and salad was simple—one of these days I'll become a gourmet cook, right after learning to play the bagpipes—but it seemed to suit Laura.

She said, "A home-cooked meal seems so blessedly heavenly. After eating restaurant food or takeout or room service for a while, it all starts to taste the same. One of the first things I do when I get home is to camp out in the kitchen and just cook to my heart's content. Some people get fat while they're away. Not me. I eat poorly, and I definitely don't eat enough."

"And where is home?" I asked.

"Don't laugh. A condo in a suburb outside of Las Vegas. Real estate still relatively cheap, and it's an easy commute to work."

"Live alone?"

"Of course."

"So that story about your boyfriend, that wasn't part of the cover story?"

She had her fork about halfway up to her mouth when I said that, and then she lowered it down to her plate. "I may be guilty of a lot of things, Lewis, but telling lies about Tom isn't one of them. He really did go to MIT. He was in Air Force ROTC and was studying aeronautical engineering. Only way he could afford to go to that place and get the brass rat. We . . . we managed to spend a lot of good times together, even with me working in the DOE and him being a pilot. And yes, he did get shot down in Colombia. Hell, I even got word of it before his parents did . . . His poor mom. She couldn't understand why she couldn't see her boy in the casket before they buried him. She wanted to kiss him one last time. The poor dear didn't realize that what was left of him—was left of the boy she had loved and kissed and wiped his nose—once he and his aircraft slammed into the side of a mountain looked like a lump of greasy black charcoal. And I wasn't about to explain it to her."

Her eyes began to fill. "So that was all true. I was in fact wearing his sweatshirt. I wish to Christ it was a cover story, I wish the whole goddamn thing was a cover story, but it wasn't. Your curiosity satisfied?"

I found myself reaching over and touching her hand. "Quite. And my apologies for jumping to a conclusion."

She softly pulled her hand away, picked up her fork again. "Apologies accepted. I can't rightly blame you, considering the crap I spun your way earlier. Which reminds me, belated and hateful congratulations for sniffing out my real job. You must have been a real pisser back at the Pentagon."

I wiped at my lips with a napkin. "It had its moments."

"I've opened my life to you, my friend. How about repaying the favor?"

"Like what?"

"Like how did a nice boy like you end up working in the bowels of the five-sided puzzle palace."

I smiled at her. "You sure you have the clearance?"

She rested her elbows on the counter, leaned her chin into her folded hands. "Trust me," she said. "My clearance level is such that I know things even the President doesn't know."

"All right," I said. "Born and raised in New Hampshire. Moved to Indiana as a young boy. Went to the University of Indiana at Bloomington. Worked on the school newspaper. Was going to enter journalism when I got out. But there was . . . oh, I don't know. I had a sense that I should be doing more than just reporting on a zoning-board conflict or a car accident. I had a talent for writing, no doubt about it. But I had no talent for fiction writing and I wasn't too compelled to enter newspaper work after I graduated, but . . . let's just say I was a conflicted college youth."

She gazed at me. "Let me guess. Then a man from the government showed up with Great Lie Number One."

I laughed. "Good, very good. Close. A man from the government placed an ad in the very same newspaper I was writing for. They were looking for energetic, talented college students who wanted to make good money and do something in service of their country. So me and a few dozen others took a test in a gymnasium. I'm sure you know the kind of test I'm talking about."

Laura leaned up and picked up her wineglass. "Sure. Multiple choice. Number lines. Problem solving."

"The same. I guess I did well enough because I got an application to fill out, about two inches thick. One thing kept on leading to the next, and I ended up in the service of our country, at the Pentagon. Quite a heady time, a college student just out of school, thinking he's going mano a mano against the evil empire.

Until you found yourself in a cubicle contrasting rice-growing statistics in India and Pakistan. I got in trouble a few times and found myself transferred to an odd little unit where I actually thought I made a difference."

"The Marginal Issues Section," she said. "Where you and your cubicle mates worked on intelligence matters that fell through the cracks, that proved to be too sensitive for other people to look at."

"Yep, a motley group, but for the most part it was a lot of fun. You had a license to be a snoop, to find out anything and everything you needed to know. You read the day's newspapers and watched the day's newscasts, and you felt incredibly smug knowing that you knew so much more than the average citizen or even reporter. You had access to the most powerful computers and databases in the world, and . . ." I stopped, feeling slightly ashamed. "Listen to me. I'm beginning to sound like a recruiting ad."

"Good for you, that you had so much fun," she said.

I took a swig of wine, feeling a bit liberated at telling this young woman about who I was and where I had been, conversations I had never permitted myself to have with any other woman in my life. "Yep. Tons of fun, until we went out to Nevada on a training mission. Our group leader couldn't read a map, even if it was one given away on a McDonald's meal tray, and we ended up in a secure part of the desert. Then . . . well, you know the rest. The score ended up, U.S. Government twelve, Lewis Cole, one. And I don't think there's a Marginal Issues Section anymore, is there."

She shook her head. "If there is, then it's called something else. You lost someone out there in the desert near and dear to you, am I right?"

Cissy, my dear Cissy Manning. A fellow worker in the Marginal Issues Section. Long legs, auburn hair, a ready smile and laugh, and a mind so sharp she could do *The New York Times* crossword puzzle practically in her sleep. Cissy . . . who was going to move in with me and start a new life right after that trip to Nevada, a week of training in the desert, a week where only one of us would walk out alive. Cissy . . . "Yes, and I don't want to talk about it anymore."

This time, she reached over and touched my hand. "Not a problem. It's just that . . . well, you and I have a lot of things in common, Lewis. Besides being good at what we do, we both lost somebody we loved due to idiots higher up. Your woman due to a misread map by your section leader. My man because the idiots in charge of our efforts in Colombia won't allow our pilots to fly aircraft with antimissile technology. Thought to be too confrontational. Bah. High-priced idiots, all of them."

"Agreed," I said, picking up both of our empty plates. "High-priced idiots, all of them."

As I washed the dishes, Laura got on the phone and called over across the street, and I heard part of the conversation as I put away those few dishes we'd used.

"Well, I'm sorry if he called; I'll call him back when I get over there."

She paced the room like an angry lioness being held against her will, the phone in her hand. "The neutron flux detector? On the fritz again? Well, Gus, don't you think you can handle it?" A long pause as I wiped down a plate. "Telling me it's on the fritz isn't what I'm looking for. You telling me that it was on the fritz and that you and Tony got it recalibrated, that's what I'm looking for."

Then she noticed me looking at her, and she smiled. "My ETA? I'll be back there when I'm back there, all right? Look, gotta go."

She put the phone down and I said over the now-clean kitchen counter, "Our dessert options are limited. Either chocolate ice cream, or chocolate ice cream."

Laura sat down on the couch, picked up a *Smithsonian* magazine. "You decide."

"All right," I said. "I will."

When I got over to the couch with the coffee mugs filled with ice cream, I said, "Gus is the guy with the red hair, right?"

She gingerly licked at the side of the coffee mug, where a trickle of ice cream was oozing its way south. "Yep. The guy with the red hair and the eager-beaver attitude. That's the one. This is his first real field mission and he can't believe how boring it is."

"And how boring can it be?"

Another swipe of her pink tongue against the side of the mug, and then she picked up a spoon. "Looking through forty- or fifty-year-old records, getting dust in your eyes and your lungs. Trying to find a warehouse that existed in 1946, and which is a parking lot today. Using the best detection gear in the world, flying and driving around your target area, trying to determine where the uranium might be hidden. Locating a couple of potential sites. Going to those sites and finding out one of them was a medical facility back in the 1950s, and another place processed old watch dials in the early 1960s."

"And Gus finds this boring?"

"Can't hardly blame him," she said. "Entering NEST, you begin to think you're on the front line of squashing terrorism, and when you spend a week up to your elbows in old microfilm and newspaper files, the glamour goes away real quick."

I spooned in some of the ice cream. "You guys think the uranium is around here?"

"Sure," she said. "We know for sure it's not at the shipyard. That place has been searched and re-searched ever since the stuff went missing back in 1945. Which means it got secured somewhere in the area, if this Libyan character came here to pick it up."

"And why do you think it's being put on the auction block now, more than a half century later?"

"A variety of reasons. Most likely, the guy or guys who took the stuff, they want to cash it in before they die."

"But if it's nearby, shouldn't your detection equipment have picked it up?"

She shook her head, a slight line of chocolate about her lips. "If the stuff is well-shielded and well-buried, we could be within a yard of it and not even know. But it would have to be good shielding. And you know what? People who work at the shipyard, they know about good shielding. Which reminds me."

"Yes?"

A glance my way. "The museum up there in Porter. Why did you go there?"

Because of the button on the man's lapel, I thought. That's why. The button that was there and that disappeared between the time I saw the dead man and his photograph was taken by you folks. I supposed I should have told her everything, but I was hesitating. What I knew back when I was working in spookland, you never gave up information you didn't have to. And something didn't seem quite right here, despite her assurances that she was revealing all.

I cleared my throat. "I had a source at the Porter Police Department. He was going to see what he could learn from the people he knew at the shipyard. Between him and whatever you guys have done over there, I thought the place was pretty well-covered. So I thought, maybe an ex-worker or retiree. And that's why I went to the museum. Maybe there was a retiree's association or some old records there."

"And did you find anything out?"

"Not yet," I said, lying easily. "There's an old guy at the museum who I'm going to visit again, probably tomorrow. But when I was in his museum, that's when I saw the little display about U-boats. And not to get any of your folks in trouble, but in one of my visits to your rooms over there at the Lafayette, I saw some documents printed in German. Not the language of choice for Colombian drug cartels, is it?"

"Documents lying out there in the open," she said, speaking slowly. "That'll be something I'll be raising at our next staff meeting. Okay, go on. What else?"

"What else is just putting the pieces together. You looking for someone associated with the shipyard. You guys looking into something related to German. The shipyard once having hosted four U-boats that surrendered there back in 1945. Nothing extraordinary about those U-boats except for the cargo of one of them, which was enriched uranium. Missing for more than a half century. I made a guess, that's all. Missing uranium seemed to make a hell of a lot more sense to have your kind of guys crawling around here, rather than some bogus story about drug cartels."

She rattled her spoon around in the bottom of her mug, trying to get at the last of the ice cream. The room was now growing dark, the only faint light coming in from the kitchen. I was suddenly aware of her presence, her scent, everything about her, sitting beside me here on the couch.

"You ever feel bored here, sitting by the ocean?"

"Some days."

Laura gave me another gaze, and I forgot about the rattlesnake analogy. "Sure could use somebody like you, maybe as a consultant, when we wrap this one up."

"Laura—"

"Please, don't answer now," she said. "I know we came in like a herd of water buffalo and stirred everything up and trampled over you some. My apologies. That's the way I sometimes operate, especially when it's something concerning missing bomb material and some bad guys chasing after it. You'd think that a group like us would be overfunded and overequipped, but that's not the case. Some of our equipment is as old as I am, and we also could use some new blood. Which is where you come in. I like the way you don't take things for granted. I like the way you poke and ask questions and put things together."

I laughed. "Keep on saying that and how you like my merry smile, and maybe you'll get a deal."

"Maybe," she said, putting the mug down on the coffee table before us, the spoon rattling around. "If that's what it takes to get you on board." She looked at her watch, frowned. "Got to get a move on, or those boys across the street will come barreling through with guns drawn, wondering if you've kidnapped me."

"One visit from them was enough, thank you," I said. I got up and walked her to the door and said, "Need an escort back across the street?"

She smiled up at me, hands now holding on to her leather bag. "Last month I requalified on the weapons range, in the top one percent. I also know six forms of hand to hand combat. I think I can handle myself."

156

"I'm sure you can."

"Tell me something, will you?"

"Sure," I said, standing by the open door, the sound of the ocean now louder.

"Do you think you can do it, find Whizzer? Because right now, we are shit out of luck."

I held on to the doorknob. "I think I can. If he's around here, I think I'll be able to do it."

A nod. "Glad to hear it."

I thought for a moment. "If you can spare it, I sure could use the photo of the Libyan. A head shot that doesn't show much of the wound. When I head back to the museum.

"Sure," she said. "We'll have one ready for you tomorrow. And one more question, if you don't mind."

"Have I ever said no?"

It was nice to see the smile again. "You like it, don't you."

"Like what?"

"Being back in my world, of spooks and intrigue and finding things out. You had this energy about you, something I haven't seen before from you. I got the feeling that maybe you were bored with being here, bored with writing a magazine column each month. It just seemed like you were enjoying myself."

"You think too much," I said.

"Another flaw of mine, I'm sure."

She was still smiling at me, looking up at me, her hair softly framing her face, and I leaned down to her and kissed her. At first she just stood there, hesitant, but when I started to pull back she dropped her bag on the floor and her arms went up my back, and I returned the favor. I closed my eyes and concentrated on the taste and the sensations and the smell and the touch, and then she gently broke away and whispered, "That was nice. Unexpected, but very nice."

"I agree," I said, and kissed her again.

When she broke away, long seconds later, she took a hand and gently tapped it against my chest. "Nice, quite nice . . . but too complicated right now, Lewis. We . . . I . . . Well, it's too complicated. All right?"

I slowly let my arms down from around her slight waist. "Sure. It's all right. I'll check in with you tomorrow."

She nodded and now she looked older and taller, and was back to being Laura Reeves, section leader, Nuclear Emergency Search Team, U.S. Department of Energy. "Good," she said, tapping my chest again. "Very good."

She eased her way past me and started walking up the hill, and I waited in the doorway until I saw her look back at me and give me a quick wave. I waved back and kept on watching until she disappeared from sight.

CHAPTER THIRTEEN

After a half hour of efforts the next morning, unsuccessfully trying to get ahold of Paula Quinn, it was time to go to work. I made a slight detour by going south and returning yet another collection of unwatched adult videos, and then I reversed track. On my way north to Porter I made another slight detour and went to the Sandtree Stables in North Tyler looking for Felix Tinios. I had called him earlier and he'd said he would be at the stables, meeting up with his girlfriend Mickey. I still had a hard time wrapping my mind around that term. Girlfriend. Usually the women who entered Felix's life weren't around long enough to earn the name girlfriend.

Before starting out that day, I had gone over to the Lafayette House, where I found that the entire NEST group had left early that morning. But a nine-by-twelve manila envelope had been left for me at the front desk, with a black-and-white photograph of the Libyan intelligence operative, sitting dead in his car. I opened the envelope far away from the elegant splendor of the front desk, not wanting to upset any potential guests with a photo of a dead man with a bullet to his head. But Laura had chosen well. The photograph made it look as if he were sleeping, not dead.

I checked the envelope again. No note or letter from Laura. And I was surprised at how much that disappointed me.

At the stables in North Tyler, I parked next to Felix's Mercedes and walked over to one of the fenced-in areas near the barns. The place was well-kept, with a fresh-hay smell and the scent of horses mixed in with the salt tang of the ocean. It was a crisp day and Felix was leaning over one of the wide white planks that made up the fencing. Out at the farthest end of the enclosed paddock was a woman riding a horse, with an English-style saddle. Felix had on a short black leather jacket over a light blue polo shirt, and stone-washed jeans. He nodded in my direction as I ambled over.

"Carrying?" he asked, now looking out toward the open field and the woman on horseback.

"That I am," I said. "How come you always guess so well?"

He shrugged. "From years of experience. It's always been a good thing to spot when you meet someone that he's carrying a concealed weapon. That way, you're not surprised when it suddenly becomes unconcealed. Plus, that L.L. Bean jacket you have doesn't do such a good job of covering up your shoulder holster. It gets all bunched to the side. You should think about getting a smaller holster, wear it in your waistband."

I joined him at the fence, leaning my arms over the planks as well. Just a couple of good ol' country boys hanging out together who wouldn't know the difference between a Morgan and an Arabian. "I like a shoulder holster," I said. "Thing is, I don't like having a loaded weapon stuck in my pant waistband. Too much opportunity for something bloody hitting close to home, if you know what I mean."

"Yeah, that could suck," Felix said, watching his woman canter back and forth. "What's going on with you?"

"Looking for some advice," I said.

That made him laugh. "Me? Advice? Many a times I've offered you advice before and you've never taken it. Why should this time be any different?"

From this distance I could tell that Mickey was a redhead,

for she had a ponytail that bounced along her back in time with the horse's movement. "Always a first time," I said.

"True," he admitted. "Go ahead. What's up?"

I cleared my throat, looked around in a bit of paranoia, just making sure we weren't being overheard. "I'm involved in something delicate, something involving the feds."

"Department of Justice?" he asked.

"Can't say, I'm sorry," I said. "But I'm . . . well, I just want to make sure I'm not in over my head. I've always had the feeling that you might have had some dealings with feds in the past, some experiences you could pass on."

He gave a low chuckle. "Yeah, experiences, that's a good word. What do you mean, 'involved'?"

"It would appear that I'm now working for them."

"They paying you well?"

"I'm volunteering," I said.

"Well, that's a thought. I remember reading that there's a new spirit of volunteerism sweeping the land. Glad to see an example firsthand. They promise you anything in exchange for your help?"

"Sort of," I said. "It was more like a series of threats that won't come true if I cooperate with them."

He nodded, clasped his large hands together. "Boy, does that sound familiar. Okay, remember this, and remember it well. A couple of times I've been entangled in some federal business, and I've been fortunate enough to wiggle my way out without too much fuss. But I did learn a few things. First, feds always lie. Always. It's in their nature, because usually they're operating on a couple of different levels, and these levels don't all involve you. And if they're not out-and-out lying, they're holding things back. So remember that, and use it to your advantage."

"How?" I asked.

He turned and looked at me. "Don't give them everything all at once. And don't feel guilty if you don't come forward with some information you find out. Make the playing field level. Hold some things back on your own."

161

I mulled that over for a moment, thinking about the dead Libyan and the little button that showed he had been to the submarine museum. Good, I wouldn't feel guilty anymore about not bringing that up with Laura.

"Anything else?"

"One more thing," he said. "Always have an end game prepared, in case things go to the shits unexpectedly. You don't want to be sitting there, fat dumb and happy, being led away in handcuffs in case you were promised immunity in exchange for whatever you're doing. Remember that, too, and remember it well."

"Thanks," I said. "I will."

"Good." He smiled. "Thus endeth the lesson."

I was going to say something else when there came the sound of a loud and out-of-tune engine. We both turned and saw a van roar into the parking lot and skid to a stop. It was a light blue and had once belonged to some sort of business, for lettering and illustrations on the door and side had been painted over in black. The two front doors flew open and two guys jumped out, wearing dirty jeans, heavy boots and white hooded sweatshirts. They strode forward purposefully, the one on the left holding a tire iron, the one on the right a baseball bat. They were both heavyset and bearded, and the one with the tire iron had a ponytail.

I cleared my throat. "I do believe these gentlemen are here to see you."

Felix sighed. "Unfortunately, you're right."

I said, "Somehow, I don't think they want to discuss the differences between the Western and English style of horseback riding."

"Once again, you are correct, sir."

"Tinios!" the guy holding the baseball bat said. "You were so fucking tough with our cousin, breaking his arm like that! Let's see how tough you are now, asshole."

I was conscious of what was under my coat and I said, "You going to need some help here, Felix?"

"Yep," he said, shrugging off his leather jacket. "Hold this for me, will you?"

I did just that. "Are you sure I can't do anything else?"

He gave me a cheerful smirk. "Sure. Tell Mickey my last thoughts were of her. Excuse me for a sec, will you?"

With that, he went over to the two advancing men, and I was reminded again of just how good Felix was at what he did. He went up to them, hands held up in front of him, as if he were showing them that he was unarmed. "Come on, guys," he started. "Your cousin was shooting off his mouth about burning this place down if the owner didn't come up with some—"

And then things moved quickly indeed. Felix moved whip-like under the reach of the guy holding the tire iron, and threw an elbow into his chin. The guy grunted and dropped the tire iron and fell back against his partner. The guy with the baseball bat tried to untangle himself but Felix came in again with a flurry of punches to the man's nose. They both collapsed onto the ground and Felix went in again with fists and feet.

I moved Felix's coat from one hand to another. Felix backed away, chest moving hard, but his face calm enough, and he kicked away the baseball bat and picked up the tire iron. He went over to the van and punched out both headlights with the tire iron, and then tossed the tire iron into the open doorway of the nearest barn. Back he went to the two guys on the ground. One was looking up sourly, hand to his bloody nose, and his companion was facedown on the ground.

"Satisfied?" Felix asked.

The guy with the bloody nose used a variety of four-letter words and then said, "Whaddya mean, satisfied?"

Felix shrugged. "You wanted to see how tough I am. I just demonstrated it to you. Now, you and your bud should get up and get out, and don't ever bother me or this place again. Or next time, you'll get to see how tough I am when I'm angry."

More four-letter words and threats were issued, but within a minute or two the van was backing down the road, the reverse gear whining in a high-pitched sound, one man driving, the other hunched over in the passenger seat. Felix came up to me, hand held out, and I passed his coat over.

"Nicely done," I said.

Felix grinned. "Thanks. And if I'm lucky, Mickey didn't see a thing."

I looked over and saw the woman and her horse still prancing around at the far end of the field. She waved and I waved back. "Looks okay to me."

"Good. Hey, you want another piece of advice?"

"Sure. What do you have?"

Felix tossed his coat over a fence plank. "Just remember my phone number, that's all. You get into anything silly, give me a ring."

"Care to define silly?"

He gave me a look, one that was a cousin of the look he had given to the two previous visitors. "Like pornography, I think you'll know it when you see it."

I nodded. "You're probably right."

It was a busy day at the Porter Submarine Museum, with two tour buses parked in the lot among dozens of cars, the diesel engines to the buses grumbling, and a number of people lining up to go into the *Albacore*. I got out and went over to the museum, envelope in hand, and found a sort of roiling chaos as I got inside. Jack Emerson was bounding as fast as he could with his cane, going from his office to the telephone on the countertop. There was a small crowd about the gift counter, and from the dark looks they were shooting in Jack's direction, I figured he hadn't been over there in a bit.

I stood self-consciously there for a moment, and then made a quick decision. I went to the gift counter and maneuvered my way through the people and stood there looking at their angry faces. Now I knew once again why I'd never liked working at any type of service job.

"So," I said. "Who's next?"

A heavyset woman with glasses hanging by a thin chain around her fleshy neck tapped the top of the glass. "We've been for a long time! Where have you been?"

"Sorry, I'm late."

The woman wouldn't let it go. "And why are you late?"

I looked back at her. "Water buffalo got loose in my garden. Please, who's next?"

She looked suspiciously at me, and then tapped the glass again. "One of those coffee mugs, please."

I reached under the counter, pulled out a white mug with the *Albacore*'s name and profile painted on the side.

"How much?" she asked.

I turned the mug over, which revealed a tiny price tag stuck on the bottom. "Five ninety-five."

She shook her head, the dangling eyeglasses moving to and fro. "No, I mean how much with the tax and all."

"That's it, that's the price," I said. "There's no sales tax here in New Hampshire. Or an income tax."

The suspicious look came back. "Then how do you folks pay your bills?"

I shrugged. "Beats the hell out of me. Look, do you want the mug?"

"I'll take two."

"Two it is," I said.

Within a half hour most of the people had cleared out of the lobby, either going into the museum proper or heading outside to the submarine, which offered a self-guided tour. My feet ached, my hands were cramped from wrapping up coffee mugs and shot glasses, and I had paper cuts on a few of my fingers. Jack came over, leaning heavily onto his cane, and slapped me on the back.

"Man, you were a lifesaver today," he said. "I rightly do appreciate it, Lewis. Honest, I do."

"Glad I could help," I said, handing over a pile of bills and change. "Sorry I piled everything up here in the corner. I figured I didn't have enough time to learn how to run the cash register. Here, I also kept track of what I sold."

He took the paperwork and the money and went to the cash register, and started punching in the sales I had made. As I watched him work, I said, "Are you always by yourself when it gets this busy?"

"Nah, not really," he said. "Lucky for me that today a couple of Boy Scouts are in the submarine, helping make sure the people go through the submarine without getting themselves into too much trouble. Some of these tourists we get, they show their appreciation for the sacrifice of the sailors that manned the *Albacore* by trying to steal something from the boat, or scratching in their names on an instrument panel."

"How charming."

"Yeah, how friggin' charming. Anyway, Ross Termin, he was supposed to come help me this morning, but he woke up puking his guts out and couldn't make it. And my idiot son Keith said he'd be over this morning as well, and as you can see, he ain't here. So there you go. Hey, did you come back here to do a story, or what?"

"More like 'or what,' " I said. "I'm still trying to track down a visitor you might have had a few days ago."

He shook his head, his gnarled fingers still punching the keys to the cash register. "Did you see what kind of day we're having here today? Lewis, I could have had a guy come in here wearing a sombrero, and within a half hour I'd forget his face and what color the hat was. That's what kind of day we're having."

From the countertop I picked up the envelope I had brought in and took out the photograph of the dead Libyan. I handed it over and Jack gave it a look. "This the guy?" he asked.

"It is."

"Is he sleeping or what? It looks like he's in a car."

"He was in a car," I said. "And this photo was taken just before they took his body out."

"Oh. Dead, then." He held it up closer to his face. "How'd he die?"

"Someone shot him."

"The hell you say. Really?"

"Really," I said. "Look, does it—"

Jack interrupted me. "You know, he does look familiar. And you want to know why?"

"Sure."

He handed the photo back to me. "The suit. It was a pleasant day and he came in wearing this suit, and no necktie. I find that strange. Why would anybody go to the bother of putting on a suit and not put on a necktie? Yeah, I remember him now. Came in real quiet. Didn't speak English that well. Spent a while in the lobby, looking out the windows. Like he was supposed to meet someone here. And he went through the exhibits real quick, and then he barreled out to the parking lot, like the guy he was meeting had finally arrived."

I put the photo carefully back into the envelope. "Did you see who he was meeting?"

"Nope, not a thing. Minute he went out the door, he just disappeared. You know, standing back there behind the counter, you really can't . . . well, look who the cat just dragged in."

I looked over to the museum entrance and a man came in, with the careful walk of someone who is either drunk, or who is trying to bluff his way through a terrible hangover. He had on soiled khaki pants frayed around the edges, dirt-encrusted sneakers, and a blue nylon windbreaker zippered up the front. He hadn't shaved for several days, and his eyes were large and slightly protruding, like the eyes of some sort of aquatic animal. His thick brown hair looked as if he had cut it himself.

"Keith," Jack said, deep disappointment coming out in that one syllable. "So glad you could show up."

"Sorry 'bout that, Dad," Keith murmured, rubbing a large hand across his face. "Damn clock radio didn't go off."

Jack looked as if he was trying to keep his temper in check. "Then you should get a new clock radio, son. It seems like that one always breaks down just when you have to be somewhere."

Keith rambled over to the countertop and stopped, and then slowly eased his hip against the side, so he could have some support while standing. "Jesus, Dad, could you lay off the guilt shit already? I just got here."

"You certainly did, and hours late." Jack took a deep breath and said, "Lewis Cole, I'd like to introduce you to my son, Keith Emerson. Formerly of the U.S. Marine Corps. Former apprentice welder at the Porter Naval Shipyard. Former productive member of the community. Any other formers you can think of, Keith?"

Keith burped and said, "Whatever. I'm sure you can think of a few more, Dad. Hey, I misplaced my ATM card. You got a twenty I can borrow?"

I said, "Nice to meet you, Keith."

He looked over in my direction. "Yeah, well, fuck you very much, too. You got twenty I can borrow?"

I moved to my wallet and Jack said, "No, I'll handle this." He awkwardly leaned his cane against the counter and pulled out his wallet. "Here. Ten is all you get. If you had gotten here on time and helped me out like you promised, then I would have given you forty."

Keith snapped the offered ten-dollar bill from his father's hand and then suddenly shoved him in the chest, making him stumble back against the near wall, the metal cane clattering to the floor. "Thanks a fucking lot, old man! You think I enjoy your charity, do you? You think I like being your friggin' chauffeur, the guy who answers the phone here, do you?"

By now I was around the display cases and out in the lobby, and Keith was reaching over the counter, trying to grab his dad. I got a double fistful of his nylon jacket and pulled him back, and remembering how Felix had operated just a while ago, I tried to duck under his swinging punch.

But I'm no Felix, and the punch popped me in the chin, making my teeth clack with a horrible noise that echoed inside my ears. I stepped back a few paces, breathing hard, still holding his jacket, and I managed to wrestle him to the ground. I still had my weapon in my shoulder holster, which is where it was going to remain for the time being.

"Stop it, stop it right now!" Jack yelled.

I got up from the floor, moved away from the kneeling figure of Keith, who was trying to catch his breath while flinging an impressive number of obscenities my way. Jack moved over, cane back in his hand, and he reached over with the tip of the cane and, with a gentleness that surprised me, touched his son at the side of his ribs.

"Keith, can you get up?"

A slow nod, and then he stood up, weaving around. Saliva

was running down his chin. Jack went on. "You go on home, now. All right? I'll give you another ten dollars when I get home."

His son's eyes were filling up. "I hate it, you know. I hate being poor in this city! All the tourists and rich types coming here and the yuppie homeowners, and look at me. Almost forty years old and I'm begging money from my dad. Jesus . . ." He caught me looking at him and the tone of his voice changed. "And you, you fuck . . . I ever catch you in Porter again, you're a dead man. All right? You're a fucking dead man and you won't have a chance."

"You keep on drinking like you've been doing, I'll have a chance the size of Montana."

"Lewis," Jack said quietly, and Keith wiped a hand across his face. He muttered a few more things and then went outside. By then a group of chattering senior citizens came out of the exhibit area, laughing and talking to one another, and I touched the edge of my chin. I gingerly moved my jaw back and forth and let my tongue examine each of my teeth. All seemed solid, though I was sure my jaw would hurting like hell tomorrow.

I joined Jack back behind the counter and he said, "My apologies."

"None needed," I said.

Jack took out a handkerchief the color of old snow and blew his nose and wiped at his eyes. "I wish you had known him when he was younger. He was smart and tough and quick on his feet. He entered the Marines right when he turned eighteen—though I was sure I could have gotten him a job at the yard without any trouble—because he said he wanted to prove himself."

He carefully folded up the handkerchief and replaced it in his pocket. "The Marines seemed to suit him. Gave him discipline, gave him a purpose. When he was in high school, he could be a wild one when he wanted, and I was glad the Marines made something out of him. Then he entered aviation school, and actually became a pilot. My son, a pilot. Oh, how proud I was of him."

I stepped closer to the counter so he wouldn't have to raise his voice so much around the visitors crowded by the brochure stand. "What did he fly? Helicopters?"

"Nope. Jets. F/A-18 Hornets. Flew them off the USS *George Washington*."

"I'm impressed."

A satisfied nod from Dad. "You should be. An aircraft carrier is a huge vessel, but when you're up in a jet, coming in for a landing, it looks like a postage stamp. And remember, too, that this postage stamp isn't stable. It's moving up and down, side to side, and crowded on that postage stamp are other aircraft, people and equipment. And you're coming in at hundreds of miles an hour . . . A controlled crash, Keith once told me it was like. A controlled crash. And then there's night landings . . ."

Jack stopped for a moment, and then I quietly said, "Did something happen to him in the Marines?"

Another nod, but this one wasn't as satisfied as the previous one. "Yep. Never got the whole story, but Keith told me some of it once, a couple of years back. He was coming in for a night landing in the Persian Gulf and there were problems with the electrical system on his Hornet. Batteries were supposed to supply emergency back-up power, but they were drained for some reason. He was practically flying deaf, dumb and blind when he put her down on the flight deck, inches away from rolling off and killing himself . . . It shook him, shook him so bad that he lost his confidence. He tried getting into the jet the next day and he got the shakes. And it got worse, much worse . . ."

He stared at me. "It was like he was on a slippery slope he couldn't get off. He got transferred out of flying status, but even working at a desk made him get the shakes. Then he got discharged and came back home. I pulled a few strings and got him a job at the yard. Didn't even make it through a year before he was out of there. Now he's on some sort of disability pension, living in a crappy apartment, and begging for a few dollars off me every now and then. Not much of a life, is it?"

I tried to think of what kind of answer to give him, and decided the truth would work all right. "You're right," I said. "Not much of a life."

He rubbed at the hand that held his metal cane and said,

"Tell me this, why don't you, speaking about lives. You're a magazine writer for *Shoreline,* am I right?"

"Yes," I said, knowing where this was going.

"Yep," he said. "Came in here with a business card and everything. I even went to the trouble of going over to the smoke shop, see what kind of magazine you were. You see, some scamsters out there, they like to think the older you get, the stupider you get. Every now and then some clown comes in trying to convince me to buy an ad in their magazine or brochure. And most times, these magazines and brochures don't even exist. But yours existed, that's for sure, and I even saw your name and photo on your column."

"But you still have questions, am I right?"

"Yep. Like what's a magazine writer doing sniffing around for some visitor I had a few days back? Okay, you said it was confidential, and I can go along with that. But here you come again, still looking for info, but this time you've got a photo of this guy. Dead in his car. Which means that it came from a cop or something. So, are you a cop, or are you working for the cops?"

"I'm not a cop, and I'm not working for the cops."

"Then who the hell are you?" There was no anger in his voice, just a strong sense of wanting to know up and down, right and wrong, black and white.

"I'm a writer," I said. "Just like you saw in the magazine, just like you saw on my business card. But sometimes . . . sometimes I get involved in some things that are quite confidential. Sometimes it's best for a writer to ask questions, instead of an investigator or a detective. It's more casual that way, doesn't raise a lot of fuss. Which is why I'm working on this particular story, about this particular visitor."

He picked up the photo, put it back in the envelope and handed it over to me. "This guy a friend of yours?"

"No, not at all."

"But it's important, right?"

"Yes, quite."

He shook his head. "I'm sorry. I really can't help you,

Lewis. And it pisses me off to say that, it really does, considering how you helped me earlier today and how you put up with my son." Jack stuck out his hand and I shook it. "Tell you the truth, I think of anything, I'll let you know. And remember this."

"What's that, Jack?" I asked.

He smiled. "You still get a free tour of the *Albacore* from the other day. You can take it now, if you'd like."

I headed for the door as it was opening up and a group of kids came tumbling in. "Not today, but later. I look forward to it."

He looked to say something in reply, but in a moment he was engulfed by the kids, all demanding admission, all demanding attention.

Outside, the spring air was nice and clear, though it was lightly scented from the belching diesel engines of the tour buses. I looked across at the highway and over to the port of Porter. A lot of ports up and down the New England coast have been touristed and condoized and yuppied up, but not this one. Porter had its share of coffee houses but it also had its share of diners, and while there were a few high-priced condos overlooking the harbor, by God it was still a working harbor.

And part of the working harbor was the mass of buildings and cranes, over at the other side of the harbor, marking the Porter Naval Shipyard.

As I got to my Ford I checked the time, saw it was almost noon. If I raced south I might be able to meet up with Paula Quinn and buy her an expensive lunch and offer her an explanation for last night, when she had called and Laura Reeves had answered the phone. In spite of the little good-bye kiss, there was nothing there, not really . . .

Oh yeah? a little voice inside of me said. When I got to the Ford I decided to retrace my steps back to the museum and use the pay phone and officially set up a lunch date with Paula. I didn't want to leave this one to chance.

And as I turned away from my Ford, there was a deep-sounding *pong* as a bullet whizzed past my ear and struck the driver's door.

CHAPTER FOURTEEN

No time to think, no time to debate, no time to look about and say out loud, "What the hell was that?"

I dropped to the asphalt on my belly and rolled underneath my Ford Explorer, and when I got to the other side I sat up against the front tire, where a whole lot of engine and steel and other heavy things were between me and my assailant. I scrambled underneath my coat and pulled out my Beretta, finding it extremely heavy. I laid it across my knees, tried to remember how to breathe. A bit of tradecraft from Felix popped into my head. "Sometimes you get into things, you don't have the luxury of figuring out what in hell is going on. So you default to your primary response. Which is saving your hide. A number of years ago I was at this party in West Roxbury and this lovely young lady was putting the moves on me. She really wanted me to stay, but I was rude and left her and the party. Couldn't explain it, couldn't put my finger on it, but something was making me uneasy. So I bailed out and I'm glad I did. Later I found out that there were a couple of guys in the basement with ropes and blowtorches who were waiting for this fine young lady to bring me down. So always go to the basics. Protect yourself. Even if you piss off some people and look foolish."

Well, I certainly might have looked foolish scrambling underneath my Ford, but at least I was breathing and my body was unpunctured. And as for pissing somebody off, I think I had done that a while earlier. Maybe Keith had come back, ready to come through on his promise.

I sat there breathing hard, the tremblings beginning to ease some in my hands, when I heard the sounds of sirens. They seemed to be coming my way, which was surprising, unless some passing tourist had seen me with a pistol in my hand, which I didn't think had happened.

There was also the chance that someone had heard the gunfire that caused me to perform my groundhog imitation, but I was thinking that was also unlikely, since I hadn't heard the shot either.

Which meant somebody had been out there, gunning for me, with a silencer-equipped rifle.

I took another deep breath and listened as the sirens got louder.

A while later I was handcuffed and was sitting in the rear of a Porter police cruiser, which was the best thing that could happen to me after I was shot at. The cops had arrived in good form and I had initially ignored their commands to stand up and put my hands on my head. I compromised by kneeling and putting my hands on my head, because I didn't want to expose myself to the guy on the other end of the telescopic sight, wherever he might be. By then I had also kicked my Beretta underneath another car—presenting yourself as armed to a cop who has just raced in with lights and sirens on is a short recipe for a big disaster—and after I had been cuffed I was stuffed in the back of a Porter cruiser. Fair enough. By now there were enough cops and other people milling around that the chances were pretty good that the shooter had given up.

For now, of course. But I wasn't being greedy.

I looked around the parking lot as best I could. Jack was out there, talking to one of the uniforms, and a bunch of senior citizens were trooping into their tour buses. A couple even stopped and took my photo, and I obliged them by not turning my head. The back of the cruiser smelled like old cleaner, and the upholstery was dark blue plastic. Nothing fancy back here, just something that could be easily cleaned of whatever bodily fluids might be left behind while transporting a prisoner.

The rear door suddenly opened up and someone leaned in to look at me. It was Detective Joe Stevens, wearing a long rancher's coat and brand-new, pressed blue jeans. His detective shield was hanging from a chain around his neck. I decided this wasn't the correct time to ask him if he had come across any information on the mysterious Whizzer.

"Lewis, how's it going?"

"I can't complain," I said.

He nodded, his face showing neither a smile nor a frown. Fairly neutral. He said, "If you get your legs out, I can get you standing up here and get those cuffs off."

"You sure that's a good idea?" I asked, now hearing the chatter of police radios with the door open.

"Why, you like being cuffed in the back of a cruiser? Is that a better idea?"

"No, I don't like being in here. But I even like less the chance of that shooter out there going for another try."

The detective shook his head. "Not to worry. From the trajectory and such, it looks like the shooter was over by one of the warehouses, down by the salt piles. We've got a crew searching it right now, and so far they haven't found anybody. But with all this activity around here, if I was a shooter, I'd be long gone. So. You want to spend the rest of the day in there?"

I shifted my weight, put my legs outside. "Nope, not at all."

Getting out was a chore, with my hands cuffed behind me and my body bent at an awkward angle. But Detective Stevens grabbed my shoulders and helped me up, and I turned around and heard the nice *click-click* sound of the handcuffs being undone. He took the handcuffs away and I rubbed at my wrists.

Stevens said, "What did you see?"

I leaned back against the rear fender of the cruiser, feeling tingly and alive and breathing, and feeling almost childishly safe with all the police officers around me. "Not very much. Came out from the museum to my car here, and then I decided to head back and make a phone call. That's when I heard the round snap by and hit the car."

"What did you do next?"

"Made like a high school kid from the fifties and ducked and covered. Ended up on the other side of the Explorer while your uniforms showed up. Tell me, how did your guys get here so quickly?"

He eyed me. "What do you mean?"

"I mean that from the time of the shot until the first cruiser showed up here was only a minute or two."

He opened up a tiny little black-covered notebook and said, "Dispatch got an anonymous call of gunfire at the submarine museum parking lot. That's what happened."

I rubbed my wrists again and looked across the roadway, at the brick warehouses down by the harbor. "Odd . . ."

"And what's so odd?"

"Because I didn't hear the sound of a rifle, that's why. Just the bullet whizzing by and hitting my Ford."

Now there was a frown on Stevens's face. "You sure? Maybe the sounds of the traffic drowned it out. A gunshot can sound like a car backfiring, or a piece of heavy equipment operating."

"Maybe, but I'll bet you that when you do your canvass of the neighborhood, you won't find a witness who heard a gunshot."

"Sorry," he said, returning to his notebook. "Since the Red Sox last year, I'm not a betting man. And I'm also not a man who likes the thought of a nut running around with a rifle that has a silencer on it. About the only good thing, besides the fact the shooter missed, is that the bullet went through the door and dropped on the upholstery. It's pretty dinged up, but ballistics should be able to do something with it once we get it to the state crime lab. Okay, anybody you know out there who'd feel like putting a bullet in your head?"

"None that come right to mind."

"How about Keith Emerson, the son of the museum director over there? You think you're on his enemy list?"

"Well, I don't know if I'd go that far—"

"Look, we've already talked to Jack Emerson and some of the visitors who saw something going on back in the museum lobby. The two of you got in a little scuffle and he threatened to kill you. Any reason why you're defending him?"

"I'm not defending him, it just seems unlikely."

Now his tone was getting sharp. "Unlikely? Why unlikely?"

I rubbed at my wrists a third time. "All right, he made some threats. But I don't know how sober he was when he made them. He had a hard time standing up and walking around. And when he left and when I came out here, maybe just a few minutes had passed. It doesn't sound right that he'd be in a position to go over to the warehouses, pull out a rifle, and pop one in my direction."

"Doesn't sound right, is that what you said?" he asked, the neutral tone now back in his voice.

"Exactly," I said. "Guy like Keith, it seemed like he'd be the type to be in your face, with a fist or a knife. Not from a distance and with a high-powered rifle."

"Okay, Lewis, what doesn't sound right is you coming in here and getting shot at. That doesn't sound right. And I don't care what you think about Keith Emerson, he made threats against you, and a bullet came your way just a few minutes later. So we're going to pick him up and bring him in for a little chat." He paused, and added with exaggerated politeness, "If that's all right with you, I mean."

"I understand," I said.

"Good. I need to ask you one more thing."

"Go ahead."

Stevens looked around at the cops working the scene, talking to witnesses. I saw Jack Emerson talking to another detective, leaning on his metal cane by his small pickup truck. The museum door was fastened and a CLOSED sign had been put up.

"First time I met you, you asked me questions about the

local drug trade and about a guy in particular, named Whizzer. You poking around the local drug managers, making them upset? Trying to put a little sting in their business?"

"No, I'm not," I said. "But having said that, you find out anything about a guy named Whizzer?"

He paused as a truck went by, heading out of the parking lot. Jack was driving, staring ahead, not looking in our direction at all.

"Not a word," Stevens said. "You think this Whizzer guy might be the one who tried to pop you?"

"Could be," I said. "But so far, I haven't met anybody or anything with any kind of connection to anybody named Whizzer. Could be a ghost, for all I know."

"Maybe," he said. "But there's another thing." He reached into one of the deep pockets of his rancher's jacket and pulled out my Beretta. Even holding the small notebook, he worked the pistol expertly, popping out the clip and then working the action, ensuring there wasn't a round in there. He passed both the full clip and the pistol over to me.

"I take it you have a carry permit?"

"In my wallet, if you'd care to look."

"Nope. That's okay. Do me a favor and just put it away, and don't replace the clip until you're home, safe and sound. Second Amendment or not, having a citizen with a pistol in his possession at a crime scene tends to make us cops nervous."

I put the Beretta back into my shoulder holster and stuffed the clip into a coat pocket. "Not a problem," I said. "Always glad to cooperate with the local police."

"If that was a joke, it was a bad one," he said, his eyes narrowing down. "You get along now. Don't take this too personally, but if someone's gunning for you, I don't want it to take place in Porter. The paperwork would be a real pain. And with this little incident and my little search for Whizzer for you, my favor quotient with Diane Woods and you is used up. Understood?"

"Loud and clear," I said.

Then he shifted his feet and said quietly, "All right, enough barking on my part. Here's my business card." I took it from his outstretched hand and pocketed it next to the Beretta clip. "Anything else happen," the detective went on, "you let me know. Immediately, if not sooner. Like I said earlier, I don't like the thought of a sniper loose in my town."

"Neither do I," I said, and went over to my Ford, now sporting a round little hole in its door.

About halfway home to Tyler, driving on the interstate, I suddenly got the shakes and had to pull over to the breakdown lane. As traffic roared by me, heading south, I got out of my Ford and went down to a drainage ditch at the side of the highway, surrounded by cattails and tall grasses. I dropped to my knees and then had the dry heaves for a long minute or two.

Then I sat down in the grass, hands still shaking. I got the clip out of my pocket and popped it into the handle of the Beretta, worked the action so there was now a round in the chamber. I let the hammer down on the pistol and it took both of my hands to replace it in the holster.

I wiped at my face with a handkerchief and took a couple of deep breaths, as my stomach tried to make up its mind as to whether or not to revolt again. When it seemed to settle down, I sat on my hands and looked around. A redwing blackbird was moving about the cattails, chattering at me. Good for him.

Inches. Just a matter of inches and instead of digging a round out of the upholstery in my Ford, a medical examiner from Wentworth County would be doing the same to what was left of my bloody head.

Inches. And that woman who had called my home a few nights ago, warning me off on what I was doing, working with the feds. An empty threat at the time, but now . . .

Inches, maybe even just millimeters. I wished I could have sat down and talked more with Detective Stevens from Porter. Tell him about the NEST team secretly working in the area. About the dead Libyan in North Tyler. About the missing uranium.

I wished I could talk about a lot of things, and I remembered a time when I was working for the Department of Defense and had the very same wish.

I freed my hands and held them out. The shaking had mostly subsided. I had things to do, and the time for shakes was over.

I got up and looked at the redwing blackbird one more time, then went up the embankment to my Ford.

In the parking lot of the Tyler *Chronicle*, I noticed a familiar green Volkswagen Jetta in the lot with a Tyler Police Association sticker in the rear window. I sat for a while in my Ford, listening to talk radio from Boston and wondering what the host would say if I called down there to report an attempt by the Libyan government to secure uranium from New Hampshire to make their very own atomic bomb.

I'd probably be hung up on, and the host would go to a caller complaining about seat-belt laws in Massachusetts. After all, one has to keep these kinds of issues in perspective.

Then the door to the *Chronicle* opened up and Diane Woods came strolling out, wearing khaki slacks and a short black leather jacket, her hands stuck forlornly in the coat pockets. I got out and was rewarded with a small smile as I met up with her at her car. I thought about telling her what had just happened to me and then decided not to. This was her time, not mine.

"Here to renew your subscription?" I asked.

"Now there's a thought," she said, leaning back against her car. "I plumb forgot to do it after I spent the past half hour in there, being interviewed by your friend Paula on my history as a detective, why I work to help out the people in this town, and why I happen to love women instead of men. Care to guess which one of these three issues will be highlighted on the front page one of these days?"

I felt a chill tingle along the back of my neck, seeing the expression on my friend's face. "They made you do the interview here at the newspaper, instead of your office?"

She shook her head. "No, not at all. I made them do the interview here, that's what. I'll be damned if we were going to do it at my office or at my home, or at some restaurant. I thought if they were going to do something like this story, then by God I'd do it on their turf, not mine. Make them look right at me."

"Diane . . ."

She held up a hand. "No, it went okay, as okay as one could get. Your friend Paula tried to do the best she could, and both of us knew that it was her new boss pushing her to ask those questions. To be fair, she did talk most about my career in law enforcement, and the kind of cases I've worked on. But she did toss in a few questions about my personal life, which I did answer, as much as I didn't want to answer."

"And how did you answer?" I asked.

She laughed for a moment. "All these years, wondering if and when I'd ever publicly come out of the closet . . . I always thought that I'd be the one in control, the one in charge. Deciding when it would be a good time. And I didn't think it would happen like this, and I didn't think I'd be alone while doing it."

"Kara still away?"

"Yep. She won't be back yet for a few days. But I've talked to her a couple of times, and she's given me some advice."

"Like what?"

She folded her arms, smiled. "Kara can be even more strong-willed than I can, and sometimes she favors the direct approach. Like taking a full-page ad out in the *Chronicle*, showing a photograph of the two of us in a lip-lock. Like those milk ads. Instead, ours would say, 'Got lips?'" She laughed. "You know, that wasn't half-bad, except a full-page ad is so damn expensive. So I went in there and did my own thing."

I had an urge to go over and just put my arm around her, but I stood still, not wanting to disturb her moment. So I said, "And what was your thing?"

Diane reached up, pulled away a strand of her fine brown hair. "My thing was to be truthful, to a point. Paula was about as diplomatic as one could be asking me about my personal life, if I was dating anyone. I told her that if it was anybody's business, I was currently involved in a committed relationship with one Kara Miles of Newburyport, Mass., and that beyond that, I wouldn't say a damn thing. Which I didn't." She tugged on another strand of hair. "All in all, you know, it went okay, except when I was leaving the office, and I saw that new editor. Rupert Holman. He looked at me as I was heading out, and you know what that look was?"

"Undressing you with his eyes?"

That got another smile from her, and I felt good about that. "Oh yeah, that's my big wish. To be a turn-on for a hetero male. Nope, it was an odd look. Those few men who know about me and who I love, sometimes I do get that undressing look—though not from you, God knows. Imagining what it must be like, to see two women go at it, hot and sweaty. They don't imagine the other ninety-five percent, like doing laundry together or fixing a leaky faucet. Nope, it's always the sexual thing. Fine, let them have their fantasies."

"But Rupert wasn't giving you that, was he."

"No, he wasn't. He was looking at me like a thing, an object that he and his newspaper could use to further his career and the newspaper's sales, and it gave me the creeps. Almost made me wish that I was back as a uniform, so I could follow him driving around Tyler and pull him over for crossing over the double yellow line. Lewis, looking at that guy . . . what was going on behind those eyes made me wish that he was fantasizing about me and a can of whipped cream."

"Anything I can do?"

She shook her head, turned and opened the car door. "Well, lunch on the day the story appears would be wonderful. It'd be nice to be with a friendly face when that little storm breaks."

As she got into her car, I reached down and touched her cheek. "Anything, anything at all," I said. "All you have to do is ask."

Diane reached up and squeezed my hand, tight. "I know. Now, let me get back to work, okay?"

I stood back as she backed up the Jetta and headed out to Route One, and when I turned to head into the Tyler *Chronicle* building, the rear door opened up and Paula Quinn came out.

Talk about timing.

She stood in the doorway entrance as if she was debating

whether to come outside or go back in, and then she pulled the door shut and said, "Hey."

"Hey yourself."

"It looked like Diane Woods's car was just leaving. Am I right?"

"That you are," I said.

She had on jeans and a brown corduroy coat, and her large black purse was hanging off her shoulder. "Let me guess. The two of you have just spent the past few minutes talking about the inquisitive and cold-hearted Paula Quinn, and how she was going to ruin Diane's life because her newspaper is turning into tabloid trash."

"No, not at all."

"Gee, I find that hard to believe," she said, her voice sharp.

I took a deep breath. "Then believe this. If you must know, we talked about the interview. She said it went well, as well as it could. She doesn't have a grudge about you or the job you do. Honest."

She seemed to ponder that for a moment, then said, "Well, we'll see, after the story appears next week and Rupert gets to write another one of his patented headlines about the decline of morals in small-town America. Jesus, I'm getting so tired of this crap. After that story appears, I'll be frozen out by the police department, the fire department, and about half the elected officials in this town, and my job is going to be as much fun as going to the dentist every day for a month. How about you, Lewis? Coming by to check up on me?"

"Yes, I am," I said. "You called my house last night. A woman answered. I called you back but all I got was your answering machine or voice mail, here or at home."

She shifted her purse on her shoulder. "My prerogative, deciding whether to answer my phone or not. Especially after someone's promised a drink and conversation, and blows off both and ends up at home with another woman."

"And it's my prerogative, too, to give you an explanation. I tried to make it in time for drink and conversation. The woman visitor was unexpected and unscheduled. She's someone I'm involved with on doing a story for *Shoreline,* and nothing else."

"What kind of story?"

"A story about the drug trade," I said, not liking these lies to Paula, not knowing what else to say. If I mentioned anything about NEST and Libyans and missing uranium, Paula the reporter would politely tell Paula the friend of Lewis to shut up and get to work.

"The drug trade?" she said, exaggerating the words slightly. "That sounds soooo interesting. What is she, a dealer? A druggie? A cop?"

"She's with the federal government," I said.

"The federal government, and she's meeting with you at your house?" she said incredulously. "I guess the government really is improving public service. Who is she with? Department of Justice? The drug czar's office?"

Now I felt fairly miserable. "I can't say, sorry."

A crisp nod, and she walked by me, heading to her Escort. "Oh, I get it. Another mysterious Lewis Cole story, another attempt by Lewis to be the hero and the fixer, and us mere mortals can't be let in on his little secret. Well, here's my secret, Lewis. I'm late for an appointment with the town counsel, and I don't like being bounced around by you, no matter how noble your intent."

"Paula . . ." I said, not knowing what else to say, knowing she had nailed me pretty well. "It's more than that, honest."

She got into her car, started it up, and then was gone without once looking in my direction. I put my hands in my coat pocket and bounced back on my heels, and decided to get the hell out of this cursed parking lot before Rupert Holman came out and arrested me for trespassing or some other damn thing.

At home there was just one message on my answering machine, a message that made the backs of my legs quiver for just a moment. That female voice from the other night: "Mr. Cole. A reminder. I do hope you have your affairs in order." Then the hang-up. I looked at the machine and said aloud, "If you say so, hon," and I made a point of checking all the windows of my house, making sure they were locked. Then, even though it was mid-afternoon on a nice sunny day, I drew all the shades and switched on the lights. With shades drawn, anybody out there with a high-powered rifle wouldn't have an easy time of it gunning for me a second time.

I also loaded up my 12-gauge Remington shotgun and stood it up against the headboard of my bed for easy access. A pistol is fine, but in close quarters, when someone's trying to get into your house and cause you harm, a shotgun and its pattern of shot is much more effective. In what seemed to be a long time ago, Paula had asked me why I had such a collection of weapons—a pistol, a revolver, the shotgun and my FN FAL 8-mm assault rifle—and I said, "Tools. That's all. They're tools with different functions in case I get into trouble." When she asked, "Wouldn't dialing nine-one-one be easier?" I had shrugged and said, "What do I do if the phone is out?"

True. And what would I do if someone was trying to nail me and I couldn't say much about it because of the Holy God of National Security? I then had a Molson Golden Ale and some cheese and crackers for a meal. It was too late to call it lunch and too early to call it dinner—or supper, if you prefer—and all I knew is that it eased up my stomach some.

I sat and watched television, deciding that the current crop of talk-show hosts would have done quite well in the old Roman coliseum— "Live! This afternoon! Cultist Christians reveal their sex secrets as they are devoured by lions!"—and when I decided my stomach had calmed down enough, I made a call and then walked across the street to the Lafayette House.

Before I could see Laura Reeves, one of the musclemen who met me when I knocked at the door—Clem—gave me a look and I gave it up right then and there. "I'm carrying," I said. "Nine-millimeter, holster under left arm. Do you want it?"

He nodded, not saying a word. I cleared my throat. "Do you want to retrieve it, or should I hand it to you?"

Clem just eyed me, as if he were gauging both my weight and my intentions. "Sure. Just hand it over, using two fingers of your left hand, on the barrel end. All right?"

"Not a problem," I said, though it was very awkward, removing the Beretta as he had requested. But that was his intent. An awkward man with a gun is much less of a threat than a confident man with a gun. After I handed it over he opened the door wider and let me in. I asked, "Do I get a receipt for that?"

"Tell you what, sport. You get to have it back when you leave. That okay with you?"

"That sounds fine."

"The room next door; go on in."

Which I did, opening up the interconnecting door, but instead of Laura Reeves, Gus Turner was there, sitting at one of the conference tables. He looked up at me and smiled as he started putting papers away in envelopes and manila folders. I guess security had improved here since I had last visited. "Sorry, Lewis. Laura's in a call right now. She asked me to keep you company until she's free. Have a seat, why don't you."

I sat across from him, saw the wrinkled nature of his shirt and trousers, and his red-rimmed eyes. "Gus, you've got to get out more."

"Hah," he said, picking up a can of Coke. Empty cans of Coke were scattered across the large table like little red lighthouses. He went on, "Ever since I've been here, out is what it's been like. Either driving around in a van or flying overhead in a rented Cessna, all I've done here is been out and about. I know this is your home turf and all, but I'm beginning to hate this little state of yours."

The room was showing signs of being seriously lived in. The wastebaskets were overflowing with fast-food wrappers, old newspapers, and additional empty cans of soda. For some reason the place looked quite familiar to me, as if I had worked in here before instead of coming by earlier for brief visits. "What's Laura up to?"

He picked up the soda can, took a deep swig. "Beats me. You know the drill, right? Need to know. That's what guides us and everything we do. All I know is that she had to take a call. You want a drink? Nothing alcoholic, but I could rustle up something for you."

"No, I'm fine," I said, now noting the smell inside the room, of unwashed bodies and clothes, pressed together for a long time. The glamour of government work.

"Hey," Gus said. "Can I ask you something?"

"Go right ahead."

He looked sheepish, like a kid who saw his parents playing somersaults in the bedroom. "I've read through your service record, when you were in the Marginal Issues Section. You sure had your hands full back then. It sure was impressive."

I put my hands in my coat pocket. "If you call reading a lot of reports and writing your own reports impressive . . . well, if you say so."

He looked eager as he kept on talking. "Yeah, but even if it was dull work, it was all to a greater purpose. Fighting the old evil empire, the Soviet Union. It was all so clear back then. Us and them. Allies and adversaries. West Germany versus East Germany. Contras versus Sandanistas. Quite crystal-clear. It must have been invigorating."

I sighed. "Did you read the whole file, especially the part about what happened to me and the other members of my section? What happened to us was pretty crystal-clear as well."

He took another swallow from his Coke. "Sure, and sorry about that and all. But look what I signed up to do. Skulking around in the shadows, trying to make sense out of poorly microfilmed documents more than a half century old. Flying around in circles with detection gear, trying to ignore readings from hospitals or industrial facilities that use radioactive materials. Tracking down high school students over the Internet who've made a bomb threat against Cleveland. Man, when I signed up for this gig, I thought I'd be doing something, you know. Searching out bomb material in Kazakhstan or Iraq or someplace. Not friggin' New Hampshire."

I was trying to think of a suitable retort when another door opened up and Laura Reeves strode in. "Gus," she said crisply. "If you'd excuse the two of us."

"Sure," he said, but while his tone might have been cheerful, his eyes told me another story. I got the feeling that among the things red-haired Gus Turner didn't like about this assignment included being bossed around by Laura Reeves.

When Gus had gone out into the other room, Laura sighed heavily and sat down, hooking one leg over the arm of the chair, letting her leg swing back and forth. "Well, I just got off the phone with the Secretary. Of Energy, in case you were wondering."

"Go on."

"It seems things are moving quickly in other arenas, and poorly."

"Poorly in which way?"

She rubbed at her face and sighed again. "Poorly in that if we don't get this uranium back and soon, it looks like a nice little war is going to break out in North Africa. That poorly enough for you?"

My mouth got dry and I wished I hadn't turned down that drink offer.

"Yeah," I said. "That's poorly enough for me."

CHAPTER FIFTEEN

Laura Reeves rubbed at her face again and started talking. "Here's the deal. Our little friend out in the North African desert, the one who's hot to trot to get ahold of this uranium, it seems like he's made more progress than anybody thought. The necessary equipment and machinery have been assembled and are in a series of caves at the base of a range in the Atlas Mountains. Intelligence estimates show that they've geared up, and they're waiting for one little piece of the puzzle to start work on a North African bomb."

"The German uranium."

She took her hands down, clasped them across her flat belly. "The same. So the boys and girls down south in DC are getting nervous, quite nervous. If we don't get a handle on this uranium soon, and I mean quite soon, Lewis, then something is going to happen to that installation in the Atlas Mountains." She reached over and poked through the piles of folders and envelopes, and then flipped over a photocopy of a newspaper article. "See this? It appeared in today's *Washington Post*. You don't get that paper up here, do you?"

I picked up the paper, saw that it was a facsimile. "I see it on the Web, when I feel a need to see what's going on in DC. Thankfully, that doesn't happen that often."

I scanned the article. It was buried in one of the A sections of the newspaper, and the small headline said CARRIER GROUP ON MANEUVERS, and mentioned that the USS *George Washington* and its support fleet had left a port-of-call visit in Tel Aviv a day early to conduct maneuvers in the central Mediterranean. I looked up at Laura. "Gulf of Sidra again?"

She smiled. "Very good. Sure we can't get you a job here when this is all over?"

"Positive."

Laura shifted some in the chair. "Gulf of Sidra, back in '86, was just a little exercise, looking for an excuse to punch al-Qaddafi in the nose. Al-Qaddafi claimed the entire Gulf as his own, and we sent in a carrier group to quote, exercise the right of free passage through the seas, or some damn thing. He sent up a couple of MiGs to tangle with a couple of our Tomcats—always a bad idea—and those MiGs were shot down. A couple of more clashes later we sent in a flight of F-111s to give him a heavy dose of punches in the nose. But still he's there, and every now and then he makes trouble. Lewis, one of our raids back in the eighties killed an adopted daughter of his. You think if he had the bomb, he might not use it over here somewhere?"

"This carrier group, I take it, is not going to be tooling around the Gulf of Sidra on some routine exercise."

A quick shake of the head. "Nope. And a reminder about the non-disclosure form you signed, Lewis, because it covers everything and anything we discuss. Such as the fact that the carrier group is going to be in a certain position in a few short days, and they aren't bringing flowers."

It was as if the whole hotel room and the two of us had been picked up and transported back in time, back when I worked at the Pentagon and dealt with these kinds of issues all the time, month after month. Now I knew why this room had seemed eerily familiar to me. I had been in similar rooms before, years ago.

"If you don't get the uranium under your control soon, the carrier group is going to attack, won't they?"

"They will."

I thought for another moment. "If I read correctly last week, the current Mideast peace negotiations are in a rather delicate phase, aren't they. I'd imagine they'd collapse for a long, long while if our bombers and cruise missiles are going into North Africa and killing Libyans and blowing up installations."

"So true," she said. "And after that happens, you can bet that the news will come out that we went ahead and blasted an aspirin factory or baby-milk factory or textile factory, and whatever low prestige we have in the Arab world will get even lower. It might be another four or five years before the peace negotiations get back on track, if then."

"Some pressure," I said.

"Some understatement," she said.

"You getting any additional resources coming your way?" I asked.

"Yeah, another NEST team is winging its way east, and the local FBI offices have been placed at my disposal. But you know the FBI guys are more experienced dealing with mob matters or bank robberies or white-collar crime. There's a special unit coming up from Quantico, but by the time everyone's landed and gone to the rest room and been debriefed, it'll be a couple of days before they can make a contribution. By then, the trade-off most likely will have taken place, and that uranium will be out of the country. And then the bombers and the missiles will start flying."

"No news on who the new contact might be?"

She shook her head, kept on moving her leg back and forth. "We were lucky once. We weren't so lucky again. Speaking of luck, you got anything for me, anything at all?"

I began to tug nervously at the end of my coat zipper. "I know this sounds melodramatic and all, but someone tried to kill me today. Plus, I've gotten two threatening messages at home, from a woman who wants to know if my affairs are in order. Would you call that luck?"

Her leg stopped swinging. "Are you serious?"

"If you want, I can take you over to my house and show you the bullet hole in my Ford. Came a few inches from taking off the top of my head. I'm afraid I've erased the threatening message."

Laura moved around in the chair, eyes now excited. "The gunshot. Where did this happen?"

"At the submarine museum in Porter. I was trying to get more information from the museum director on leads to retirees who might have been at the shipyard when the German U-boat was brought in. The guy running the place didn't have anything for me, and when I left and got to my car, that's when it happened."

"The cops up there in Porter know what happened?"

"They do," I said. "It's under investigation, but I'm not sure what they can do."

She clasped her hands together and squeezed them tight, her eyes still excited. "That's the best news I've heard all day."

I said, "I hope you wouldn't have been so excited if I'd ended up dead."

"Oh, no, no, no, you don't understand," she said. "Sorry, I know it sounded cold and all that. But you getting shot at was good news. It means that whoever's out there, in control of the uranium, he's nervous that you've been poking around and asking questions. It must mean you're on the right track. Retirees, right?"

"Yeah, that's right," I said. "I figured—"

"You figured well," she said, picking up a pen and starting to make some notes. "Gus was in charge of looking through the retiree records, trying to see if anything out there matched. There were thousands of people working at the shipyard when those U-boats came in. Thing is, it'd be very easy to overlook something." She looked up from her note-taking and grinned. "This is great. I've got some FBI agents heading over here in a few hours, and I'll get them to work on tracing those old records. That's what they're experts at, seeing old connections, old evidence. Damn it, Lewis, I think you might have given us the key."

I tried to keep my voice even. "You want I should get shot at again?"

Now her smile was affected. "I was told by Clem that you're carrying a weapon. True?"

"Quite true."

She wiggled the pen some in her grasp. "I wish I could say I had the resources to give you twenty-four-hour protection. But I'd be lying. I'm stretched thin as it is, and even these new bodies won't help that much. Maybe you should take a couple of days off, go on a trip."

"And not see this one to the finish?" I asked. "After all you clowns did to me to get me to sign up, you think I'm going to bail out?"

"No, but I'd think—"

I stood up. "Nope. I get the message. I'm on my own, right?"

Now her eyes were locked on to me, cold and clear. "My objective is to get the uranium back as soon as possible, and prevent lots of people from being killed, either in this country or overseas. I have to work with the resources I have. Sorry."

"Understood," I said, and I started heading for the door. Before I got there, she said, "One more thing?"

"Yes?" I said, turning, and damn if her smile hadn't come back. "The other night. At your place. I enjoyed the meal and the kiss. No matter what I might have said at the time. I'd like a chance for a repeat performance, if you don't mind."

I was going to shoot something back about it only happening if I didn't get killed over the next few days, but that seemed too obvious, so I said, "Sorry, right now I don't have the resources to even consider it."

Then I left.

Outside, armed once again, I slowly walked back home in the gathering twilight. The April air was getting cooler, teasing the residents of the New Hampshire seacoast once again. During the day the sun would warm things up, tempting one to break out the shorts and T-shirts, but when the sun went down and the wind came up from the ocean, one was thankful for a nice jacket and a heating system at home.

I stopped at the side of Atlantic Avenue, waiting for the traffic to ease up before crossing the street. Of course, having a nice jacket also worked to hide one's weapon, and the weight of the Beretta was clearing up my mind. So. I was on my own. Nothing new, nothing I hadn't encountered before.

When the road was clear, I strode across and stopped for a moment in the parking lot of the Lafayette House. In the darkening sky, Jupiter was making its appearance in the west, accompanied by the dimmer star that marked Saturn. I looked up there for a bit, waiting to see if I could spot a fast-moving dot of light that'd mark the space shuttle *Endeavour,* but nothing was there. No doubt she was on the other side of the planet at this hour, and when I got home, I'd fire up my new Macintosh and get on the Web, to find out the latest orbit information.

I stopped looking up at the night sky and headed past the parked cars to my dirt driveway. All right, then, I thought. Once I had the computer work wrapped up, then what? Maybe a call to Paula, a peace offering. Maybe a call to Felix, to see how his love life was doing.

Maybe. And what about the missing uranium? It was just a few days before a North African desert would blossom with flames and explosions, death and destruction, all because of a secret almost six decades old on this stretch of coastline. A well-hidden secret, one that someone was ready to kill for to keep it hidden.

As I reached the edge of my driveway, I stopped thinking for a moment as a heavy weight blasted me across the backs of my legs.

I tripped and fell on the dirt, started rolling and rolling, reaching underneath my coat, grabbed the Beretta as a shape came running after me, and I yelled out, "Freeze, right there, or I blow your damn head off!"

The shape stopped, came closer, formed itself into Keith Emerson. His hands were empty, and he swayed a bit as he stood over me. "You serious?"

I clicked the hammer back on my pistol, the sound of metal on metal quite loud. "That I am."

He stood there for a long moment, still swaying, hands empty, staring down at me, and then he shook his head and went over a few feet and sat down on a boulder marking the edge of the parking lot. He shook his head again. "Damn it. You're not serious, not at all."

I sat up, kept my pistol aimed at him. "What makes you think that?"

He sniffed a few times, and I realized he was weeping. "I was counting on it, just for a moment or two, that you'd splatter me. That you'd end it for me, make me have some quiet nights for once in my life. And now it ain't gonna happen."

Keith crossed his arms and squeezed himself tight, and then started rocking back and forth, murmuring to himself. I got up on my feet and walked over to another boulder, about six feet away from Keith. I sat down and held the pistol down between my legs.

"Why are you here, Keith? Coming through on your threat?"

He slowed his movements, looked over at me. "So I did do that, huh? I threatened you, right?"

"Yes, you did, back at the submarine museum, earlier today."

"Knew it!" he said, his voice triumphant. "Knew it, knew it, and that's why I came here. Took me a bit to track you down. I came here to apologize to you, for threatening you. I don't remember it that well, but when it came to me, I decided to come down and apologize to you, face-to-face."

I touched my own face, where I had scraped it some against the gravel of my driveway. "That's a hell of a way to apologize, by knocking me off my feet."

His back-and-forth movements slowed even more. "Oh, I had a reason for that, a very good reason. You want to hear it?"

"Sure," I said.

"Well, I figured I was here to apologize to you, for what happened up at the museum. But suppose I hadn't done anything wrong to you at the museum? Then my trip here would be a waste of time. And time . . . Lord, how I hate to think of wasting any time, any time at all. So I figured I'd knock you ass over end, and if I hadn't threatened you, then I'd have something to apologize to you for. Make sense?"

I touched my face again. "About as much as anything else has today."

Now he had stopped moving. He said, "I can tell by your look, and by your tone. You think I'm nuts, don't you?"

"No, I—"

"Please don't insult what little intelligence I have left, Mr. Cole," he said. "I know what I am, know quite well. A long time ago I was something else, something to look up to."

"Your dad told me. You were a Marine pilot, on an F/A-18. That must have been something, to fly jets on and off aircraft carriers."

"You have no idea," he said, his voice toneless.

"You're right," I said. "I have no idea."

"It's . . . it's . . . ." He paused, seemed to look over my shoulder. "It's a like a tall pyramid you're climbing, day after day. When you first start out, as a recruit, the pyramid's pretty wide and the steps are real easy, to get up to the next level. Then you become an officer, then you enter flight school. The pyramid gets steeper, the steps narrower. You suck it in and keep on moving, no matter what. Then you fly solo, then you fly jets, then you fly carrier jets . . . The ocean's a big place, Mr. Cole, especially at night when you're looking for a place to land. By then the pyramid's so steep and the steps are so narrow . . . Doesn't take much to fall off."

"Your dad told me a little bit about it. You had an electrical problem in your jet, right?"

He grinned. "Sounds so innocuous, here on the ground, nice and safe, doesn't it? Electrical problem. Like a refrigerator light burned out, or a fuse that needs replacing. Let me tell you what an electrical problem is, my friend. Flying a huge piece of machinery at night, everything in your grasp and under your feet, everything you can control. A flick of the wrist here and you're heading to Oman. Another flick of the wrist, and you're heading to Qatar. All that power. All that authority. In your little hands. And this night, you've done your patrol, you're heading back to the ship, heading back to that couple of acres of moving steel on a wide ocean, heading back to your squadron and your buds."

I kept quiet, letting him talk, now trying to hide the fact that I was still holding the pistol, firm behind my legs. Keith went on. "Amazing thing, from one second to another how things can change. Second one, you're a spit-and-polish Marine aviator, flying a multimillion-dollar piece of machinery. Second two, your electrical equipment fries out. Second three, you're a frightened little child, wondering how you're going to get home and live."

I spoke up, trying to keep my voice calm and not accusatory, not at all. "Did you consider ejecting?"

It looked as if he shivered. "Sure I did. But you've heard stories . . . about guys snapping their spines, breaking their legs, drowning in the water with the parachute wrapped around your head . . . Plus, well, it's hard to explain. There's a sense of pride in what you do. You want to bring that jet home to the carrier. You don't want to dump it in the water and face all that bullshit later on. So. Electrical problem pops up and you go through your training, and flip on the backup battery systems. And you look at your dials, and you can't believe what you see. The battery system is dying. You have just a few minutes to land that plane, before everything fails on you . . . I . . . I'm sorry. I can't go on anymore or I won't sleep at all tonight. Let's just say I got on the carrier and they had to carry me out of the cockpit. And I never flew again. Never."

"What did you do then?"

He shrugged. "I tried a couple of times to get back into my Hornet, and I couldn't do it. My legs would just freeze as I'd walk across the flight deck. Could not move. So I was assigned to desk duty. First tumble off the pyramid. Then I started having the shakes just thinking of everything that could go wrong on the ship. Even in peacetime, military people die all the time, don't they."

"Sure," I said. "Training accidents. Equipment problems. Aircraft collisions."

"You're so very right," he said. "And a two- or three-paragraph story in the newspaper later, and nobody cares anymore. It got so I couldn't stand being on the carrier anymore. All those steam

197

pipes, the live ammunition, jets taking off and landing . . . I started spending more and more time in my bunk staring at the bulkheads, just with the shakes, imagining everything that could go wrong . . . Pretty soon I was shipped back to the States, to a regular base, and after that, I was discharged . . . More and more tumbles off the pyramid."

"The Porter Naval Shipyard," I said. "It must have been just as hard there. All the machinery. Hazardous waste. Radioactive materials. Welding and cutting of metal. You couldn't stay, could you?"

"Nope. Nobody understood, nobody. The world is such a dangerous place, especially when you've been dumped off that pyramid and are down in the mud. Am I right?"

I turned for a moment and looked at my house. Remembered how it had been the first few months I had lived there after my own little tumble off the pyramid, when my little world had been destroyed and people I knew and had loved had been killed. The long hours spent just looking out at the ocean, or, at night, up at the stars. The hurried trips to the bookstore and grocery store, to pick up reading material and food, so I could stay hunkered down in my new home without having to speak to or see anyone.

Oh yes, I knew it well. Living down there at the bottom of the pyramid, living in the fear and mud and squalor. I looked over at Keith, now saw him almost as a brother. We had both been there. I had been lucky enough to fight and find my own path out. This poor ex-Marine, ex-member of a group dedicated to the service of their country, was still a lost soul. I felt a flush of shame, remembering how quickly I had grabbed him and wrestled him to the ground.

I spoke up. "Yes, Keith. You're absolutely right. The world is a dangerous place."

His rocking motion started up again, slowly this time. "I knew it, always knew it. Thanks for agreeing with me. Not everybody else does, not hardly. And the place is getting more and more dangerous, you know. Strange cars. Strange lights. People from afar poking around and asking questions. All looking for something."

I froze, not even daring to breathe, wondering if I was over-reacting to what I had just heard. "Really?" I slowly asked. "You've spotted these things?"

I couldn't see it, but I sensed his smile. "Sure. I'm not stupid, Mr. Cole. If you asked me, I could give you the step-by-step procedure for starting up a General Electric Model 4-A turbofan jet engine for an F/A-18 Hornet without missing a step. I get around. I see things. I see a lot."

"And what have you seen?"

"Strangers. Lots of them. In planes and helicopters and dark cars. All looking for the same thing, all of them asking lots and lots of questions. You too, am I right? Even asking my old man. All hunting the same thing. And you want to know a funny thing? Nobody's asked me a thing. Me, who stands in the shadows, who moves around this entire seacoast without being noticed, who sees things, who's ignored. Nobody's asked me a thing."

The hand holding my pistol was starting to fall asleep, getting the pins-and-needles feeling, but I wouldn't move it, would not disturb the moment. "All right, Keith. I'll ask you. Do you know what everyone's looking for?"

He giggled. "Sure. Ten boxes, metal, sealed with metal pack straps, nine inches by nine inches by nine inches, marked on the outside by a swastika and the phrase 'Eigentum der OKW.' OKW means 'Oberkommando der Wehrmacht.' The German High Command. Sure, I know where it is. I even tried to talk to my dad and he blew me off. Thought I was drunk or something. You think I'm stupid?"

I could no longer hear the ocean or the traffic on Atlantic Avenue or any other damn thing. "No, you are definitely not stupid. Where is it?"

"Around," he said.

"At the shipyard, where you worked?"

"Look," he said, his voice rising up a bit. "It's around, okay?

Why are you asking me so many questions? Are you trying to steal it from me?"

"No, no, not at all," I said, thinking furiously. "Look, did you know there's a reward for those boxes?"

Now I had his attention. "A reward? Are you sure? How much?"

"How much do you need?"

"Hmmm," he said, "that's a question. Do you think the reward could be a weekly stipend? Tax-free?"

Knowing what was going through Laura Reeves's mind right at this moment, I said, "Sure. That wouldn't be a problem."

"Okay."

We sat for a few long moments, until I said, "Okay . . . okay what, Keith?"

"Okay, I'll turn the boxes over. But only to you. You've taken the time to talk to me and I appreciate that. Plus, well, I mean, well, the reward's all mine, right?"

"Absolutely. Turn the boxes over to me, and the reward belongs to you and nobody else."

"Okay."

Another long pause. I took my free hand and rubbed at my face, winced at touching the scrapes from where I had fallen. "Keith, I'm not pushing you or anything. I'm just trying to plan my day here. When you said okay, did you mean you're ready to turn the boxes over to me?"

"Shit, yes, didn't you get that?"

There was a pounding in my chest when I heard that. "Fine. Can we do it now?"

His voice lowered. "Hell, no. Not now."

"Why?" I asked.

" 'Cause it's in a dark place, that's why. A very dark place indeed. And I won't go in a place that's dark, no, sir."

"I could bring some strong floodlights, make it look like it's light."

He shook his head. "Nope. Suppose your lights burn out? Like the batteries on my Hornet? Then where would I be? Nope. Daylight. Tomorrow. That's when we go in. And don't ask me anymore. I'll think you'll be trying to get the reward money."

Despite the emotions racing through me, I was trying to keep my tone nice and calm. "All right. I can see that. Tomorrow it is. What's the best time for you?"

"Ten o'clock," he said firmly. "I get up and watch the morning news shows—I love those girls on the 'Today' show—and then I have my breakfast and wash my face. By ten o'clock, I'll be ready. You can pick me up at my apartment. Fourteen Seward Street in Porter. Apartment twelve. That's a one and a two. You'll remember, right?"

"Sure I'll remember," I said. "But Keith . . . wouldn't it be better if you spent the night here, at my place? You could have my bedroom, I'd make you breakfast and we can watch the 'Today' show together. Wouldn't that work?"

He laughed. "That's a fair offer. And if you were one of the girls on the 'Today' show, I'd take you up on it. But I know my place. I know where the bad things are and what's in the shadows. And if I was at your place, I wouldn't be able to sleep at all. I wouldn't feel right. No, don't you fret. We'll meet tomorrow and you'll get your boxes and I'll get my reward. Fair enough?"

Keith stood up and held out his hand, which I shook. I kept the hand holding my Beretta behind my back. "Fair enough. Tomorrow, ten A.M. Apartment twelve at Fourteen Seward Street. I'll be there."

He started heading out to the parking lot. "So," Keith asked, "what's in those boxes that is so important anyway?"

I thought for a moment. "Something that needs to be in the right hands. Something that could make this world a very dangerous place."

"Okay." And another quick nod. "That's good enough for me. See you tomorrow, Mr. Cole. And oh, one more thing."

"What's that?" I asked, feeling foolish standing there with the pistol still hidden behind my back.

He waved at me. "I'm glad you didn't shoot me. And I'm sorry for the trouble I've caused. I won't drink anything tonight, promise. And you can put your gun away. All right?"

I did just that. "All right. See you tomorrow."

And he didn't answer. He just kept on walking, a vet and a man who had once been in the service of a grateful nation.

I turned and went the short distance home.

CHAPTER SIXTEEN

After cleaning up my face and locking the doors and windows, I sat down to make some phone calls. The first was to Laura Reeves, and once again, she was not available. Gus Turner—ever cheerful, though no doubt still wishing he were fighting the forces of evil in an Iraqi desert—asked if he could help. I said no, having earlier decided that this was between me and Laura. And besides, I wasn't sure how much I could trust Keith. He had seemed coherent and cogent in talking to me about what he knew about the missing uranium. The problem was, I still remembered how he had looked earlier that day, threatening his father at the museum.

Besides, if things did go well, I didn't think Keith would appreciate the extra company while we went out to the so-called "dark place" where the uranium was hidden, and by now, so close to getting the prize, I didn't want to jeopardize anything.

My next call was to Paula Quinn, who wasn't home. I hung up and thought things through again, and then made another call. "Paula, it's Lewis. Look, I know I haven't been the best of friends or companions these past few days. Things are going on that I can't talk about right now, but I do promise I'll explain it as best I can when it's over. And I promise to make it up to you. Honest."

I hung up and then sat for a while, remembering the look on Paula's face when last we talked in the *Chronicle* parking lot. If I really wanted to make it up to her, I should grab some flowers and take-out Chinese and camp out in front of her apartment building on High Street.

Sure, I thought. That'd be a lot of fun. Right up to the point where the mystery sniper blows off my head in front of her, and then decides to kill her for good measure.

Not the kind of relationship that gets written up in *Cosmo*.

Then I made a fourth call, and the person I was looking for wasn't home. So another message was left, and then I sat again, in my empty home. Waiting.

I got up and even though it was pleasant enough, I built a fire in the fireplace, and then rustled up dinner. My insides were still tense and quivery from the day's events, so I had a couple of scrambled eggs and mixed in some cheddar cheese and bits of ham, with two pieces of toast on the side. I ate in the living room, in front of the fireplace, and the night dragged on as I tried to get tired, tried to get sleepy.

But a lot of thoughts were racing through my mind like cheetahs, coming and going, and mostly I thought of an ancient ocean halfway across the world. I imagined the ships in formation, steaming to the southwest, heading for a place that we had fought over many times before, once almost two hundred years ago. Shores of Tripoli and all that. Plans were being prepared, missiles aimed, and aircraft armed. And in the desert, men and women were at work or at sleep, not knowing that they were days away from being obliterated.

All because of what had been lost here in my own land, decades ago.

I stretched out on the couch, watched the flames flicker and begin to die away. Years ago, when I had worked at the Pentagon, I had experienced the same feeling. A hollowed-out, gaunt feeling, where you sense forces and people are on the move, all because of what you have or haven't done, and you are powerless to stop what is about to happen. I swallowed, felt the taste of fear. It had been easier, back then in the Pentagon. At least I had been part of a section, part of a department, part of an entire defense structure. Back then I had a lot of other shoulders at hand to share the burden.

But not tonight. I felt terribly alone, terribly responsible.

The phone rang, jangling me up in terror. Again and again it rang, and I answered it.

"You rang?" the voice on the other end said.

"Yes," I said. "I need to see you. I . . . I need some help."

"All right. When?"

"Tomorrow morning."

"An early breakfast suit you?"

"Yes, it does."

"All right." And after a time and place had been settled, I hung up the phone and lay down on the couch again. I stared at the dying flames for a while, and then went upstairs and got a thin down comforter. Back on the couch I went and I pulled the comforter over me. I think I fell asleep, for when my eyes looked at the fireplace again, the logs were dead, charred black, and light was coming in through the shades on the windows facing east, to the ocean. I lay there still, listening to the sounds of the waves, the killer waves, waiting for all of us.

At the Breakfast Nook on Atlantic Avenue in Wallis, we sat in a rear booth, Felix Tinios across from me. The windows in this tiny restaurant usually have a great view of the ocean just above Wallis Harbor, but a heavy rainstorm was obscuring almost everything. The place was doing a reasonable business this early in tourist season, and on such a rainy day. Felix had a cheese-and-vegetable omelette that seemed about the size of my head, while I made do with scrambled eggs, yet again. My cholesterol level was no doubt taking a serious hit this week, but I had more important things to worry about.

Felix sighed as he drank from a big mug of coffee. "You've had an interesting few days. You want to remind me again why you haven't packed up and taken a flight to Bermuda for a week or two?"

"Because I feel responsible, that's why."

He shook his head. "That's the way the feds operate," he said. "It's practically a seduction, the way they get you into their power and control. Smartest thing you could do is to tell them to go to hell, and watch out for number one."

"Sure," I said. "Then they'll take my house, my job and my savings account. Maybe even put me in jail to round everything off."

"Yeah, and you'll still be breathing. I'd miss not having you around, but if you did get into prison, I'd make sure to visit you at least once a month, and I'd make sure you got protected on the inside."

I munched on the last piece of toast. "For a moment, I almost took you seriously."

"You should've, because I was quite serious. Sure I can't change your mind?"

"Positive."

Another sigh. He reached into his coat pocket, took out a cell phone not much bigger than a pack of cigarettes. "Here you go. Are you sure you know all the nice little features of this before I pass it over to you?"

"Yes."

"Good," he said, sliding it across the breakfast table. "Because it's quite special and quite expensive, and Uncle Felix doesn't want to have to go through all the time and trouble to replace it if you lose it."

"Thanks," I said, picking up the phone and putting it in an inside pocket of my jacket. "I won't lose it. How's things with you and Mickey?"

"Great," he said, wiping his hands on a napkin. "We're seeing each other for lunch today, but I'll be available if you need anything. All right?"

"Fine," I said. "Look, Felix, I really—"

He waved a hand. "Spare me the thanks and good wishes. First, it's good to stretch my mind and abilities. You stay stagnant, you rust. Second, you can pick up the check for breakfast and we'll call it even. Deal?"

"Deal," I said, and when the waitress dropped off the check not five minutes later, I left a ten-dollar bill on the tabletop and we went outside, to the front steps. The rain was still coming down steadily and I drew my collar up. Felix stood next to me as we looked out over the parking lot. "Remind me again how much you're getting paid for this little adventure?"

"Not a thing."

He shook his head. "A hell of a way to run a business. If I pulled something like that . . . well, what's this?"

A black Lincoln Town Car with Massachusetts license plates came into the restaurant parking lot and pulled to the side, away from the parking spots. The windshield wipers moved back and forth in a quick rhythm, and the driver flashed the car's head-lights at us, and then honked the horn. The window rolled down and a heavyset man in front beckoned at us.

I said, "A friend of yours?"

Felix seemed to squint his eyes. "You know . . . hold on, I'll be right back."

He sprinted across the parking lot, splashing through two puddles, before he reached the driver's side. Felix leaned over, hunched up against the rain, and talked to the driver. He motioned with his hands a few time, and then sprinted back, as the Town Car sped off and made a right onto Atlantic Avenue. When Felix came back up to the steps, his face was flushed and his eyes were dark. He didn't look particularly happy.

"Jerk," he murmured, stamping the water off his shoes.

"What was that all about?"

"Jesus, look how wet I got . . ." He wiped his face with a handkerchief and said, "From the Town Car's plates and the way the driver looked, I thought it was an acquaintance of mine from down south. But no, it was a lost tourist, looking for the fabulous dining room of your neighborhood hotel."

"The Lafayette House?"

Felix blew his nose. "The one and only. So the guy honks at us and expects me to come over in the rain and give him detailed directions on where he can go for a nice hot brunch, all the while sitting fat and dry in his car."

I thought over what I had just seen and said, "But he turned right."

"Huh?"

"The Town Car turned right, heading north. He should have turned left, and gone south. To Tyler Beach."

"Yeah, well, I wasn't feeling in a particularly charitable mood and when he started bugging me about where the Lafayette place was, I gave him detailed and firm directions that should, if he's lucky, bring him to the Porter Town Dump in about an hour. You all set?"

The rain seemed to be slowing down. "About as set as I'll ever be. And you?"

Now he smiled. "You know what I say. Every day you're alive and breathing is a good day." He gently tapped me on the shoulder. "And making sure you end the day alive and breathing is even better."

"Thanks for the advice."

"Well, it's free."

"Sometimes that's the best kind," I said, and I headed off to my Ford.

The rain stopped as I made my way north. I checked the dashboard clock of the Explorer as I headed up I-95 to Porter, now feeling a bit of a buzz of excitement, thinking that maybe everything could be wrapped up before lunchtime. It was quarter of ten and I would be in Porter in just a couple of minutes to meet up with Keith. From there, if he had kept his promise to be home and sober, it would just be a short time indeed to get the missing uranium and make that wonderful phone call to Laura Reeves.

I got off at the Porter traffic circle, and after some nimble driving through the rotary I was in a part of Porter that the tourist dollars had passed by. There were a couple of brick factory build-ings, shuttered up and closed, the windows broken and doors boarded over. A few abandoned cars, resting on flat tires, were scattered along the narrow street. The apartment buildings here were built close together, with full clotheslines flapping in the breeze from the porches on each of the three floors. Knowing the history of this city, I knew these buildings had been tossed up around the turn of the nineteenth century for the immigrant population coming in to work in the mills and shops. A century later, these buildings had hardly changed.

I made it onto Seward Street and slowed down until I found number 14, where I stopped the Ford and switched off the engine. Number 14 was four stories tall and built like one large white box, with tiny windows that didn't even have shutters. I got out and walked across the street, noting the crumpled beer cans and other trash in the gutter. A couple of blocks away were places where tourists bought five-dollar cups of coffee and designer T-shirts that could pay my grocery bill for a month, and for all the differences between that place and here, I could have been on Mars.

The door to the foyer rolled back with no problem, the spring being broken. Small black mailboxes on the walls, overflowing trash cans, and a bicycle missing its front wheel cluttered the entranceway. I went upstairs, hearing the noise of a television as somebody listened to one of these mid-morning talk shows that—hard to believe—featured guests who had even stranger stories to tell about their lives than I did. The stairs and the hallways smelled of wet carpeting and disinfectant, and then I found number 12, up on the third floor.

I knocked on the door. No answer.

"Keith?" I called out. "It's Lewis Cole. It's ten o'clock. You in there?"

Still no answer. I checked my watch, saw that it was running, and then turned around, looked up and down the hallway. Nobody. I rubbed at my face, knocked again.

No answer. Damn.

I was debating in my mind whether to wait up here in the hallway, or downstairs in my Ford, when I reached down and gave the doorknob a spin.

And it spun quite smoothly, and the door to number 12 opened right up.

"Keith?" I called out. Still no reply. I softly stepped in and closed the door behind me.

209

Then I started breathing through my mouth. The odor in the small apartment was overwhelming, even though a window in the kitchen that overlooked the fire escape was half open. I stepped in, looked to the left and then the right. Clear. To the right was a small living room. The carpeting was a yellow shag type that had been popular back at a time when most dance floors had spinning ceiling bulbs. The furniture included a heavy wooden coffee table, a black leather couch repaired in several places with gray duct tape, and a television set. There were also walls filled with bookshelves, paperbacks clustered one upon the other, spilling out even on the floor. Magazines and newspapers were piled up in tottering piles that looked as if they would collapse if a heavy truck drove by.

Before me was the kitchen and I stepped in closer. Dishes and spoons and glassware were submerged in a pool of yellow water. The table was scarred with drink rings and cigarette burns, and I went in and looked to the right, past a narrow door. Bathroom. Everything had been empty so far. My chest felt tight, as if I had raced up those stairs with concrete blocks balanced on my shoulders.

"Keith?" I called out, my voice sounding quite small in this empty apartment.

I retraced my steps into the kitchen, glanced over to the left, where there was another door. "Keith?" No answer. My chest felt even tighter as I nudged the door open with my foot, leaned in and looked around.

Empty.

I stepped in farther, sniffing at the air. It smelled metallic in here, as if someone had been burning some odd type of incense. Bed in the center, sheets and blankets piled up at the end. A bureau with a small black-and-white television set balanced on top. More paperback books on shelves. I spared them a glance. Fantasy and science fiction. Sure. Made sense. Seeing how trembling and nervous Keith had been last night, in the Lafayette House parking lot, I could see how books about fantasy worlds would be attractive. I stepped around the bed, heading to another bureau. There were photos on the bureau, of a younger

Keith in his Marine dress blues, and Keith in the cockpit of an F/A-18 Hornet. I wondered quickly if he kept those photos displayed to torture himself on what he had once been, or to show him how he could someday recover what had been right within him.

I was still wondering when something grabbed my ankle.

I fell back with a shout, stumbling into the bureau, making one of the photos fall over, and there was a gurgling and wheezing sound and a faint voice. "Lewis? Is that really you?"

I looked down at the bedding where a hand had emerged, soiled and brown with . . . with blood. I knelt down and picked up the bed and the mattress and box spring and managed with one large shove to move the damn thing to the other side of the room, and Keith Emerson looked up at me, blinking hard, his other hand clasped tight against his throat. Blood was oozing out between his fingers and dribbling down his wrist and falling upon the soiled white T-shirt he was wearing and he shook his head and whispered again, "Lewis . . ."

"Hold it right there," I said, standing up. "I'll call—"

"No," he said, grabbing on to my ankle tight again. "Wait . . . I've got to tell you . . . the battery room . . . that's what caused it all . . . a . . . a . . . the battery room . . ."

I knelt down again and said, "What battery room? The one on your aircraft carrier? Is that what you mean? Keith, who did this to you? Who attacked you?"

He looked up at me, grinning despite the wound in his throat, the blood still oozing about his fingers, staining his beard and even his teeth. The wheezing and rattling seemed to echo in my ears and I leaned down to him.

"Keith? What do you mean? The batteries on your fighter plane? What battery room? Keith?"

He looked up at me, still smiling. His eyes fluttered and I called out again. "Keith? Damn it, hold on."

I stood up and fumbled inside my coat, remembering the cellphone that Felix had given me, and I took it out and unsnapped the cover. And as I started punching the numbers for 911, I paused. The room was quiet. The gurgling and the wheezing had stopped. Keith Emerson, a volunteer for service to his country and one of the very few who could call themselves carrier fighter pilots, lay there unmoving, an ugly gash in his throat.

I stood still, looking down at the body. No movement. Keith had been right. Time wasted on making a phone call for an ambulance wouldn't have made any difference. And if I had done that, I would have missed those last words.

A battery room. That's what caused it. A battery room.

"Damn it," I whispered down to the body. "I thought you said you wouldn't be drinking again."

I realized I was still holding the telephone. I could make a call to the Porter Police Department, get things rolling over here, get the investigation started. I might not be able to avenge this poor guy's death, so maybe it was time for the professionals. I moved to the phone again and was going to make the call, and then I stopped. I thought it through. Detective Joe Stevens and the State Police coming in. Lots of questions at the scene. Interrogation in a smoky little room at the Porter Police Department. Even more interrogations, questions after questions, hours being spent answering their demands.

Hours and hours. While a carrier task force in the Mediterranean continued steaming to the southwest, ready to make war.

I put the phone back in my coat, wiped at my eyes, which had suddenly gotten moist. I backed out of the bedroom and went into the kitchen. I went to the door and thought quickly, and pulled out a handkerchief. I wiped the doorknob and used the piece of cloth to open the door. Out in the hallway, I closed the door softly, wiped down the doorknob again, and walked quickly downstairs. Nobody had seen me, not yet, anyway, and when I got into my Explorer I started up the engine and smoothly drove away.

I went a couple of blocks and found a small convenience store. I pulled into the parking lot just as my legs started trembling uncontrollably, and I stayed there, my eyes wet yet again. I wiped at them with my handkerchief, and then I—

The chiming of the cell phone startled me so much that my head shot up and struck the roof of the Ford. I fumbled again getting the phone out, and after unsnapping the cover and extending the little antenna, I managed to croak out a "Hello?"

"Yeah," said the male voice on the other end. "Is Freddy there?"

"Who?"

"Freddy."

"Sorry, there's nobody here by that name."

" 'Kay," said the voice. "Sorry."

After shutting the phone off and putting it back in my coat, I started up the Ford and went back into Porter traffic. I had at least one more place to go before calling up Laura Reeves and letting loose with everything I knew.

At the Porter Submarine Museum, a group of people were clustered around the entranceway. Two tour buses were in the lot, diesel engines running. Some of the people were pressed up against the glass windows and doorway, peering in with their hands clustered about their faces. I drove by slowly and saw the two bus drivers, each with a cellphone up to his ear.

On the doorway was a little red-and-black sign that said CLOSED. I stopped and looked around the parking lot. Jack Emerson's little pickup truck was missing.

"Damn this morning," I said, and I drove out, leaving the disappointed tourists behind me.

It took some long minutes for me to find this particular house, for the guide I had the last time wasn't with me. I had to go to two convenience stores to find a phone book and get the right street address, and then I went to a gas station to buy a local map of Porter. By then I was sweating from nervousness and fear, and the weight of my pistol digging into my side wasn't even close to being a comfort. About a half hour after I had left the submarine museum, I was on the right street in Porter, driving slowly, checking out the houses. There. Small two-story home with the sagging couch and rusting refrigerator on the front porch.

And parked in the driveway an old pickup truck with the bumper stickers that still said bravely: SUPPORT THE PORTER SUBMARINE MUSEUM and THERE ARE TWO KINDS OF BOATS: SUBS AND TARGETS. I parked halfway down the block and got out, walking quickly up the street, dreading what I was about to discover. Up to the front porch, where I spent a couple of minutes ringing the doorbell and rapping on the door. No answer. I took out the cell phone and placed a call to the number I had lifted from the phone book. Thirty rings later I gave up. I leaned over and peered through the windows, which were blocked by white curtains. Nothing.

I looked around and then got off the front porch, and went out to the rear. The yard was tiny, with a small brick patio that had a picnic table and a gas grill covered by a plastic tarp. At the rear entrance the door was open, leaving a storm door closed. It was fastened shut, but only by a hook-and-eye clasp. From my wallet I took out a credit card and slid it up through the crack between the door and doorjamb, and the clasp popped free. I opened the door and called out, "Jack? Are you home? It's Lewis, Lewis Cole."

No reply.

The entranceway opened into a laundry room, and from there, the kitchen. Unlike his son's, Jack's kitchen was clean and tidy. No dishes in the sink, nothing on the table except a napkin holder and a small collection of bills and letters. From the kitchen I went into the living room. Typical couch and chairs and television, and books, lots of books, piled up neatly on shelves. Most were hardcover and almost all had something to do with World War II or the Navy or submarines. A few newspapers were piled neatly at one end of the couch. The house smelled dusty but tidy.

"Jack?"

In the living room was a door that led down to the cellar. The cellar had a dirt floor—not uncommon in a lot of old New England houses—and it held some trunks and a workbench and a dusty collection of rakes, shovels, and an old push lawnmower. The ceiling was low and I was hunched over as I walked about. There was a *Playboy* wall calendar from 1972 over the workbench and no sign of a human being.

Back up on the first floor, I spotted the stairs and then released my 9-mm. from my holster and started going up to the second floor. I stayed to the side of the stairway, so my weight wouldn't cause the steps to creak, which was stupid, since I had been calling out Jack's name and rambling through the house for the past ten minutes. But it was comforting to do that, and comfort was mighty hard to find this day.

Top of the stairs, a bathroom. Empty. What looked like a guest bedroom to the right. Nothing. Closet empty, bed just covered with a bedspread, and a quick check showed nobody under the bed.

Which left one other bedroom, where the door was closed.

I walked over, the hand holding the Beretta trembling a bit. With a handkerchief covering my other hand, I opened up the door and said in a normal voice, "Jack? You in there?"

Silence, except for the slow creak of the door opening up on the hinges. I knelt down and looked in, not wanting to give anybody a quick and easy target. The door opened up to reveal a carefully made bed with a white bedspread. I scurried in, saw that the place was empty. I took another quick look under the bed and saw a few dustballs. The thumping in my chest started to ease off and I had a quick look into the closet. A spare cane, shoes, pants and shirts and two suits, carefully hung up.

I replaced my pistol into my holster, sat on the edge of Jack's bed. "Damn it, where are you?" I said aloud.

On the other side of the room was a large window that overlooked the tiny backyard, and next to the window was a large oak chest covered by a lace cloth. There were three framed photos up there. One showed a very young Jack Emerson in the Navy, and the other showed Jack in an ill-fitting tuxedo and a woman in a white wedding dress. Both Jack and his bride were smiling widely.

The other photo was similar to one I had seen earlier, at Keith's apartment. It showed Keith in his flight gear, standing in front of an F/A-18 Hornet on the deck of an aircraft carrier. Again I was drawn to the man's face and look, seeing the cocky self-confidence of a jet fighter pilot ready to take on the world.

A battery room, he had said. A battery room.

I looked around the sparse room and then, for no reason at

first, I found myself looking at the photo of Keith. It was similar, but it was different from the one I had seen at his apartment. For in this one, it looked as if Keith was ready to go out on a mission, for he had his pilot's helmet underneath his right arm, like a soccer ball or basketball. The helmet had jagged lightning stripes along the side, and like most military pilots, it had his nickname or call sign emblazoned on the front, in big bold letters—

Now I was standing in front of the bureau, holding the photo close up in my hands, not even remembering the few steps I took from the bed to this bureau, to this photo, which showed a young Keith Emerson when he was a fighter jock and an air god, master of his universe, holding his helmet, showing the world what his nickname was, what his call sign was in the pantheon of his fellow air gods:

WHIZZER.

CHAPTER SEVENTEEN

On the way south back to Tyler, I had called Laura Reeves twice—using the cell phone supplied by Felix—and had spoken to Gus Turner both times. "She's still out and about," he had said during the last call. "Anything I can help you with?"

"No," I had said, not wanting to explain over the very-eavesdroppable airwaves what I had been up to. "When I get home I'll come over and wait for her."

"Oh," he had replied. "Well, if you want . . ."

"Sorry, Gus," I had said, "this call's breaking up," and I had hung up on him.

Now I was on the streets of Tyler, heading home, trying to keep both my speed and my emotions in check. Coming down on the interstate, I had easily exceeded the speed limit by twenty miles an hour in my rush to get home, but after taking the Tyler exit, I realized I had to take it easy. I had found out who Whizzer was. The man identified as Whizzer had even told me that he knew where the uranium was hidden. True, his last message was cryptic and made no sense—a battery room—but it was a hell of a lot more than I and Laura Reeves and the other NEST members had known at the start of this morning. If Laura had the resources that she said were now coming to her—a second NEST team, another squadron of FBI agents—then the chase would be on for real. Poor dead Keith Emerson's life would be dissected and examined and traced, and everybody he knew and every place he had visited would be checked and rechecked. He had been the contact man for the Libyan. He knew what the missing uranium looked like. And he said it was in a dark place, a place that he was afraid of.

Put enough investigators and agents on that set of information, and I was sure the uranium would be found within a day or so. And with such good progress being made, maybe that carrier group would get other orders in the next several hours, orders that would mean a great number of people—strangers all—would live to see another day.

I was on Atlantic Avenue and drove by the Lafayette House, and through the hotel's parking lot to my private driveway. As I got closer to my house, I saw that someone was waiting for me on the front steps, somebody who stood up and waited for me to park my Ford in the nearby garage.

Detective Diane Woods, Tyler Police Department.

I came out of the garage and Diane nodded at me as I came closer. "You having an okay day?"

Let's see, one missing old man, one man who just died an hour or so ago in front of me. I shook my head. "I've had better."

"So have I," she said. "I got a call a little while ago from Joe Stevens, detective up in Porter. All kinds of hell are breaking loose up there. Seems like a museum director is missing, and his son has been found dead in his apartment. Detective Stevens said you've had contact with both of these individuals. True?"

"Quite true," I said.

It had gotten cloudy again and the wind was picking up. Diane had on a knee-length leather coat that she was holding closed by using her hands in her pockets. "He also said somebody took a pot shot at you the other day, and that the dead guy—called Keith—had threatened you just beforehand. Also true?"

"Yes, also true," I said, now standing in front of her by the entrance to my home.

She gently kicked at one of the many rocks that littered the landscape that really couldn't be called a lawn. Diane said, "Now, in reply to all this, I told Detective Stevens that you were a trustworthy, honorable man, and that while you might have been on the fringes of whatever was going on up there, that you wouldn't have done anything criminal. That you wouldn't have anything to do with the death of that guy or the disappearance of his father. That he should trust me on this. Is that also true?"

"You're batting a thousand," I said, thinking now of that damn carrier task force, trying to remember what time it was in the Mediterranean at this hour. Was it still dark and would they attack in the next few hours?

A small nod. "Then that's the first time in days that I've batted anything well. Look, don't make me look like an idiot, all right? Get in there and call up Detective Stevens and go on and see him. Clear everything up. I went out some distance to do some favors for you. Don't make me regret it."

"I won't."

"Good." And then she added quietly, "Of course, next few days, it might not make one hell of a difference."

"Story coming out in the paper about you?"

"Three more days. On a Friday, most popular day in the week for newspapers. Make sure it gets a lot of good coverage. Ain't I lucky?"

Off in the distance, the faint sounds of thunder approaching. "Maybe something will happen between now and then. Paula Quinn might find something else to report about, something that will bump your story into the dead file."

Now she smiled. "You still trying to do the best for your friends, aren't you?"

"Always."

She looked at her watch. "Time to get going, my friend. Look, let's get together in a couple of days for lunch or something. Maybe you could give me some advice on how to market my skills."

I smiled at her, still cooling my heels. "Lunch sounds good, and don't be so quick about worrying to market anything. Okay?"

Diane didn't reply, just waved a hand in my direction as she trudged back up the hill to the parking lot. I waited a decent interval of about a second or two before I went into my house.

Inside, as I was taking my coat off, I had about the third or fourth coronary of the day as that damn cell phone started ringing again, making me drop the coat on the floor. I got down on my knees and pulled the phone free. "Hello?"

"Yeah," said the male voice on the other end. "Is Tony there?"

"Who?"

"Tony."

Jesus, of all the times . . . "Sorry, there's nobody here by that name."

"'Kay," said the voice. "Sorry."

I snapped the phone shut so hard that I was sure I had broken it—and wouldn't Felix be displeased—and then I went over to my own phone and the answering machine that glowed steady with a solitary "1." I hit "play" and Laura Reeves's voice filled my living room: "Lewis? It's Laura. Understand that you're trying to get ahold of me, but in about ten minutes I'm going to be in a helicopter and fairly unreachable. Look, talk to Gus. He can handle anything you've got. That's what he's there for. All right? Talk to you when I get back on the ground."

I stopped the answering machine and went into the kitchen, realizing I was starved but also wasn't very hungry. An odd combination, I realized, but there you go. I had a banana and a Granny Smith apple, and a large glass of water. I felt constricted, closed in. Opening the sliding glass doors, I went out onto the deck, looking out to the ocean and to the wooded hills of Samson Point. This was where it had all started just a few days ago, when I had been out here in the middle of the night to see a space shuttle go overhead. I wondered how the mission was going, and I had a feeling it was going much better than Laura's.

I looked out to the ocean, but for some reason my gaze returned to Samson Point. Storm clouds were moving in again, after the rain showers of this morning. The wind was stronger, making me shiver, and I rubbed at my arms and kept looking at the nature preserve. That's where it had started. Right there, with the Libyan agent being found dead in the parking lot.

A battery room, that's what Keith Emerson had said to me.

A battery room.

A. Battery. Room.

I rubbed at my eyes and looked at the trees and the low hills, hiding the bunkers and gun emplacements and tunnels and—

I turned and went back into the house, and upstairs to my office. My fingers flew across the bookshelves until I found a slender volume that I remembered reading a couple of years ago. Back downstairs, I went to my phone and dialed for across the way, and Gus Turner came back on the line. "Yes, what is it?"

"Gus, it's Lewis Cole," I said. "Is Laura there?"

A slow sigh. "No, she's not. She's on another reconnaissance mission. Look, what do you have? I'm pretty busy over here."

I couldn't help it, I was smiling. "How does this sound? I know who Whizzer is, and I know where the uranium's hidden. Is that good enough for you?"

A pause, making me wonder if the phone line had suddenly broken, and then he whispered, "You better not be joking."

"I'm not. I guess I should come over there, right?"

"Jesus, you better believe it."

I hung up and grabbed my coat and looked at my Beretta and the shoulder holster hanging in the closet. I shrugged, took my weapon and holster, and pulled it over my shoulders. As I was getting my coat on, my phone rang. I looked over and thought for a moment, and then waited a few more rings, until the answering machine clicked on. As my outgoing message did what it was supposed to do, I walked over to the machine, to see if it was a hang-up, my threatening caller, Laura Reeves or Gus, or just someone trying to get me to change my long-distance carrier.

Click. A woman's voice. "Lewis? Are you there? Pick up, will you."

Paula Quinn. Damn. I looked at my watch and imagined

again that carrier task force moving into position, getting ready to launch death in a half dozen ways.

"Lewis? Pick up, will you? I really need to talk to you. Really."

I looked down at the book I had in my hand, *A History of Samson Point Coast Artillery Station,* and then turned on my heel and walked out the door. As I closed the door behind me, I heard her quiet voice, "Oh, okay, please call me, okay?"

Sure, I thought, walking up my dirt driveway. Soon as I can. Honest.

One of the NEST guards, Clem, was standing inside the hotel room with the door barely ajar, probably to make sure I wasn't abducted as I made my way down the hallway. He opened the door wider and called out, "He's here, Gus."

I went in, wrinkled my nose again at the smell. When these folks moved out of here in a day or two, the staff of the Lafayette House were going to have their hands full. They'd probably have to borrow some decontamination gear from the nuclear power plant at Falconer down the coast.

Gus looked up at me from his chair at the long conference room table, a nervous smile on his face. "I got a call into Laura and she said, 'Congratulations, Lewis, and I owe you dinner.' She'll be back here in about a half hour, but she told me to get right on it. And another thing she told me, too."

"What's that?" I said, pulling a chair out and sitting at the table.

He motioned to Clem standing by the door, his large hands clasped in front of him. "She also told me that if you were playing games with us, that I should have Clem kill you and dump your weighted body in the ocean. And I don't think she was kidding."

"And I don't care if she was or wasn't," I said. "Because I got the real deal. Look. Whizzer was one Keith Emerson. His dad is the curator of the submarine museum up in Porter. I went there to check on any leads he might have about Navy Yard retirees who might have been around when the U-boat was brought into Porter Harbor."

Gus said, "We jumped on those retirees, first thing we did

when we set up shop here. Why did you go to that museum? Why not the retiree's association?"

I thought about the hesitation I had before, decided it didn't make any sense anymore. "Well, there was one other thing, too."

Gus was writing furiously on a yellow legal pad. "And what was that?"

"Remember the first time you met me, Gus?"

He looked up from his scribbling. "Sure. The night the operative's body was found."

I nodded. "Besides the two cops and the EMTs, I was one of the first ones there. I looked at the body in the front seat of the car. The guy was wearing a button on the lapel of his suit coat. I didn't think much of it, and later, when Laura showed me the photos you guys took there, the button was missing. I guess it had fallen off or been removed."

"Go on," Gus said. "I wasn't in charge of removing and ID'ing the body, so I can't help you there."

"Well, I found out later that the button is used to control admission at the Porter Submarine Museum. And the curator remembered someone matching the description of the Libyan visiting there, the day he arrived here and later got killed. So obviously he was there to meet somebody—the curator's son. Gus, the son, was a Marine aviator a few years back, before being medically discharged. His call sign was Whizzer."

That seemed to get even Clem's attention, for he seemed to be leaning his large bulk closer into the room to hear better. "Whizzer," Gus said, his eyes bright with excitement. "After all these weeks . . . where is he now?"

"He's dead."

Gus blinked hard. "He's *what*?"

"He's dead. I went to meet him this morning, because he told me last night he knew where the uranium was hidden, even what it looks like. And before I got there to meet him, somebody took a knife to his neck. But he managed to tell me something before he lost consciousness. He said what caused everything was a battery room."

"Hold on," he said, sitting up straighter in his chair. "You were meeting with someone who said he knew where the uranium was, and didn't tell Laura or anybody else here?"

I shot back, "We can discuss my investigatory techniques later, Gus. The thing is, he said a battery room. That's what caused it. A battery room."

He glared at me. "That doesn't make sense."

"No, it doesn't," I agreed. "Because I was hearing him wrong. He wasn't saying 'a battery room.' He was trying to say, 'Battery A room.'"

I slid the book across to him. "Look at pages fifty and fifty-one. A schematic design of a gun emplacement at the Samson Point nature preserve, which was once a coast artillery station. One of the batteries was known as Battery A. Your Libyan was killed within a hundred yards of that gun emplacement. That's a hell of a coincidence, isn't it?"

He opened the book up and looked at the drawings, looked at me, and then went back to the book. "An underground vault, covered with yards of concrete and dirt . . . no wonder none of our detection equipment could spot it." He closed the book. "This Keith Emerson. Did you report it to the police?"

"No," I said.

That really got his attention. "Why the hell not?"

"Because I didn't do it, and about the only lead I could give the Porter cops was the possibility that another Libyan agent in-country did it. And if I started talking to the cops, I wouldn't be here, letting you in on what I just found out. And that wouldn't help you guys get the uranium to beat the deadline, would it."

He whistled. "Jesus, you're a cold one."

"Only when the circumstances count. Plus, there's the matter of Keith's dad."

"The museum curator? What about him?"

"He's missing. The museum's closed up and he's not home."

Gus looked over at Clem as if seeking reassurance. "It sounds like the Libyans are here and are definitely playing for keeps."

I said, "Look, shouldn't we saddle up and get going? The nature preserve is all of a ten-minute drive away."

Gus slowly slid the book back to me. "Procedurally, we shouldn't. We should wait for Laura to get back, to get more reinforcements along the way. We should have a meeting, design our options, our game plan, and draw a map so that everybody knows what they're doing."

I stared at Gus's tired eyes. "So what are you telling me?"

He grinned. "Fuck procedures. Let's get the hell out there."

Clem and I went out first, and as we walked down the hallway to the elevator, Gus called out after us, saying, "One more call. I'll meet you at the car."

Inside the elevator I looked over at Clem, who was standing as if he were all alone, hands clasped in front of him, eyes looking straight ahead. I said, "Clem, have I ticked you off lately, or in some previous life?"

"What do you mean?" he said, thereby doubling the number of words he had ever said to me.

"You don't talk, you don't smile, you don't do much of anything when I'm around," I said. "I'm just curious what's going on."

He didn't move. "I do lots of things. I spotted that you were carrying the moment you came in the room. I heard every word you and Gus Turner said. I also kept watch on the door. That's what I do. It's my job. Besides . . ."

Now he looked over at me, and his face seemed to soften. "It's just a job, all right? I'm tired of being cooped up here all day and all week long . . . I miss my wife and kids and grandkids. I'm retired Marine Corps, put my thirty in, and I still can't make it with my pension. So here I am. I'm doing my job, and in a year or two, when we've socked away enough money, it's back home to Pensacola and I'll never go anywhere again. You satisfied now?"

Luckily, by then the elevator had stopped and we were out in the lobby of the Lafayette House. "Not a question of being satisfied. Just wanting to know."

"Well, all I want to know is when I can get home again."

"Soon," I said. "If what I think is going to happen is going to happen, it'll be soon."

As promised, Gus caught up with us in the parking lot, as we made our way to a dark blue Ford LTD, parked in the area behind the hotel usually reserved for employees. He had on a dark leather coat that looked warm enough for the cooling weather that was heading our way.

"Okay, procedures or not, I made another call," he said, tossing a set of car keys to Clem. "We've got a crew of FBI agents coming down from Porter. They should get there about five minutes after we do. Just in case our friendly Libyans are having a cookout in the parking lot, I don't want to be outnumbered."

"Sounds good," I said, climbing into the backseat of the LTD. Gus sat up forward and Clem got behind the wheel of the car, and in a matter of seconds we were heading north.

Along the way Gus tossed some more questions back at me, and I did my best to answer them. "Samson Point started off as government property back in the eighteen hundreds. They had a Lifeboat Rescue Station there, which served ships coming in and out of Porter Harbor. Lots of sinkings took place out there over the years. Then, during the Spanish-American War, the government got concerned that the big naval yard at Porter and the harbor were vulnerable to attack. So they started building the coastal artillery base here, and at other places up the coast and in Maine, to guard the harbor and its approaches."

"So, did the Spanish ever get here?"

"Only as POWs," I said. "War was over by the time the first concrete was poured. But the place expanded during World War One and World War Two. They had some of the largest guns in the world emplaced up there. Story is, whenever they test-fired the cannon, windows would shatter in houses up and down the seacoast."

"What happened after the war?" Gus asked, as Clem kept on heading us north. The clouds were thicker, making the sky look as if it were ten minutes away from dusk. Clem put the wipers on intermittent to clear the windshield as we got closer to the park entrance. To our left marshland stretched out to a line of woods in the west, and to our right the ocean view was mostly blocked by a berm of rocks and earth.

"Eventually the military decided that threats weren't going to come from raiding warships, but from aircraft. The cannons were taken away and the place was turned into an early-warning radar station, looking for Soviet bombers. But when ICBMs started getting deployed in the sixties, the place was finally closed down, and then eventually was turned over to the state as a park. The cannons and barracks are gone, but there are still heavy concrete emplacements, and the underground service rooms and tunnels to service them."

Gus turned in the seat, admiration in his voice. "Man, you do know this place. I know Laura has mentioned having you join us as a consultant when this gig is up. You interested?"

I folded my arms. "Not today, thank you."

Gus laughed and flipped through the small book I had brought over. "What do you think happened, then, that the uranium ended up there?"

"The war was over in Europe," I said. "People around here, they had worked long hours and weekends turning out submarines and other weapons to fight the Germans. Then . . . it seemed like peace was at hand. I read that when those four U-boats were brought in here after they surrendered, the yard workers stripped every imaginable souvenir item from them, anything that could be unbolted and taken off. Sure, there was tight security, but you had thousands of workers there, most of whom knew that they'd be out of a job once Japan surrendered. Things might have gotten loose. Who knows. The uranium itself disappeared and the government, to cover up such an embarrassment, did just that. How it got resurrected all these years later . . . who knows."

Clem slowed the LTD down and made a right into the park entrance. A large wooden beam that served as a gate was across the entrance. WINTER HOURS. PARK OPEN FROM 9 A.M. TO 4 P.M. I checked my watch. It was four-oh-five.

Gus said in disbelief, "Winter hours? Hell, it's spring!"

"State parks around here have just two seasons. Summer and winter."

"Maybe so," Gus said, "but the federal government has its own idea on timekeeping. Clem, think you can work some magic?"

Clem eased his large bulk out of the car. "Back in a minute."

The ex-Marine went up to the gate and pulled a small leather case from his coat pocket and went to work on the lock and chain holding the gate closed. Gus said admiringly, "That guy hardly ever talks about what he's done and where he's gone, but I can tell you one thing. I'm sure as hell glad he's on our side."

Clem undid the chain and swung open the gate, and Gus slid over to the driver's side and moved the car in a few yards. The gate swung shut and I noted how Clem just looped the chain around it and didn't relock it. Good stuff, leaving the place unlocked for the backup FBI crew, which was heading south from Porter.

Back into the car Clem came, Gus slid back to his side of the car and we went past the closed gatehouse and into the empty parking lot. I shivered for a moment, remembering how empty the place had looked just a few days ago, when I had walked over here and came across the crime scene. I wondered how the North Tyler cops who had been here were doing, and if they ever whispered to each other on a night shift about the strange things that had happened here.

Gus said, "Clem, why don't you pull over to the left, as close as you can get. From the map in this book, it looks like this is where the emplacements are located."

Clem did just that and we pulled into the farthest spot to the left and switched off the engine. Seagulls were overhead, looking as if they were seeking shelter from the approaching storm. There was a grumble of thunder. To the right was the large empty lot, and then a field with picnic tables scattered around, and near the edge of the ocean was the park's visitors' center. Before it was an artificial hill, made by Army engineers decades ago. Up top was a concrete cube marking a spotting station for artillery observers, and before us, set in a concrete revetment, a metal door that looked as if it had been welded shut. Small saplings and grass covered the hill, and to the left of the hill was a gravel path leading farther into the park, where there were similar hills and structures.

Gus said, "Place is pretty overgrown. Can't imagine it was this green back when the Army was here."

"If anything," I said, "it was even more overgrown. The brush and the trees served as camouflage for any approaching ships or aircraft. If the place looked peaceful enough, they hoped the warships would get close enough to get sunk."

"Really?" Gus asked. "And do you think that would've worked?"

"This place was built in the middle of a resort area in New England. You can pretty much guess that a lot of tourists that came through here during the nineteen thirties were working for the Germans, the French, the English and the Russians. Hard to keep such a thing a secret, but the government does what it can."

"Ain't that the truth," Gus said, glancing at his watch. "Tell you what, let's get out and get some of the gear out of the trunk. I want to be ready to roll the minute the FBI shows up."

We all got out of the car, and it felt good stepping out to the cool air of the ocean. The salt tang seemed sharper than ever, and Gus motioned to Clem and me. "Hey, can you guys give me a hand? Some of this gear is pretty heavy."

I nodded and we joined Gus at the rear of the LTD. Off to the west I caught a flash of light, as lightning jagged its way through the thick clouds. Gus stood behind Clem, as Clem took a key and opened the trunk. I was on the other side of Clem, and when the trunk lid popped open, I thought Gus was a mighty weak guy, for there were only two small black cases in there.

I was going to say something about that to Gus, when he stepped back, pulled a pistol from underneath his coat, and shot Clem in the back of his head.

CHAPTER EIGHTEEN

The sound of the report was quite loud, and Clem jackknifed forward, falling to his knees, his upper torso dropping into the open trunk. I backed up just a step and stopped, my legs quaking with horror, feeling as if I was going to throw up and scream all at once. Gus spun on his heels and pointed the pistol at me, the damn thing looking about the size of a semi trailer.

"You move, you shout, you do anything right now except nod your head, then you're a fucking dead man," Gus said, staring right at me. "Understood?"

I nodded.

"Good." He sighed loudly. "Jesus, working with all these feds, it's refreshing just to get a yes or no response. Here's the deal. You reach in there, and get those two cases. Get 'em out and put them on the pavement. And move slow. All right?"

I nodded again and gingerly reached in to do as I was told. There was blood spray on the underside of the trunk lid and some blood and tissue matter on the bottom of the trunk, but I felt blessed, just for a moment, that both cases were clean. They were fairly heavy and made of thick black plastic, with metal clasps. I set them both on the ground and stood up, trying not to look at Clem's body or the back of his head. But that brief reprise lasted just a second, for Gus waved his pistol at me and said, "Good job. Now, grab this poor slob's legs and shove him into the trunk. Can't have him getting wet out here, can we?"

I found that my mouth was now working. "I was going to call you a bastard, Gus, but words fail me."

Another wave of the gun. "Oh, I'm sure you'll figure out something eventually. Now, get a move on. Get him into the trunk."

I knelt down and grabbed Clem's legs. I closed my eyes and grunted and huffed as I raised him up, this former Marine from Pensacola who was just here doing a job, trying to provide for his family by being in service to his country. If I had my wits about me I would have offered a quick prayer, but the only prayer coming out of my consciousness began and ended with "Oh, God." I had a hard time of it getting his legs to fit in, and tears were rolling down my face by the time I was done. I backed away again and Gus nodded in satisfaction.

"Good," he said. "You're now two for two. God, I would have loved it had you been my boss instead of that witch Reeves. Bitch, bitch, bitch, all the fucking day long."

"If I had been your boss, you'd be in prison now."

"Well, we all have our dreams," he said. "Now. I know you're carrying. Poor Clem here told me earlier, and you know what? I had nothing against Clem. He even played cribbage with me, late at night, waiting for Reeves to come back with more orders, more directives. But he was in the way, that's all. In the way of getting things done. So that's why he had to go, and that's why you're going to remove your pistol with your left hand, and toss it in the trunk. All right?"

Sure. I slowly and awkwardly reached up with my left hand and pulled my Beretta free. It made a desolate thunk as it landed inside the trunk, and Gus nodded again. "Well done. Close the trunk, will you?"

I slammed the trunk down with both hands, probably harder than I had too. The wind was now whipping up gravel and sand on the parking lot, making Gus's red hair flutter. Another motion with his hand. "Okay, your job now is to make me happy,

Lewis, and right now, it would make me terribly happy if you would pick up those two cases. All right?"

"I don't think I have much of a choice," I said, picking up the two cases, the plastic handles cutting into my sweaty hands.

"You're right, you don't," he said. "Now. Lead on."

I looked at him. "Lead on where?"

"To Battery A. Wherever the hell that is."

I looked over at the hills and trees and high grass. "Sorry, Gus. I just know it's over there, to the east. What are you expecting, a sign saying 'This way to the German uranium?'"

"No," he said, stepping closer. "I expect you to find Battery A and a way inside, or you're going to join Clem in a few minutes. Got it?"

I started walking toward the interior of the park.

"Gotten," I said.

A gravel-lined trail led from the parking lot to a sign that showed a schematic diagram of the park, and as I recalled, Battery A was one of two large artificial hills toward the eastern side of the park. But getting to Battery A and getting inside was going to be hard indeed. Decades of tourists coming through this old military site had prompted the state to weld shut old doors, pour concrete down ventilation tubes, and put metal bars on gunports, to prevent teenagers or whomever from gaining access to the underground tunnels and chambers. Even in the relatively short time I had lived nearby, I had noticed how, each year, more and more barriers had been constructed on the old structures in the park.

Now I had a madman behind me with a pistol, eager and ready to kill again, looking for an easy way in to a place where the uranium had been hidden more than a half century ago.

I said aloud, not looking back, "I gather there's no squad of FBI agents racing their way south to meet up with us."

"You got that right," he said.

"And Laura Reeves. She knows nothing of what's going on. She doesn't know that I found out about Whizzer or anything else, right?"

Gus laughed. "Good deduction work there as well. Too bad it's about a half hour too late."

The rumbling of the thunder grew louder as we made our way into the darkening interior of the park. "So why are you going renegade? You don't like your pension plan?"

"Close," Gus said, keeping right in step with me, his legs sometimes bumping into the cases I was carrying. "I look at the money I make, I look at the shitty places I travel to do the government's bidding, and if this job and what I do is so important, I should be compensated for it. Not living on a daily stipend, exaggerating your mileage report, trying to stretch out your daily meal payment. The hell with that. So I found out about the uranium, and here we are. One big payoff and I can retire. Brazil looks good this time of year."

I quickly looked back at him. The trees arched overhead, making a tunnel-like effect. "The uranium. How did you find out about that?"

A laugh. "Never you mind. You're asking way too many questions as it is. Let's just say I'm the agent of change, getting that stuff where it belongs."

"Libya? You're going to help Libya get the bomb?"

He shrugged. "If I don't, somebody will. Why not get paid for it?"

"And Libya gets the bomb, that's a good thing?"

"Not my concern," Gus said. "You see anybody shedding tears that Pakistan and India have the bomb? Let 'em kill each other all they want, and let God sort it out. Looking out for number one has done well for me so far. And that's how I intend to close out the day. Now, get a move on, before I decide I don't need you anymore."

With the fading light from the storm it was hard to see where we were going. Woods and brush made a thick tangle on both sides of the trail, and I had a quick fantasy of spinning around and popping Gus on the side of the head with the black plastic cases. Then, when he was stunned, I would run past the trees and bushes and make like a scared bunny and hide in the underbrush. An attractive fantasy, one that unfortunately would no doubt end with a few bullet holes blasting into my hide.

Rain came down for a moment or two, and then let up. The trail widened, and to our right a concrete overhang appeared. Wide metal doors were set into the concrete. I set the cases down on the ground and rubbed my hands.

"Gus," I said. "You carrying a light of some sort?"

He chuckled. "Man, I got this thing nailed. Of course I do. What's up?"

"Shine the light up there, at the concrete overhang. At the upper lip."

A rustle of clothing and then a beam of light shot out. Carved in the upper portion of the concrete overhang was BAT-TERY B. "Nice," Gus said. "Getting close, aren't we?"

"We are," I said.

Gus lowered the flashlight beam down to the tall metal doors, and I made out the thick bead of welding material, extending top to bottom, closing the doors forever. He let the flashlight beam rest on the weld for a long moment.

"You better hope things are better at Battery A," he said quietly. "Now, get going. I don't want to get rained on."

I picked up the cases without a word and kept on walking.

People, I thought. Where the hell are all the people? Knowing the cantankerous nature of the local residents and tourists alike, I was sure that not everyone had left the park once the gate had closed. There was no fence around the preserve, meaning anyone walking down Atlantic Avenue could wander in without any questions or problems. I had another quick little fantasy, of a little group of hard-drinking construction workers coming up the trail, so many that even Gus wouldn't think of shooting them all.

The landscape lit up, as if a gang of photographers had suddenly taken a picture of the surroundings, and it only took a few seconds for the rumbling to reach my ears. There's the answer, I thought. Who wants to be out in the woods waiting to get rained on during a thunderstorm?

And meanwhile, the FBI agents are doing their thing up in Porter, and Laura Reeves is probably landing in her helicopter, and everybody's doing their own thing, while the uranium is about a few minutes away from leaving this country and heading overseas. Not to mention that the pilots of the fighter bombers were probably getting their briefings, and the final mapping coordinates had been plugged into the cruise missiles.

All this destruction, all this death, all focused on this rainy stretch of land in New Hampshire.

Another flash of lightning. Another concrete overhang approaching on the right. Gus noted it as well and I didn't have to say a word. He lit up the concrete and the old carved letters appeared in the gloom. BATTERY A. He lowered the light and there were the same tall double doors.

Welded, top to bottom.

"Guess it's not your night, Lewis," he said.

"I've had better. Can I borrow your light?"

I could see the grin on his face. "Why? You planning on blinding me? Planning on upgrading the flashlight to a laser beam and cutting me in half?"

"No," I shot back. "I'm trying to find your goddamn uranium. You give me the flashlight, I'll do the work. There's more than one way in and out of Battery A. You want to blunder around by yourself, go ahead. This way, I do the grunt work."

No answer. More grumbling of the thunder, and another spray of rain, wetting my hands and hair. I said, "You still got the book I brought, showing the diagrams of the buildings?"

"All right. Hold on. The light and the book, I'm putting on the ground. You do anything quick or unusual, and you're—"

"Yeah, yeah, I know the drill. I'm a dead man. I'm tired of hearing it. Get on with it, okay?"

Gus did just that and I knelt down in the wet gravel, flipping through the book written by a local historian who probably in his wildest dreams never thought his work would be used in such a fashion. I found the schematic of Battery A and B easily enough, but the drawings were old engineering sketches from the 1930s. I looked down at the drawings and over at the main entrance, and looked back and forth twice.

"Well?" Gus said.

I got up, flashlight held down, so he wouldn't think I was trying to blind him. "Let's go for a walk. The sketches show some outbuildings in a perimeter around this emplacement. Question is, are they still here, more than fifty years later?"

He didn't answer, so I handed over the light to him. I picked up the containers again, feeling the sharp bite of the handles in my palms. Now a drizzle was coming down, and the warmth of the April day had disappeared. I shivered, and kept on walking into the darkness.

Something bumped on my side as I walked, and I remembered Felix's cell phone, nice and secure in my jacket. Thank God Clem hadn't noticed this little instrument, or it would have been tossed in the LTD's trunk back in the parking lot, next to Clem's rapidly cooling body.

But so what? I doubted Gus would allow me to make a phone call, and if there was a point where I could break free—quite doubtful—I'd use that time to bail out and hide, and not to call 911.

The phone kept on thumping me as I kept on walking.

The first outbuilding was a concrete foundation filled with cement and beer cans, the second was a pile of bricks. Gus spent a few minutes poking around the bricks, looking for any kind of opening. Nothing. The drizzle had changed to a light rain, and Gus said, "This book's falling apart in the rain. Where to next?"

"Keep on walking, following the trail," I said, tired and achy and still terrified at the easy and casual way Gus had ended Clem's life. My knees and legs were quivering from all that had happened, and as we went on, the trail came to a fork. The one to the left was well-traveled, while the one to the right was narrow and overgrown.

"Which way?" Gus said.

I didn't say a word for a moment, feeling a burst of resentment and anger boiling up, being treated like a pack mule and a native guide. If I could have led him into the ocean, I would have gladly done it. I dropped the cases for a quick rest.

"To the right," I said. "The left looks like it goes out to the ocean."

He grunted, and I gathered that was an affirmative sign.

I picked up the cases and made my way to the right. This trail was hard going, rocky and with branches snapping at my face. The light from Gus was moving around so much that it was hard to see where we were going. We were now close enough to hear the sound of the waves crashing in, and the thunder's rumbles had eased up. My throat was dry and my chest hurt from the heavy breathing, from carrying these two damn cases and everything else. Then my feet got wet and I felt mud ooze up past my ankles.

"Hold on," I said. "Shine the light over here."

He did just that, and my heart ached at what I saw. Swampy marshland, with nothing in view that looked man-made, nothing at all.

"I'm running out of patience," Gus said.

"I can imagine."

We retraced our steps back along the trail, heading for the intersection, when something caught my eye. I stopped suddenly and Gus nearly bumped into me, and I had a quick, terrifying thought of his finger accidentally tightening on his pistol, blowing a hole through my back. I had no illusions that if that happened, Gus wouldn't do more than just grab the two plastic cases and keep on walking even without my assistance.

"What's wrong?" he said. "Why did you stop?"

"Shine the light over there, to the right."

The beam went over and I saw what had caught my eye: freshly trimmed tree branches, the white stumps shining brightly in the light. A trail barely wide enough for one skinny man made its way into the woods, and I wasn't surprised we had missed the opening on the way in.

"Another trail," Gus said, walking around me to take a better look. "And it seems pretty new. Does it match the drawings in the book?"

"How the hell should I know?" I snapped back at him dropping the heavy cases again. "The only way to find out is to start walking."

He took the pistol and tapped the end of the barrel against my neck. "Then start walking."

My hands cramped up some as I picked up the two cases and blundered my way into the new trail. More branches and limbs snapped at me, and Gus kept close by, no doubt ensuring that I wouldn't break away and start running. But the underbrush and brambles were so thick, it'd probably take me about five minutes to go five feet, plenty of time for him to choose which body part of mine he wanted to shoot first.

The rain was coming down heavier as the trail zigged and zagged its way through the woods, and my arms and shoulders were aching and crying out for relief as I went through, trying hard not to think of what might happen if the trail opened up to a clearing with a couple of picnic tables and a barbecue pit.

The thunder returned, and so did the lightning. I saw a square shape up ahead, and so did Gus. "I see something, real close."

I didn't say anything in reply. It didn't seem necessary. The trail abruptly widened out to a clearing about the size of an acre. A small hill rose up in the middle of the clearing, covered with grass and shrubbery. Another concrete abutment, another metal door. We walked up to the door and I dropped the two cases, not caring at that moment what was going to happen.

Gus came around me again and used the light to illuminate the old metal door. This one was small and looked as if it was used for an entrance for people rather than trucks or tanks. The two hinges looked unimpeded, and Gus whistled in delight as he ran the light up and down, looking at where the edge of the door met the concrete.

There was no weld, but there was a padlock. And the padlock looked shiny and brand-new.

"Fair enough," Gus said, putting the flashlight under his arm and going into his coat pocket again. "This looks easy enough to pick, and if that schematic was close enough, this should bring us right into Battery A."

I rubbed my hands together and then rubbed at my shoulders. I was going to speak up but then something interrupted me.

It was the harsh *snick-snack* of someone priming a pump-action shotgun, and then a sharp voice: "Hold it right there, or I'll blow off your damn head."

I couldn't help but grin. It looked like the cavalry had arrived.

CHAPTER NINETEEN

Then the clearing lit up, as a man came out from the underbrush carrying a gas lantern, which he placed down on the wet grass. The man walked true and fair, and I had to look twice before I believed what I was seeing: Jack Emerson, curator of the Porter Submarine Museum, carrying a shotgun and no cane, no cane at all.

"Hey, Jack," I started. "It sure is great to—"

"Shut up," he said, aiming the shotgun in my direction, and I felt like a lost Union soldier suddenly realizing he's been rescued by the Confederates. I swallowed and felt like an idiot. Whizzer. The first time I had met Jack at the museum, he had denied all. Had never heard of Whizzer.

"Nice to see you, Jack," Gus said.

"You were supposed to call to set up the meet," Jack said, swinging the shotgun over to his direction. "What happened?"

Gus gave a cheerful shrug. "Circumstances changed, that's all."

Things were clicking inside my head, one right after another, and it was not a pleasant feeling. Jack stepped forward, saying, "I should shoot you down right now, you fuck. I know what you're doing here. You found out where the stuff is hidden on your own. You're trying to back away from the deal, am I right?"

"Shoot away," Gus said. "And you won't get what's in those cases. They're triggered, my friend. You don't punch in the right combination in the little dials under each handle, and a thermite charge explodes. Fries your face and burns off your eyebrows and, oh yeah, every single hundred-dollar bill inside is destroyed."

Jack said, "Whatever's in those cases isn't enough, and you know it. I get a finder's fee, you get the delivery fee. That still ain't fair."

"Whoever said fair had anything to do with it?" Gus said.

Now Jack turned his attention back to me. "What's he doing here?" he asked, and the cheerful and helpful face I had seen back at the museum had gone, replaced by a cold look that chilled me.

"He's my mule, that's what. Not to say that I don't trust you, old man, but I don't want my back exposed while moving that stuff out."

Jack snorted. "A hell of a thing, trust. Ain't no such thing. Just a deal, and you coming here by yourself, without setting up the meet like you said, tells me a lot."

"Look, you want to chat all night here in the rain, or do you want to wrap this deal up?" Gus demanded.

I spoke up, "Damn it, Jack, your son Keith's dead. Also known as Whizzer. You know who did it, don't you. And you're still dealing with him?"

Jack moved the shotgun back in my direction. "Keith's been dead a long time, boy, ever since he came back from the Gulf. What Gus did . . . I can see why. I don't like it, but I can see why. He was going to pull everything down, threaten everything. And we couldn't risk that. I told Gus Keith was a problem, and that was that."

Gus said, "Hey, this is all special and nice, but can we get out of the fucking rain? Please? You got a key, old man, or what?"

"I do," he said. "But I'm not gonna open it and have you put a bullet in me."

"Nor I," Gus said. "Lewis, it looks like you're drafted. Old man, toss the keys over to him."

Jack kept the shotgun trained on Gus while he poked around in his pocket, came out with a key attached to a length of chain. He tossed it over to me and I caught it one-handed. I noted how Gus moved so that I was between him and the old man. Nice job description, I thought. Human shield for a couple of criminals. I went over to the door, fit the key in the lock and popped it open. I grabbed the metal door handle and the door slid open effortlessly, not a squeak or a squeal. Somebody had kept it well-lubricated. With the door open, I smelled old things, dust and dirt and things kept moist over decades.

"Reach in," Jack commanded. "To your right is a light switch. Pop it up and then we can all get out of the rain."

My hand went in and felt slimy concrete. I moved it up and down and then felt a switch, which I threw. I blinked as lights clicked on, leading down at an angle. It looked like a temporary job, black wire fastened up on the concave concrete roof, small lights dangling down every five feet or so. I looked down and saw car batteries, lined up.

"Nice work," I said. "I can't see how you did that with your cane and all."

Jack laughed. "For the past twenty years I've fooled the yard, the government, and even you into thinking I got injured. A nice little pension every month and all I had to do was play around with a cane. Seemed like a small price to pay."

"And giving up your son?" I demanded. "And helping an overseas dictator go nuclear, are those small prices to pay?"

"Shut up and get inside," Jack said. "I don't want to talk about Keith no more."

"Hold on there," Gus said. "I go in first. Lewis, you come in after me with the cases."

Gus elbowed by me and I gave one more look to Jack and said, "All that stuff about service to your country, about vets and doing your part, so much nonsense, right?"

The shotgun was aimed at my midsection. "If so, I didn't make it nonsense first. Plenty of others did. I worked and slaved and sacrificed for this country, all for a pension and a Social Security check that might disappear next year or the year after that, 'cause we give billions each year to idiots overseas. Time for me to take care of myself. Now, get on in there."

I picked up the two cases, my hands wincing from the familiar pain, and in I went. Jack followed, swinging the door behind him, the clanging noise as the door closed echoing down the cement tunnel.

I took in our surroundings. We were in a dome-shaped alcove, with the tunnel leading down into the darkness at a slight angle. Once again, Gus maneuvered himself so that I was between him and Jack. The old man shifted the shotgun in his grasp and said, "Here's the deal. I lead the way down the tunnel, and you follow. Lewis behind me, and you in the rear. The uranium is well-secured, and if you have any ideas about arriving there by yourself, Gus, just know that it's secured by more than just a combination lock."

Gus smiled. "Makes sense to me. And why do you get to go first?"

Jack's answer was interrupted by a shrill ringing noise, emanating from me, of all places, and both men stared at me and Gus said, "What the . . . you carrying a cell phone?"

"I guess I am," I said. "All right if I answer it?"

Gus smiled again. "Tell you what. Hand it over and I'll answer it, okay?"

I set down my cases and took the ringing cell phone out of my coat pocket and handed it over to Gus, and even though I was expecting it, his move startled me, it was so quick and sudden. He threw the phone against the wall, where it shattered, and then he stomped three times on the pieces. The ringing finally stopped.

"I guess the caller is either busy or has left the service area, huh?" Gus said.

Jack spoke up. "Let's get a move on. Gus, you get behind Lewis. I'll lead the way."

"You didn't answer my question, old man," he said. "Why do you get to go first?"

"Because I know the way," he said.

Gus looked around him. "I only see one way in and out. What's the big deal?"

This time, Jack was smiling. "Like I said, I'm the only one who knows the way."

Then the lights went out.

Gus started yelling and shouting and threatening and when there was a pause in the cursing, Jack said from the darkness, "Are we going to talk, or are we going to just listen to you go on?"

"Turn on the lights, turn on the lights right now."

"No," Jack said. "They're on a timer. They kick off ninety seconds after they're turned on. And I'm the only one who knows where the other switches are."

"Fine, I've got my flashlight and—"

"Turn on that flashlight, and you're dead," Jack said. "Honest to God, I mean it. Turn it on and I see where you are, and you are dead. I keep the uranium, I get the cases with the money, and it may take a year or two years, but I'll figure out a way of getting that money out of those cases without triggering whatever kind of booby traps you have."

A hand grabbed me by the throat, and Gus's voice was louder. "I got Cole, right here in front of me."

Laughter. "I gave my son up to you, and you think I give a shit about a stranger? Go ahead and stand there and use your light. This shotgun's got a nice wide pattern. Guaranteed to knock both of you down, and then I can take my time with whoever's left alive."

Dark—I could not believe how dark it was. Even in a dark room in the middle of the night, there's ambient light, coming in from streetlights, the moon, the little LEDs on your VCR. Here, surrounded by concrete and a heavy metal door, there was no light, nothing at all.

The grip on my throat eased up. "Not bad, old man," Gus said, his voice loud in my right ear. "Not bad. How do you want to work this?"

A chuckle from the blackness. "There, now that's what I call cooperation. Tell you what. First, drop your pistol. Then, you take your flashlight out and light it off, pointing it at the floor. Okay?"

I could sense movement and there was a thunk as Gus dropped his pistol. Then I shut my eyes against the sudden glare when Gus switched on his flashlight. Jack was over by the door, shotgun pointing right at the two of us. He nodded with pleasure. "Very good. All right. Now, drop it on the ground, kick it over here."

The light fell down, and Gus gave it a swift kick. The motion across the floor tossed lights and shadows about us on the concrete, and then Jack bent over, picked it up, and smashed it against the wall.

Darkness returned, seeming blacker than before.

Jack's voice came out from the void. "Lewis, pick up the two cases and come out three steps."

I bent down at the knees, flailed around with my hands, found both cases. I stood up and took the requested steps. Jack's voice was now quite close. "Good. Put the cases down, and reach out slowly with your right hand."

I did that and felt cloth. Jack's coat. "Raise your hand up and grab my shoulder."

I felt like asking Gus whether, if I attacked Jack, he would call the whole thing off, but I didn't want to push what little luck I had remaining. My hand went up and grasped the thin shoulder, and from the way he was talking, I could sense he had turned around, so his back was facing me.

"Your turn, Gus," Jack continued. "Come forward until you touch Lewis."

I cringed, waiting for his touch, which came at me a few seconds later. Jack said, "Got his shoulder?"

"I do," came the voice.

"Then that's how we're going inside," Jack said. "One happy little family, like three little elephants, tail to nose, to tail to nose. We'll shuffle right along, and it'll take some time, but that's how we're going to do it. Lewis, grab one of the cases."

I did that and said, "That leaves one behind."

"Sure it does," Jack said, "and that's what Gus is going to pick up."

Gus muttered something and I yelped as a black case banged against my knee as Gus retrieved it. Jack called out, "All set?"

"Yes," I said, and Gus said, "Yeah, yeah, can we get a move on?"

"Sure we can," Jack said. "We can get a move on, and it's going to be my move, setting my pace. I know the tunnels and the rooms inside of here, and I'm not going to say a word for the next ten or fifteen minutes, 'cause I'm going to be keeping count of my steps. And don't get any nice ideas of overpowering me and then finding your way out. You move around in the dark and pick the wrong turn, you'll be heading into some dangerous areas. Some of the work in here has collapsed over the years. One wrong turn and you might fall down a deep hole where there's water and no way of coming up. Or you might fall down and there's no water, just chunks of broken concrete. Either way, you're going in with me and you're coming out with me, or you're going to end up dead."

My legs were quivering again, my mind racing with the thoughts that I was trapped, trapped inside this dark and closed-in space with two men, either of whom would kill me in a second if it suited him. I kept my eyes open, looking around, trying to make out my surroundings, to see anything, but there was nothing. Just blackness. It was as if I had been struck blind.

"Off we go," Jack said. "We move slow and take it easy."

My left hand held onto the case and my right hand stayed on Jack's shoulder, as we started shuffling our way into the unknown. We moved slowly, the sound of our feet rasping against the concrete echoing back and forth, almost matched by the sound of our breathing. I was reminded of a famous painting by John Jay Jasper, called *The Gassed,* depicting British soldiers in World War I, blinded on a battlefield, being led off to a medical aid station. And here we were, effectively blinded, being led into the depth of an old gun station that had never fired a shot in anger, veterans of a sort of different conflict.

Except for the time in Nevada, I had never been on a more terrifying journey in all my life. We stopped when Jack said, "Rest break, just for a moment," and I dropped the case I was carrying and lifted up my hand to my face. The old cliché of not being able to see one's hand before one's face came horribly alive. There was nothing but the darkness, nothing at all except the smells of decayed objects and wet concrete, and the sounds of our breathing and of our feet on the ground and of dripping water, and the touch I had of the person in front of me, and the touch on my shoulder of the person behind me.

Gus spoke quietly. "Hell of a thing, ain't it."

I turned my head, replying just as quietly. I didn't want Jack to lose count. "Let me guess. Among the other lies you've told me, you were in charge of photographing and removing the Libyan body. And you took off the lapel pin, right?"

Gus just laughed, for a moment. I went on. "How did you two get hooked up? Did you intercept the first contact between him and the Libyans?"

Gus laughed again, but again kept it short. "Man, you are as dumb as the day is long. What do you think, that old yard worker up there dropped a postcard to Libya and they opened up negotiations? Hell, no. He contacted us. Found an article about us in *Popular Science* or some damn thing, sent a threatening letter to NEST. Said he had this uranium and would dump it in Boston's water supply if we didn't pay him a half million dollars."

I took a breath. "And the letter came to you, didn't it."

"Uh-huh. Nobody else saw it except me. So I decided to take some initiative. Contacted him and offered something a bit more rich. A million-dollar finder's fee if he turned the uranium over to me, and I would turn it over to the Libyans. Keep it nice and simple and quiet, just the two of us. But the damn Libyans, I thought they had a more secure communications system than the one they used, 'cause having Laura Reeves and the other fools crawling around here wasn't part of the plan."

"Killing the Libyan contact, was that part of the plan?" I asked.

"No, that was the idea of the idiot in front of you. Jack

demanded a one-on-one with the Libyan guy, sort of to size him up. You know, man-to-man crap, stuff like that. I thought it was a dumb idea. Just made sense to get the deal done. But Jack had the uranium, and I didn't. And they had the meet and it went wrong, didn't it, Jack."

No answer, just breathing from the old man in front of me. Gus continued. "From what little that geezer told me, it seems Jack took offense at some things that the Libyan was talking about. You know, stepping onto the grounds of the Great Satan, dealing with whores and thieves, blah-blah-blah. I guess Jack lost it and popped him one. Right, Jack?"

Again, just the steady breathing. I spoke up. "And what about the pot shot at me yesterday? Whose idea was that?"

"Oh, his, who else?"

"And you were the shooter, right?"

"Right." Gus squeezed my shoulder and I felt nauseous. "Lucky you, Jack didn't want you dead. Just wanted to scare you away, make you go to ground for a couple of days. Looks like you guessed wrong, Jack, huh? It would've been better if I had splattered ol' Lewis's head across your museum parking lot."

There was another squeeze of his hand and I shook my shoulder in irritation. I said, "Next time, Gus, you're going to be in my gun sites, and I promise you I won't be as agreeable as you were."

"If there's a next time, sure," Gus said.

Jack spoke up. "Stop your yapping, both of you. It's time to get moving."

The shuffling started again.

Over the next few minutes my mind began to play tricks on me. At first I imagined I was seeing a glow out in the distance, like a burning candle or lamp, and only if we moved faster would it get brighter, and I was frustrated by the slow pace. And then the glow would disappear and I wouldn't see anything, and I knew my mind was trying to bring something to the fore to reassure me. Other times I was convinced that I had gone blind, that something in the dark bowels of the tunnelworks had caused me to lose my sight, and that Jack's method of getting us to the uranium would fail and we would wander in the darkness, getting tired and hungry and thirsty, finally dying in here listening to one another's yells and shouts.

The sound of our footsteps seemed to change, to get more dim, and I sensed that we were in a larger room. Jack stopped and said, "We're moving to the right. You move along with me and we'll get there just fine. Any problems, I might choose the wrong corridor, and you'd end up in the bottom of a gunpit, broken bones and all, dying of thirst 'cause nobody comes down here. Nobody at all."

"But Keith did, didn't he? How did he know about the uranium down here?"

Jack ignored me but Gus took the question. "Sure he did, but who's going to believe a fool like that? Ol' Jack's dad, he was the one who stole the uranium out of the shipyard. The war in Europe was over, massive layoffs were coming down, and some of the less-legal members of the workforce started taking souvenirs. Jack's dad grabbed the uranium and stashed it here, just as this place was winding down and being decommissioned. And here it sat, year after year, gathering dust, 'cause old Grandpa died in a drunk-driving accident a year or two later. The old man's grandson Keith, he started going through dear old Grandpa's papers and found out what had been stored here. He passed that along to Jack, and then Jack wrote a letter to me."

Jack said, "Let's get a move on, now. Come along."

My right arm ached from being placed on Jack's shoulder all this time, and my left hand was cramped from carrying that damn black case. Again, we began the shuffling motions and I almost groaned in pain and dismay at what we were going through. My mind's tricks started again, especially when Jack called out, "Water coming up. Don't worry, it's only about ankle-deep," and we splashed through cold water that had a foul smell. After going through the water, I imagined again that Jack was lost, that he didn't know where he was going, and that he would tumble us over into a pit that was a hundred feet deep. My toes began to curl back against themselves, as I was thinking of what it might feel like to step out into nothing but deadly air.

I was afraid I was going to start moaning in fear, moaning out loud and making noises like a coyote caught in a leghold trap, when Jack said calmly, "We're here. Close your eyes and cover them with your hands. It helps."

I dropped the case and almost sighed out loud in relief as I brought my hands up to my eyes. Yards, I thought, I was literally yards away from my comfortable home and safe bedroom at Tyler Beach, and here I was, buried underneath tons of dirt and concrete, living at the whim of two killers, each of whom seemed eager as hell to strike out at the other.

Suddenly light glared through my fingers and my closed eyelids, like being on a Nevada test range as an atomic bomb goes off. I blinked hard and slowly opened my eyes, which were tearing from pain, and looked around. We were in what seemed to be the central area of the emplacement, with concrete-lined corridors running out like spokes on a wagon wheel. More homemade lights were hung from rusting pipes, and cable conduits from the cement ceiling. Gus was off to my right, and Jack was to my left, and again I had the feeling of being a target, as both ensured that I was between them.

I looked around some more. The place was a mess. Graffiti—WORSHIP SATAN, 666, WORK SUCKS—had been spray-painted in large looping letters on the walls, along with the names of Freddy, Jen, Krystal and Byron, and the usual cryptic graffiti symbols that look like relatives of Egyptian hieroglyphics. Beer cans, broken whiskey bottles and crumpled cigarette packages and snack containers were scattered across the floor. Faded black paint in careful block letters above some of the corridor openings said PLOTTING ROOM, RADIO ROOM, OOD STATION. Despite all that was going on, I felt a flash of anger at what years of teenagers had done here, trashing a place where men had come to work every day, defending their home, their soil. It was like seeing a graveyard being desecrated.

Near where Jack was standing was a rusted metal door, bowed in at the center, which looked as if generations of troubled youth had tried to kick it in. A grate was placed at eye level in the door, and Jack—keeping the shotgun trained on us—poked around the trash on the ground until he came up with a short length of pipe. He inserted the pipe at a particular angle through the grate, and something made a loud click. Jack had a satisfied smile on his face as he took the pipe out and dropped it to the floor.

"My dad was handy with tools and such," he said, grabbing hold of the grate and swinging the door open. "Nobody knew anything was back here for nearly a half century. A little spring lock and pressure plate. That's all it took."

The door opened up and more lights came on. A shorter concrete corridor extended in, and the floor was covered with empty beer and soda cans, no doubt tossed in through the grates. Jack kicked them aside with practiced moves, heading to another metal door at the end. This one was in better shape, and a combination lock was holding it in place. Gus and I followed Jack in, each of us carrying one of the black plastic cases.

"Lewis," Jack said. "Not that I don't trust my partner in crime here, but please keep your distance between us two as I get to work."

I moved back, as I was getting that tingly feeling, as if a large bull's-eye were painted in the middle of my spine. Jack worked the combination lock and popped it open, and I sensed Gus looking around me as the door swung wide.

And there they were, illuminated by a single bulb dangling from the ceiling. Lined up against a wall were ten metal cases, nine inches to a side. Such a small collection of containers, such a small thing that had caused all this death and deceit and hate. And as if to symbolize all the death and hate, emblazoned on the side of each container, just as Keith Emerson had told me, were the German eagle and swastika, and the words: EIGENTUM DER OKW. There were other items in there as well: a couple of furled flags or banners leaning against the wall; a small pile of what looked like uniforms in the corner, and a moldering collection of pamphlets and books, all in what looked to be German. Near the door was a long metal handcart with four wheels, and by the cart were some old canvas sacks.

From behind me Gus seemed to sigh in satisfaction. He said, "Jack, I need to ensure that those boxes contain what we both think they do. If they contain sand or rocks or Spam, it sure'd be a hell of a thing."

Jack said, "Makes sense."

"One of these cases has detection equipment. I'll open it up in full view of you, just to make sure nothing . . . well, make sure nothing untoward goes on. All right?"

Jack nodded and moved in with Gus, shotgun still in hand, as Gus knelt down and laid out the case flat on the soiled concrete. He deftly went through the combination and undid the side latches. Jack looked on intently as the lid was slowly lifted up, revealing dark gray foam-rubber protection and some instrumentation, and what looked like a metal probe, about a foot long.

"Lewis," Gus said, without looking at me. "Go on over and grab one of those cases. Bring it to me."

I wanted to tell him off, but kept my mouth shut. I stepped into the tiny room and lifted up the case with no problem. Unbelievable. More than a half century ago, German technicians had carefully packed away this uranium, confident that they were helping their Axis ally get the Bomb. Thousands of miles and decades later, these careful packages were soon going to be on their way to a place that, like wartime Japan, wanted the Bomb and hated America.

I placed the metal container down and stepped back. "It's welded shut," I said.

"Doesn't make any difference," Gus said, placing the end of the probe against the container, and working some of the instrumentation inside the case. "This close up, it . . . aaah, that's nice. Jack, my friend, you are now officially one million dollars richer; by this time next week, I should be humping two young things from Ipanema."

Jack smiled, for the first time I had seen him smile tonight, and he said, "The money. Pass it over. That's the deal. You've got the uranium, and I get the cash."

"Sure," Gus said, sliding the other case over to him, but Jack shook his head and slid it back. "Nope. You open it."

Gus said, "Hell, I'll tell you the combination. You can open it just as easy as I did this one."

Another shake of the head. "And have that damn thing blow up in my face? No, you open it."

"Gee, you're being awfully distrustful tonight," Gus said in mock disappointment, and he went to work on the case. He popped it open, and piled in tight rows were bundles of hundred-dollar bills, the benign face of Benjamin Franklin looking up at me. He slid the case back, and once again Jack didn't look happy.

"Lewis, that money sure looks good, but I wouldn't put it past this character to have some sort of pressure switch on the bottom, set off a charge once I start emptying it. So . . ." He reached back into the small room, past the handcart, pulled out a bag. He tossed the bag at me and I let it fall to the floor. "Please be so kind as to transfer the money from the case to that bag."

"No," I said.

Jack looked right at me, and moved the shotgun closer in my direction. "I'm afraid you don't have any choice."

"Maybe not, but I'm tired of being everybody's gofer tonight," I said. "So to hell with you, and to hell with putting that money away. You want it so bad, do it yourself."

Gus laughed. "Well, good for you, Mr. Cole."

Jack wasn't laughing. "I'll shoot you down if you don't."

I tried for a casual shrug, wasn't too sure if I achieved it. "Maybe you will. And then what? You shoot me down and then Gus is out a mule, and then you'll have to put the damn money in the bag yourself. So save yourself a pull of the trigger and a kick of the shoulder. Do it yourself."

Jack stared at me. "Your last chance."

"For all that talk you gave me about being part of a noble generation, of not being appreciated for all that you've done, you sure are a cold-hearted bastard. Not much of a memory there, right? Or did you forget how I helped you out that day in the museum, when you were all by yourself? Or was that all part of your cover all these years, pretending to be a noble veteran, and just being a noble thief?"

He kept that cold stare, started moving the shotgun up to

253

his shoulder, until Gus broke in. "Oh, for Christ's sake, I'll do it. Lewis, untwist your panties. Jack, let up on the trigger finger. I'll take care of it."

I kept my own look at Jack, and he gave a crisp nod. Gus flopped open the canvas bag and started tossing in the bundles of hundreds, one right after another. "Lot of money here," Gus observed, as the bag started to bulge from all the hundred-dollar bills being stacked inside. "You got any grand plans? Gonna get some new teeth? A new truck? A new house?"

"All that and more," Jack said, looking at the money with hunger in his eyes. "All that and more. You just keep on shoving it in."

"Sure," Gus said. "Hey, one more thing."

"What's that?" Jack asked.

"You want to make sure I'm not cheating you, right?" Gus juggled one of the bundles in his hand. "You'd hate to see that it's just one hundred-dollar bill on the top and bottom and green paper in the center. Right?"

"Well, shit, yes," Jack said.

"So, here you go," Gus said, "check it yourself."

With that, Gus tossed the bundle of bills at Jack. Everything seemed to move as if we were all in amber. The bundle rolled end over end, and Jack looked almost pleased with himself as he reached up to catch the money. His eyes were on the money, were on the bundle of Ben Franklins, but I kept looking at Gus, Gus whose hand flew back into the case and came out with a revolver.

CHAPTER TWENTY

I fell to the ground as Gus fired and didn't see what happened next, though I sure as hell heard it. There was a teeth-rattling boom as Jack fired his shotgun, and then another two sharp reports, as Gus returned fire. I rolled on my back and got up and started to think of sprinting away, when Gus called out, "You stay right there, Cole. Right fucking there."

I slowly turned. There was hazy smoke in the air. Gus got up from a combat crouch, lowered his revolver. Jack was sprawled against the near concrete wall, head lowered, chest splotched with blood. The shotgun was on the floor next to him. I rubbed at my eyes, looked over again at Gus. He smiled.

"Jeez, that was fucking close," he said.

I took a deep breath. "How in the world did you ever get through the psych testing for your job?"

"Just lucky, I guess," he said. "Looky there, up on the ceiling."

I did just that, saw fresh marks on the dirty cement ceiling. "Not even a ricochet?" I asked.

"Nope, not even a ricochet. Think about that. A couple of dozen shotgun pellets go overhead, and not a single one hits me. Guess this is really my lucky day, huh?"

I looked over again at Jack, lying there still. "The day's not over yet," I said.

"Well, it's close enough. C'mon, you've got work to do. Start loading up that handcart, and let's get the canisters out of here. Seeing that old fart there is spooking the shit out of me. Get a move on."

I thought of how bravely I had stood up to Jack a few minutes ago, and how that bravery had melted away with the second murder I had witnessed on this dark evening.

I shook my head and headed into the little room, started packing up the canisters. No time for bravery. No time for action. Just enough time to stay alive as long as I could.

As I worked, I think Gus noted the glances I was sending to the shotgun on the floor, and with a smile he picked it up and casually placed it in the far corner. It was hard work, putting the canisters up on the handcart, and I took a moment to catch my breath. Gus was putting the money back into the open case, and I said, "That sure was some planning. What would you have done if Jack hadn't asked for one of us to unpack the money?"

Gus said, "Then he would have gotten a free revolver, that's what. Besides, I had another revolver in the detection case. I was going to pull a similar stunt before he left. No offense, but not having to spend that money on Jack will mean a lot more months of fun for me in Brazil. I thought I could use it better than he could."

"And where did you get a million dollars?"

He grinned as he snapped the case shut, still holding the revolver in a free hand. "Trade secrets, Lewis. That's all. You gonna finish up in there?"

"Sure," I said, grabbing one of the last canisters and putting it down on the handcart. "Helicopter, right?"

Gus stopped on his way to the other black case. "Huh?"

"Helicopter. There's no way you're going out of here putting this stuff in the rear of the LTD and just driving away. Nope. And there's no harbor close enough for a boat pickup. You must have a helicopter around here. Somebody waiting for a pickup, on a signal from you. A radio concealed in the case that had the detecting equipment. Libyans?"

"Nope," Gus said, snapping the cover shut of the instrument case. "Ex-French Foreign Legion. Having a couple of guys hanging around at a small airport who speak with a French accent is easier to explain than having those guys speak with an Arabic accent. Plus, they're easy to hire. They don't rightly care what they're doing as long as they get paid for it. A nice philosophy. Ready to move out?"

"Move out where?" I asked.

"Where else? The way we came in."

I tried to see if he was joking, and failed. "Did you keep track of how we came in?"

"Didn't have to," he said. "We got lights now, don't we? We'll just get a move on. C'mon, I don't have time to waste."

My hands and arms ached, and I was terribly thirsty. I was also terribly aware of how this evening was going to end for me, and decided that arguing with Gus wouldn't buy me anything, except a quicker end to things.

"Okay," I said, grabbing the twin handles of the handcart. "You're the boss."

Gus swung both black cases onto the top of the uranium canisters. "That's the nicest thing you've said all night."

I leaned in and pushed, and the weight of the uranium and the two cases made it slow going. But the handcart was fairly new and the wheels seemed well-lubricated, and after I got it started, it moved well. I tried not to look at the still form of Jack as we headed away from the small storage room. Gus stayed right behind me as we moved down the corridor, brushing aside empty beer and soda cans. When we came out to the large center room, I let the handcart roll to a stop.

"Where to?" I asked. "We've got six corridors to choose from."

"That one," Gus said, indicating the closest one.

"You sure?"

"Who gives a fuck?" he said. "There's only six. Process of elimination. C'mon, doggy, get a move on."

I dug in with my feet, and the cart slowly began rolling. I thought about asking Gus again about why he was doing this, when he knew that he was helping a government gain a nuclear device, a government with a unique view of the world and its place in it. A government that every now and then declared war on the rest of the world. A government that was now going to have a weapon that could kill tens of thousands in seconds. A hell of a thing to do. I still wondered how Gus could be doing what he was doing.

But I was too tired to ask anything. I just bowed down and kept pushing down the corridor, and after a couple of minutes I realized it was getting harder and harder to see. I raised my head and looked back, where Gus was silhouetted in the lights coming from the large center room. I let the handcart roll to a stop again.

Gus came up to me. "What's the problem?"

"The problem is that we're running out of light. Look, the corridor must curve. See how dim it's getting? We keep on going like this and we're going to be in darkness again."

"Well, I guess we'll have to keep on—"

I interrupted, "Look, you idiot, I keep on pushing your precious cargo down this corridor without any lights, and I may drop it down a hole. Or I might get stuck in a rough patch. And how will that affect your schedule?"

I could sense what was going on in Gus's mind, knowing the pressures that were starting to bear inside him. I rubbed my hands, trying to ease the muscle cramps.

Gus said, "Okay, it makes sense. Turn this rig around and let's head back. I've got an idea."

I was going to say something snappy in reply, but remembering Clem's and Jack's fates, decided against it.

It seemed like a week of steady pushing before we were back in the circular room, and Jack said, "Come along and leave the cart here. I want to check something out."

He motioned me to the short corridor where we had just been, and I started heading in. Gus came up behind me and said, "We're going to take another look at poor dead Jack."

I stopped and turned. "Excuse me?"

The pistol was back in Gus's hand. "You heard me. I can't

believe the old man didn't come in here without a flashlight or a lighter or matches. You're going to take a look. If he's got a flashlight, fine. If he's got matches or a lighter, then we can make a torch or something."

"You want I should take his rings and gold teeth while we're at it?" I asked.

"Hah, hah," he said, with no humor in his voice. "Get going, before I decide I can do this whole thing by myself."

I looked at his face, memorizing the expression, the anger and dead look in his eyes, and I turned around and resumed walking. I got back into the room and then looked back at Gus, a smile suddenly erupting on my face. "Tell you what: Was this part of your plan?"

Gus looked shocked, and I could hardly blame him.

For Jack was gone, and so was his shotgun.

Gus elbowed past me, looked into the small room. Empty. He turned on me in a fury. "Where the hell is he? Where in hell did he go?"

I kept silent, just enjoying this little drama play itself out for as long as I could.

"Well?" he demanded.

I said, "As I mentioned before, you're the boss. What do you think, I snuck him out in one of the canisters?"

He shoved the pistol into my ribs. "Now. Back to the uranium."

I walked at a quick pace down the corridor, past the empty cans and trash of the current generation showing its appreciation to an earlier generation for its service. When we came out, there was Jack, stumbling out of one of the side corridors, one hand held against his chest, the other dragging the shotgun by its wooden stock, heading over to the collections of batteries and instruments that controlled the lights. Darkness. I knew what he was planning. Darkness, his only chance.

I moved left and Gus moved right, and Jack turned, raised the shotgun, but Gus was quicker, firing off two shots. I couldn't tell if they struck home, but Jack did fall down, sitting back up against the batteries. Gus ducked and took cover behind the handcart. I froze, out in the open, as Jack coughed blood and looked over at me. The shotgun in his hands wavered, then started drifting over in my direction. I was exposed—no cover, no weapon, nothing at all.

Jack stared at me. Whispered something. I think he said "Thanks." I wasn't sure.

Then the shotgun moved around to the direction of the handcart, and he fired off another round. Gus returned fire and Jack's head snapped back. No doubt he was dead now, no doubt at all, and he fell to the side, right against the batteries, and once again we were plunged into darkness.

"Lewis?" came Gus's voice. "You over there?"

I started crawling away, knowing this was my chance, my only chance.

"Lewis, say something, or I'll start shooting." I heard clicking noises as he reloaded his revolver. "I can hear movement over there. One lucky shot on my part, and you're a dead man. Speak up. You're closer to Jack than I am. You can get the power up and running if you can crawl over there. Do that and we'll see what we can do. Lewis?"

I froze, knowing he was right, knowing he could hear things, but damn it, this was as good as it was going to get. I wasn't going to give him any satisfaction. Let him sit there and stew.

But Gus had other plans.

"Hey, Lewis," he called out. "You say something, right now. Or I'll turn on the lights myself, and when you pop up it'll be over, real quick. Last chance."

I started crawling, moving one agonizing foot at a time, and I really thought I could make it. I could hear Gus moving about, knowing he was heading over to where Jack's body was lying, over the power supply. Get a move on, I thought. Get a move on and we can be down one of these corridors; and then options, lots of options.

I was still thinking that when I brushed against an empty

beer can, which made a hell of a noise as it rolled away. Gus started laughing and called out, "Lights, camera, action!"

Sure enough, the lights came on and I sat up, blinking my eyes, and I was at the juncture of another corridor. I could try to duck down the corridor and maybe make it, except that Gus was looking over at me, a sharp smile on his face.

"Thanks for your help, Lewis, but it's time for me to go on my own," he said, raising his revolver.

Then gunfire erupted, fast and furious, and I fell back and Gus fell back, and I realized with amazement that Gus wasn't the one firing. I crawled into the corridor, looked back, and the room was empty, except for two things. One was the handcart and its load.

And the other was a man strolling in, night-vision goggles hanging around his neck, wearing black combat fatigues, with what looked to be an Uzi in his hands, and one serious expression on his face—the face of Felix Tinios.

"Felix!" I whispered loudly. "Over here!"

He came at me in a half-trot, head moving around like a radar station, looking for and evaluating any potential threats. He looked down at me, grinned. "You owe me one very good cell phone, complete with tracking device. I found what was left of it when I got here and spent the last half hour going up and down these damn corridors."

"I'll reimburse you the minute we get the hell out," I said, standing up.

"Which sounds good, so let's get a move on. Who was that character I shot at?"

I got up, feeling so good and alive, so damn alive with Felix standing next to me, well-armed, larger than life, having come after me after my not answering the phone the last time it had rung. A nice little defensive plan we had cooked up over our last breakfast. "That was Gus Turner, employee of the Department of Energy, and definitely not on the short list for employee of the month."

He looked over at the still form of Jack. "Guess I got here just in time. And who's the guy on the ground?"

"Gus's former partner. They had a falling-out."

"Yeah," Felix said, his head still turning around. "Things like that happen a lot."

I went over to Jack's body, picked up his shotgun. Now I felt even better. "You know how to get out of here?"

"Yep."

"Then let's get going."

And we did, about three feet, until I looked over at the handcart. One of the black cases was missing. The one with the detection gear. The one with the radio.

The radio.

"Hold it," I said.

Felix turned to me. "Hold what, Lewis? C'mon, let's get a move on."

"We can't," I said, trying to think of which corridor Gus might have run down. "We've got a problem."

Felix said, "Way I see it, we've got a number of problems. Which one is first on your list?"

I nodded in the direction of the handcart. "One of these days I'll give you a history lesson of how this got here, but trust me when I say that this is uranium oxide, the basic material for making an atomic bomb. The guy that was holding the gun on me, he's getting ready to turn it over to the Libyans."

Felix was standing still but his eyes were still moving about. "No offense, but that's what we pay tax dollars for. To take care of matters like that. Government doesn't tell me how to dress, I don't tell them how to deal with rogue nations."

I felt a rising surge of frustration, did my best to control it. "By the time we blunder out of here and find a phone and get some help in here, it'll be too late. The uranium and that guy will be gone."

"So, what in hell are we going to do?" Felix asked.

"We need to find him," I said. "Right now, if not sooner. If we don't, then the world is going to be made a much more dangerous place in just a matter of hours."

Even in the dim light I could make out the range of conflicting emotions playing across Felix's face. He said, "You know, my rule has always been to look out for myself and those I offer my protection to. I'm going a bit out of my area here, looking for this guy."

I shifted the shotgun in my grasp. "Sorry. Because I'm in my area, and I'm going to have to do something about it. With or without you, Felix."

He seemed to sigh. "You would do something like that."

"No time to talk," I said. "You got a flashlight I can use?"

He reached into one of the bulging pockets of his fatigues, pulled out a small black flashlight, tossed it over to me. He looked over and said, "Way I see it, he went down one of these two corridors. I'll take the one on the right, you take the one on the left. Anything special I should do if I hook up to him?"

I switched on the light. "I'm sure you'll figure something out."

"Smartest thing you've said so far," Felix said.

I nodded and got a move on.

Faded black paint over the archway of the corridor stated EAST PASSAGEWAY, and like the corridor earlier, this one banked smoothly to the right. I traveled as far as I could with the benefit of the light from the central room, and when I could go no farther, switched on the flashlight. Patches of cement had fallen free from the wall and the ceiling, revealing rusting strands of rebar. Parts of the floor had buckled as well, and where the ground water had come up, caused long puddles to form. This forced me to keep close to the side as I moved in deeper into the tunnel. With the flashlight on, I found myself moving ahead in spurts, breathing hard, keeping the shotgun trained in front of me, both dreading and anticipating seeing Gus in front of me, phone in hand, trying to make his way out.

Something brushed against my hair and I bit hard to force down a yelp. I raised the light and saw old lengths of cable hanging free from a broken light fixture. More graffiti spoiled the smooth walls of the tunnel, most either promising or boasting of a variety of sexual exploits. More broken glass on the floor, more empty beer containers, more cigarette butts, but no sign of Gus.

I shifted the light in my grasp and had just started moving again when the gunfire started.

Pow. Pow-pow.

Three shots. Just three shots. And none of them had the deep sound that I remembered from Felix's Uzi.

I got a move on, started splashing through the water, almost tripping, and then I slid to a stop. A shorter tunnel, leading to the right. Black paint announced CONNECTOR C. I leaned over, gave a quick flash of the light. More water but at least the sides of the tunnel were dry. There was no bottomless pit here. I moved in, again trying to keep to the side, again getting soaked in the process. Something slithered away in the water and I paid it no mind. I stopped at the intersection, the shotgun now weighing about as much as a length of concrete. I gave another ducking look with the flashlight. Nothing. I moved into the intersection, flashed the light up and down. Still nothing. I moved the light down and something heavy seemed to ooze through my throat as I saw what was there.

Felix's weapon.

But nothing else.

"Felix?" I called out softly.

No answer. I moved to the other side of the small intersection, where another tunnel seemed to lead away, and I took a step in and stepped on nothing, quickly windmilled my way back, breathing hard, trembling.

Oh. Oh, no.

I knelt down, held the flashlight out, saw where the concrete flooring disappeared after about two feet. I got closer to the rough edge and looked over. The drop wasn't much, maybe five or six feet, but it ended in a pool of water. There was a body in the water, floating facedown, wearing black fatigues and boots. There was a smear of blood at the base of the skull, and the body wasn't moving.

Oh, damn. Damn it all to hell.

Then there was another noise, farther down the hallway. Of metal striking metal.

I had a soul-deadening moment of regret, of sorrow and loss and anger all rolled into one, and then I heard that noise again.

I got up with the shotgun and went back hunting.

I didn't have far to go. The tunnel widened up to another connecting hub, and there was Gus, flashlight clenched in his mouth, as he was trying to get a clasp off a metal door. He had a length of rebar in his hands, his revolver in one rear pocket and what looked to be a radio in the other, and he quickly turned as I came in. I raised up the shotgun and worked the action, *snick-snack*, and an empty shotgun shell flew out and struck the floor.

"My, you're looking some serious there, Lewis," he said, smiling.

"Damn right I am," I said. "Drop the rebar and sit down on your hands."

"Why?" he asked.

"Sorry, I'm not in the mood," I said.

"Look, it makes sense," he said. "Let me out of here so I can use the radio. Looks like all this metal and concrete's blocking the signal. You wait with me until the helicopter arrives, and then I'll hand over the money that Jack was going to get. Then I get the goodies and leave."

"And what about my friend back there, floating in the water?"

He shrugged. "Got in the way. Sorry. Least he did was to give me this flashlight 'fore I tossed him into the water. Look, you can do well here. You telling me you don't care about the money?"

"Maybe I care about something else," I said, moving in closer. "Down. On the ground."

"Why?" he asked, his voice sounding almost reasonable. "Why do you care so much that the Libyans get the bomb? That a bunch of desert nobodies eventually bomb the shit out of a bunch of other nobodies? You actually care about that?"

"Last time, Gus," I said. "On the ground—now!"

"Or what? You gonna shoot me?"

"That's what I'm thinking . . ."

He shook his head, started to turn back to the door with the rebar in his hand. "You don't have the fucking stones. I've read your record. Nothing but an analyst, a reader and writer. You wouldn't fucking dare."

In a blaze of a second, I thought about all the bodies I had seen today, ending up with that of Felix, and I raised the shotgun to my shoulder and braced myself, and pulled the trigger back.

The shock of the sound almost floored me. I had expected a gut-wrenching blast, the force of the stock against my shoulder, and the sight of Gus falling down from the shotgun pellets striking him.

Instead: a tiny click.

Gus whirled around. "Man, I guess you did have the stones, huh?"

I worked the action, and nothing happened again as I pulled the trigger. Empty. The magazine was empty. Nothing.

I raised the shotgun as a club and advanced toward him, and Gus started laughing and said, "Man, this day just keeps on getting better and better. And you doubted that this was my lucky day."

I moved forward as fast I could, but Gus's practiced hand moved back to his rear pocket, going for his revolver, and though I knew in less than a heartbeat that I wasn't going to make it, I sure as hell was going to try.

Then something funny happened to Gus's shirt. Three red dots appeared, bright red and wavering, and then they suddenly blossomed wide into black, torn holes. Gus stumbled back, eyes wide open, and fell against the metal door he had been trying to open. His stolen flashlight fell to the ground, as did his weapon. He slid down to the dirty concrete, eyes still expressing surprise at all that was happening, and then things got busy and confusing and loud, as I turned around.

Hooded men in dark fatigues came trotting through, carrying stubby automatic weapons with silencers on the ends of the barrels, their laser sights cutting through the darkness, and I couldn't quite make out their shouts, but I guessed their intent. I dropped the shotgun and raised my hands, and from behind the advancing group of armed men was a very happy-looking Laura Reeves.

There was a flurry of movement and sounds, and two of the armed men grabbed me by the elbows and started propelling me back down the corridor as Laura and a couple of others went up to Gus's body. Other men were setting up powerful lights on tripods along the corridor and in the main hub, and as I moved down the corridor I saw another group, clustered around that short corridor piece that ended in a pool of water. I closed my eyes and felt something inside me shudder as I went by. I wanted to stop, had to stop, but it was easier to let the armed men take me away.

In the center room more lights had been set up, and Jack's body was being examined, poked and prodded. The handcart and its cargo were also being taken apart, and a crew of two started working with a welding torch. I rubbed at my face, tired of it all, and sat down and leaned against the cold concrete wall. Lots of thoughts were crowding their way into my mind and I didn't want them to come up and play with me, so I focused on looking around me, at the burst of activity. Some of the men had pulled free of their black hoods and were talking together, hands moving in expansive gestures. The cutting crew was still at work on one of the canisters. There was a flap-flap noise as a rubberized body bag was undone and rolled out for Jack's body. Some photographs were taken. Another guy in black fatigues started putting together a communications setup of some sort. All of them ignored me.

That was a good thing.

Then Laura Reeves came strolling by, talking to one of her armed escorts, who looked a bit silly with an automatic weapon slung over his back as he was taking notes with a Palm Pilot in his huge hands. Laura noticed me and gave me a big smile. I'm afraid I didn't smile back. She had on khaki slacks and a blue turtleneck, and the cut of the turtleneck was spoiled by the black protective vest she was wearing. She went over to the guy with the radio and said, "Set?"

"All set, ma'am," he said, pulling away.

Laura picked up a handset, started talking rapidly into it: "Comanche, Comanche, Comanche. This is Field One, Field One, Field One. Items are secured. Repeat: items are secured."

I could hear the buzz of conversation from the other end,

and then Laura snapped her fingers at one of the guys, who came over with another Palm Pilot for her to look at. She nodded and said, "Comanche, Comanche, this is Field One. Confirm all items are here, all items are here. None missing. Repeat: None missing."

Then she listened just a bit more, nodded twice, and said, "Roger that. Field One out."

She gave the handset back to one of her crew and then walked over to me and sat down on the concrete next to me. "You okay?"

"I'm breathing," I said.

Laura reached over and squeezed my hand. "You done good, my friend. You done good."

I pulled my hand away. "The hell I did." I remembered again that view—of that body floating still in the water. Tears started to form in my eyes.

"The hell I did," I said again.

CHAPTER TWENTY-ONE

Laura seemed almost hurt at what I had just said, and I added, "Not that I'm ungrateful, but how the hell did you end up here?" As I wiped at my eyes, she said, "We knew there were problems this afternoon, with Gus and Clem gone and out of contact, and with you missing as well. Word got out, and then, well, God bless the local cops."

"Why?"

I could feel her shift her weight next to me. "Remember the two local cops who found the body of the Libyan agent last week?"

"Yep."

"Well, one of them came back again on patrol and saw an empty car parked where it didn't belong. Plates came back odd, as you know, and then he saw blood on the ground, underneath the trunk. Talk about coincidences, huh? We got the word and we flooded this area, my friend, we really did. Sound and thermal sensors, even in the rain, and we got right to work."

"Yes," I said. "God bless local cops."

She turned to me. "Did you hear what I was saying back there on the radio, just a few minutes ago?"

"Telling your bosses that you've secured the uranium. They must be very happy."

"More than that, Lewis, more than that," she said, her voice exasperated. "Don't you know what almost happened?"

Now I remembered. "The bombing raids against Libya."

"Right. The bombing raids against Libya. I'm not sure of the time frame, but I'm sure we were pretty close to killing hundreds of people. And thanks to you, that was stopped. So, again I say: You done good."

I was starting to feel cold and my arms were cramping up again from all that exertion, and I was going to say something sharp to Laura in return, when my mouth refused to work.

Coming out of the hallway, dripping wet and with a compress against the back of his head, was one very alive Felix Tinios.

I stood up, legs trembling. Laura stood up next to me. Felix broke away from his armed escorts and came over to me. He got right to the point.

"That guy dead?"

"Yes," I said.

"Good." Dried blood was on his wrists. "You do it?"

"No, but it wasn't for lack of trying," I said. "I drew him down with Jack's shotgun. But Jack was low in the ammo department. The only thing I did was to scare him with the sound of a firing pin slamming shut on an empty chamber."

"Well, shit like that happens," Felix said. His clothes were dripping wet on the concrete, his hair was matted and dried blood was on his neck as well. "I guess I have to thank the fed shooters, huh?"

"Looks that way," I said.

Laura spoke up. "Excuse me, and you are . . . ?"

Felix gave her a chilly smile. "Sorry, miss, I'm talking to this gentleman here. Don't you know it's rude to interrupt?"

Which I did, just then. "What happened?"

Felix shook his head, seemingly in admiration. "That little bastard was good. I was heading down the corridor, scanning on both sides. Good things about night-vision goggles is that you can see in the dark. Bad thing is that you've got shit for peripheral vision. You know that swimming hole I ended up in?"

"That I do," I said.

"Little bastard was crouched down in that hole. Lots of hand- and footholds on the broken concrete. I went by and he got up and popped me in the back, and then a couple of more times for good measure. I fell in, and without my Uzi, well, I figured the best approach would be to play possum."

With his free hand, he unbuttoned the front of his shirt, revealing a Kevlar vest. "These things do work, but I know I've got a couple of bruises back there. Damn, it hurts."

Laura spoke up again, "I'm sorry; I really have to ask. Who are you?"

Felix smiled, bowed in her direction. "Ma'am, I make it a rule never to talk to the feds without my lawyer present. And since my friend here Lewis is not a member of the New Hampshire or Massachusetts bar, then I must be going."

"Oh, no, you don't," she said.

Another smile. "Oh, yes, I will. The name is Felix Tinios, I reside on Rosemount Lane in North Tyler, and if you'd care to stop by, do. You can try to take me into custody, and I'll go willingly, but the only thing you'll hear from me is what I just said. I never talk to feds without my lawyer present. Otherwise . . . Lewis, I'm sure I'll be seeing you."

"You certainly will."

He smiled again for both our benefit, I suppose, and then ambled down the exit corridor, now well-lit and bustling with people who seemed to know what they were doing and why. I almost envied them. Laura looked at me and said, "Who the hell was that?"

"A friend of mine who came in to rescue me," I said. "He's also someone who you don't want to piss off."

She gave me an odd look and said, "You know, I do think you're right. How are you doing?"

"I'm doing all right," I said.

"That's fine," she said. "Look, we need to talk and debrief, and—"

I wiped at my face again. "No."

Laura said, "Lewis, it's been a long day and—"

"No, no, and still, no. Tell me, how are you doing?"

"Me?" she asked, surprised. "What do you mean?"

"I mean, all of this," I said. "You're in charge, right?"

"Yes, of course I am. What are you getting at?"

In the strong lights now in this concrete chamber, I tried to gauge what was going on behind those still brown eyes, and I failed. I could not understand who she was and what she had done. "What I'm getting at is how your gun crew came in at the last moment. What I'm getting at is that you weren't interested in capturing Gus, or interrogating Gus, or putting him on trial and embarrassing you and the Department of Energy. It would have been easy to capture him. But that didn't happen. Which tells me that your boys with guns got specific orders. Am I right?"

"No," she said slowly. "No, you're not right."

"Good going, Laura," I said. "That was the same tone of voice you used on me when you first said you worked for the Drug Enforcement Agency. Which is why I asked how you were doing. Considering how Gus was set up and terminated, without too much fuss. Pretty cold, Laura. Pretty cold."

"We do what we have to," she said. "That's the nature of our business. All right, we'll talk tomorrow. Give me a couple of minutes and I'll get a car and driver for you."

"Sorry," I said. "No again. I'd rather walk."

Laura said, "It's pouring rain out there. You'll be soaked."

"That's right," I said. "And I'll be soaked on my own, without owing you or anybody else. See you later."

And with that, I turned around and started heading out.

While the trip in with Gus and Jack in the darkness had seemed to take hours, the trip out took only a few minutes. Earlier in the darkness I had imagined the vastness of the tunnels and chambers, wondering how Jack had gotten us here, and I felt slightly sheepish as I easily made my way back. Other serious-looking men and women kept on streaming in, carrying cases of equipment, more lights, photographic paraphernalia and who knows what. At the entrance the door was propped open and more lights were set up outside, the rain streaming down highlighted in their strong beams.

A couple of men looked over at me and started coming

toward me, but I just kept my look down and went out into the rain.

Some long minutes later, soaked and with my clothes sticking to me and my shoes squishing in the mud, I made it out to the parking lot of the Samson Point nature preserve. I stopped, coughed a bit, and looked around. I had earlier thought of walking out onto the parking lot and then ambling down Atlantic Avenue, keeping to the side of the road, making my way home quietly. But the lot was full of LTDs and dark vans, and beyond the gate other cars were parked as well, cruisers with lights flashing and what looked like a couple of television news vans.

Not much chance of a quiet walk home.

The rain seemed to come down even harder, and I only hesitated for a moment. The longer I'd wait, the wetter and colder I'd get. I turned and started heading out to the low dark hills beyond which my home was. I walked across the parking lot, dodging through the parked vehicles, and as I started climbing up into the darkness, I looked back. The last thing I saw was a little pool of light around a parked LTD with its trunk open, where people were looking at the body of a dead ex-Marine who had died this evening at the hands of a trusted coworker.

When I got home, before I did anything else, anything at all, I made sure the telephone was unplugged. No talking tonight, no, sir. Shivering and cold, I went upstairs, stripping off my wet clothing and footwear as I got up to the second floor. I turned the shower on as hot as I could stand it, and spent what seemed like a half hour or so scrubbing and washing and rinsing, repeating the process over and over. When my hot water heater finally surrendered and the water started to cool down, I got out and automatically began checking my skin, the way I did after every shower, looking for the bumps or swellings that meant that the bio agent from my long-ago exposure had finally bitten me again.

My skin was clear, at least this night. I rubbed my body dry and wished there were a way I could reach in and check my mind, for what I had seen today would be with me for a very long time—the bodies and the blood and the shooting and that terrible, cold-blooded moment when I had raised that shotgun ready to kill another man, and how disappointed I had felt when the firing pin fell on an empty chamber.

Dressed in a blue terry-cloth robe, I went downstairs and built a fire in the fireplace, piling in the oak chunks as high as I dared. In my kitchen I grabbed an unopen bottle of Australian Merlot, a package of saltine crackers and from the refrigerator a chunk of cheddar cheese. I got back to my couch, listened to the crackling of the fire and the rain still coming down in sheets, and got to work on the only food and drink I cared about. I sipped from the wine bottle without benefit of glassware, and ate the cheese and crackers, as I looked at the fire, its flames rising higher and higher. I watched the flames for a long time, keeping my eyes open as much as possible, for whenever I closed them, I saw the same things.

Clem, jackknifed and dead in the trunk of the LTD.

Jack, collapsing and dying in the central chamber.

Gus, stumbling back, as bullets tore into his chest.

I drank and ate and stared at the flames as long as I could.

Sometime during the night I woke up on the couch. I didn't remember stretching out or pulling a down comforter over me. I woozily stood up and went upstairs and used the bathroom, and then came back down. In the kitchen I drank two glasses of cold water and then went to the sliding glass doors that led out to my deck. The rain had stopped and it seemed the clouds had moved away.

I got out on the deck, the wood wet under my bare feet. I hugged myself and looked out at the ocean, at the swelling of the waves, coming in again and again. I looked up at the stars, the bright and beautiful stars, just imagining what lay out there in the universe, what wonders and mysteries. Staring up there, I saw a tiny dot of light moving, fast and unblinking. Perhaps it was the space shuttle. Perhaps it was the International Space Station. Perhaps it was just a weather satellite. But it didn't quite matter. What was up there belonged to us, had been sent up there and now resided up in the heavens.

I looked over to the north, where Samson Point was, and

there were plenty of lights over there, as whatever work was being done by Laura and her crew was continuing. I remembered a night some days ago, when the lights I had seen over there had drawn me, like a curious moth to a flame. Well, this particular insect was still living, though singed.

I looked at the lights and then went back to looking at the stars.

In the morning I had two cups of tea, three scrambled eggs and an English muffin, and throughout the morning I kept the phone unplugged. If someone wanted to talk to me, they could damn well come down and talk to me in person, though I knew eventually I would have to talk to them. Laura Reeves. Felix Tinios. Even Diane Woods, my detective friend, and Paula Quinn. Always, Paula. I owed her a lot and I knew I had blown off her last phone call, when she had said she needed to talk to me.

But I had a little work to do. I went up to my office and got out some paperwork I had collected over the past few days, I got to work, typing up a long letter about things I had seen and things I had collected. When I had printed out these documents, and I got the other paperwork together, I put them into a nine-by-twelve manila envelope, sealed it, and then left my house, after making sure I had plugged in the phone. The day was a pleasant, sunny April morning, a day I would usually spend on my back deck, getting some sunshine and enjoying the cool ocean air.

But not this morning.

I drove back to Porter and went to the offices of the Porter *Herald*. I hope Paula would eventually forgive me, but what I was going to supply to a newspaper I couldn't possibly have given to her editor. The Porter *Herald* is in a one-story brick building a couple of blocks away from the harbor and just a few blocks more from the Porter Submarine Museum.

I parked in its large lot and went up to the front entrance. Near the entrance was a newspaper box, and after dropping in two quarters, I retrieved that morning's issue. I don't read the Porter *Herald* that much—its copyediting staff relies too heavily on computer spell-checking—but I needed this particular issue. I opened it up to the editorial page, where I scanned the little box that listed the top editors. I skipped the chief editor's name and went down to the news editor: Alan Sher. Knowing how newspapers operate, I knew that the chief editor would be too busy juggling different items from personnel to budgets to office politics to look seriously at what I had to offer. Which is why I scrawled Alan Sher's name on the brown envelope and went inside.

The receptionist was a young man with a blond crew cut and earrings on both ears, wearing baggy khaki pants and a dungaree shirt with a red necktie. He had on a headset and sat behind a waist-high counter, and through a glass door on the left I could make out the computer terminals and the reporters in the newsroom. I came in and handed the envelope over to him.

"Could you see that Mr. Sher gets this right away?" I asked.

He glanced down at the envelope and said, "Certainly. May I ask who's dropping this off?"

"You may," I said, and left.

Outside I felt both antsy and tired, a strange combination. There was a pay phone and I made a phone call to Paula Quinn at the *Chronicle*. No answer. I left a message on her voice mail.

"Paula, it's Lewis. I know I've been a pain lately, and you have my apologies. I'd like an opportunity—ah, make that a bunch of opportunities, to make it up to you. Please give me a ring as soon as you can."

I hung up and rubbed my hands, and kept on walking. At a small restaurant on Congress Street I had a quick bowl of chowder for lunch, and then walked around downtown. Lots of cars, lots of people, lots of everything. It made my head hurt. Coming to the brick-and-glass building that marked the Porter Public Library, I went in. This was what I needed. On the first floor was the periodicals room, with plenty of comfortable chairs, and magazines displayed on racks all around the room. I looked at where they started—*Astronomy*—and where they ended—*Yachting*—and decided this was the place for me.

I sat down and started looking at pictures of Saturn, wondering how the shuttle was doing overhead.

Hours later, I left the Porter Public Library, after reading about the newest dock facilities in the British Virgin Islands. I wandered back to the Porter *Herald* parking lot, curious how the news editor's day was going, and I got in my Explorer and headed south once again.

The drive seemed to take just a few seconds before I was back at Tyler Beach and turning into the parking lot of the Lafayette House. A woman was there, sitting on the trunk of yet another government-issued LTD. She had on black high-heeled shoes and a short black skirt and black stockings, and a leather jacket. I thought about racing past her or backing back onto Atlantic Avenue, but instead I slowed down and rolled down the passenger's side window. Laura Reeves yawned and got off the car trunk and came over.

"Hey, there," she said.

"Hey yourself," I said.

"I was wondering if you could spare some time my way," she said.

"If you're looking for a formal debrief, forget it," I said. "Not today. Maybe tomorrow. Maybe next week. But not now."

"Understood," she said, leaning against the open window, her hair hanging into my Explorer. She had on a gray sweater and a strand of pearls about her neck. "Look, it's almost time for dinner. Or supper, as you New Englanders call it. How about my treat?"

"What kind of treat are you offering?"

She nodded back in the direction of her car. "We can go to the fanciest restaurant around here, or, back in the car, I've got a cooler with dinner fixings. Your choice. Either out or down to your house. You decide."

I looked at her face, tried to remember the look she had given me late last night, back in the gun complex. "Do we talk business?"

"Only if you want to."

I felt my fingers squeeze the steering wheel. "All right. My choice. My house."

She smiled. "I hoped you were going to say that. Hold on."

And in a matter of a minute or two she was in my Explorer

as we bounced down the rough driveway, a small cooler rattling around in the backseat.

She took over my kitchen and when I tried to lend a hand, she shooed me away. "No, you can have this place back when it's cleanup time. Other than that, leave me be."

So I poured both of us a glass of wine, as she made a roast pork tenderloin dish with rice and a small Caesar salad, and she noticed how I watched her as she cooked. She had shed the leather jacket and looked a hundred degrees away from the woman who had taken control of a crime scene in an underground fortress. "You got a problem with a woman in your kitchen, Cole?"

"Maybe not," I said. "Maybe I have a problem with this particular woman. I realize I'm not being PC and all that, but after seeing the way you work, watching you worry about the temperature of my stove is a bit amusing."

"Well," she said, washing some lettuce in the sink. "When I'm on a job, living far from home, I get tired of other people cooking my meals. I don't mind restaurants and I don't mind hotel food, but I do get tired of it after a few weeks on the road. It gets quite monotonous. So I actually find some joy being in a kitchen, cooking something the way I like it. You got a problem with that?"

"Nope," I said.

"Good," she said, tearing the lettuce into small pieces. "And I especially enjoy it when I'm cooking for someone else, and I certainly hope you don't have a problem with that."

"Not yet," I said. "Not yet."

We ate out on my deck, watching the shadows lengthen as the sun set in the west, on the other side of the house. A couple of seagulls hovered overhead, looking for a handout, and we sent them along their way disappointed. Laura looked out and said, "A hell of a view. You ever get whales through here?"

"Occasionally, though I've never seen them this close to shore," I said. "You've got to take a whale-watch boat out to get a good viewing."

She smiled. "If I had the time, that sounds like fun."

"And what kind of time do you have now?"

Laura shrugged. "Not much. It only took some threats on my part to get this evening off, considering all the hours I've been putting in. But there's reports to be filed, witnesses to be interviewed, evidence to be collected. Right now the uranium's being flown out to Los Alamos, and I still have a couple of people left to talk to. Including you."

"Lucky me," I said.

"Yes, lucky you," she said. "And what do you plan to do when this is all wrapped up?"

"Plans? I didn't know I was suppose to have plans."

"Sure you do," she said confidently. "Everyone's got plans. You mean to tell me that when this is all over you intend to go back to your quiet little existence, doing whatever it is that you do?"

"Exactly," I said, cutting a fresh piece of roast pork. "That's exactly what I plan to do. What do you think I want to do, come work with you?"

She eyed me as she chewed delicately on a piece of meat. "To repeat a phrase, that's exactly what I'm thinking. Not full-time. I wouldn't want to take you away from this coastal paradise. No, what I'm thinking is a contract force. Come in when we have particular problems to look at. I like the way you handle yourself, I like the way you poked around and answered questions."

"Did you also like the way I tried to kill your coworker?" I asked.

She raised an eyebrow, while the faint breeze off the ocean blew hair across her face. "I liked the way you handled yourself back there, when your back was against the wall, so let's leave it at that. All right?"

"All right," I said.

She toyed with her fork some and said, "I know you're going through a shakedown after all that happened. But be glad with what you helped do, Lewis. You saved hundreds of lives, you saved the lives of American servicemen and women who were about to fly into harm's way, and you also helped keep some important Mideast negotiations on track. You should feel proud."

"Maybe I should," I said, still thinking of what it had been like looking at the still form of Felix Tinios floating in that flooded chamber. "But it's too soon. It really is."

She smiled. "Okay. I get it. But I also need a commitment from you on an official debrief. Nothing too fancy. Just me and nobody else. Does tomorrow sound okay?"

I thought and said, "Tomorrow afternoon. I might be busy in the morning. Is that all right?"

"Sure. Two P.M.?"

"Two is fine."

We ate some more and chatted about the weather and the foibles of working for the federal government, and what kinds of hotels have the best room service. Nothing too fancy. Then the wind picked up some and clouds began to roll in, and when I saw her shiver, I suggested it was time to go in.

It happened just as we were in the kitchen area, after the dishes had been piled up. She looked at me and said simply, "I'm cold," and then she was in my arms. We kissed for long seconds and then stumbled into the living room and onto the couch. I was on my back and she was on top of me, surprisingly strong, and I enjoyed the sensation, enjoyed the taste and feel of her, of the long hair gliding through my fingers, the strong muscles of her back as I held her close.

Her legs were entangled in mine and we kept on kissing, her hands now unbuttoning my shirt, and then it all just faded away. I thought about Paula Quinn, a few miles away, maybe coming home from a planning-board meeting or something, and finding my message on her answering machine. I imagined her smiling slightly as she picked up the phone and dialed me back, and then the smile slowly fading away as the phone rang and rang and rang without being picked up.

Paula. Wanting and needing to talk to me, by a silent phone.

Laura raised her head. "Well, permit me to introduce myself. The name is Laura Reeves."

"I know," I said.

"Then why have you suddenly departed? Something wrong?"

I sighed and rubbed at the sides of her head. "Yes. Several things. All wrong. It's like this, I—"

"Hush," she said, touching her fingers to my lips, sitting up on the couch. "I don't need to hear anything else. I know the drill. It's one of a few reasons, tried and true. There's somebody else. There's not somebody else, but you don't fit the bill. You're going to be leaving soon, what's the point. You're a hard, tough woman, and sorry, I can't get past that."

She tugged at her sweater, pulled it down back over her skirt. She kissed me quickly. "I've heard it all before and I don't want to get into a lengthy blah-blah-blah session over the ins and outs. All right?"

Laura got up and grabbed her jacket and said, "I'll see you tomorrow at two. And thanks for the company. I really enjoyed myself."

"I did, too," I said, but by then she was already out the door. I was on my feet now, the scent of her still on my hands, the taste of her still on my lips. I went to the kitchen and started slowly washing the dishes, waiting for the phone to ring, and its silence mocked me during the rest of the evening.

I called Paula Quinn one more time, just before going to bed, and hung up without leaving a message on her machine.

CHAPTER TWENTY-TWO

The next morning I felt better, and after a quick stand-up breakfast of tea and toast in my kitchen I took my Explorer out and drove the thirty seconds up to the Lafayette House, where I went into the small gift shop and purchased that day's Porter *Herald*. I folded the paper in half, and from a pay phone in the hotel's lobby, I called Paula. Still no answer. I rubbed the paper against my leg and thought for a bit. Knowing Paula, she also had the habit of letting messages pile up on her answering machine when she didn't want to be disturbed. I checked the time. A little before 8 A.M. Should be up by now, and I thought she'd want to see that day's *Herald*.

I got back into the Explorer and headed south and made a right-hand turn onto High Street and drove the short distance to her apartment house. Her Ford Escort was still in the parking lot, and by the time I was in the building and going upstairs to the second floor, I was smiling like a glad uncle, ready to present his favorite niece with a magnificent gift.

It took two knocks on the door before it opened up, and there was Paula, yawning, wearing a short yellow robe. Her face seemed surprised and she said, "Lewis, what is—"

"Hold on," I said. "Before you say another word, another syllable, I want to show you this."

I handed over the *Herald* to her and she muttered, "This better be good, or—Holy Christ, look at this."

I craned my head to look over her shoulder as she looked at the front-page headline and accompanying news story. The headline said, CHRONICLE EDITOR LINKED TO PORN SHOPS, and the lead of the story began, "Documents supplied to the Porter *Herald* yesterday show that Rupert Holman, the new executive editor at the Tyler *Chronicle* and a prime mover behind the county-wide decency program, has himself been renting adult videos from local video rental stores. Copies of receipts—with Holman's name, address, phone number and what appears to be his signature—show that Holman rented nearly a dozen videos in the last week alone. The videos were of the most explicit possible, and even the names of the videos cannot be published in this newspaper."

She looked up at me, her face pale with shock. "This can't be true. Can it?"

I proudly looked back at her. "If it's printed in the newspaper, it must be true, right?"

Now her expression changed. "You. You had something to do with this, didn't you?"

"Well, maybe a little—"

"Lewis, do you know what this means? Do you?"

"Sure I do," I said. "Somebody who's been giving you and the rest of the newspaper grief these past few weeks has just been hoisted by his own petard. Someone who's been sitting in judgment is going to get a brief taste of—"

"Spare me, will you?" she said sharply. "What this means is that my newspaper is going to be the laughingstock of the seacoast. What this means is that—sure, Rupert might be heading out over this embarrassment, but we've gotten used to him. Which means that we now have to get used to some other jerk who—"

"Hey, Paula," came a voice from inside her place. "Where do you hide the coffee around here?"

Paula's face seemed to flush and I looked into the apartment as a young man wearing a towel wrapped around his waist came into view. He stopped quickly, his face now the color of Paula's, and I wished right then and there that I had overslept that morning.

"Lewis," she said, "I'd like you to meet—"

"Yes, I know who it is," I said. "Mark Spencer, town counsel. Am I right?"

"Yeah, I'm, uh, I'll just leave you two be," he said, backing away, and I held up a hand. "No, that's fine, I was just leaving. Right now."

"Lewis," Paula said, holding the newspaper, clasping her robe close against her. "Look, I'll call you, we'll chat, okay?"

"Yes, of course," I said, and I turned around and the next thing I knew I was back in my Ford, driving away, not sure of where I was going or why, but just knowing I had to be away from there at any price.

The next person who saw the newspaper had a more cheerful response than Paula, and Diane Woods laughed over and over again as she read through the story. We were having an early lunch at the Whale's Fin, a small restaurant at the Tyler Beach Palace, right in the center of the Strip at Tyler Beach. Large windows looked out over the sidewalk, where the first trickles of tourists began their yearly trek to visit the shore.

Diane had on a tan business suit and white blouse, and she chuckled again as she read the ending of the story aloud to me. "'Reached at his apartment late last night, Holman refused to comment and hung up on the phone on this reporter.'" She looked over at me, still smiling. "Don't those yahoos in the media know any better? It's always the cover-up that gets you in trouble, not the crime."

I tried to get my hands around a sloppy steak-and-cheese sub that was oozing out over my plate. "You're enjoying this way too much, you know."

"I know, I know," she said, returning to her salad. "There's a German word about taking joy in the misfortune of others, and I wish I knew it right now, because I sure am feeling this. Hah.

Self-appointed guardian of the town's morals, exposed for all to see. Except . . ."

I chewed, swallowed. "Except what?"

She eyed me. "Except that I don't think he even could have been that stupid, to rent videos from stores that he tried to send protesters to. Which tells me that he must have been set up. I'd first think that one or two of the stores might have done it on their own, but three different ones? Doesn't make sense."

I took another healthy bite of my sandwich. "Yeah, you're right. It doesn't make sense."

"Uh-huh," she said. "Which tells me that somebody with a grudge or ax to grind did it. Somebody who doesn't like bullies. Someone who doesn't like a person from out of town coming in and raising hell with the locals. Someone I'm looking at right now."

I made chewing noises and pointed to my mouth, and Diane smiled in return. "Oh, I'll wait until you swallow. Lewis, you had to know that this wasn't going to work that well. A day or so later, he'll be able to prove that he didn't rent the videos. So what was the point? A temporary embarrassment?"

I finally swallowed, wiped my chin with a paper napkin. "There's an apocryphal story about Lyndon Johnson, back when he was first running for some statewide office in Texas. It was a close race and he asked somebody in his campaign to start spreading a rumor, that Johnson's opponent enjoyed . . . um, a special relationship with his barnyard animals. Johnson's adviser was horrified. 'No one will believe that,' he said. And Johnson's supposed reply: 'That's all right. Let's make the son of a bitch deny it.'"

Diane seemed to nod in appreciation. "I see. And after a day or two of denying that he was renting *Leather Lesbians from Hell*, Holman wouldn't be so quick to print stories about people's private lives. Lewis, quite noble, but I'm a big girl. I could have handled myself."

"Having seen you knock around a robbery suspect or two, I have no doubt about that."

"Still . . ." She reached over and touched my hand. "It was

285

greatly appreciated. Greatly. The less stress in my life and Kara's life, the better. And how did your friend Paula handle this news? From what you told me, she's no fan of her new boss."

"Right now, I don't think she's a fan of Lewis Cole, either," I said.

"Oh?" she asked, and I spent a couple of minutes telling her about what had happened earlier that morning, and she said, "Ouch. You should have called again, before going over."

"I should have stayed home, that's what," I said.

"Poor you," she said. "Women problems, yet again."

"Yeah, you're right. Tell me, whenever you figure women out, you let me know."

Another smile. "Deal."

A few more minutes later, she said, "I heard there was quite a hoo-ha over in your neck of the woods last night, over at Samson Point. True?"

"Quite true."

She toyed with her salad. "You involved?"

"Quite involved."

"Anything you can talk about?"

"Nope."

She put her fork down. "Maybe that's why Paula ended up with our new lawyer in town. No big secrets, except maybe a trust fund or two. Maybe you should think better about playing spook man. You're a long way away from your old job and old life, you know."

I wiped my hands on a bunch of napkins. "No, I didn't know."

At 2 P.M. on the dot, Laura Reeves knocked at my door and I led her upstairs to my office. Like Diane, she had on a business suit that covered up the charms she had been displaying yesterday, but unlike Diane, she was cool and to the point.

"You don't want to do this downstairs?" she asked.

"No, if you don't mind," I said. "I'm wrapping up a column for my magazine, and I'd rather hold court in my office."

So we stayed in my office, my new computer still humming

away, and we sat across from each other, less than a yard separating us. From her large bag she took out a fresh yellow legal pad and started from the beginning, asking me questions about why I had come out to the Samson Point nature preserve on that night almost a week ago, through my poking around with the local cops, up to the time when I went down to Boston and found out the truth about her and NEST, which made her raise her eyebrows some. Sometimes the questions were repeated, and sometimes they weren't, and as she talked, I couldn't help but admire that bulldog tenacity she took in asking me the questions.

When she was done, about an hour later, she flipped through the pad again, made a few checkmarks, and said, "Okay, I think we're done here, Lewis. Once again, I offer you the thanks of a grateful Department of Energy. You did an exceptional job."

"Gee, thanks."

"Again, my offer still stands. You can come work for us anytime. You still have my business card?"

"I do."

"Okay, please don't lose it."

"No chance of that," I said. "Permission to ask a question?"

"Sure, go ahead."

"I got a couple of hang-up phone calls over the past week. Nothing serious, nothing too threatening. But they started right after I signed up with you. Can I spare a guess?"

"Go ahead."

"The calls. They came from you, or someone who works for you. Right? What was the point? To keep me sharp?"

A quick nod. "Exactly. To keep you a bit off-balance, so that you'd be more energetic in doing what had to be done. We couldn't have you sitting home doing nothing, hoping to wait us out."

"Could have just trusted me."

"Sure," she said. "But we didn't have the luxury, not then. Fair or foul, Lewis, we needed you to work with us. No hard feelings?"

I didn't answer. Just looked at her. She sighed and said, "Look, one more thing."

Laura rummaged around in her large bag and pulled out a large folder. "I've got some items to show you. Here." She passed over some papers and I slowly went through them. Two were the non-disclosure forms I had signed, once while in Nevada, the other just a while ago across the street. The other papers were copies of bank statements and IRA statements and the title for this house, and all reflected what had happened after I had first turned down Laura's request to work for her. The balances in all the accounts showed zero, and the title—instead of displaying my name—had the Department of Interior inked in.

I handed the papers back to her. "A threat?"

"No, a promise, and a reminder. You've agreed to keep your mouth shut about everything that went on, in return for our promise to leave you alone. Break your promise, and we can do what we did earlier, just as fast. You'll be broke and homeless. Got it?"

"Surely do," I said. "Tell me, if things had progressed last night beyond a little kissy-face on the couch, would you have done this little presentation just the same?"

Her face was expressionless. "Absolutely. And I make no apologies. Whatever I do isn't for spite or anger. It's to defend this country and its people. Killer waves. Remember?"

"Sure, I remember," I said. "Oh, one other thing. I've changed my mind."

"About what?"

"About compensation. I know I made a big show earlier about tearing up that check and all, but I've changed my mind. I've decided I want to be paid for my work."

"Oh. Well, that's a bit out of the ordinary, but I'm sure we can tap into some discretionary funds—"

"Hold on," I interrupted. "Who said anything about money?"

Now I had gotten her attention. "What do you mean?"

"What I mean is this," I said, taking her legal pad and pen from her hands. I scribbled something at the bottom of the first page and passed it over. "There. I wrote it down so there's no confusion. That's what I want, and it's non-negotiable."

She took the pad from me and looked down, and just as quickly looked up. "Impossible."

"No," I said. "Difficult, but not impossible."

"What you've asked for can't be gotten," she said. "It's the property of the people of the United States."

"And you represent the government of the United States, and you can get your hands on it, if you really try."

"No, I'm afraid we can't. It's impossible."

"Nothing's impossible if you put your mind and talents to it, Laura, and you've shown me that you have an impressive amount of both. Like I said, it's non-negotiable. That's what I want."

"Really? Or else, right?"

"Right," I said, and I spun my chair around and reached over to my new computer. A few mouse clicks later, and a familiar voice came out of the computer's speakers: *"All right then, here it is. You're right, you bastard, about the enriched uranium. One of the many little secrets from the end of the Old War and the start of the Cold War."*

Laura did not say a word. I smiled and said, "Not bad sound quality, right? Here's another demo." And I clicked on a few more keys.

"Our job is to analyze the threat, respond to it, and make sure that little snot-nosed sixteen-year-old gets in a world of hurt so much that he'll never go near a computer again. Our job is also to respond to the threats that come from some adults—to go into cities with detecting devices and search out where a bomb may be hidden. Thank God that particular scenario hasn't come up recently. It's not often that we get to respond to a real deal."

"Oh," I continued. "If you're wondering, everything we've said here today as well has been recorded. Amazing what built-in microphones and sound systems these new computers have, and what they can do. So that was my little demonstration. And since you were so big on making promises earlier, here's mine: The moment I get what I want, those files are trashed. The files that are being kept in some friend's hands, they'll be trashed as well.

And the files that are being stored on a Web site, set to be automatically E-mailed in a week to some major news organizations, those will be trashed as well. All in exchange for one little item. Not a bad deal, is it? In exchange for keeping you and your folks and what went on over at Samson Point out of the newspapers. Pretty fair, don't you think?"

Her hands were clasped tightly in front of her. "You son of a bitch."

I shook my head. "No, my parentage is fairly well established. What I am is somebody tired of being pushed around by people who think they're my betters, especially those whom I employ through my tax dollars. People who break down my doors, shanghai me, threaten me, and lie to me. So you've had me and everything I had to offer this past week. What I'm looking for is fair compensation. And what you're looking for is peace and quiet. Like I said, sounds fair to me."

Her hands seemed to loosen up some, and then she laughed. "Boy, I'd really like to have you come work with us, Lewis."

I laughed in return. "Not a chance. Are we done here?"

"Yep," she said, standing up. "And I'll see what I can do about your request. You're right, it does sound fair, and I'll make sure you get it."

"Great."

I walked her downstairs, and at the door I said, "Walk you back to the Lafayette House?"

"No, I'm all set." She gently placed a hand on my chest, kissed me on the cheek. "All in all, it's been quite an adventure. Thanks."

I grasped her chin in my hand, bent down and kissed her on the lips. "True. A real adventure."

"Maybe I'll see you again," she said. "If I ever come back here on business. Or pleasure."

"Make sure it's pleasure," I said. "If it's business, I'll be hiding out."

She laughed again and stepped out, and then began walking

up my driveway. I watched her for a second, and then closed my door.

I suppose I shouldn't have done what I did next, but I needed to get out of the house for a while. I spent a few minutes at a combo drugstore/convenience store down at the beach, and then went to the Tyler Professional Building, where I saw that Paula Quinn's car was missing from the parking lot. No matter.

Following the rules like a good boy, I went through the front door and waved cheerily at the receptionist, who called out after me, "Can I help you? Can I help you? Can I help you?"

In the newsroom Rollie Grandmaison was working at his cluttered desk, strands of black hair still plastered across his skull. Over his head the front pages of the Dover and Porter papers still hung from the ceiling, the fake blood and the plastic dagger, the sign saying, IT'S WAR! Rollie looked over at me and I said, "Rupert?"

He motioned to the closed conference room door. "In there. Having a hell of a meeting, I'd guess."

"Well, I'll go check on it for you."

He grinned. "That'd be great."

I opened up the conference room door without knocking and I could smell it right away: trouble. Rupert was sitting at the head of a shiny conference room table, and the suits were there, on either side of him. One woman and three men. Sent over from the home office no doubt to see what the hell was going on with their porn-loving editor. Rupert's eyes were puffy and even his bow tie looked droopy.

"Hey, Rupert, how's it going?" I said.

His voice was hoarse. "This is a private meeting, Cole. Get the hell out."

"Oh, it'll only take a second," I said. "I just got three quick things to pass along. First of all, congrats on the circulation boost this week for the *Chronicle*. I'm sure it'll be a doozy. Second, next job you get air-dropped in, try to keep what snipers call a low pro-file. Or somebody else might feel a need to take you down when you've decided you're the king of the county. And third . . ."

I tossed the little package over to him, and he caught it and slammed it down on the table. "Yes?"

"A little going-away present for you," I said. "Head cleaner for your VCR. Something tells me that you might need it right about now."

He started yammering to the suits about how he had been set up, and they were yammering back, but the female suit had a hard time hiding a smile behind her hand. I went out of the conference room and left the door wide open, so Rupert the Ruthless could see me leave by the employee's entrance. When I got there I turned and he could still see me. I waved bye-bye at him, like a three-year-old. By now Rollie was on a stool, taking down the newspaper and plastic knife, and just for the hell of it, I waved bye-bye at him as well.

Later that night, the phone rang, and it was Paula. "Hey," she said.

"Hey yourself." I was on my couch, trying to get an update on the shuttle mission from CNN, and so far I had to sit through segments on a Paris fashion show, a calf born in Iowa with the sign of a crucifix on its head, and an interesting bit on some unexpected naval maneuvers in the Mediterranean, off the North African coast.

"I understand you said farewell to our fearless leader this afternoon. I'm sorry I missed it."

"Me, too," I said, muting the sound on my television. "Is he still there?"

"Nope. Cleared out about five P.M. Took one box and that was that. Spent the whole day protesting his innocence. But the powers upstairs don't care. He's an embarrassment, so he gets tossed over the side."

"For once the powers upstairs sound okay."

She sighed. "Yep. And this morning, remember how pissed I was, about how now we'd have to get someone new in and learn to deal with his or her foibles?"

"I remember," I said.

"Well, forget it," she said. "When I saw that arrogant and smug man walk out of there, his career in tatters, after all he did to us and the towns around here . . . I hate to say it, but it made me feel good. *Schadenfreude.*"

"Excuse me?"

"*Schadenfreude.* A German expression at feeling joyous at someone else's misfortune. Not a very nice feeling, but when I saw how Rupert the no-longer-so-Ruthless was leaving, that was the only feeling I had. So there you go."

"Uh-huh."

There was the sound of her breathing, bringing back a memory of the first night she had spent in my bed, more than a year ago. "Lewis?"

"Still here," I said.

"About this morning . . ."

"No explanations necessary," I said.

"I don't care if they're necessary or not, but they're coming your way. I like Mark. I really do. And it wasn't just a one-nighter, that's not the way I operate."

"I know."

"It's just that with my job so up in the air and everything so crazy, I needed something stable. Something warm. Something dependable. Lewis, you are a dear in so many ways, but—"

"Dependable I'm not," I said. "Especially this past week."

"Right," she said, and she spoke louder, "Oh, sometimes you can be so damn secretive and mysterious, and I hate it."

On screen there was a familiar face, a space-shuttle mission commander whom I knew personally being interviewed from out in orbit. I kept the mute button on. I cleared my throat. "Ask away," I said. "Ask away and there'll be no more mysteries, no more secrets."

She paused for a moment, and her voice was quiet again. "No, not now. I don't want to know. Earlier, maybe, but not now. Look, we'll have lunch tomorrow, maybe talk some more. You're a special man in my life, Lewis, but I needed something more. Do you understand?"

"Yes, I do."

There was a noise in the background, and she said, "Um, somebody's at the door. Gotta run. Tomorrow?"

"Yes," I said. "Tomorrow, and any day after that."

" 'Kay," she said, and she hung up.

I slowly put the phone receiver back in and switched the sound off. I had missed the segment I had wanted to see, and I spent the rest of the night on the couch, finally falling asleep in my clothes, and it never repeated.

CHAPTER TWENTY-THREE

A few days after that evening phone call with Paula, Felix Tinios was over at my house. He walked slower than usual from having a couple of cracked ribs and there was still a small bandage on the back of his neck. Other than that, he was his usual self, and he was standing in my living room, a bottle of Molson in his hand, complaining. "The steak tips are getting colder with every passing second," he said. "How much longer?"

"Just another minute," I said. "Just another minute."

On the screen CNN was showing the space shuttle *Endeavour* gliding into a landing at the shuttle landing strip in Florida, its mission successfully completed. Another round of truck drivers back from low earth orbit, passing time until we decided to go back to where we had once belonged. Felix grumbled something and took a swallow from his beer. In his other hand he juggled a small black rock.

I tore my eyes away from Felix and looked at the television. On screen the shuttle flared down and its landing gear poked down. The voice of the NASA commentator said, "Main gear touchdown," and was followed a few seconds later by, "Nose gear touchdown." I watched and felt something tug at my throat as the braking parachute deployed, and then *Endeavour* glided to a halt. I looked over at Felix. "Okay. Now we can eat."

We ate outside on the rear deck, consuming a complicated steak-tip-and-pasta dish that Felix had prepared. I suppose we should have had wine with our meals, but it was the first real warm April day we had this rainy spring, and beers seemed in order. The Red Sox were playing in Boston that afternoon and I had a small radio set outside. It was a pleasant way to spend the afternoon, eating and drinking and listening to the sounds of baseball and the waves and the seagulls. Earlier Felix had said that baseball just seemed more real if one listened to it over the radio, and I had agreed.

Felix now looked over at me, tilted back in his chair. He was still juggling that small black rock. "Something's going on with you, isn't there."

"Always," I said.

"Something to do with me?"

I balanced my own beer bottle on my belt buckle as I tried to avoid looking at him. "Yeah, you're right. Something to do with you."

"What is it?"

Now I looked over at him. "You really want to know?"

"Really and truly," he said. "What is it?"

"It's guilt."

"Guilt?" He leaned his chair back down flat on the deck. "Guilt over what? Not the cell phone, I hope."

"No, not over the damn cell phone," I said. "Over the way I left you behind, back at the gun emplacements. I should have tried to rescue you. You might have been alive. You might have been slowly drowning. I should have done something. Instead I looked at you and went away. That's why I felt guilty. That I left you there to die."

Felix took another small sip of his beer, continued juggling the rock. "If I was dead, there wasn't much you could do, right?"

"Right."

"If I was wounded, what would you have done? Tried to drag me up out of that hole?"

"Maybe. I could have done—"

"Wait," he said. "What did you do, then? Did you hide? Run away? Wet yourself?"

I ran a finger over the top of my beer bottle. "No. I went after Gus. I wanted to kill him."

Felix nodded with satisfaction. "Good. You did exactly right, and if we're ever in a similar circumstance again, do the same thing. Don't worry about my corpse. Don't worry about my wounded body. Go find the son of a bitch who took me down and take care of business. Guilt? Forget it. You did the right thing."

"Maybe so, but—"

"Hey, Lewis. End of subject, okay? I want to see how the Sox can lose this one. All right?"

"Fine," I said, and I cleared the dishes and piled them in the sink and came back with fresh beers. "How's Mickey?" I said.

"Mickey's fine," he said.

"You seeing her tonight?"

"Nope."

"You seeing her tomorrow?"

"Only if I catch a flight to Denver," he said.

From the radio came a tinny roar as somebody had hit a home run over the Green Monster. I had lost track of who was up. I said, "Colorado?"

"Very good," Felix said. "That's where she is, and that's where she's going to be for a few weeks. Then Montana, and then Wyoming. All summer long. She's on some horse exhibition tour that goes on the whole summer, state to state, out west."

"Oh," I said.

"Don't say it like that," he said. "It's not like she's dead or anything. It's just that . . ." And Felix's words, so unlike him, just dribbled off.

"It's just what?" I asked.

He shrugged, though his shoulders didn't move much, as if they were weighted down. "She wanted me to come along with her. Go on the road, go to these horse shows, keep her entertained at night in the motel and hotel rooms. I tell you, I was tempted, very tempted, to take her up on it. She's quite a woman."

"And why are you here, and not there?"

He took another swig from the bottle, looked around at my house and the deck and the big ocean. His voice got quiet. "Because I belong here, my friend. That's who I am. I'm content in who I am and what I do. Sometimes what I do doesn't make sense. Sometimes what I do I can't share with anyone at all. Sometimes what I do involves violence. But I'm content with all that. Finding a woman to share things with who can say the same . . . well, I doubt she's out there."

"So what's left?" I asked.

"What's left?" he asked, raising his eyebrows. "What's left are the moments, the special times, the encounters. That's all, my friend. And I'll tell you a secret. You know exactly what I'm talking about, don't you."

Another roar from the crowd on the radio. I wish I had been paying more attention to the damn thing. I spoke up. "Maybe. Maybe I do."

He laughed and juggled the rock again. "Speaking of secrets . . . Tell me you're not lying to me."

"Okay, I'm not lying to you."

He held the rock up to the April sun. "This rock, this is an honest-to-God moon rock?"

"It surely is."

He tossed it over to me and I caught it with one hand, and then rubbed at it gently, thinking of the many hundreds of thousands of miles it had to travel to end up in my grasp. Felix said, "I thought moon rocks were controlled tighter than the gold at Fort Knox. National treasures, and all that."

"You are correct, sir," I said.

"Then how did you get it? Steal it?"

"Not hardly," I said. "I made a deal."

He laughed. "Over the uranium and that woman who wanted to debrief me a few nights back. Am I right?"

"I can't say," I said. "Not right now. Maybe later. Hey, I've got an idea. Let's just listen to the game and drink our beers. Does that sound all right with you?"

"It sounds perfect," Felix said.

So that's how we spent the afternoon on the first warm day of April, relaxing and letting the sun caress our faces, while I held a chunk of the universe in my fist and watched the waves softly roll into the cove beneath me, killer waves no more.

AUTHOR'S NOTE

The author wishes to express his deep gratitude to Ron Thurlow, for his technical advice; to the staff of the Exeter, New Hampshire, Public Library for their cheerful assistance; and to his wife, Mona, the best first reader an author could ever wish for.

The Porter Submarine Museum as mentioned in this novel does not exist. However, the USS *Albacore* is on display and can be visited in Portsmouth, New Hampshire.

The story of the German U-boats being interned in New Hampshire after World War II is true, as is the tale of the U-234 and its cargo, including the uranium to be used for a Nazi atomic bomb.

This uranium did in fact disappear after the U-234 was brought to the Portsmouth Naval Shipyard. Its whereabouts are still unknown.